Praise for Janet T

"Janet Tronstad pens a warm, comforting story."
—*RT Book Reviews*

"An emotionally vibrant and totally satisfying read."
—*RT Book Reviews* on
Snowbound in Dry Creek

"This enchanting story…has delightful humor, suspense and a warm and wonderful fortysomething romance."
—*RT Book Reviews* on
Silent Night in Dry Creek

"Tronstad's story is riveting…and will stick with readers long after the last page is turned."
—*RT Book Reviews* on
Lilac Wedding in Dry Creek

"This great story filled with kindness, understanding and love is sure to please."
—*RT Book Reviews* on
Mail-Order Christmas Brides

Janet Tronstad grew up on her family's farm in central Montana and now lives in Pasadena, California, where she is always at work on her next book. She has written more than thirty books, many of them set in the fictitious town of Dry Creek, Montana, where the men spend the winters gathered around the potbellied stove in the hardware store and the women make jelly in the fall.

Janet Tronstad

SNOWBOUND IN DRY CREEK
and
SILENT NIGHT IN DRY CREEK

HARLEQUIN® LOVE INSPIRED®CLASSICS

Recycling programs
for this product may
not exist in your area.

ISBN-13: 978-0-373-60972-7

Snowbound in Dry Creek and Silent Night in Dry Creek

Copyright © 2014 by Harlequin Books S.A.

The publisher acknowledges the copyright holder
of the individual works as follows:

Snowbound in Dry Creek
Copyright © 2002 by Janet Tronstad

Silent Night in Dry Creek
Copyright © 2009 by Janet Tronstad

www.Harlequin.com

Printed in U.S.A.

CONTENTS

And the angel said unto them, Fear not: for, behold, I bring you good tidings of great joy, which shall be to all people. For unto you is born this day in the city of David a savior, which is Christ the Lord.
—*Luke* 2:10–11

SNOWBOUND IN DRY CREEK

This book is dedicated with love
to my good friend Darlene Hanson.
She is a warmhearted woman with lots of class.

Chapter One

The last thing Jenny Collins needed was rain on her windshield, especially since her old car had just hissed and then died in the middle of what was clearly the only street in this postage-stamp of a town. She and her children had begun this move to Dry Creek, Montana, with high hopes, but their enthusiasm had deserted them a thousand miles back down the road.

It was the middle of the afternoon and the day itself was gloomy. There wasn't another car in sight except for the ones parked beside the road.

"The car stopped," eight-year-old Lisa announced calmly as though her mother might not have noticed.

"I know, dear."

"I don't like the rain."

"I know that, too, dear."

Jenny had figured there was no point in packing

their old, beat-up umbrella. By spring, she would have a job and could buy an umbrella that actually stayed open without someone's thumb constantly pressing on the button at the bottom of the rod. So she threw the broken one away.

And now, suddenly, it was clear she'd made a mistake. The lack of that old umbrella seemed to symbolize Jenny's whole disastrous plan. She hadn't thought things through. In her first rush of enthusiasm, she'd told herself that their move to Dry Creek would be a shining example to her children of the way God was taking care of them after their father had died. But after the car's muffler gave out in Nevada and the radiator overheated in Utah, she had no longer been able to convince herself that anything was going as it should. And now she hadn't even got the umbrella right.

"It'll be fine," Jenny said for the sake of her children. She prayed that she was right.

She had started to wonder in Idaho if she'd misunderstood God. Maybe what she thought was God's provision for them was nothing more than a widow's foolish dream. She knew why she thought the move here would be good, but maybe God didn't agree. Even though she had given up on Stephen's love for *her* long before he died, she refused to give up on it for their children. She didn't want them to think that their father hadn't cared enough to make any kind of a plan for them when he knew he was dying.

The old farm that Stephen had inherited from his uncle was really all they had left after Jenny had settled their debts in Los Angeles, so she finally decided in her own mind that it was Stephen's final gift to their children—a gift she wanted them to experience to the fullest. She believed all children needed something from their fathers, and her children would have this farm and the knowledge that their father had spent many summers on it as a boy. In time, she hoped the farm itself would look like evidence of Stephen's concern for them.

"Don't worry. We're almost there." Jenny pushed her thoughts aside and kept her voice upbeat. She looked back and smiled at her children. Lisa was strapped into the middle of the backseat and four-year-old Andy was in his car seat to her right. The rest of the backseat, like the trunk, was filled with their belongings. "We'll be warm and dry in no time at all when we get to your father's farm."

Lisa looked at her.

"We'll get the car going again soon, too," Jenny assured her daughter as she slipped the key out of the ignition. "It's probably nothing serious. But we need to stop and ask directions to our place before we go farther, anyway. These people might have known your father when he was a boy. Imagine that."

Lisa didn't say anything.

It worried Jenny that neither Lisa nor Andy had said anything about their father after he died. Was that normal?

"There's no school here." Lisa craned her neck to look out the side window. "If there's no school, I'm going back home."

Home to Lisa was their old apartment in El Monte, southeast of Los Angeles. They'd moved into that run-down two-bedroom apartment a year and a half ago. Jenny had thought at the time that it was as low as their little family could go. She'd been wrong. What she had seen as temporary housing until Stephen was able to work again turned into an apartment she tried, and failed, to keep after he died.

Her receptionist job hadn't paid much even before her hours were cut back. Stephen had been dead for six months by then. That's when she'd decided God must want them to move to Dry Creek. The farm was all they had left. Even with her doubts now, she couldn't think of any other options they might have had. If they'd stayed in Los Angeles, they would have needed to move into a hotel room. Apartment rents were too high, but some of the older hotels rented rooms by the week.

Jenny didn't want her children to grow up in a hotel room. Not when there was a choice.

"There has to be a school someplace," Jenny answered as she, too, took a better look out of the windows. It was raining harder by now, but she could still see the buildings. There was a church; she could identify the white frame structure by the steeple on top of it. There were a dozen or so houses, all of them obviously occupied either because of their porch lights or the dogs in their yards.

But Lisa was right; there was no school. No library, either, and Lisa loved to read. Jenny supposed it was too much to hope that they had a ballet class anywhere within fifty miles of here. Lisa loved to wear her pink tutu and pretend she was a princess.

Jenny hadn't expected Dry Creek to be quite so small. The only building that looked like it might belong in a bigger town was the café. She would have taken the children over there instead of bracing herself to go into the building straight ahead except for the fact that a café usually meant money and she didn't want to part with any more of hers than was necessary. Besides, they still had some apples and cheese in their cooler, and she could heat up a can of soup when they got to the farm.

No, the other building was better for what she needed. If the sign over its door were to be believed, it was a hardware store. Surely, the children wouldn't want anything from the shelves of a hardware store.

"There's Thunder," Andy said, with reverence in his voice, as he pointed to a sign she hadn't noticed on the side of the store. It advertised some brand of animal feed and, sure enough, there was a black horse staring right at them.

The two heroes in Andy's young life were the cowboy Zach "Lightning" Lucas and the man's faithful black horse, Thunder. Pictures of the two of them were always on the box of Ranger Flakes, Andy's favorite breakfast cereal.

"It's a different horse, sweetie," Jenny said before Andy could ask if they were finally going to meet his idols. Andy was so awestruck by them he had even started mentioning the cowboy and horse in his evening prayers. Jenny hoped there were some young boys around here who could be Andy's friends. If he had more flesh-and-blood people in his life, maybe he would give up the cardboard ones.

At least Andy had been happy to leave Los Angeles once she'd told him there were cowboys and horses in Montana. Jenny only wished Lisa had something like that to make the move easier for her. Unfortunately, the street outside didn't have anything a princess would like.

Jenny took a last look at the afternoon sky. It was getting darker. "Put your coats on and we'll go inside the store."

The only things she'd bought before she left Los Angeles were two heavy coats for the children. She might not have an umbrella, but she was ready for snow. That should count for something. Jenny reached behind her and pulled the flannel shirt off the seat. She'd wrap that around herself.

"Careful of the mud," Jenny said as she opened the car door. "And wait for me on the porch."

They all ran as quickly as they could and stood a minute under the overhang that sheltered the porch. Jenny could hear the rain beating on the roof. She took a deep breath and then opened the door.

Warm air pushed at her as she stood in the doorway. She smelled stale coffee and burning wood. Lisa was a little in front of her and Andy was to the side. Both children were wide-eyed as they looked around. Jenny didn't blame them; she'd never seen a store like this in her entire life, either. There were the usual shelves of things for sale, like bins of nails and brooms and shovels. But that's where everything normal stopped.

In the middle of the plain oak floor there was a potbelly wood stove that had a couple of old men sitting around it with their boots off and their stocking feet stretched out to the stove's warmth.

"Well, it's not the same thing for all women," one of the men protested loudly. He obviously hadn't heard Jenny and the children enter the store. "Every woman is looking for something different in a husband. Just like horses with their feed. They're particular."

The other old man snorted. "And you just happen to know what that something different is?"

The first one reared back. "That's what I've been sitting here telling you for the past half hour."

Jenny almost felt as if she should clear her throat to let the men know someone was there. Then she remembered how cold it was outside and closed the door behind the children. The door gave a loud click as she shut it. That was as good as clearing her throat. By the time she turned around, the men were all looking at her and the children.

"Good. Here's a woman," the first man said. "We'll ask her. Then you'll see what I mean."

"I'm afraid we're just here for directions," Jenny mumbled. Lisa and Andy were already walking toward the fire's warmth. She couldn't blame them; they'd all gotten damp in the rain.

Neither man looked as if they were listening to Jenny.

"Okay, prove it," the second man finally said. He pointed at Jenny. "You tell me what she wants from a husband and we'll see if you're right."

"It would be my pleasure," the first man said with a smile in Jenny's direction. "Elmer Maynard at your service, ma'am. Now, if I may—"

"Charley Nelson, here." The other man nodded at Jenny.

"I really don't think—"

Elmer had his eyes closed and a deep frown on his face. "Now, a woman like her—" he managed to point at Jenny even with his eyes still closed

"—she's apt to want a man who's good with children."

The other man, Charley, barked out a quick laugh. "Well, any fool can see that. The kids are sitting right here in front of us. Obviously, she wanted kids."

Lisa and Andy had been given prime seats next to the woodstove and they were watching the old men as if they were in the middle of a *Sesame Street* episode.

"I'm just getting started." Elmer opened his eyes and glared at the other man. "She probably also wanted a husband who was athletic, someone who would be a good father and play catch with her son—"

Elmer stopped to smile down at Andy. Jenny figured it was a kindly gesture, but it was also the older man's fatal mistake. Andy had a one-track mind these days.

"Ohhh, could he be a cowboy?" Andy asked breathlessly, his eyes wide with hope as he looked up at the older man. "With a black horse?"

Andy wiggled as though he was suddenly overcome with the possibilities and then he continued in a low whisper. "Could it be Zach Lightning Lucas?"

"Who's that?" Elmer turned to Jenny with puzzled eyes.

"You'd have to eat cold cereal to know," Jenny

said with a smile. "He's just some guy pretending to be a rodeo star."

"Well, tell your husband not to worry then. All boys like cowboys when they're little like this. I would have traded my father for the Lone Ranger when I was this little guy's age. But we all grow out of it. What does your husband do, anyway?"

Jenny stood up. "Nothing."

"Well, I'm sure he'll find work," Elmer said as he smoothed back his hair. "Tell him not to lose hope."

"He doesn't need hope, he's dead."

"Oh," Charley said in dismay.

"Oh," Elmer echoed in shock.

Jenny wished she'd worked up to that revelation. She'd let her unease with the conversation come between her and these new neighbors.

"Well—" Charley mumbled.

Elmer cleared his throat.

"It's been a while since he died," Jenny added flatly. She didn't need any words of sympathy. "We're fine. We just stopped in to get directions to a farm he inherited. I'm sorry, but I don't really need a husband."

"Well, but surely a husband—" Elmer started to say before Charley gave him a fierce look.

"Don't pay him any attention," Charley said quietly to Jenny. "We believe in minding our own business here in Dry Creek. Elmer's just trying to prove he's a matchmaker. Next month he'll be back to worrying about what color of blue to paint his Cadillac."

"Well, I'm sure other women will be happy if he finds them a husband," Jenny said politely. "But all I need is directions."

"Of course," Charley said as he reached into his shirt pocket and drew out a small stub of a pencil. "If the place is around here, we can tell you how to get there. I'll even draw you a map. I'm getting pretty good at maps now that I'm the relief mail driver. I know the quickest way to every place."

Meanwhile, Elmer reached into the top pocket in his bib overalls. "Anyone want some candy?"

Jenny recognized the gesture as a peace offering and nodded to Andy and Lisa, letting them know they could each take one of the wrapped chocolates the man held in the palm of his hand. She wanted to be friendly to the first people she met in the area. After all, these men would be their neighbors.

By the time the men had drawn a rough map showing her how to get to their property, Jenny was beginning to feel more optimistic about settling in this community. They all remembered little Stephen Collins who had visited his uncle every summer for years.

The fact that the men seemed to have fond memories of her late husband gave Jenny the courage to mention that her car had stalled out front in the middle of the road. The men had to walk to the window to look, and they seemed to agree that the car was in trouble. She asked for the number to call a tow truck operator, but the men waved that idea away. The nearest tow truck, they said, was in Miles City, and the way business was backed up there it would take twenty-four hours before it'd come to Dry Creek.

Instead, Charley offered to help get the car started and then follow her out to the Collins farm, just to be sure they all got there in one piece, he said. Jenny and the children walked with him out to the porch.

"Are you always this kind to strangers?" Jenny asked Charley.

"You betcha," Charley said with a nod and a grin. "We make it a policy around here."

He had their car running in twenty minutes.

Four weeks later, Zach "Lightning" Lucas stood on the same weathered porch and scowled as the same gray sky darkened. "Whatever happened to that small-town hospitality I've heard about? You know, that kindness to strangers thing?"

"What about it?" Charley shrugged as he cheerfully slipped another handful of candy canes into the mail bag Zach had slung over his shoulder. "You're able-bodied."

"Don't you require people to pass some test if you want them to deliver your mail?"

"We had the foresight to have people sign forms

saying that, in an emergency, civilians could carry
their mail. Today, that would be you."

Zach grunted. At least the man realized a sick
horse was an emergency. Charley was apparently
the closest thing to a vet in this small town and he'd
agreed to treat Zach's horse, Thunder.

The two men were far enough down on the porch
that Zach could look into the window of the hardware store and see a group of old men sitting around
that potbelly stove. Fortunately, older men like these
tended to eat oatmeal instead of cold cereal, and
none of them had recognized him or Thunder. Of
course, they might have treated them with more respect if they had.

When he first stepped inside the store, Zach
hadn't even gotten his piece said before those old
men were asking him if he was a single man. They
got that one question out there faster than most
women did in the pick-up bars down in the panhan-
dle. And those women prided themselves on being
brazen. Zach knew it was true from experience.

Zach told the men he didn't need any help with
his love life; he had a sick horse.

At the mention of Thunder, Charley had sat up
straight and paid attention. It had taken a few minutes, but finally Zach had laid out his problem. His
sick horse had to have veterinary care as soon as
possible.

Charley was willing to tend the horse, and the

other men all agreed he was the closest thing to a vet this small town had, so Zach relaxed. That is, until he realized that Charley had a problem of his own. It seemed Charley was the relief mail carrier, as well, and needed to deliver the mail one last time before Christmas. If Charley was going to tend Thunder, someone else needed to take around the mail.

Zach hadn't realized it was December 23rd already, but he figured the date didn't mean too much. Charley asked for a volunteer to deliver the mail, and not a man inside the store had done anything except stare at the floor as if he was suddenly deaf. Zach thought maybe there was a lot of heavy lifting because of last-minute packages or something.

Well, he could understand that. If those boxes were heavy, he wouldn't want any of these older men to strain their back muscles. Having a bad back might interfere with them sitting there and harassing strangers.

So Zach volunteered. He said he'd be happy to help out. How hard could it be to toss around a few boxes? He was in prime lifting shape.

Zach couldn't help but notice that he'd barely got his offer out before the men sitting around the stove started grinning like a bunch of renegade dogs that had trapped an unsuspecting cat.

Five minutes later, Zach was standing on the porch and he understood why the men were so full of glee. Charley had promised the regular mail carrier that he'd deliver the mail the way she always did on the last day before Christmas. She, a Mrs. Brown, always made it look like Santa was out there delivering the letters himself on that day.

Zach figured Charley would have offered to treat a rabid skunk if it meant he could convince someone else to take his place on this particular mail run.

Zach pushed his Stetson hat lower on his head. He didn't know anyone in this crazy one-stop town, but he still didn't like the men looking at him from inside that store. Suppose one of them recognized him even now. He was Zach "Lightning" Lucas and he had a reputation to uphold—a reputation that didn't include a fuzzy red fat-suit and a black plastic belt. It was bad enough that the four-wheel-drive postal truck had a fake set of reindeer horns tied to the grill and a ball of mistletoe swinging from the antenna. He didn't need Christmas fuzz all over himself, too.

Zach grimaced as red and green flashes met his eyes. The lightbulbs hanging from the reindeer horns were on a timer. When he first saw them, he'd hoped they were merely ornamental. No such luck. The men inside the store had all come to the window to see the show when he'd tried out the lights. If it hadn't been for all of the green lights flashing, they would have thought the town was on fire because of all the red lights flashing.

Zach didn't know how much holiday nonsense

he could take. He just wasn't a Christmas kind of a guy. After all, he had more gold-plated champion belt buckles than most men had ties. He had fans who knew his name—lots of fans since he'd endorsed that Ranger breakfast cereal. Those fans obviously didn't live in Dry Creek, but people in many other towns recognized him in grocery stores and in Laundromats. He was Zach "Lightning" Lucas. He was *famous*. He was entitled to some dignity.

Unfortunately, Zach had a feeling his dignity was about to be covered in padding and thoroughly ignored for the day.

And it was all because of Christmas. Not that Zach should be surprised. Christmas had been giving him trouble for years. It always depressed him with all that family stuff. Not that he had anything against families—it's just that family stuff wasn't for a man like him.

That's why, this year, he had made a plan. He should have thought to tell the men inside the store that he had his own way of dealing with love during the holidays.

Zach and Thunder were only passing through Montana, heading over to Interstate 15 for the long stretch down to Las Vegas. Once there, Thunder would board at a ranch some miles outside of Vegas while Zach hit the Strip. The neon lights and showgirls—well, if her return message were to be believed, one showgirl in particular—would make him forget the holidays were even here.

He and Thunder had been making good time, too, Zach thought mournfully, until the horse got a fever.

"You've got the map." Charley patted his pockets as though the slip of paper showing all the county roads might still be there instead of taped to the dashboard of the postal truck.

"Yes, sir."

The winter air had a bite to it, but Zach was in no hurry to leave the porch and get into that decked-out postal truck. He might as well ride around in a clown's cart and be done with it. Which made him think of something.

"I can't be driving the postal truck," Zach said. "Isn't that against some kind of a law? Government property and all."

"The thing belongs to Dry Creek, so it's not postal property. We got it in some sale last year. Rural carriers out here aren't generally issued postal vehicles."

"Well, then, I'd be glad to drive my truck," Zach said.

"Don't have time for that. I can't pull your horse trailer with my pickup. So I need to drive your truck if you want your horse to get into the barn before the snow gets any worse."

Zach hung his head. He couldn't be choosy, not when Thunder needed help.

Both men were silent for a moment.

"Well, then, let me get that apple pie my fiancée, Edith, baked for the Collins family," Charley said as he stepped back and opened the door of the store. He reached inside to pick up something sitting on a chair by the door. It was a foil-wrapped package. "Remember that name—Collins. That'll be the last stop on your list. And the box in back is for them, too. Their car is broken. Radiator. So Edith said she'd pick up some things for them and send them out in the mail truck." Charley lifted the pie. "There's two of the cutest kids you'll ever meet out there."

Zach nodded. He'd already met every kid on the planet—both the cute and the ugly. The ones he missed at the rodeos he met because they ate Ranger Flakes breakfast cereal. Not that he was complaining. He liked kids better than he liked most adults. He did glance over at the window of the hardware store though. Apparently, the men had got tired of laughing at him and gone back to sit by the fire. They were probably deciding who to torture next.

Charley smiled and looked at Zach slyly. "'Course, one look at their mother and you'll see why they're so cute."

Zach grunted as he turned back to the old man. Now that was the part of meeting kids he didn't like—their mothers. Even the women who were married always seemed to have a scheme to get him married off to someone. You'd think there was something wrong with a man choosing to live in hotel rooms and wash his socks in bathroom sinks.

Charley must have known what he was thinking because he shook his head. "The poor woman. Such a pity—"

Charley looked at Zach as though he expected some curiosity.

Zach had none.

Charley ploughed ahead, anyway. "Jenny Collins is a widow. Not that she's old, mind you. No, sir. Moved up here a couple of weeks ago—surprised us all. She'd been married to Jeb Collins's nephew." Charley nodded at Zach as though Zach had known this Jeb, whoever he was. "Jeb had left the place to his nephew, but we all thought the nephew would have sense enough to sell it before he started dying of that cancer of his. But he didn't. Stephen was his name. Don't know what he was thinking. Surely he didn't expect his widow to move up here with the two kids. What do you think a city woman's gonna do with a place like that, anyway?"

Zach shrugged. He didn't like to get involved in the problems of strangers.

Charley had no such hesitation. "I hear she's been getting magazines on farm management!" He shook his head. "She's a game one, I'll give her that. She had so many questions, Edith gave her an old guide book on living in Montana. But it's no place for her and the kids—even old man Collins used to move into town here for the winter months. The house doesn't even have a decent road leading up to it. Ruts a mile deep, and it drifts closed every time there's a blizzard."

Charley took a breath before he continued. "The regular mail carrier, you know, the Delores Brown I told you about, always drives the mail right up to the house for the Collins family. But with the next hard snow they won't get mail for a week. The county snowplow doesn't go that far out. Most farmers out that way have plows on their tractors or something. But all the woman's got is that car of hers—and with the two little ones—well, Edith is worried about their car not working."

Between Edith Hargrove and Delores Brown, Zach had already concluded, the two women pretty well worried about everything and everybody within a hundred-mile radius. He was surprised they didn't go into politics. They could form their own party.

Charley stopped suddenly and squinted at Zach. "What Jenny Collins needs is a husband."

Zach looked at the other man in amazement and then pushed his hat farther down on his head. "Don't look at me. I'm just trying to get my horse fixed up. Besides, from the sounds of it, she needs a tractor worse than she needs a husband."

Charley shrugged. "I doubt you'd stand a chance,

anyway. I hear Max Daniel is planning to ask her out after Christmas—he's a rancher north of here. 'Course Tom Fox might beat him to the punch. A good-looking woman like Jenny can have her pick of the bachelors around here once folks decide we've given her enough time to settle in. Most folks think Christmas is time enough for a young woman like that to start dating again."

Zach grunted. Ever since he started making money at rodeoing, he'd had folks trying to get him to settle down. Made him nervous as a rope-tied calf every time a woman talked about it. Anyone with any sense could see that the life he'd led didn't prepare him for marriage.

Not that he didn't like women. He did. He just had sense enough to know his limitations. He didn't even have a year-round mailing address; he'd be a fool to think he would be any good at marriage.

"Yeah, well, it was only a thought," Charley said as he pointed to the back of the postal truck. "Now, you remember what I said about the camera back there. Edith promised Jenny pictures of her little boy with Santa, and I'll never hear the end of it if you don't remember to take one with him."

"Pictures." Zach grimaced. "I'm not much good at pictures."

"What? You can't tell me that. If you've ridden the rodeo circuit, you must be used to getting your picture taken," Charley said and then lowered his eyes. "That is, if you've ever won anything."

"I win," Zach said. He should tell the old man how many times he won.

"Well, then, you must have had your picture taken at least once."

Zach grunted. Once? Try a hundred times. "Well, the win photos—they're all right. But they're not, well, personal."

Zach didn't know how to explain his reluctance to have a picture of him in some family album along with pictures of babies and grandmas. He'd feel a fraud. A family photo album was one place he didn't belong.

"There's nothing to a Santa picture," Charley said, pushing ahead, anyway. "It's one of those cameras that prints out a picture while you wait. Jenny will even take the picture for you. And Edith said to leave the camera, in case Jenny wants to take other Christmas shots."

Zach nodded in defeat. He hoped Thunder would enjoy being taken care of by Charley here.

"And don't forget about old Mrs. Goussley. She has a sweet tooth. We always give her a few extra candy canes." Charley winked. "Say they're for her cats. She'll give them back if you say they're for her."

"Cats," Zach repeated bleakly.

"Mrs. Goussley likes her visit from Santa. She

gets a kick out of the suit." Charley eyed Zach. "I know Delores got carried away this year with putting those flashing lights around Santa's belt, but you can keep them pressed off if you want. Plus the suit's warm—all that padding. Still, it might not be enough. Gets cold out there. Could drop to below zero before you get back."

"I've got a sheepskin coat if it does." Zach had put his duffel bag and the coat in the postal truck. The sheepskin was imitation, but of good enough quality to be worth a pretty penny. It wasn't something he'd leave behind. Not that he didn't trust the older man, but he'd worked enough rodeos to know never to leave his duffel with strangers.

"Oh, well, then," Charley muttered as he stepped closer to the truck. "I'll just put this pie inside and let you get going. Remember, now, the brakes turn a little to the left if you happen to be going downhill."

Zach nodded. He was definitely going downhill. Playing Santa to an old lady and her cats. Zach "Lightning" Lucas. He shook his head and pulled his Stetson down farther.

He sure hoped no one who had the teeth to be eating something besides oatmeal saw him today. He didn't want to be recognized. People always wanted pictures of him. The real him. A snapshot of him dressed in a Santa suit might even make it onto a grocery store tabloid. He shuddered to think what the rodeo world would say if they saw him looking like this.

The reporter probably wouldn't even be kind enough to say Zach was doing it all for his sick horse. No, Zach would just be there looking like a fool for no good reason.

Chapter Two

Jenny looked out the kitchen window again. Gray storm clouds almost covered the square butte west of their place. It was starting to snow, and the mail hadn't come yet. Mrs. Hargrove had told her that Charley might be late with the mail, but he'd see the package Jenny was expecting got to them. It wasn't much, but it had the few presents she had been able to get for the children, and she was anxious for them to arrive. Tomorrow was Christmas Eve day and, since it would be Sunday, there'd be no mail delivery then.

Mrs. Hargrove had driven out to see Jenny and the children the day after they'd arrived. She'd brought some homemade bread and jelly, which had won over Andy's heart. She'd then won over Lisa because she had a bridal magazine for them all to look at. Mrs. Hargrove and Charley were getting married on the first Sunday of April and the older woman glowed when she spoke of it.

"You're all invited to the wedding, of course," Mrs. Hargrove had said. "We want to have lots of children around."

"You're sure?" Jenny had asked. "They can be distracting."

Mrs. Hargrove grinned. "I'm hoping they will be. Charley and I are simple folks. We don't need everyone staring at us."

That's when Mrs. Hargrove had won Jenny over. Since then, the older woman had become Jenny's closest friend. Just knowing that there were people like her in the small town of Dry Creek had convinced Jenny that God did want her and the children here.

Mrs. Hargrove had done some shopping for Jenny in Miles City. The box coming with the mail should have what she had ordered—a water pistol for Andy, a paint kit for Lisa and much-needed mittens and scarves for them both. Andy really wanted a cowboy outfit with a hat, and Lisa really wanted a princess tiara, but they were both too expensive and nowhere to be found in Miles City, anyway.

Maybe next year, Jenny consoled herself. She'd surely think of a way to make some money soon. She had to. She'd just spent everything except a few hundred dollars filling the propane tank so the furnace would keep going for the next few months.

If nothing else, she thought, *I want to be generous with heat when it comes to our place.*

Our place. She repeated the phrase to herself in satisfaction. Stephen had left them a wonderful place. This Christmas it would be enough that they had a home that was all their own, even if the roof leaked on the south side of the living room and the linoleum in the kitchen had more cracks than color left. Still, the place had three bedrooms and no landlord. They didn't have to worry about making too much noise or keeping the walls beige. Or paying the rent.

There was even a huge barn that would be useful if she got some goats. In the meantime, a cat from someplace had taken up residence in the barn, and the children had both started leaving food for it.

The barn was the final thing that convinced her that the move here would turn out all right. The agricultural guidebook Mrs. Hargrove had given her said this country was good for sheep, so Jenny supposed it would also be good for goats. She wasn't sure if she could make a living from raising goats, but she intended to find out. She'd already found a recipe in one of her farming magazines for goat cheese.

And, of course, she'd also need to look for a job after Christmas. She was hoping she might find something in Dry Creek since she'd have to go there every day, anyway, once she enrolled Lisa in the school in Miles City. The school bus stopped at the café to pick up the Dry Creek children and take them to the bigger town. Jenny had talked to the third-grade teacher, and they'd agreed Lisa could start in January. Surely by then Jenny would have the car running the way it should.

In the meantime, they were adjusting.

"Mom, I see her coming!" Andy's voice carried from the back bedroom. He was obviously looking out the window himself.

"Get down off those boxes, Andrew Joel." If he could see out the window, it meant he was standing on the boxes again. Jenny hadn't intended to leave everything in boxes for long. She just hadn't been able to buy dressers or bookshelves or cabinets— none of the furniture that stored things.

Jenny had sold all their furniture before leaving California. Stephen had said in his ramblings that there would be furniture in the house already.

He had been wrong, of course. Nothing had been as he described. She wouldn't have recognized the farm from his memories when she took her first look at the place that late afternoon several weeks ago. The day had been starting to grow dark and she had her headlights on when she drove over the hill to the property. Charley was following behind her.

Jenny doubted anything but thistle had grown on the place for the past ten years. The acreage was fenced, but half of the fence was down. The only trees were short scrub ones, and she'd already heard from someone before they left the store in Dry Creek that the creek Stephen remembered at the bottom of the coulee, the Big Dry Creek, had been dry for the past two years.

Still, this was to be their home. Charley had stayed that first day to help Jenny light the furnace. The electricity was off, but she had candles, and she told Charley they would be fine until she had a chance to sort things out the next day.

The older man had welcomed her again to Dry Creek and left. From that first day, things got better. It only took a few days for the children to figure out that they didn't need to stay inside the house. They had a freedom they had never known around Los Angeles.

If the children were content, Jenny could live without furniture for a few months. She'd told the kids they'd pretend they were camping. So far, they hadn't complained.

"But she's coming!" Andrew said as he ran out of the bedroom door and down the small hallway. "She's coming to get my letter."

"Oh, dear. I forgot." Jenny remembered that Mrs. Brown had promised Andy she'd take his letter special delivery to the North Pole so that Santa could read it before he began his trip tomorrow. Jenny had helped him write the letter, so she had known for days what it said. She just hadn't realized he wanted the letter mailed until recently. "I'm afraid it won't be Mrs. Brown getting the mail today. Charley is taking the route for her."

"Does he still have that runny pig?"

Charley had had a pig in the back of his pickup truck the last time he'd brought the mail.

"*Runt.* The pig was a runt. And, yes, I think he still has him."

"Can he find the North Pole?"

"I'm sure he can," Jenny said. Charley was a nice man. She was sure he'd play along with Andy's fantasy. She'd wondered if Andy should still believe in Santa. If it weren't so soon after Stephen's death, she probably would have explained to him that Santa Claus wasn't real. After all, Andy would be five soon.

But it was all so complicated. Jenny worried that Andy never talked about Stephen's death. He was as closemouthed as Lisa. Jenny had tried talking to them both, but they just didn't seem to have much to say.

Jenny knew Stephen had been a distant father, but surely the children felt something.

Stephen had made it plain to Jenny shortly after they married that he wasn't a family man. She wished he'd said so before they married. But he hadn't, and Jenny had hoped he would change— surely a man would care about his own children. But Stephen never had. Stephen had lived his life apart from the family as much as possible ever since their oldest, Lisa, was born.

No, it wouldn't hurt Andy to believe in Santa for another year.

Zach twisted the wheel to keep the postal truck on the road. Charley hadn't exaggerated when he'd complained about the ruts to the Collins's place. No wonder the woman's car was down for the count. There probably wasn't a nut or bolt in the whole vehicle that hadn't been shaken to within an inch of its life.

The road matched the house at its end. A bright patch of white paint around the door made the rest of the house look even more faded. He suspected this Collins woman didn't know that paint needed to be applied in warmer, dryer weather. Of course, he supposed it did get the message across that someone was living there. Without that paint and the yellow curtains in the kitchen window, the place would look deserted.

The huge red barn a few hundred feet from the house looked as if it was in better shape than the house.

The land itself looked as though no one had ever cared for it. Flat and gray, it stretched out in all directions with nothing but half-melted lumps of old snowdrifts and a few scrub trees on it. The gray patches were gathering a coating of white as the

snowflakes started to fall. In the distance Zach saw
a few buttes rising up from the ground, but they
were so far away he didn't pay them any attention.

A woman opened the door of the house as Zach
pulled the postal truck to a stop. She was hugging
an unbuttoned man's flannel shirt around her shoulders and was wearing a T-shirt and jeans. A young
girl stood on one side of her and an even younger
boy on the other.

Zach unlatched the side door and stepped out of
the postal truck. The north wind was already turning bitter, so he walked along the south side of the
truck until he reached the vehicle's back door. Cold,
hard flakes of snow hit against his face.

Zach had given up and put the Santa beard and
hat on before he even got to Mrs. Goussley's. It
was the cookies that had done it. Every place he
stopped, someone shoved a plate of homemade
cookies into his hands. He explained that he wasn't
Mrs. Brown—why, he wasn't even Charley—he
wasn't entitled to any cookies. But no one listened.
It was Christmas, they said, and he looked like a
nice young man.

He hadn't been called a nice young man since
he'd started riding rodeo. He was getting soft, he
thought glumly as he yanked the furry red cap farther down on his head and snapped the fake white
beard into place. The cardboard box marked "Collins" and the pie were all the mail left to deliver.

Zach lifted the two things up. It would only take a minute to get the box up to the porch. Once there, he'd see about a quick Santa picture with the kids and head back to town. Maybe Thunder would be able to travel by then. If Zach was lucky, he'd be in the arms of that showgirl by Christmas after all.

Even from a distance Zach could see the woman was younger than he'd thought she would be. He'd guess her age at twenty-seven or twenty-eight. He shared Charley's surprise that she'd taken on a farm in the middle of Montana. He would expect someone like her to move into one of the cities like Billings or maybe Missoula. Someplace that had a video store and a beauty shop.

Not that it was any of his worry. She could live on the moon for all he cared.

"Package," Zach said when he got close enough to the porch to thrust the package at the woman. Short blond curls blew around her face, and up close he confirmed his opinion of her. Even in the cold, she would draw some attention in a crowd. The wind had turned her nose pink to match her cheeks.

Zach had a momentary wish he'd taken the Santa suit off before he'd made his last delivery. Lots of women had a weakness for cowboys. He'd never heard of a woman yet who thought a fat, polyester Santa was sexy.

Not that he was interested in what this woman or any woman in this part of Montana thought about him. What he'd told Charley had been true—he was just delivering the mail and then passing through.

If Zach had been paying attention to what he was doing instead of admiring the woman in front of him, he would have seen her eyes sooner. Startled blue eyes looked straight at him.

"It's the mail," Zach clarified. No one else had greeted him with anything remotely like panic. Maybe she thought he was some kind of kook. "The suit's for the old ladies. Well, that and the pictures. Mrs. Hargrove wanted you to have one with your kids."

"Where's Charley?"

"In some barn someplace looking after my horse."

"You've got a horse." The young boy looked around his mother's thigh and up at Zach. His eyes shone with wonder. "A real horse."

The two children stood on either side of the woman. The boy's jeans were neatly patched at the knees, and he obviously took his fair share of tumbles; the girl's clothes were well washed but showed no sign of stains or tears. Not even little ones. The boy's eyes had already welcomed Zach, but the girl's were more careful.

"He's as real as a horse can be, even when he's sick," Zach said. "In his day, he was the best bucking bronc around."

"Santa has reindeer—not horses," the young girl

pointedly corrected Zach as she crossed her arms. Zach pegged her age at seven. Maybe eight. "You need to get the story straight."

"It's no story," Zach protested. "I'm not—"

The woman's eyes widened in even more alarm and Zach stopped. He looked back down at the young boy.

"—in a hurry," Zach fumbled. Were there still kids left that believed in Santa Claus? Apparently so. "I'm not in a hurry at all."

The woman smiled in relief.

Now, that woman should smile more often, Zach thought. She was pretty without the smile, but when she smiled she made him think of one of those soap ads where they try to picture springtime. It might be twenty degrees below zero on this porch right now, but when he looked at Mrs. Collins he could almost see the green meadow she should be walking through.

But, Zach reminded himself, he wasn't here to think of meadows. He was here to deliver the mail, snap a picture and give away the last of those bothersome candy canes.

"I have something for you in my pocket." Zach had moved the last of the candy canes from the bag to his pocket several stops back. "Just let me set this box down inside the house and I'll get it out for you."

Zach didn't notice that the alarm on the woman's face turned to dismay.

"I can take the package," Jenny offered. She wasn't ready for company.

"No problem. I've got it," Zach said as he stepped up to the door the boy was opening.

"But I can—" Jenny started to repeat even as she watched the man walk into her kitchen. Great, she thought. Just what she needed—some man in a Santa suit seeing her house. Every man she had ever known expected a woman to keep a neat house. Stacks of boxes and fold-up furniture would hardly qualify as neat. She hoped the beard would hide his disapproval. Although, she told herself with a tilt of her chin, it wasn't any of his business what kind of a housekeeper she was.

Chapter Three

"I haven't had a chance to get to town much yet," Jenny said defensively as she stepped through the kitchen doorway behind the man. She hadn't minded when Mrs. Hargrove had come inside and sat on one of the folding chairs, but a strange man was different. "I've been meaning to find some used furniture or something."

The man set the box and a foil-wrapped pie down on the kitchen counter and started patting his pockets.

The kitchen counter was covered with tiles so old the white had turned yellow, but Jenny had scrubbed the grout clean. The floor, too, was spotlessly clean even though the linoleum was cracked. No one could say the place was dirty, she reminded herself, even if they could say it lacked almost everything else to recommend it.

"I've asked about garage sales—then I'll be able to buy a few things," Jenny continued before realizing the man was not only not listening, but he hadn't even taken a good look around. He probably didn't realize that all that stood in the kitchen was a broom in one corner and the folding card table and chairs that sat square in the middle.

"I must have another candy cane here someplace." The Santa man turned and held up one candy cane. The plastic around the red-and-white cane was wrinkled and looked as if it had been slept on. "I'm sure I couldn't have given them all out already."

The man continued patting his pockets a little frantically. "I gave one for each of the cats—that was five—and a few extra when she said one of the cats was going to have kittens—and then she gave me that plate of cookies, and I had to give her some for that—but I should still have—"

Zach made another pass at checking the pocket on his right. The suit only had the two large pockets, and they had both been full of candy canes. He shouldn't have given so many to Mrs. Goussley and her cats. Not when two children were waiting at the end of the route. "Maybe one dropped out in the truck. I'll go see."

Zach smiled at the kids to show they could trust him. The boy smiled back, so excited he was almost spinning. The girl eyed Zach suspiciously. No smile there. She clearly had her doubts about him and the promised candy cane. Well, he didn't blame her. At least she wasn't whining about it.

Zach walked toward the door.

"I'll go with you," Jenny said, as she turned to the two children. "You two stay here."

"But, Mom, I gotta—"

"Stay here," the woman interrupted the young boy. "We'll be right back. I want to talk to Santa."

"But, Mom," the boy persisted. "I gotta—"

"Later. I need to talk to Santa alone." The young woman used her best mother voice. Gentle but firm. Zach forgot all about the candy canes. Maybe Santa did have a little sex appeal if an attractive young woman was willing to take a walk in freezing temperatures just to talk to him privately.

Of course, he knew that a woman like her was trouble. He'd feel hog-tied after the second date. He'd have to tell her he was just passing through. Zach took another look at the woman's face and hesitated. Maybe he was being too cautious about dating. Just because a second date was out of the question, that didn't mean a first date was impossible.

Even a woman like that wouldn't have expectations on a first date, would she? A first date was a test with no commitment whatsoever. And that's all it would be. One date. He could put off starting down to Vegas until morning and still make it. Maybe he should ask her out for dinner tonight.

The one restaurant in Dry Creek looked a little casual for a big date, but people must go somewhere.

"Where do people go around here for fun?" Zach asked as he opened the door for the woman.

It was only four o'clock in the afternoon, but the cold pinched at Zach's nose and he was grateful for the warmth of that beard on his face. The temperature had dipped a few degrees just in the time they had been inside. A full-fledged storm was coming.

"Fun?" The woman looked at him blankly. She crossed her arms against the cold and walked out the door, headed toward the postal truck.

Zach closed the door and hurried to follow. He could see the goose bumps on her neck in the strip between her collar and her hair. Pinpricks of snow still swirled around in the wind. "You need to wear something heavier than that flannel shirt when you're outside."

The woman walked faster. Her teeth chattered so he could hardly make out her words. "It'll do."

Zach opened the passenger door to the postal truck. The handle was icy to his touch. "Here. Sit inside."

Zach closed the passenger door and quickly walked around to the driver's side.

"You've heard of the North Pole?" the woman asked when Zach was inside and seated.

"That some kind of night club?" Zach was feeling more hopeful. Now they were talking fun. Maybe he wouldn't even need to go to Vegas to find some Christmas cheer. The North Pole must be a place in Billings.

"Huh?" the woman looked bewildered.

"Charley there could watch the kids," Zach thought out loud. He felt a little bad about the kids, but Charley would treat them fine. He probably even had more of those candy canes. The kids could do without their mother for one night. Some kids would actually be glad to spend a night apart from their mother.

"The North Pole," the woman repeated as if she had doubts about his mental abilities. "You know—that place where Santa Claus makes his toys."

"Oh." So much for night clubs. Zach reached up and turned on the heat. The engine was still warm and gave off a soft wave of hot air. "I didn't know you meant *that* North Pole. Sure, I know it."

"Well, Andy is going to give you a letter to deliver to Santa Claus at the North Pole. Just go along with it, okay?"

"Sure," Zach shrugged. "I'll tell him I ride my horse, Thunder, right up there every night."

Jenny frowned. "Don't overdo it. He's four, but he's not gullible."

Zach refrained from pointing out that the boy still believed in Santa Claus. "Anything you say."

Zach smiled.

Jenny frowned.

Zach got a glimpse of himself in the rearview mirror and frowned, too. No wonder the woman was still cool to him. He looked like a lunatic. His beard was crooked and looked as if it was made of yarn that some cat had chewed. Zach pulled the beard down past his chin and let it settle around his neck. He pushed the Santa hat far enough back on his head so that she could see his hair. That should make her relax.

It didn't. Jenny's frown turned to an expression of alarm. "You look just like that…that cowboy on the cereal box."

Zach relaxed. He was home free. She'd seen the Ranger boxes. "He's me—I mean, I'm him."

"But you can't be." Jenny tried not to stare at the man's face. His cheekbones were high; his eyebrows black and fierce looking when he wasn't smiling. It was the middle of winter and his tan was only partially faded. The golden flecks in his brown eyes saved his face from being too severe. Nothing saved it from being the handsomest face she had ever seen.

Jenny had dreamed of that face ever since Andy had convinced her to buy the first box of that cereal a year ago. She must have bought three dozen boxes this last year alone. And that wasn't the worst of it. She'd been talking to the box.

Jenny was a private person and she didn't admit her unhappiness to anyone. But, one morning at a solitary breakfast, she'd poured out her troubles to the face on the back of the box and she'd been talking to it ever since. Only the face on the box knew about her disappointment with her marriage. To the rest of the world, her marriage was fine and her husband was the good-natured man he appeared to be to others. But the box knew the truth.

She'd told that box things she wouldn't have admitted to a minister, and now it sat before her. She felt betrayed. Pictures on cereal boxes were not supposed to spring to life in front of your eyes.

"You just can't be him."

"Well, everybody's got to be somebody."

Jenny panicked. Not only was the face here, it was—unless she missed her guess—also teasing her. Maybe even flirting with her. It was awful. "You'll have to go."

Okay, Zach thought to himself. Definitely not a night clubber. Which was fine. He had his good time waiting in Vegas. "Just give me a minute to find another one of those candy canes and I'll be happy to head out. I need to get back before the storm hits, anyway."

Jenny looked up. "I thought you said you'd take a picture with Andy."

"I did, but I thought you were, well, in a hurry for me to leave."

"No, I'm just, well, I don't want to take more of your time. But a picture only takes a second."

Jenny forced herself to look the man in the face.

It wasn't his fault she'd started talking to his picture. She had a moment's wild suspicion that Elmer, the old man who thought he could tell what every woman wanted, had sent this man out here to finally prove his point. But that was silly. No one could possibly know about her and this man's face. Could they?

Zach was talking. "Okay. Fine. I'm happy to take a picture. Whatever you want."

Jenny forced herself to smile. "It's just that you're the only Santa around."

Zach grunted. "No problem."

"And I appreciate you bringing out everything for Mrs. Hargrove. And the candy canes, too. That was very nice of you."

"The mail carrier bought the canes. Delores Brown. I'm just passing them out for her."

"Still…"

Zach noted that the woman's face had relaxed. The goose bumps had left. The air inside the truck wasn't white with trails of exhaled air. "Not a problem. I'll even tell that boy of yours I'll take his letter to Santa."

Jenny frowned. "You're not related to Elmer, are you?"

"Huh?"

"Never mind. I'm sorry I can't—I mean, I don't date, anyway—not that you were asking me out." Jenny stopped in embarrassment.

"Oh, but I *was* asking you out. At least I was heading in that general direction."

Jenny couldn't help but notice he sounded a little too cheerful for someone who had just been turned down. "Well, I appreciate that. I'm just sorry I can't accept."

"It's okay," Zach felt around the side of his seat and found not one but two candy canes. Hallelujah! He'd soon be out of here. "I suppose you tried the cereal and didn't like it—or you thought the manufacturer shouldn't say it is the cereal real cowboys eat when everybody knows cowboys don't eat anything but beans and trail dust."

"No, actually, I like the cereal. And I think cowboys would like it if they had a chance to try it. It's great—real nutty."

Zach nodded and didn't make the obvious comparison. "So you like the cereal. You just object to the box."

Jenny nodded sheepishly. "I guess it is kind of odd."

"No problem." Zach smiled to show it was okay. He'd been bucked by broncs. He'd learned how to take his lumps in life. If the woman was that set against him, he'd let it be. Better times were waiting for him. "I'll just take this other candy cane into the house and pick up the letter from—what's the kid's name again?"

"Andy."

"So I'll pick up the letter from Andy, do our bit with the camera and be on my way back to Dry Creek."

"Thank you for understanding."

Zach shrugged as he opened the driver's door on the postal truck. "Don't mention it."

To show there were no hard feelings, Zach walked around and opened the passenger door, as well. "Some folks think the picture on the box is just some dress-up modeling job. But it isn't. The cereal company asked to put my picture on the box because I won the All-Pro Championship in bronc riding five years in a row."

"Oh, I didn't think they used your picture because of your looks." Jenny gracefully stepped out of the truck and almost immediately folded her arms in front of her for warmth.

Zach admitted complete defeat. Most women found him attractive. He wasn't fool enough to go after one who didn't. Especially not when he was out in the middle of nowhere and the sky was turning a serious gray.

"Storm's coming," Zach offered as they walked toward the house. He suddenly understood why everyone in Dry Creek worried so much over this little family. He felt some of that same worry tugging at him. There wasn't another house around for miles. "You got enough supplies stored up and everything? A winter storm in southern Montana can be a fierce thing."

"I know that."

Zach wondered how she could know that. He didn't ask, but she must have caught the drift of his disbelieving thoughts.

"I may not have lived through one of the storms here, but I have a guidebook about Montana. It's got lots of information." Jenny told herself she had learned from her lack of an umbrella. She'd read the guidebook cover to cover. She was prepared now.

Zach groaned inside. The woman had learned about Montana storms from a guidebook. The few snowflakes that were falling had a dry sting to them. Zach knew that meant the coming storm would be cold enough to freeze a person. Some folks thought the large wet flakes signaled the worst storms, but they didn't. The wet flakes generally meant more snow, but the dry ones foretold a swift and merciless drop in temperature. And with the wind that could be dangerous.

"The electrical will probably go out. Are you set for that?"

Jenny turned to look at him squarely and lifted her chin. She was standing on her porch and she could still feel the pinch of the cold in her nose. She could see the sky was going deep gray and she could hear the grumbling in the air. "We have a propane furnace. And I have some oil lamps if the lights go out."

Zach grunted.

The door on the house popped open when they stepped near it. The little boy had been waiting for them to come back and must have heard their steps on the porch.

"Hi, there, Andy." Zach stepped inside behind Jenny. At least the boy liked him. Zach revised that opinion. Andy was looking at him as if he'd sprouted a second head.

"Santa Claus?"

Zach grabbed for his chin. He'd forgotten the beard.

Jenny met his eyes in alarm. She took a quick breath. "Santa shaved."

Zach slipped the beard back over his chin. But it was too late. The kid was bewildered. Then the confusion on Andy's face slowly cleared as though he finally understood a big secret. Zach felt a momentary pang, but then decided it was just as well the kid learned the truth about Santa Claus.

Zach looked over at Jenny. She was signaling him desperately to do something. Zach figured there wasn't much to be done.

"He'd find out someday, anyway—now that he's a big boy." Zach threw the boy a bone. He knelt down until his eyes were level with the boy's. "Isn't that right? You're a big boy and big boys can handle the truth about Santa Claus, can't you?"

Andy nodded happily.

Zach threw Jenny a self-righteous look. He might not be a parent, but he did know some things about little boys. "You're a real smart big boy to figure out Santa's secret." Zach noticed the girl who stood beside her mother. She rolled her eyes as if Zach was hopeless.

Andy nodded eagerly and leaned forward to whisper. "I know the secret. Santa's a cowboy— he's you—Lightnin' Lucas."

"Well, now, that's not exactly true." Zach stalled. Maybe he didn't understand a little boy's mind as much as he thought he did. "I am Zach Lightning Lucas—that's true—but I'm just wearing a Santa suit. I'm a pretend Santa."

"I have cowboy pajamas." Andy nodded happily as he danced from one foot to the other. "That's pretend. Want to see?"

"Sure, I guess." Zach looked up at Jenny to get direction.

Jenny gave a reluctant nod. The pajamas had been Andy's present last Christmas, and they were still his most prized possession. "Why don't you bring them out here and let Mr. Lucas see them when you give him your letter? I think he'll still take it for you."

Jenny lifted a questioning eyebrow at Zach.

Zach bristled. He was a man of his word. "Of course I'll still take the letter. I'll see the letter gets to the North Pole tonight. Before Santa leaves on his trip tomorrow. I'll take it personally."

"Can you fly?" Andy looked at him in awe. "Like the reindeer?"

Zach swallowed and shifted his weight onto his knee. "No, but I know the way to the North Pole and I can drive fast in my truck. Zoom. Zoom. Of course," he said, fumbling, "nobody should drive too fast."

Zach hoped the kid forgot this conversation before he turned sixteen and got his driving permit.

"Will you take me with you?"

Zach looked over at the little boy looking at him with such shining trust. Like a shy deer, the boy had edged closer and closer to Zach as he knelt beside him until now the boy was practically leaning against Zach's shoulder. Zach had to swallow again. "Not this time."

"Why not? I'll be good."

Jenny looked down at the man and her boy and felt sad. Andy never said anything, but he clearly yearned for a father even more than he yearned to be a cowboy. Maybe after Christmas she should accept a date from Max Daniel, that single rancher up north who Mrs. Hargrove had mentioned might be interested in her. Max attended the Dry Creek church and Jenny had spoken with him briefly on the three Sundays she and the children had gone there. Even if Jenny didn't find him very exciting, he was stable.

Jenny knew she didn't want to marry, but she had the children to think about.

Besides, a date didn't mean she was making a commitment. And it would make her feel as though she was at least open to God's leading in that area. And who knew? Maybe she would go on a date with the man and feel something that might eventually lead to being willing to get married again. The whole thought depressed her.

"Of course you'll be good," Zach was saying to Andy. "But you see, well, you have to stay and help your mother. There's a storm coming and she'll need a big boy like you to help her."

"Lisa's bigger. She can help."

Jenny looked at the helpless expression on Zach's face and almost laughed. Just watching him lifted her spirits. Not many men were a match for a determined four-year-old.

"Of course she can." Zach searched the room for the girl and didn't see her. He wondered where she had gone. "It's just that—" Zach had an inspiration "—Santa's too busy to see people before he takes his trip. He only talks to the elves."

The boy looked up in sudden worry. "But my letter."

"Oh, I'm sure he has time for letters." Zach

started to sweat. He decided he was better off facing a bucking bronc like Black Demon than a child like the one in front of him. He understood a thousand pounds of angry horse better than he did this little boy.

"I'm sure Santa reads all his mail." Jenny took pity on them both. Andy had labored for a full afternoon on his Santa letter, patiently copying the letters Jenny had printed for him.

Jenny hoped that Mr. Lucas understood how precious the letter was he'd offered to deliver. Andy hadn't thought of anything for days since he wrote that letter.

"Lisa can come, too." The little boy leaned closer to Zach and confided, "She told me there's no Santa at the North Pole." The boy's voice dropped to a whisper. "She has to do dishes for a month all by herself if I show her that Santa lives there. It's a bet."

Jenny saw her son's blond head leaning close to the man's dark one. The man's arm had gone around her son's shoulders and they were whispering about something she couldn't make out. She knew children liked their secrets, but she wasn't sure she wanted this cowboy to share them.

"Mr. Lucas needs to leave soon, Andy," Jenny reminded her son as she picked up the camera from the counter. Lisa had insisted she was too old for a Santa picture, so Jenny only had to worry about

Andy. "Why don't you go get your letter for him, and I'll take your picture while you give it to him."

"It's here," Andy said as he moved away from Zach enough to pull a crumpled letter out of his pocket. He handed it up to Zach. "I've been saving it."

The camera flash went off as Jenny snapped a picture.

"I'll deliver it express mail." Zach blinked as he took the letter in his hand. The woman hadn't even given him time to force a smile. "You can trust the U.S. Postal Service." Zach saluted the boy even though, as far as he knew, the postal service had never had a salute of any kind. But it seemed to reassure the boy.

Zach stood up and looked at the woman. "If you want, you can try a second picture."

Jenny looked at him.

"I wasn't smiling." Zach almost swore. It wasn't his idea to have his picture in some family album, but if his picture was going to be there it seemed only right that he be smiling.

Jenny shrugged. "The beard covers most of your face, anyway."

Zach nodded. If the woman didn't care if Santa was smiling, he shouldn't care. It did make him wonder what Christmas was coming to, however. If anyone should be smiling at Christmas, it was Santa and his helpers. "It's your picture."

"Did you get my letter in the picture?" the boy asked.

The woman nodded.

"I drew the stamp myself." The boy looked up at Zach. "Mom said it was all right."

Zach bent down and shook the boy's hand for further assurance. "It's just the right kind of stamp."

The kitchen had a window by the sink and one on the opposite wall. The sky was gray out of both windows, and Zach heard the rattle of the wind as it gathered force.

He watched as Jenny pulled the stub of a picture out of the camera.

"Here." Jenny held the camera out to him.

Zach shook his head. "Charley said you were to keep it over the holidays in case you want to take more pictures."

"Well, that's kind of you."

"Not me. It belongs to Mrs. Hargrove." Zach shuffled his feet. He wasn't used to getting so much credit for things he didn't even do.

"I better get out of here before the storm hits." Zach pulled his Santa hat back on his head. No one had flipped any light switches, and the light coming into the windows was thin. Fortunately, he could hear the hum of the furnace and a floor vent blew a steady stream of warm air into the room. At least the family had heat.

Zach looked over at the woman who held a still-developing picture in her hand. "You're sure you'll be all right now in this storm? If you need to call anyone on the phone to come sit this storm out with you, I'd do it now. The lines might go down any-time now."

"Thanks. I'll do that," Jenny said. She smiled confidently as if she had someone to call.

Zach nodded. He figured that the cereal box wasn't the only reason the woman wouldn't go out with him. She must have a boyfriend. Well, he shouldn't be surprised. Charley had as much as told him she did. Some rancher—what was his name? Max something.

"Well, I'll leave, then," Zach said as he walked toward the door. "I'll close the door quick behind me so you keep your heat in."

Jenny watched the man walk to the door. Sud-denly she didn't want him to leave. There was a bliz-zard coming and she didn't know what to expect. Even a cereal-box cowboy was better than no one when it came to facing a storm. But she couldn't ask him to stay. He was a stranger, for goodness sake. Just because she was used to telling her troubles to his face didn't mean he had any obligation to her.

"You've got holiday plans?" she squeaked out as he put his hand on the doorknob.

He turned around and looked at her. "Vegas."

"Oh. I see. Well, have fun."

Jenny could kick herself. Of course, the man had plans. It was Christmas, after all. Everyone had plans.

"Thanks." Zach hesitated. "I could change them if—"

"Of course you can't change them." Jenny stiffened her resolve. "I was just asking because I…I mean we…we have plans of our own and I was hoping you had plans, too."

"I see. Thanks." Zach turned the knob this time. No sense staying where someone had plans that didn't include him.

Zach leaned into the wind as he walked to the postal truck. The sky was getting darker in the east. A spray of snowflakes hit his face, even with the beard pulled up. He noticed that he hadn't closed the back door to the postal truck completely. He walked over and snapped it shut. He didn't want a chill at his back while he raced this storm back to Dry Creek.

Zach started the engine on the postal truck and released the brake. Time to get back. It was probably too late to beat the storm to the pass. Unless he missed his guess, he'd be sleeping in the horse trailer tonight while Thunder boarded at Charley's barn. In a few hours no one would be doing much driving. Zach just hoped he made it back to Dry Creek before the roads were snowed shut.

He could feel the hard boards of that trailer on his back already. It was going to be some merry Christmas.

Chapter Four

Andy wanted a peanut butter sandwich.

"Just let me be sure the oil lamp is filled and I'll make you one," Jenny said as she watched the tail-lights of the postal truck pull away. The red lights were the only bright thing in the dark gray of the afternoon. A layer of snow had already fallen and she could see the tire tracks of the truck.

Jenny had made a mental list over a week ago of the things she needed to do to prepare for a winter storm. Making sure the lamp was full was the first one. The other was to be sure the curtains were drawn on all the windows so that there was a little extra insulation. Mrs. Hargrove had insisted Jenny buy a case of tuna and another of assorted soup when she moved here. The older woman had also urged her to always keep the propane tank that fed the furnace at least half-full.

"Heat and food is all you really need," the older woman had said. "If your pipes freeze you'll more than likely still have snow around that you can melt for water. Not that it's as pure as you might think. I'd get some water filters if I were you and run the melted water through them. Outside of that, keep healthy and you'll do fine."

Jenny didn't feel as if she was doing fine. She hadn't been able to get any filters for water. But the small stove in the kitchen fed off the propane tank out back so she could use that to boil the water if necessary.

Just keep focused, she reminded herself. Like Mrs. Hargrove had said, she'd do just fine. Ten minutes passed before she realized Mrs. Hargrove was wrong. Jenny wasn't fine. She'd made one big mistake. The number one rule of surviving a blizzard with your children was to actually have your children inside the house with you. Andy was here, but Lisa was gone.

Jenny searched every room in the house twice before Andy confessed that Lisa had sneaked out the door in the laundry room and hid in the back of the postal truck. Jenny was accustomed to watching Andy. He was the one who got into trouble and scrapes. She never had to worry about Lisa.

"We got a bet going," Andy explained without a trace of worry. "Lisa's gonna go see all about Santa and let me know."

Jenny's heart stopped. "You mean she went off alone!"

"The Lightning man's with her," Andy said calmly. "He'll take care of her until they get to Santa's."

"But Mr. Lucas is going to Las Vegas!"

"Not until he takes my letter to the North Pole. He promised."

Jenny was speechless. Her daughter had run off with some cowboy on his way to Vegas, and she was only eight years old.

"He'll bring her right back," Jenny promised herself aloud. *Dear Lord. The man has to bring her back.* "When he sees her in the truck, he'll bring her right back."

But what if he didn't see her? Lisa was obviously hidden or she'd be back already. Unless the man was—Jenny stopped herself. No, she wouldn't even think that. She was sure he wasn't that kind of a person. After all, she knew he hadn't deliberately taken Lisa.

Jenny looked out the window. The tracks left by the postal truck had been filled in with new snow.

He's not going to see Lisa in time to bring her back, Jenny thought to herself in despair. Oh, she supposed he would leave her with Charley—when Jenny thought about it she wasn't completely worried that the man would actually want to take Lisa to Las Vegas with him—but still, Lisa would miss

Christmas. Lisa had never been away from home at Christmas before.

Jenny looked around. She wished now that she had swallowed her pride and asked someone to bring them a Christmas tree from Miles City. She had told herself it would be okay for this Christmas to be plain. Her children would understand and share her gratefulness that they had a new home. They'd hang their stockings and read the Christmas story and that would be enough.

But she was wrong. Lisa wouldn't have come up with a ridiculous bet like this for Andy if they had both been busy decorating a tree or putting gumdrops on cookies. Her children needed Christmas and she had failed to give it to them. It wasn't even grief that had stopped her from doing what she should. She had just been so intent on proving that they belonged here on this farm that she'd forgotten how important Christmas was.

Zach swore under his breath. The snow blew thicker every minute. Enough of it covered the road so that he couldn't make out the ruts. He was lucky to keep this tin can of a postal truck on the dirt road. But the snow wasn't his big problem. His big problem sat on the passenger seat next to him.

"I knew you couldn't go to the North Pole," the girl said smugly as she bit into another oatmeal cookie. "There is no North Pole."

Zach gritted his teeth. "Didn't your mom teach you not to go off with strangers?"

He'd been halfway back to Dry Creek when he'd heard the muffled sneeze from the back of the postal truck and had been so startled he'd almost driven off the road. In fact, he did pull to the side of the road so he could twist around and take a good look back there. The girl had been hiding under his sheepskin coat.

"We're not in Los Angeles anymore." The girl took another bite of cookie. "There aren't any strangers here. Only farmers."

Zach had given her the plate of cookies he had gotten from Mrs. Goussley. So far she'd managed to polish off half of them.

"There are things to be careful about in Montana, too."

"I know." The girl brushed the crumbs off her jacket sleeve. "My mom read about them in that book. There's snakes in the coulee. And bees in the summer."

"And strangers. Weird people are everywhere. You can never be too careful with strangers."

The girl shrugged. "You got any milk?"

"Of course not, this is a postal truck not a lunch truck."

Zach strained to see through the snowstorm outside his windshield. He'd guess there was four inches of snow so far on the ground—maybe more.

He hoped that was the final turn to the Collins place up ahead.

"Your mother's going to be worried. She won't know where you are."

"Andy will tell her. He can't keep a secret."

Zach hoped the girl's mother didn't jump to any wild ideas like that maybe he had asked the girl to come with him. He had given her the candy cane, but no mother would think that would be enough to entice a child to climb into his truck. Of course, Zach slowly realized, he had said he was going to see Santa. A court of law might see that as enticement enough for any child.

Zach started to sweat. He'd best get this little one home soon. "Ah, good, that *is* the turn."

The snow was blowing so much he could only make out the outline of the house and the yellow glow of the windows.

Jenny thought she heard the sounds of a car and ran to the window. An hour had passed since Mr. Lucas had left, and the day had turned to evening. Jenny opened the door to see better. Stinging snow hit her face, but she only leaned out farther to try to see more clearly. If it weren't for those red and green lights on the postal truck, Jenny wouldn't have been sure it was Mr. Lucas coming back up her long driveway.

The truck stopped a few feet from the porch, and

the lights went out. The driver's door opened and Jenny breathed easier. It was him.

"Lisa!" The wind blew the call away from Jenny and she wasn't sure her daughter would hear it, but the man did and he gave her a reassuring wave as he walked around to the passenger side of the truck.

Her daughter started to walk to the porch, but the wind made her stumble. The man picked her up and took her up the steps in long strides. Snow clung to her daughter's hair as the cowboy brought her across the porch and into the door that Jenny held open.

The temperature had dropped even more than Zach had figured when he was inside the truck. He knew that was why the girl clung to his neck. All that Santa suit polyester was warm and fuzzy. Still, he liked having her nestled there. It made him feel, well, a little fatherly, he thought defensively. Nothing wrong with that.

"Lisa! Are you all right, honey?" The woman opened her arms, and Zach reluctantly gave the girl to her.

"She's fine," Zach said curtly.

"I don't feel so good," the girl moaned.

"What'd you do to her?" Jenny shifted Lisa in her arms and glared at Zach.

"Me?" Zach looked around. Even the boy was looking at him suspiciously. "All I did was give her the candy cane and some cookies."

"You did find Santa's!" Andy gave a triumphant

war whoop and jumped down off the chair where he was sitting. "No more dishes."

"The cookies came from Mrs. Goussley. Honest, you can call her up on the phone and ask her."

"That won't be necessary." Jenny set Lisa down on the floor and knelt at her eye level. "How many cookies did you eat?"

Lisa gave Zach a look of appeal.

"They were oatmeal cookies," Zach offered in her defense. He hadn't even counted how many were on that plate. "Oatmeal is good for you. Builds bones or something."

Jenny reached over and smoothed down her daughter's hair. It had been a long time since Lisa had been disobedient. Or done anything like eat too many cookies. It was good to see her daughter be a child again. "I guess a few extra cookies won't hurt anything."

A gust of wind rattled the house, and the overhead light flickered.

"I hope you have that lamp handy." Zach looked out the kitchen window. The sky was completely dark now, but he could see flakes of snow being whipped past the glass by the wind. "I should call Charley, too, before everything goes down."

"The phone's over there." Jenny pointed to the wall opposite the sink.

"Did you get a chance to make your call earlier?" Zach stepped over to the phone. Whoever she had been planning to call hadn't been much help to her. If she had called Zach with a storm like this on the way, he'd have been on her doorstep by now.

"I, ah, I thought I'd wait."

Zach pulled a slip of paper out of his pocket. Charley had written his phone number on the same page he'd written the other instructions. Zach dialed.

"This is Zach Lucas." The phone only rang once before it was answered; Charley must have been waiting for a call. "I'm at Jenny's—"

"I'm so glad someone's there! Edith just called. There's a real blizzard coming through and she's worried—"

Another gust of wind hit the house and the phone went dead. Then the overhead light in the kitchen flickered again before it went out. Jenny's heart stopped. Her house was completely dark. There was no moon outside to provide even a soft hint of light. There was nothing. Just the howl of the wind and the rattle of the windows. Followed by a whimper and the shuffle of little feet.

"Stay still, Andy, I'll come to you." Jenny said as she slid one foot out across the kitchen floor. Andy didn't like the dark. She had to get to him. He had nightmares.

"That's okay. I've got him," Zach said as he felt the boy's arms grab his thigh and hug tightly. Zach bent down to lift Andy up in his arms. "We're just fine, aren't we, partner? It's just a little darkness."

The boy burrowed into Zach's fuzzy suit. There was something about a Santa suit, Zach thought to himself. Even a crazy Santa suit like the one Mrs. Hargrove had put together. It made the kids feel at home with him. He realized with surprise that he kind of liked it.

"I don't like the dark," Andy whispered softly.

"It's okay," Zach muttered as he shifted his arm so one of his hands would be free to feel the grooves along the belt of the Santa suit. If he remembered Charley's words correctly, there was a switch here someplace that would turn on the flashing lights surrounding the belt. Zach had only seen the lights flash for a minute or two when Charley first asked him to put on the suit.

Jenny kept taking small steps in the general direction of her son. What had made Andy slide over and grab on to the cowboy? She had been as close to Andy as the cowboy had been. "Mama's coming."

Zach's hand found the switch on the belt at the same time as he smelled the perfume. He stopped to take another breath. It was a simple perfume— peach, if he wasn't mistaken. But it made him want to keep the darkness around him for just a minute or two longer.

Jenny reached out to where she thought Andy was and touched the cowboy's arm instead. The softness of the Santa suit could not hide the solid steel of the man's muscle. Jenny knew she should move her hand when she discovered it was the cowboy she was touching and not her son, but she didn't. It was dark all around her and he was an anchor.

"Jenny?"

Jenny snatched her hand away from his arm. She was glad it was dark enough to hide the fierce blush she was sure was on her face. "I'm just worried about Andy."

"Of course," Zach shifted the boy's weight in his arms. "He's right here."

Jenny was close enough to sense the cowboy turning his body slightly so that her son was in the arm closest to her. Jenny reached out her hand again. This time she felt Andy's soft hair. She also felt the edge of Zach's shoulder.

It was ten degrees below zero outside and only about fifty degrees above zero inside the house, but Zach felt as if he didn't need to see another fire again as long as he lived. Jenny's touch had been tentative, but it scorched him.

"Can you hold him while I get the lamp?" Jenny asked.

"You got oil in the lamp already?"

"It's right next to it." Jenny felt disoriented. The sink had to be in that direction. "Under the sink."

Zach groaned. "You better light me up, then, so you don't break your neck walking over there."

"What?"

"It's the belt," Zach interrupted. "It's got built-in Christmas lights. I had the switch a minute ago, but I had to let go when I moved Andy."

"But how do I...?"

"Just feel along the belt until you come to a clicker kind of a thing. It attaches to the batteries."

"Your belt?"

Zach's mouth went dry at the breathless way she said it—as if he were asking her to do something a whole lot more intimate than turn on some lights. "It's about where Andy's feet are."

Jenny moved her hands away from Andy's hair and let them slide down Andy's back until the man shifted her son in his arms and suddenly her hands were sliding down the man's torso. Even the softness of the Santa suit couldn't hide the lean muscles of his chest and then his stomach underneath.

"I can't find it." Jenny stopped. It suddenly occurred to her she didn't want to go too low. But she left her hand on his stomach. The whole world was dark around her and she wanted an anchor. Besides, she could hear his breathing.

Zach felt his breath catch. He shifted slightly to balance Andy in his left arm. He put his right hand over the one that Jenny had on his stomach. It wasn't until he touched her that he felt her pulse. Her heart was fluttering like a bird's.

"Scared?" Zach whispered.

"Me?" Jenny braced herself. It was only a man's stomach for goodness sake. "No, I'm fine."

"Good. I'd begun to worry I scared you with what I said about storms earlier. There's nothing to worry about. We'll be fine."

Jenny had completely forgotten about the storm. "Of course."

Zach reluctantly guided Jenny's hand to his belt buckle. He realized he could have just flipped the switch on his belt himself, but it was much more satisfying to feel Jenny's hand under his.

"I found it." Jenny felt the ridge of a button on the side of the smooth plastic of the belt. She slid the button to the right.

"That's it!"

A dozen tiny lights flickered. The kitchen was no longer dark. Instead, long shadows filled the corners and a soft glow surrounded Santa.

"Mama." Lisa ran to Jenny and stood beside her.

Zach felt as if time had stopped. There was just enough light in the kitchen to see Jenny's eyes. Zach didn't even realize he was staring at her eyes until she blinked.

"I better go get the lamp." Jenny didn't move. She meant to move, but she didn't. In the light coming from Zach's belt, the man looked more like his cereal picture than he had since he'd pulled down his beard. It was his eyes, Jenny thought to herself.

He was looking at her as if she'd just given him a championship trophy.

"I didn't know those lights would work so well." Zach tried to rein his mind back to the present. He would start counting to ten if he had to—he couldn't stand there staring at the woman. She'd think he was a lunatic.

"Oh." So that was it, Jenny thought. That's what pleased him so much. Men and their mechanical toys. "Yeah, they're something. Great lights."

Zach felt Andy squirm in his arms.

"I'm hungry," Andy said as he wiggled his way down Zach until he reached the floor.

"Let me get the lamp set up first." Jenny patted Andy on the head as she turned toward the counter. "Then I'll see what we can fix for dinner."

Jenny mentally catalogued the cans in her cupboard. She wished Mrs. Hargrove had warned her to keep more than soup on hand for blizzards. She didn't have anything suitable for company. "I'm afraid it won't be fancy."

"I don't need fancy," Zach said.

"Mama, what about—" Lisa said suddenly as she lifted worried eyes to her mother. "I mean, I know she's a wild cat, but—?

"You have a cat?" Zach asked. This family barely looked as though they could take care of themselves. What were they doing with a pet?

"She's not ours, but she lives in our barn," Jenny

said. "We feed her and—well, I'll put together a dish of something."

"I'll take it out," Zach said. He couldn't bear the thought of Jenny going out in this kind of weather. "You could get lost on the way back."

"I wouldn't get lost. I already strung a rope out to the barn from here."

Zach grunted. At least the guidebook had one good tip in it.

"Maybe," Jenny hesitated and then pressed on. "Maybe you could build a fire in the wood stove when you're out there. It's in the side room with the bed. Charley brought us a load of wood one day and we put most of it out there. It's going to be cold tonight."

"You'll burn the place down doing that if no one's out there. Tell me you haven't been doing that."

"Well, no, but it hasn't been this cold yet. I'd say you should bring the cat into the house, but I don't think you could catch her."

"She's wild," Andy added solemnly.

Zach nodded. Of course, this little family couldn't have an easy pet if they had to have one. "I'll take a look when I'm out there."

Jenny opened a can of tuna and gave it to Zach for the cat.

"We'll have something hot to eat when you get back," Jenny said as Zach started for the door. "And the end of the rope is tied to the post by the porch. The guidebook—"

"I know," Zach said as he opened the door. "The guidebook said to tie it there."

One hour later they sat down to the table and there wasn't one hot thing on it. Even soup was impossible. "I never thought the pipes would be a problem. I should have kept the can of tuna for us."

The outside pipe on the propane stove had shaken loose in the wind. Zach had capped it off when he came back from the barn, but he needed better light to fix it completely.

"This is just fine." Zach grinned. They were having cereal for dinner. His cereal. "I didn't know you ate this stuff."

"It's my favorite." Andy pushed his chair closer to Zach before he climbed up on it.

"I thought we should use up the milk up since the refrigerator is off." Jenny set a plate of bread on the table and sat down. "I had a coupon for the cereal."

"So you're just trying the cereal out?"

"I wouldn't say that exactly." Jenny casually turned the cereal box so the man's face wasn't staring at her. "We eat lots of kinds of cereal."

"It's my favorite," Andy repeated as he picked up his spoon and waved it around. "Cowboys eat it."

"It's only your favorite because Mom bought a ton of it." Lisa unfolded the napkin by her plate.

"Mr. Lucas doesn't want to hear about what we eat." Especially not how much of his cereal we eat, Jenny thought frantically. "Let's pray."

Zach looked around. Three heads bowed in unison. And then three sets of hands reached out to grab a hand. Zach was new to this prayer business, but he figured out he was supposed to link up with Andy and Lisa. That wasn't so bad.

"Lord, we thank You for the food You have provided," Jenny prayed. "Keep us all safe and warm—"

"The cat, too," Andy added.

"The cat, too," Jenny agreed. "Be with us in this blizzard of yours. We ask this in the name of our Savior, Jesus Christ. Amen."

Zach blinked when he looked up and opened his eyes. His rodeo friends wouldn't believe he'd just prayed. Well, maybe *he* hadn't prayed, but it was as close as he'd come in his life. It made him kind of nervous. He wondered if God had been listening.

Zach had nothing against God. He guessed he just didn't know anything about Him. Not that he was about to display his ignorance on the matter right here at the dinner table. He'd sometimes wondered what kind of people believed in God, though. Really believed. Now he knew.

Jenny noticed Zach was looking at her as though he wondered what he was doing here at the table with her and the children. She supposed this wasn't the kind of situation he was used to. Well, they'd just have to make the best of it.

"We should talk about—" She tried to remember what single people like Zach talked about. "We should talk about… That's it…" Jenny turned to face the man. "How was your day today?"

Zach watched Andy take a spoonful of the cereal dry. He could hear him crunching away. "My horse got sick, but I ended up having a good time delivering the mail. Met some nice people. How was your day?"

"Oh, your horse. Did Charley get a chance to say how he was before the phone line went dead?"

"I'm sure he's fine. Charley said earlier he thought it was just a low-grade fever." Zach noticed Jenny hadn't answered his question. Now what would a mother with small children do during the day? "And your day was no doubt spent getting ready for Christmas."

Jenny gasped and dropped her spoon on the table.

"What'd I say?" Even in the dark of the kitchen, Zach could tell he'd asked the wrong question.

"Nothing. It's just—" Jenny looked at her two children sitting one on each side of the stranger who should be a stranger but who wasn't because his eyes were looking straight at her just the way he did from the cereal box. She couldn't keep it in any longer. She was used to making her confessions to that face. "I'm a terrible mother."

Zach saw the tear in her eye before she bent her head down, and he said the only thing he could. "That can't be true."

Jenny looked up at him. "I don't have a proper Christmas for my children, and that's why Lisa ran away with you."

"Lisa didn't run away with me. She didn't even run away, really. She had a bet she wanted to win."

"Yeah, Mama. I wouldn't run away. I just wanted to show Andy that there's no Santa at the North Pole."

"See what I mean?" Jenny wailed.

Zach half nodded. He didn't see at all, but he could tell the woman needed sympathy. "It's a shame they make all this fuss about a day—all it is is December twenty-fifth. Just the day after December twenty-fourth. No need to go on so."

Zach heard three gasps all at the same time. One good thing—he was pretty sure Jenny's tears had stopped.

"But Christmas is the birthday of Jesus," Lisa announced primly. "The Savior of the whole world."

"All children need a Christmas," Jenny said at the same time.

"Don't you believe in Christmas?" Andy cut right to the important question. His eyes were wide in shock.

Zach squirmed and did the only manly thing he could. He lied. "Sure I believe in Christmas."

Jenny looked at him skeptically.

"Christmas just doesn't believe in me," Zach added softly.

"Well, surely you're going to celebrate Christmas," Jenny said. It was really none of her business, but everyone needed to celebrate something. And then she remembered that he was. "Of course, that's why you're going to Las Vegas."

Zach snorted. "I'm not going there to celebrate Christmas. I'm going there to forget there is such a miserable day."

"But I thought you had plans. That you were meeting a friend, or…" Jenny squinted at him. Surely nobody went to Las Vegas to be alone for the holidays. Come to think of it, it wasn't that easy to just go alone to Las Vegas at Christmas, especially without planning. "You won't get a hotel room, you know. Not over the holidays. All the hotels will be booked."

Hotel rooms all across the country were booked on holiday weekends. Everyone knew that.

"Patti already has a room for me."

"I see." Jenny's voice tightened.

Jenny didn't know why she cared that the person he was driving hundreds of miles to see was a woman. And not just any woman. A woman with a name. She should be glad he was driving off to meet some woman. It would keep her focused. The last thing she or her family needed was a man like him around. If they had a man in the family at all, they needed someone stable. Someone who would be a good husband and a father. Someone who didn't make her feel this way. "Well then, you don't have to worry about reservations."

Zach nodded.

Jenny knew she should let it go, but she didn't. "Maybe you'll see a show while you're there. I hear they have some wonderful Christmas shows. Ice skating, I suppose."

"You're thinking of the family shows. The kind of show Patti and the girls do isn't what you'd call family fare."

"This Patti—she's a singer?"

Zach shook his head. "Naw, she's just one of the showgirls."

"With the feathers in her hair?" Jenny knew what those showgirls wore and didn't wear. "She must be very pretty."

"I suppose so."

Jenny stiffened. "Of course she's pretty. They all are."

Zach told himself Patti would have to be pretty. He'd only spent several hours with her last year. He knew she was a blonde. But outside of that… "I don't remember her eyes."

"Well, maybe you should try looking at her eyes instead of—" Jenny broke off. Her children were at the table. Besides, it was none of her business who or what the cowboy admired. "Would you like some more cereal?"

"You know that showgirl stuff is mostly aerobics." Zach took the cereal box that Jenny offered.

"Aerobics?"

"Like cheerleading," Zach said firmly as he poured more cereal into his bowl. "Yeah, it's like cheerleading. Only with feathers in the hair and a swimsuit full of sequins."

"Mama was a cheerleader," Lisa offered proudly as she paused with her spoon halfway to her mouth. "Weren't you, Mama?"

"A long time ago."

"Really?"

"A very long time ago."

"We still have her pom-poms," Lisa said as she set down her spoon. "She didn't have any feathers or a swimming suit. She was a great cheerleader, though."

"I'm sure she was." Zach had a vision of Jenny bouncing around doing cheers. He wasn't sure it was at all the sort of vision he should have while he sat at the table with her children eating cereal. "She must have been wonderful—even without the feathers."

Jenny could feel the blush on her cheeks. She needed to change the subject. "I don't know why I kept those pom-poms. I didn't even pack an umbrella and I had those silly things along."

"Memories," Zach said.

"I guess." Jenny remembered she'd been happy in high school. Sometimes just looking at the pom-poms made her smile.

Everyone was silent for a bit.

"The snow should be gone by tomorrow," Jenny finally said. "It's too early to have a blizzard that sticks. You should still be able to make it out of here and catch your show."

Zach looked at her as if she was crazy. "What makes you think that?"

"The guidebook says—"

Zach snorted. "You have that guidebook here? Let me see it. I can practically guarantee you that this blizzard will last forty-eight hours."

"But that's impossible." Jenny looked stunned. She had come to rely on that guidebook. "Montana doesn't have long blizzards before Christmas."

"Tell that to the sky," Zach said.

Jenny would tell it to the sky if she thought there was any hope the sky would listen. "So you'll be here for Christmas."

"Looks like it."

"I'm afraid it won't be nearly as exciting as Las Vegas," Jenny said. Surely he would be able to leave tomorrow. The postal truck was a four-wheel-drive. It could go places her car couldn't go even when it was running. The house suddenly felt much too small, and the Christmas she'd planned much too humble to share with this man. "We don't even have a tree."

Zach felt the collar of his shirt get smaller and he swallowed. "I'm not worried about a tree. They aren't anything but a fire hazard, anyway."

"You don't like Christmas trees?" Lisa asked him in a voice that suggested he hated babies.

"Well, I…I don't have anything against them, I guess." Zach tried to make amends. "Especially if they don't have lights on them."

"No lights!" Lisa scoffed at him. "If there's no lights, it's not even a Christmas tree. Everyone knows that."

Jenny knew she should have tried harder to get a tree. Christmas was important to children. Well, it wasn't too late. "I'm going to go out tomorrow and get us a Christmas tree."

"Really?" Lisa turned to her mother breathlessly. "You are?"

"Of course," Jenny said. "This is Montana. There's lots of trees around. It might not be a pine tree like the ones we used to have in Los Angeles, but I can find something to decorate."

"It'll be twenty below zero tomorrow." Zach thought he should mention the fact. "You'll freeze to death."

"Tomorrow will be a fine day." Jenny lifted her chin. "Montana blizzards this time of year never last."

Zach groaned. Even if the sun did shine tomorrow, he couldn't leave this family in this kind of weather. They'd never make it through Christmas without help, the way they were carrying on. Jenny would freeze out there trying to chop down some fool sage bush. "And don't try baking any Christmas cookies until that propane line is fixed."

"Cookies," Andy sighed blissfully as he looked at Zach. "Are you going to make us some Christmas cookies?"

"Me?" Zach didn't like the trusting look in the boy's eyes. "I don't cook."

"I'll help you," Andy said, his trust not wavering. "I know how to stir. We can make cookies, can't we, Mom?"

Jenny looked at her son. She'd never seen him this anxious to spend time with a man before. It must be because Zach was a cowboy. How could she explain to her son that this man was not the kind of man to put on an apron and bake cookies with a little boy. "Mr. Lucas might be busy."

Fortunately, Andy didn't ask what the man would be busy doing. "Busy" was the excuse his father had always used when Andy asked to do anything with him.

Zach watched the joy flow out of Andy's eyes, and he found he didn't like it. "I guess I could learn to make cookies. How hard can it be?"

"Really?" Andy's eyes shone again.

"What?" Jenny stared at Zach as if he'd offered to fly to the stars. "Are you sure?"

Zach nodded. He wasn't going soft, he told himself. He was snowed in with this family. Snow-bound, really. He was just making the best of a bad situation. Anyone would do the same. It was that time of year, after all.

He sure hoped he wasn't going soft.

Chapter Five

Jenny had no choice but to follow the cereal cowboy and her son deeper into the house. They'd all cleared their bowls off the card table, and there was nothing to keep them in the kitchen.

"We haven't been here a month yet." Jenny carried a flashlight even though Zach and his lit belt showed everyone the way. The living room was almost empty. She had a cork bulletin board hanging on one wall that was covered with snapshots of the kids, but it was the only thing hanging on the walls. A few boxes stood along the other wall. The flaps of the boxes were pulled up and showed a jumble of children's books. They didn't have a television set, so the children each picked a favorite story each night and they sat together while Jenny read to them. Lisa loved fairy tales. Andy liked animal books.

"We're camping," Andy confided in a loud whisper as he led Zach through the living room. "That's why we don't need furniture."

Jenny winced. The one piece of furniture that had been there to welcome them was a rust-colored sofa that sagged and had a grease spot on the right cushion. Jenny had covered it with a light-blue afghan she had knit when she was pregnant with Andy. It was a baby's afghan, but she'd made it large and it almost covered the sofa. "I plan to get some used furniture just as soon as I can get to Billings."

"Yeah, I hear your car isn't working," Zach said as he followed Andy's lead and sat down on the sofa. "Charley said it was the radiator."

No sooner had Zach settled on the sofa than Andy burrowed into the cushion next to Zach's elbow and whispered, "Charley—he's got a pig."

"Is that right?" Zach looked down at the boy. The living room was full of crazy red and green shadows from the Christmas lights on the Santa belt, but no matter what shade of light surrounded the boy's face it just seemed to keep shining. Zach had a pang of wistfulness knowing he'd never been that trusting. Certainly not at four years old. Maybe not even at four months. Not with the kind of parents he'd had. He'd had to learn to take care of himself early. By the time he was Andy's age, he was taking care of his alcoholic parents as well as himself.

"I've got pigs, too," Andy said as he jumped off

the sofa and headed toward the books. "They huffed and puffed."

Zach felt as if he'd fallen down a rabbit hole.

"It was the wolf that huffed and puffed," Jenny clarified. She had to admit that the cowboy was taking her sparse furnishings better than she would have expected. He didn't look around with anything like pity in his brown eyes.

Andy found the book he was looking for and waved it at Zach. "Read me the story."

Andy brought the book over to the sofa, sitting down close to Zach.

"Mr. Lightning might not have time." Jenny wished Andy wasn't so intent on relating to the cowboy. She supposed Andy would be that way with any man these days. But a drifter like Zach would have no patience with a little boy, and she couldn't bear to see Andy hurt. "He's resting."

Andy put his book down easily and looked at Zach with round eyes. "Is he sick?"

Zach heard Jenny's quick intake of breath at the same time as he saw the worry flare in Lisa's eyes as she stood next to her mother. Then he remembered what Charley had said about Jenny's husband dying of cancer. "Don't worry. I'm not the kind of guy who gets sick. I'm healthy as a horse."

"Your horse is sick," Lisa reminded him as she walked over to the sofa and stood on the other side of Zach.

"That's just Thunder's disposition," Zach said. He couldn't help but notice how the girl came close to him, but not too close. "He just likes to complain about his aches and pains. He's not a sunshine kind of guy like me."

Zach saw the quick smile that crossed Lisa's face before she rolled her eyes.

"My daddy got sick," Andy said quietly as he snuggled closer to Zach's side. "He died."

Jenny caught her breath. This was the first time either one of the kids had mentioned their father's death.

"That's what people do," Lisa said, her voice flat. She sat down on the sofa next to Zach. "No need to cry about it."

Zach wished he were a smarter man. He looked over at Jenny, but she didn't seem capable of speech, either. So he looked down at Lisa. "It's always okay to cry when you're sad."

Zach moved his arm so there was room and Lisa scooted closer until his arm was around her.

Everyone was silent for a few minutes.

"Here, let me see that book," Zach held his hand out for the book Andy had picked up again. "No reason we can't all read it together. I've always wondered about wolves. Thought I might get one for a pet one of these days."

"Wolves aren't pets," Lisa informed him. She moved a little farther away from Zach until her back was straight and she was perched cautiously on the edge of the sofa. "They're dangerous animals."

Zach had no idea how it happened, but the wolf led to some ballerina Lisa was anxious for him to read about.

"She has a tiara," Lisa told him solemnly as she pointed to the shiny circle on the girl's head in the book. By this time, Lisa had snuggled close to his elbow again.

"She looks like a real princess," Zach agreed. Zach decided he liked being enclosed by the kids. Now if only Jenny would join them on the sofa.

Jenny sat on a folding chair and looked at the cowboy and her children. She could not remember a scene like this one in her whole life. Even if her late husband, Stephen, had unbent enough to relate to one of the kids, he never included them both at the same time. He had certainly never read to them.

Who was she kidding? Reading was only part of what Zach had done. He had listened to her children. Maybe now that they had started talking to him about Stephen's death, they would talk about it some more with her. Maybe her children would find healing on this farm, after all.

It was past bedtime for Andy, but Jenny let the time pass. If it wasn't that she thought she might destroy the moment by capturing it, she would take a picture of the three of them. Her children would remember this cowboy reading and talking to them for a long time.

"I asked Santa for a tiara," Lisa sighed as Zach finished reading the last page of the book. "But it's too expensive."

"Santa doesn't need money," Andy said cheerfully as he wiggled even closer to Zach. "He's got elves. They'll make you up one of those things."

"Elves can't make tiaras," Lisa said as she straightened her back and took the book out of Zach's hands. "They don't have any jewels. You need jewels for a tiara."

"Oh." Andy thought about this. "But they have cowboy stuff. Cowboy stuff doesn't take jewels. You could ask for some of that, like me."

Lisa stood up to take the book back to the box. "I hope you didn't write that in your letter. If I can't have a tiara, I at least want something that's pretty. I don't want anything cowboy."

Jenny knew what was coming and tried to head the question off before it was formed. "Time for bed, Andy." Jenny stood up and added another distraction. "You can wear your cowboy pajamas." Jenny kept her voice cheerful and calm, but she could see the frown forming on Andy's face.

"When are you going to take my letter to Santa, Mr. Lightning?" Andy asked in a soft voice. "Lisa said you had to bring her back. You never got to the North Pole."

Zach reached out automatically and patted the pocket that held the letter. Uh-oh. He'd forgotten it was still there. He looked to Jenny for help.

"Mr. Lightning did his best," Jenny said softly as she walked over to her son. "But there's a blizzard outside. The roads are all full of snow. He had to turn back before he got to the North Pole."

Andy looked up at Zach in alarm. "But you're still going to take my letter, aren't you? It's almost time for Santa to come. He has to get my letter or he won't know what to bring me."

Zach knew he was a sucker. There was no longer any doubt. "I'm just waiting for everyone to go to bed. Then I'll crank up the old truck and make a quick trip."

Andy looked up at Zach in relief. "It won't take long. You can go fast. Zoom, zoom. You said so."

"That I did."

Lisa rolled her eyes and Jenny opened her mouth to protest, but neither of them said anything.

"The quicker you get to bed, the sooner I can get going to the North Pole," Zach said.

Jenny had never seen her son so anxious to get to bed. Andy ran into his room and changed into his pajamas in the thin streaks of light that shone into his room from the living room. Even Lisa seemed content to go to her bedroom. Jenny had managed to get a single mattress for each of the bedrooms, but she hadn't prepared for company. "I'm sorry, I don't have a guest room or anything."

Zach smiled. "That's all right. I think I better sleep out in the barn and keep the fire going for that cat."

"At least there's a bed out there," Jenny said. "And I know the children will be glad you kept the cat warm."

"I don't suppose the beast has a name," Zach asked. He'd seen a white face looking at him from behind a stall, but he hadn't gotten close to the cat.

"She's not ours to name."

"She's living in your barn."

"Well, still—maybe she belongs somewhere else."

"She probably belongs to Mrs. Groussley. The cat probably wanted some solitude."

Jenny walked over to a box and pulled out several wool blankets. "I have some blankets, of course, that you can use. I don't have a spare pillow, but we can roll a blanket up and—"

"I'll be fine," Zach said.

Jenny had been worrying. The Santa letter had become more complicated than she'd ever imagined. "Andy can be persistent."

"That's a good thing."

Jenny kept her voice low as she gave the blankets to Zach. "We'll just tell him in the morning that you went to Santa's while he was asleep."

"You think he'll believe that?" Zach whispered in amazement. "If I know him, he's going to lie awake in there until he hears me leave." Zach shook his head in pride. "He might only be four, but he's awfully sharp."

"But what else can we do?"

Zach no longer bothered to lower his voice. "In just a few minutes, I'm going to go out to my truck and start driving it away."

"Oh." Jenny knew she shouldn't have expected him to stay. "I see."

Jenny swallowed before it occurred to her that even if the man wasn't the kind who stayed around, he didn't look like the kind who was crazy enough to head back to the main road in this weather.

"There's a blizzard out there," she whispered just in case he had forgotten. "You won't get halfway to Dry Creek without getting stuck."

"Ah." Zach smiled and winked at her. "But I don't need to get to Dry Creek. I only need to get to the North Pole."

They both heard the sigh of deep contentment that came from Andy's room before they heard the boy's voice. "It won't take long."

"No, it won't, partner," Zach agreed as he stood up. "It won't take long at all."

"Mom can go with you," Andy offered from the bedroom. "Just in case you get lost on the way back. She knows the way back here real good."

Now that's an idea, Zach thought to himself, before he realized how unlikely that would be with the kids in bed. "Your mom probably needs to stay with you."

Zach glanced sideways at Jenny just in case she was the kind of mother who was willing to leave her kids alone on a dark night so she could go for a freezing-cold drive with a bachelor.

Zach had known women who would have left their kids in strip joints if it meant they could spend time with a cowboy. Not that he was passing judgment on those women. He knew plenty of men who were just as irresponsible. Who was he fooling? He was one of those men who were just as irresponsible.

"It sure would keep me warmer if I had some company," Zach said softly as he followed Jenny out into the kitchen. If Jenny was the kind of mother willing to leave her kids, she'd be the kind of woman to give him a friendly kiss or two out there under the night sky. He had a sudden, powerful urge to know if her wide blue eyes changed colors and danced with stars when she was kissed. "I wonder how cold it is out there, anyway."

"Give me a minute and I'll let you know. I've gotten pretty accurate at guessing temperature." Jenny turned back to look at Zach.

Zach stepped closer. He wondered if Jenny could tell how much the kitchen had heated up since she'd turned to face him. He knew his temperature had risen by ten degrees. Her face was dusted with pink. And it was from more than the red in the lights on his belt. The kitchen was still in shadows but her face looked petal soft. He could almost taste those kisses. He figured her for a sweet kisser. He couldn't wait to find out just how sweet.

It took a second or two for Zach to get past his thoughts of kissing and realize Jenny was willing to leave the kids and go off with him for a long ride into the night. It took another second for his disappointment to settle. He'd have wagered his saddle that she was a better parent than that. Not that his disappointment would stop him from showing the lady a good time, he told himself. "It doesn't matter how cold it is out there, I'll keep you warm."

Now that Zach realized Jenny wasn't a saint, he figured the same old lines would work with her that he'd used in the rodeo for years. He was back in the game.

Jenny rolled her eyes, but didn't even respond to him. She just turned and walked toward the far kitchen wall. "I hope you don't mind if I drive the postal truck. The kids will be fine with you here."

"What?" Zach couldn't believe it. He was still stuck in his fantasy of her warm lips in the cold night. What had she said? He followed her through the kitchen. "You're going without me? Without *me?* Out there—into that blizzard?"

Was the woman crazy?

"Do you know how cold it is out there?" he asked, just to be sure. "It isn't anyplace for a woman alone—not on a night like tonight. This wind chill is nothing to mess around with—especially for a woman alone."

Zach knew he had said the wrong thing even as he saw Jenny bristle. She turned to face him.

"Actually—" Jenny's voice was chilly enough to match the outdoors "—a woman alone is just fine—inside or outside. Especially if she's read her guidebooks. The fact is women are better suited for the cold than men."

Zach lifted his eyebrow.

Jenny put her chin up in the air slightly. "It's true. It's because of body fat. Women have more body fat."

"But only in—" Zach stopped. He wasn't sure Jenny would like him to tell her where her body fat was stored. Especially since it was in places that were causing him some discomfort now that the idea of kissing her had taken hold of him with a vengeance. Maybe he was the one who was crazy here.

Jenny turned and reached up to the coat hooks that were next to the door. "Well, we can't both go." Jenny lifted a drab blanket that was hanging on the hook. She'd grown accustomed to being both mother and father to her children years ago. "I wouldn't expect a stranger to do this for my children. It's my responsibility. Besides, I should have gotten the letter to Santa some other way before you came. It's not your problem."

The kitchen windows all looked out at the black night. Zach took a breath.

"It might not be my problem, but it is my truck." Zach put his hands on his hips. Let her argue with that. "I'll drive the thing."

"You hate that truck. You said so earlier." Jenny wrapped the blanket around her shoulders like a shawl. "Besides, we both know it's not your truck. It belongs to the people of Dry Creek. I know all about the mail service around here. And I *am* one of the people of Dry Creek, so it's more mine than yours."

"That truck is entrusted to my care," Zach said stubbornly. He'd moved his hands away from his hips. The extra Santa padding under that suit he still wore made him feel ridiculous. "Charley didn't say anything about me lending it out to folks to go driving around in it like it's some kind of do-it-yourself taxicab."

"I'm a good driver." Jenny held out her hand for the keys. "You can wait in the kitchen until I get back so the kids think you're gone, too. Just keep an eye on that furnace."

"Well, if they think I'm gone, maybe I should be."

"Somebody needs to be here in case something goes wrong." Jenny flashed Zach a smile. "Don't worry—the kids won't be a problem. They don't come out of their beds once they get settled. That's one good thing about it being cold. They don't want to leave their bed once they get the sheets warm."

Zach's frown turned to a scowl. Speaking of sheets, something was wrong with that blanket Jenny was holding like a shawl. "Is that what you use for a coat?"

Jenny lifted her chin as she wrapped the blanket more closely around her shoulders. "We used to live in Los Angeles. It wasn't cold enough there to need heavy coats."

"Well, this isn't Los Angeles." Zach looked at the other two hooks. They both held new snow coats, one in pink for Lisa and one in red for Andy. "You should have bought a coat for yourself when you bought the ones for the kids."

Jenny shrugged. "The kids needed the coats more than I did. I can get by until spring."

Zach didn't say anything. Boy, was he wrong to think she was an irresponsible parent. She was halfway to sainthood. Which made him proud in a funny sort of a way. Until he figured it out. If she was that kind of woman, his odds of getting a free kiss in this house were about the same as they would be at a PTA meeting filled with Republican grandmothers.

He'd learned long ago that kissing good women was complicated. They tended to take their kissing seriously. A kiss or two and they started thinking about china patterns and meeting your family. Zach didn't even know where his parents were anymore. Even if he did know, he sure wasn't going to take any woman to meet them.

Jenny lifted the blanket up to wrap it around her head as well as her shoulders.

"Andy asked me to deliver his letter." Zach pulled up the collar on his Santa suit. His hopes of a kiss might be gone, but he still would do this his way. "I'm responsible for the U.S. mail. I'm the one who's going."

Jenny looked at the man. The kitchen was in shadows, but she had no problem seeing the face before her. Faint red lines marked his cheek where the Santa beard had rubbed. A strong chin was brushed lightly with late-day whiskers. Brown eyes met hers with determination. She'd seen that same steady look in his eyes in rodeo pictures of him on those cereal boxes. He made one fierce-looking Santa.

"But it's cold out there."

"Then make me something hot to drink when I get back." Zach reached for the knob on the door. He wasn't going to argue on this one. He wouldn't be able to think straight if he let her take off in a night blizzard while he stayed in the kitchen. What kind of man would he be if he did that?

"I don't know what to say," Jenny tried again. The blanket around her shoulders was stiff, but she held it firm. "You shouldn't have to do this. You don't even like Christmas."

"Yes, I do." Zach gritted his teeth. What was it about this family? "I just don't see the need to go overboard and fuss about everything."

"You mean fuss about things like delivering a child's letter to Santa?" Jenny asked softly.

"Well, no. The letter, now that's important U.S. Postal Service business. I'm just doing my job."

Jenny smiled. "You're losing money. There's not even an official stamp on the envelope."

"It's official enough for me." He paused and added, "Besides, I gave my word. He's counting on me."

Jenny was speechless, and Zach took that as sign enough to open the door and leave.

The cold outside air lingered briefly inside while Jenny stood at the door's window and watched the red and green lights bump their way down her driveway. So that's what this man did when he gave his word. He actually carried through with his promise.

All Jenny saw of the postal truck was lights. She could, of course, hear the truck. She suspected Zach revved the motor a little extra just so it was very obvious that he was driving away.

Jenny was amazed. This cowboy was actually honoring his word. Her late husband had only considered promises made to adults to be binding. And then only if the adults were other men. Jenny was beginning to wonder if she hadn't misjudged the cereal-box cowboy. Not that it would make much difference. A man with that much sexual magnetism was not the kind of man she wanted in her life the second time around.

If and when she married again, she would marry for the sake of her children. And she wouldn't take any chances. She'd marry a solid Christian man. Someone boring would be fine. She wasn't going to be deceived if she could help it. She'd make sure the man knew his Bible and prayed. She didn't think Zach had ever even opened a Bible. He sure hadn't looked comfortable earlier when they'd prayed.

Jenny pulled the blanket closer around her shoulders as though she could press the heat into her skin. She wished the cowboy had let her make the drive. She felt beholden enough to him already and didn't relish adding a favor like this to the list. She had her pride. She just had no way to repay him.

Unless—Jenny still had a few dollars in the bank. She could write him a check. Yes, a check, she thought to herself in satisfaction. A check should even the score nicely.

Outside in the cold, Zach stopped the postal truck. He'd driven a quarter of a mile away from the house when he stopped and turned out the lights, just in case Andy had watched him leave the house. He'd leave the lights off for a few minutes so that it would look like the truck was far, far away on its way to the North Pole. He knew Jenny had said that the kids both stayed tucked into bed once they were down, but he also knew that Christmas changed the rules for kids everywhere.

Without the heater on, the temperature inside the postal truck dipped quickly. If Jenny had been sitting next to him, Zach knew he'd ask her what the temperature was just to challenge her skill. He smiled. She was some amazing lady. He wondered if she really could tell temperatures like that.

The black night, even with the cold outside, was peaceful. Zach clicked on the lights on his belt so he could read his watch. He'd had the lights off for five minutes. He wondered how long a kid would figure it would take to go to the North Pole.

Speaking of the North Pole, Zach pulled out the letter Andy had written. He wasn't curious about what the requests were. The kids had already told him what they wanted. But he was beginning to worry.

The box he'd brought out to this family hadn't been heavy enough to satisfy any child's Santa wish. Besides, he knew what was in it. The camera, a frozen ham that Jenny had already put in the unheated laundry room, the pie from Mrs. Hargrove, and two small brown bags from some store in Miles City.

Those brown bags looked awfully puny.

Zach sat in silence. He knew firsthand how it felt to be disappointed at Christmas. He'd never believed in Santa Claus, but when he was ten years old someone had sent his parents a Christmas card with a family picture on the front of it. Everyone in the picture was standing beside a Christmas tree and looking happy. That was Zach's first glimpse of what the day was like for other families, and that Christmas Zach had decided it should be that way for his family.

Zach had begged a scrawny leftover tree from a nearby lot on Christmas Eve and set it up in the living room. He'd thought a tree would make the difference. He'd believed the tree would turn his family into a Christmas family like the one on that card. But his parents had only used the tree as an excuse to drink more than usual, quarreling over who should propose the next toast to the greenery.

No one in his family smiled that Christmas, and Zach threw the tree away the next day. That was the last time he had had any hopes at Christmas. But he'd never spent Christmas with children like Andy and Lisa. They were good kids. They deserved a good Christmas.

Zach did not know exactly when in the darkness the idea came to him, but it somehow did. He, Zach "Lightning" Lucas, knew what the children wanted. They knew that he wasn't the real Santa but they had still both trusted him with their Christmas wishes. Maybe it was time Zach lived up to the red suit he wore. In this snow-covered corner of Montana he was Santa. He would see that their hoped-for presents were delivered.

At first Zach thought about driving into Dry Creek tomorrow, but then he realized he had the same limitations that had faced Jenny. The hardware store in Dry Creek would not have either Lisa's tiara or Andy's cowboy outfit. Besides, the roads wouldn't be open, anyway. And he was driving a postal truck, not a bulldozer.

Of course, the cowboy outfit—Zach looked into the back of the postal truck. His duffel bag was still there along with his sheepskin coat. He hadn't packed much for his trip to Vegas, but he did have the latest championship buckle in there that he had just won last month. He knew how to work with leather and he had a broken bridle in his duffel that he'd been meaning to fix. He might be able to fashion a belt for the boy. And he could put a thick lining in his spare Stetson hat to fit the kid. He didn't have a toy gun, but he could make a small rope with some of that postal twine in the truck.

Lisa's tiara would be more difficult. Especially because, as she'd reminded Andy, a tiara needed to have jewels. Zach grinned to himself. Now that he thought of it, he did have jewels. Zach reached into the back and pulled the duffel toward him. He unzipped the bag and felt around in the contents until his hand found what he was seeking. He'd brought a Christmas present for Patti.

He twirled the lacy leg garter on his finger and grinned. The showgirl would never miss the fancy garter he'd bought her. But Lisa would love the rhinestones that circled it. There were pink rhinestones and clear rhinestones and small pieces of real ruby. And, if Jenny had a metal clothes hanger that he could bend, he'd be in business.

By the time Zach turned the engine back on in the postal truck, he'd decided that this Christmas might be tolerable after all. Imagine Zach "Lightning" Lucas filling in for Santa Claus.

Zach said "ho ho ho" to himself just to see if he had the knack.

He didn't.

But that didn't matter. Zach would pretend to have the Christmas spirit even if it killed him. He'd do it for the sake of the kids.

He only hoped Jenny would cooperate.

Chapter Six

Jenny looked out the window again. It had been totally black outside the last time she'd peeked, but now she could see the lights of the postal truck coming closer to the house. Jenny was beginning to have second thoughts. She'd looked at her bank book and the crude budget she'd worked up to see them through the winter, before deciding to write the check for seven dollars. It wasn't much, but it was all she dared give away until she knew how much it would cost to fix the radiator on her car.

The truck engine came to a stop near the house, and Jenny smoothed back her hair. She'd put some water into her fondue pan and lit the candle underneath. She didn't know how long it would take the water to heat, but she intended to have a hot drink for Zach when he came inside. That and the check would make her feel less indebted to him.

Zach sat in the postal truck. While he was driving back up the path that led to Jenny's house, he'd noticed the ball of mistletoe someone had hung on the antenna of the truck. It would freeze solid if he left it outside over night. He might as well haul it in with his gear.

Zach opened the door and stepped outside into the snow.

The night was kinder to Jenny's house than the light of day had been. In the dark, the flickering light through the kitchen window gave the house a warm look, as if someone was waiting up for the last one of the family to come home.

Maybe, Zach thought wryly, that's why he preferred busy hotels. With all the neon flash of a hotel at night, everyone knew there was nothing personal about the fact that someone was waiting up inside. It was strictly business. Zach liked it that way. If no one was waiting up, there would never be anyone disappointed after discovering that Zach knew absolutely nothing about the things other people took for granted.

The Christmas tree failure had been only one of the lessons he'd learned as a child. It was that same year he'd discovered other families ate their meals together at a table. He'd asked his mother if they could do the same. One meal together had cured them all of the idea. His family wouldn't even have a clue what to do when Jenny's children had bowed their heads earlier today to pray.

No, Zach knew he wasn't meant for family life. He doubted God wanted someone like him saying prayers to Him on a regular basis, anyway. That was best left to church-going folks.

Of course, there was no need for him to even think about such things, Zach told himself with a shake of his head. He'd made peace with his limitations many years ago. He wouldn't wish the life he'd had growing up on anyone, but that was what he knew. Zach figured he was destined to follow in his parents' footsteps, and it wasn't a path he wanted anyone else to have to walk with him.

Besides, he was fine with being alone. The rodeo life was a good life, even if the thrill of it had grown decidedly thin in the past few years. Maybe next year he'd see about having some kind of a home base. He didn't mind washing his own socks, but he sure did miss a steady drawer to put them in.

Still, rodeo riding was what he knew and what he was good at. No one expected anything from him in the rodeo world that he did not know exactly how to give them. That should be enough for any man, he told himself as he reached Jenny's door.

Zach stamped his feet lightly outside the door, shaking the snow off them. He wore his heavy coat over the Santa suit and carried the mistletoe in one hand and his duffel bag in the other.

"What the…?" Zach muttered to himself as the mistletoe pricked him. The spikes on the holiday weed were big enough that the whole thing should be declared a lethal weapon. Zach half hung the mistletoe on his coat pocket and reached for the doorknob before he hesitated.

Polite manners were never his strong suit. But he figured even if the light in the window was for him, he was still company in this house and would be expected to knock rather than just come inside as though he belonged here. No matter how tempted he was to do just that, it wasn't right. He didn't belong. So he knocked.

The window on the door was frosted over, but the light from inside shone through the iced pattern.

"Come in," Jenny called softly from inside the kitchen.

Jenny had decided payment of a debt required some special touches. She brought down two cups and saucers from her good china set. She'd even put a lace cloth on the folding table. That should be enough, Jenny thought to herself when she heard Zach on the porch. The tea and the check should bring them about even.

When he opened the door, however, Jenny decided she should have forgotten the tea and left the check until the morning. She should have done whatever was necessary to be as far away from this man as was possible in her old house. The cold had turned the man into someone who looked as if he belonged on one of those calendars for single women. He was Mr. December.

Jenny shivered all the way down her spine. She told herself it was because of the cold wind that blew into the kitchen in the quick second before Zach turned to close the door.

But it wasn't.

Just look at him, she thought in dismay. Zach was the kind of man she had moved a thousand miles to avoid. Montana men were supposed to be farmers. Steady, reliable men with faces one learned to love. She wasn't supposed to meet a man like Zach, whose face would make a young girl swoon. But there he stood against the black of the night like some mountain man covered with snow.

The kitchen was dark except for the half dozen candles Jenny had lit, some on the counter and some on the table in the middle of the kitchen. The candlelight made the snow scattered over Zach's dark hair glisten like confetti. The cold had turned his skin to marble. His brown eyes simmered beneath strong brows, and snow had settled on his eyebrows. More snow had fallen on the shoulders of his heavy leather coat as it hung from his frame.

In that long coat, all hints of a friendly Santa were covered.

"Thanks for waiting up," Zach said as he stood

on the rug by the kitchen door and set his duffel on the floor nearby. "It was nice of you."

Jenny was speechless. Then she decided the best way to deal with the situation was to meet it rationally.

"It wasn't long." Jenny took a deep breath and walked closer to him as he tried to get his arm out of his coat. If she could only get that coat off him, she'd be fine. She could cope with a man dressed as Santa. "Here, let me help you with that."

Zach stopped in surprise. He couldn't remember the last time anyone had offered to help him with anything. He'd always had to fend for himself. "I can get it."

"Not with that Santa suit on under your coat. Believe me, I know. Andy has a playsuit out of that fuzzy material, and it's almost impossible for one person to get the coat pulled off the sleeves."

"Oh."

Zach was pretty sure Jenny was wrong, but he hoped she didn't discover the fact. She had moved so close that he could inhale the pure soap smell of her.

Jenny gripped the edge of Zach's coat sleeve and tugged.

"Something's caught." Jenny pulled on the sleeve again before looking up at Zach.

Jenny looked back down at the sleeve. Looking up was a mistake. She needed to keep focused on the

Santa material. Polyester. That wasn't sexy. Think of Andy's playsuit. "It'll come off in a minute."

Zach wasn't paying any attention to her words. He wondered if she knew what the candlelight did to her blond hair. She'd combed the short curls back and had them clipped with some combs. But little wisps of hair escaped here and there, making it look as if she wore a halo.

Zach caught his breath. His skin was still cold from outside, but Jenny slipped her hand inside the sleeve of his coat and his skin warmed up in a hurry.

"Andy's coat never did this." Jenny bit her lip as she frowned up at Zach.

"Huh?" Zach stopped breathing as her hands slid farther under the Santa suit and up his forearm. Her hands were soft as an angel's beneath the weight of both the Santa suit and his sheepskin coat.

"Ouch!" Jenny said.

"Ouch!" Zach said.

The ball of mistletoe dropped to the floor and rolled.

"Sorry. I forgot I'd hung that halfway in my pocket."

"It's mistletoe."

Zach noticed Jenny didn't sound any too happy about the fact.

"It was on the truck antenna. I think Charley put it there," Zach said.

Jenny nodded curtly. The old men of Dry Creek

were all matchmakers. They'd put mistletoe on a hearse just in case the corpse met anyone on the way to his own funeral.

"I couldn't just leave the stuff outside. It'd freeze." Zach bent down and gingerly picked the mistletoe up by the string that had tied it to the antenna. "Besides, it is a Christmas decoration. Thought you might be able to use it."

"I guess we could put it in the laundry room," Jenny offered after a moment. After all, the old men did mean well. "With the ham."

"What's a ham need with a wad of mistletoe like ours?"

"Ours?" Jenny looked up at him quizzically. The shadows in the kitchen left her eyes in darkness. Zach wished he could see them more clearly. Her eyes gave away her emotions, and he felt that he was flying blind when he couldn't see them.

"Well, you know—you and the kids," Zach stammered, before he added himself to the list. Man, this woman made him nervous. "You don't need to worry about it being mistletoe. I mean, with the kissing and all. It's not like I'm planning to kiss you."

Jenny blinked. She wasn't planning to kiss him, either. Of course not. "Good…that's good."

It was good they understood each other. Very good. She would have had to speak to him if he intended to kiss her, too, assure him that they had no prospects. That would have been awkward, and she was glad there was no need to do it. But still…

"Not that I don't want to kiss you." Zach threw that in for good measure. Jenny still wasn't smiling. "Any man would want to kiss you. I mean, you're very, ah, pleasant. Very pleasant."

Jenny frowned slightly. "Pleasant" sounded like someone's grandmother. No wonder he was stuttering and stammering all over the place. Apparently she wouldn't have had to speak to him at all. "You don't want to kiss me."

"Huh?"

"Not that it's a problem," Jenny chattered. When she was upset, she always talked too much. "Which is for the best. Of course. In fact, you shouldn't even think about it. I mean, there's no need—I mean, well, you're just snowed in for Christmas. Snowbound really. We're not even each other's type—I mean, it's not like we're—that is—you just brought the mail and I'm grateful for that."

Sometimes a man had to gamble with his life, Zach thought. Sometimes he even had to gamble with his heart.

Zach bent down and kissed Jenny.

Or at least he thought he did. Maybe she was the one who tilted her head back and arched up to meet his lips. He would never know. All he knew was that he was kissing Jenny.

Zach had never expected the rush of pure sweetness to be followed by a hint of fire. That was his only excuse for lingering over the kiss.

Jenny stood rooted to the floor. She knew it was a mistake to kiss this cowboy, knew it when she'd told herself to step back and then found herself unable to do it. What was wrong with her, anyway? She usually had more sense. Something was wrong with her. It was...

"Christmas," Jenny whispered the word to herself as if it were a lifeline. Of course. It must be because of the holiday that she was letting this man kiss her senseless. That was it. The holiday.

People did strange things at holidays. They ate fruitcake. Rang old metal bells. They even forgot their very sensible vows and kissed good-looking cowboys who were just passing through.

"Hmm." Zach smoothed back Jenny's hair. "What about Christmas?"

"It's making me crazy." Jenny tried to collect herself. What was that purring in the back of her mind? "Well, not just me—both of us—Christmas and mistletoe. You know, it's crazy."

Zach didn't like this line of thought. "Christmas doesn't make people go crazy."

Kisses like the one they'd just shared might make people go crazy, Zach conceded to himself, but a date on the calendar never would. He'd missed out on a lot of things about Christmas, but crazy wasn't one of them.

"Of course it does." Jenny stepped farther back and kept chatting. Even her teeth were nervous around this man. She was lucky she wasn't blabbing. "There's the Santa fantasy. Every kid gets carried away with Santa. Even when we're adults we expect the, well, unusual at Christmas."

"You think us kissing is about Christmas?"

Zach's voice was quiet, but Jenny didn't stop. She couldn't stop.

"Well, you know the goodwill, peace toward men—that kind of thing."

"I see." Zach turned slightly and, even with one hand holding the mistletoe string, pulled his arm away from his coat sleeve. A slight buzz of static filled the silence. So that's why Jenny had kissed him—goodwill? A man certainly couldn't go very far with that. A woman kissed her uncle for goodwill, or a child. She probably got extra points for cozying up to a sick orphan.

"It didn't mean anything. The kiss, I mean," Jenny stammered. The man was scowling about something. She supposed it was the kiss. He was experiencing after-kiss remorse. She'd seen it before. "We were just—"

"I know—" Zach hung his coat on one of the hooks and tried to stop scowling "—crazy at Christmas."

"Yeah."

Zach could vouch for the fact that at least one of

them was crazy. The bottom had sure fallen out of his stability. And people wondered why he wasn't overly fond of the holiday.

Jenny shook herself. "It was only a kiss." And a tidal wave is only a little water, she mocked herself. She felt as if she'd jumped into the deep end before she'd learned to swim. She'd never meant to be this vulnerable again. And him, he was only passing through on his way to— "You were just lonesome for your friend."

"Huh?"

"The showgirl."

"Oh, Cathy."

"I thought you said her name was Patti."

Zach didn't like the way Jenny was looking at him—as though he was such a roving cowboy that he didn't even remember names. "It is Patti. I just call her Cathy sometimes."

Now she'd think he was certifiable, for sure. Zach assured himself the only reason he couldn't remember names was because Jenny was making him nervous. Usually he did fine.

Jenny continued chatting. "Speaking of your trip…" She willed herself to stop, but it did no good. She didn't even want to think about his trip to Las Vegas. She surely didn't want to talk about it. "You'll be needing some money."

"What?" Did she think he was paying for it?

"Patti's a showgirl, but she's not—I mean, she doesn't charge."

Zach wondered if she thought he was so unattractive he needed to pay for it. She'd already made it clear she didn't particularly like his looks. But to say that—well, it was pretty discouraging when he'd just kissed her.

"I meant for gas. You'll need to buy gas to get there." Jenny willed her mind to focus. There she'd gone and insulted his girlfriend. And him, too, she supposed. "All I mean to say is that I have a check for you."

"Gas money?" Zach repeated in disbelief. He wondered if the woman knew how much money he had in his bank account. When he compared it with what was probably in hers, he was speechless. He could buy her miserable little farm a dozen times over and still have change. "I don't need gas money."

"Well, you'll need something someday—and you've done so much for us tonight." Jenny made the mistake of looking up directly into Zach's eyes. She'd heard of eyes that smoldered, but she'd never actually seen any that did until now. He was angry. The gold in his eyes sparked until it melted the brown. She completely forgot what she was going to say.

"You don't owe me anything."

"Still." Jenny gathered herself together. She needed to be strong for her children. She walked over to the counter and picked up the check. "I don't want to be beholden."

Zach saw the cornered pride in Jenny's eyes. So that was it. His face softened. "You're not beholden. You've offered me shelter in a storm. That's worth more than some ride in the dark."

"But it's just a bunk in the barn."

"I've slept on worse. Many nights."

Jenny held out the check. "I'd still feel better if you took this."

Zach didn't want to take her check. Of course, it probably didn't make any difference since he'd never cash it. "I guess."

Zach reached out to take the check with one hand. The other hand held tight to the mistletoe string.

The kitchen was quiet except for the tick of the battery-operated clock on the wall. The candles carved out pockets of golden light by the counters and the table in the middle of the room.

Zach heard a shuffle in the corner and a yawn. Come to think of it, he'd heard the shuffle for some time now. He wondered how long the little feet had been standing there.

"Mama, it's too late to give Santa a letter." Andy's voice came from the doorway to the kitchen. "Mr. Lightning, you already took the letters to Santa Claus, didn't you?"

Andy padded over to Zach and wrapped his arms around one of Zach's thighs. "You're cold."

Zach was surprised the cold didn't stop Andy from hugging his leg. "It was cold out there—going to the North Pole."

Zach let his hand rest on the boy's head.

"You should be in bed," Jenny gently scolded. Jenny didn't like the fact that her son had gone to the cowboy instead of her for the third time tonight.

"But Santa won't get your letter," Andy said worriedly as he looked up at his mother. He didn't leave his post by Zach's leg as he pointed to the check Zach held in his hand.

"That wasn't a letter. It was a check." Jenny hoped her son's fascination with the cowboy didn't turn to tears when the man left.

"Santa doesn't need a check."

"No, the check was for Mr. Lucas." Jenny hoped the formal title would remind Zach that just because her son wrapped himself around his leg at every opportunity he got it did not mean they were anything but strangers.

"It should have been a list," Andy protested. "What you want from Santa."

"Santa doesn't come to mommies," Jenny said.

Andy's eyes grew wide. "Because they've been bad?"

Jenny smiled. "No, it's just that Santa is special for little kids."

"But won't you get any presents?" Andy was frowning as he clutched Zach's leg even harder. "You've gotta have a present."

"Of course she'll have a present." Zach frantically thought about what else might be in his duffel bag that could be made into a present for Jenny. No wonder Santa was fat. The stress of thinking of all those Christmas gifts would drive anyone to eating too many cookies. "I just don't know what yet."

"We could give her the Christmas ball," Andy announced as he pointed to the mistletoe that hung from Zach's other hand. "I've seen those. They're for kisses. Mommy likes kisses."

"She does?" Zach watched the pink sweep across Jenny's face. "Now isn't that nice."

Andy nodded happily. "I kiss her every night and she sleeps with my kiss under her pillow."

"She does?"

Andy nodded as he pretended to scoop a kiss out of the air. "I blow one to her so she can catch it."

"Isn't that nice." Zach wasn't at all in favor of that kind of kissing. Not when it came to Jenny. Of course, the pillow part sounded nice.

Andy squeezed Zach's leg tighter. "Is Mommy going to keep your kiss under her pillow tonight?"

Zach heard Jenny's gasp.

"Mommy, ah…" Zach jumped in to explain before Jenny could deny everything. He knelt down so he was facing Andy directly. "Your mommy only has room under her pillow for kisses from her little boy. You give her special kisses."

Andy nodded happily. "I blow them to her."

Zach nodded. "That makes them easier for her to catch."

Andy leaned closer to Zach and whispered into his right ear, "I could teach you how to make special kisses. Then you could blow some to Mommy, too."

Jenny didn't like seeing the two heads together. Plus she couldn't hear what her son was saying. She didn't want to spoil Andy's illusions about the cowboy, but she didn't like him sharing his innocent thoughts with the man. "What's the secret?"

"Nothing." Zach knew Jenny wouldn't like what her son was saying.

Her son had no such hesitation. "I was just telling Mr. Lightning how to give you kisses that you keep under your pillow."

Jenny blushed.

"You should be back in bed," Jenny reminded her son. "It's cold out here."

"Tomorrow night Santa comes," Andy said blissfully as he continued to hug Zach's leg. "We're going to make cookies for Santa tomorrow, aren't we?"

Zach wondered when he'd become such a sucker for little boys. Maybe it was when they offered to teach him how to kiss their mothers. "Sure enough."

"I can stir," Andy offered proudly.

"You'll do a fine job," Jenny said firmly. "But first, you need to go to bed and sleep."

Andy yawned as he let go of Zach's leg and walked back out of the kitchen. "Good night, Mr. Lightning. Tell the kitty good night, too. I hope she stays warm in the barn."

"Good night. And don't worry about your kitty. I'll keep the fire going."

Zach watched Andy go. Now there was a sweet little boy, full of hope and enthusiasm. He had to be, to think of that wild cat as a kitty. The thing was closer to a mountain cat. "His father must have been something."

"What?" Jenny looked up at Zach in alarm. Now where had that come from? She never talked about her husband. She'd not even told Mrs. Hargrove about Stephen. At first, she'd never told anyone about Stephen because she kept intending to talk to him first. But then he was sick. And now she felt it was disloyal to voice her disappointment about someone who was dead and couldn't make any changes, anyway. "What about Stephen?"

"To have raised a boy like Andy, he must have been a good father is all."

Zach was surprised at the surge of envy he felt. It must have felt good to be a man like Stephen and have something steady and loving to give to a wife and kids.

Jenny bit her lip. "Stephen wasn't well."

"I heard...the cancer." Zach could have kicked himself. Jenny's face had gone closed and pale. What kind of a brute was he, bringing back painful memories? "I'm sorry. You must miss him."

Jenny nodded. That was the sore truth of it. Even though he had kept to himself, she missed him. She had loved Stephen. For years. He had been her chosen one. She'd been hopeful. She'd prayed. She'd bargained for his attention. She'd lived expecting the day would come when Stephen would look around himself and realize the value of his family. That day had never come. She always felt there had been some trigger in Stephen that she hadn't been able to find. Something she should have known that had eluded her.

Zach called himself ten kinds of a fool. "I should be telling you about my trip to the frozen north instead of stirring up sad memories—especially at Christmas."

"And I should be offering you a cup of tea." Jenny gestured to the table. "And thanking you for making this Christmas a better one for my children."

Zach tried not to notice that she didn't include herself. "The Santa stuff was all Mrs. Brown's idea."

"Do you like your tea plain or with lemon?" Jenny walked back to the fondue pot. "I'm afraid it will only be a tea bag in a cup. I couldn't get enough water to heat to make a pot."

"A cup will be more than fine."

Jenny poured him a cup of tea in silence and took it to the table. "I'm sure you'll enjoy some peace and quiet while you drink this."

Zach could have told her that he'd lived his life with peace and quiet. It wasn't what it was cracked up to be. But he didn't. She was rattled. He hoped she'd sit down at the table with him and have a cup of tea, as well.

"The tea smells good," Zach offered. "If you don't have enough water for two cups, I could get by with a half cup."

There. He'd asked her to share.

Jenny shook her head. "It's cold out there. You'll need your whole cup. Besides, I think I'm going to head to bed. Do you need anything else for the barn?"

"No, I'm fine. I already made the bed up with the blankets you gave me. I'll build a fire and it'll be fine."

"I know the cat will appreciate it."

Zach nodded. Of course, the cat. He watched Jenny walk out of the kitchen. "Good night."

Zach told himself he shouldn't mind. He was, after all, used to sitting at a table by himself and eating. He never even had a cat waiting up for him. It shouldn't bother him after all those years. He'd sat alone in coffee shops. In hotel rooms. In bars. He should be used to it. Zach looked around at the shadows in the empty kitchen. Yeah, he should be used to it by now.

Suddenly he had no appetite for the tea. He might as well go out to the barn and see about warming the place up for the cat.

Zach followed the rope out to the barn although he didn't actually need it. The snow had stopped swirling and he could see the barn clearly from the house once he had his flashlight pointed in the right direction. He opened the main door to the barn and waved his flashlight around when he entered. He figured that cat was as cautious about meeting people as he was. Neither one of them wanted to be caught unaware.

Zach heard a hiss from the area of the hay bales so he figured he'd announced his presence for the night. He then walked to the small room off to the right. He suspected the room he was sleeping in had been used by a series of hired men who had helped old man Collins before he died.

Zach had looked at the room when he was out here earlier and noticed there were odds and ends of things that had been left behind by others. An old razor—the metal kind from the sixties. A few Zane Grey westerns. An old Bible that looked like it'd been around for years. A couple of mugs and a blackened coffeepot on top of the wood stove.

Zach liked campfire coffee. He walked over to the wood stove and opened it up so he could build a fire. The metal was cold and the stove door creaked as it opened. He'd build a small fire tonight, but it would be enough to warm this room.

He heard the cat meow somewhere in the barn. It was hard to judge if the meow sounded closer than the hiss, but Zach thought so.

"Give me a minute, will ya?" Zach muttered. "It's going to take a minute to build us a fire worth anything."

Zach looked at the door to the room. He'd leave it partially open just in case the cat had sense enough to follow the heat closer to the fire. Not that the room would ever become comfortably warm with the door cracked like that.

Zach shook his head. He was going soft. The next thing he knew he'd be warming the cat's milk on that wood stove along with his morning coffee. He shook his head again.

Chapter Seven

Jenny woke with her pillow twisted around her shoulders. She'd had a dream that there were hot coals hiding under her pillow, and it took a couple of deep breaths to assure herself that everything was all right. She could feel her cheeks were aflame even though the air around them was cool.

She let herself remember where she was. She was in the farmhouse, lying on the mattress in her bedroom. The faint light of daybreak streaked into the room through the gap between her drapes. The day looked subdued. It was probably cloudy outside. Most likely the electricity was still off. At least the wind had died down.

Jenny took a deep breath to calm herself. She was surprised at the sense of contentment she felt when she slowly realized where she was. She was home.

Jenny heard the quiet giggling before she even

had a chance to turn over again. She couldn't mistake the sound of Andy's laughter, and it didn't take too many guesses to place the deeper tones. Zach.

Jenny wondered what she was going to do with her son. How did you tell a four-year-old that it wasn't wise to become attached to a man who was going to be gone in a couple of days?

Maybe you didn't, Jenny said to herself as she stood up and slipped on her robe. Maybe all she could do was distract Andy as much as possible so that he was busy with other things and stopped spending time with the cowboy.

Jenny looked at her face in the mirror on the back of her bedroom door and grimaced. Her blond hair was naturally curly, and this morning it was flyaway. Usually her hair was only like this when it was going to rain. She wasn't sure if her hair would react the same way to snow.

Fortunately, no one would notice her hair once they got a good look at her puffy eyes. She looked like someone who had been doing battle all night with her dreams. Too bad she was out of eyedrops.

She was a mess. But she wasn't in a beauty contest today. All that mattered today was getting Christmas ready for her children. She, like her son, would do well to forget the cowboy was even here.

"Whoever gets the pan out of the cupboard gets the first pancake," Jenny announced firmly as she stepped into the living room.

Three pairs of eyes turned to her. She hadn't realized Lisa had joined the other two. Her two children were in their pajamas. The cowboy was dressed, of course. The three of them were huddled around something on the living room floor.

"Mama!" Lisa squeaked.

"Don't look," Andy added in panic.

The cowboy simply pulled the afghan off the sofa and spread it over something on the floor. "It's okay now."

Jenny eyed the afghan-covered lump on the floor. "What's that?"

"Well, now," the cowboy drawled. "That depends."

My goodness, Jenny thought as she looked at him closely. Didn't the man ever have a bad day? He looked just as pleased with himself as the children did. And his excitement made his brown eyes—well, it wouldn't do to look him in the eye for too long. "Depends on what?"

"Whether or not I tell you depends on whether you can keep a secret."

"She can't keep the secret. It's—" Lisa protested before she bit off her words and looked at Zach with reproach. "You're teasing."

Zach grinned back at Lisa. "Sure am."

Lisa smiled back before she rolled her eyes.

Jenny felt the need to sit down. Lisa never took to strangers. Granted, she'd run off to the North Pole with the man, but that was only to win a bet. Now Lisa was talking to him as if he were her best friend. Jenny wasn't sure she liked it. "You've got a secret?"

"Don't you know you're not supposed to ask questions at Christmas?" Zach finally said as he stood up.

Jenny was momentarily distracted. She thought rodeo cowboys were supposed to have aches and pains in every joint. Zach moved with a smoothness that made her mouth grow dry. If he ached anywhere it was unnoticeable. His whole body was a symphony of movements. Even his hair behaved. And that little dimple she sometimes glimpsed on his chin— Jenny stopped herself.

"Huh?" Jenny looked away from the cowboy and back at her children. They were sitting on the floor and both smiling at her.

"Oh, it's a Christmas something? For me?" Jenny finally understood. Now she was completely dumbfounded. Jenny couldn't remember the last time she had gotten a real present. She'd always bought herself some soap or bath gel and put "From Stephen" on the package at Christmas. When the children asked, she'd told them all she wanted was a kiss and a hug.

"It's a surprise," Andy said in satisfaction as he stood up and walked over to her. "From us."

"You'll like it," Lisa added confidently as she stood up. "But you can't see it. Not until you open it up on Christmas morning. We're going to put it under the Christmas tree."

"I wouldn't dream of peeking," Jenny said. She hadn't seen her children so excited for months. And Zach—the man stood square in the middle of their excitement, looking just as pleased as they were. "Your secret is safe. At least until Christmas morning."

"Christmas morning should have lots of surprises," Zach said. He looked almost as pleased as the children.

"Oh?" Jenny asked cautiously as she looked at him.

"I had company last night," Zach said in triumph.

Jenny gave a quick look at her two children. She knew they were fascinated with the cowboy, but—

"The cat came inside my room," Zach continued. She had curled up right next to his boots. He had the stove door open and there was enough light so he could get a good look at the shape of her. "And I think she's going to have babies."

"Kittens! We're going to have kittens!" Lisa squealed as she stood up. "When?"

"Well, that's mostly up to the mama cat," Zach said. "But I think you're going to have a batch of Christmas kittens."

"We should at least move her onto the porch then," Jenny said. "The barn's no place for babies."

"Jesus was born in a barn," Andy said. "Remember? On Christmas Eve?"

"Well, yes, but that wasn't in a Montana blizzard," Jenny said. She had no idea how cold it had been in Bethlehem, but it couldn't have been twenty below.

"Oh," Andy said and was quiet for a minute. "We're going to read the story again, aren't we?"

"Of course we'll read the story," Jenny said. "We read it every Christmas."

Andy nodded. "Mr. Lightning can read it this time."

Zach went stiff. He wasn't even sure where the Christmas story was found. He knew it was in the Bible, but that was about it. "I'm not sure I—ah— That is—"

"We don't need to decide who reads the story yet," Jenny said. "We haven't even had breakfast."

"Where'd you say that frying pan is?" Zach asked in relief as he sat down on the sofa.

"Me first," Andy squealed as he ran out of the living room with Lisa following close behind him.

"Thanks," Zach said to Jenny when it was just the two of them left. "It's not that I wouldn't be happy to hear the story. It's just that—"

Jenny put her hand up. "I know Andy can be persistent sometimes."

"That's not a problem," Zach said. "The boy needs to be able to ask for things."

Jenny didn't answer, and Zach wondered if there was something else bothering her. She didn't look as happy now that the children were out of the room.

"I hope you don't mind us doing this," Zach said quietly as he gestured to the lump under the afghan. "Andy was already awake when I came inside this morning and we didn't want to wake you. It was early. So we had this idea of making a present. I didn't think to ask you. Maybe, as I think about it now, I should have gone in and woken you."

No, Zach said to himself, that wouldn't have been a good idea. The sight of Jenny all warm and curled up in her bed would not have been—well, it would not have been a good idea at all.

"Ah, no." Jenny felt her cheeks blush. She'd already had hot coals under her pillow this morning. "You don't need to ask permission. But Andy can be a handful."

"He's just excited. Christmas, you know. The crazy thing."

Jenny knew Christmas wasn't what was exciting Andy. It was having a grown man sit on the floor and pay attention to him.

"He's a good boy," Zach offered. He didn't want Jenny to think he minded spending time with Andy.

Zach had always liked children, but most of his encounters with kids were short and came about because the kid wanted his autograph or wanted to pet Thunder or something like that. He'd never had a chance to spend this much time with individual children like Andy and Lisa. He hadn't known what he was missing.

"I just don't want you to feel you need to spend all of your time with the children. I know you don't like all the stuff that goes with holidays."

"I don't mind the children." What did she think he was? A monster? "It's only the holiday that I said that about—just the day on the calendar. Never the children. Children are supposed to like holidays."

"Oh." Jenny tried again. "Still, if you have other things to do—reading or something."

"The only books here are the children's books."

Jenny shrugged. "I thought maybe you brought something to read."

"I guess I could go check out the mailbag and see if I forgot to deliver any letters to Mrs. Goussley," Zach teased. What did she think? That he hauled around a library in his duffel bag?

Then it hit Zach, there were some books in the barn. But he didn't want to spend his time reading, anyway, so he kept quiet.

Jenny gave up. Stephen had always found some excuse to avoid spending time with the children. She figured she had given Zach enough excuses, he could pick one up anytime he wanted. She'd given him all the help she could.

"Unless—" Zach finally figured out what was

giving the woman heartburn "—unless you'd rather I not spend time with the kids."

"What?"

"I know some women think that a rodeo man might not know how to act around kids," Zach said, ignoring the fact that even he knew he didn't know how to act around kids. "But I've been watching my language. And I don't tell them anything that they shouldn't know about."

Zach almost mentioned that he hadn't even explained what a showgirl was when they'd asked again this morning. He'd let them keep thinking a showgirl was nothing more than a cheerleader with feathers in her hair. Zach stopped himself from bringing up the showgirl, however. Jenny didn't seem to approve of showgirls. Instead Zach decided he'd list his good points.

"I might not be as well mannered as their father...and educated," Zach continued. She could stop him at any time, but she didn't seem inclined to do so. "And I'm sure they still miss him something fierce. But, one thing I can guarantee, and that is you can trust your kids with me."

Jenny was speechless. Zach wanted to spend time with her children.

"They're not perfect children." Jenny felt she should let him know. "Lisa bites her nails."

Zach nodded. "I noticed. But I think maybe she'll

grow out of it. It's not something to worry about, is it?"

"I asked Mrs. Hargrove about it. She said maybe it's just the move."

Zach nodded. "I'm sure moving around is hard on kids."

Moving around is hard on everyone, Jenny thought, but didn't say it. She'd finally decided that God wanted her and the children in Dry Creek, but that didn't mean that sometimes she didn't wonder what it would have been like if she'd dug in her heels and refused to leave El Monte. At least there she would never have been stranded miles away from the nearest neighbor with a man who cared about whether or not Lisa bit her nails.

"Mommy!" The call came from the kitchen.

"Oh, the pancakes," Jenny said. "I better get going."

"Take your time," Zach said as he turned toward where he'd laid his coat. "I need to get those pipes put back together before you can cook anything, anyway."

"Oh, I forgot."

"Now that it's light, it'll only take a few minutes." Zach walked out of the living room and into the kitchen.

Jenny stood up. "In that case, I'll dress first."

"Wear something warm," Zach called back from the kitchen. "We need to get that tree in before it starts to snow again. I told Lisa I think I know where we'll find one."

Jenny nodded. How was she supposed to protect her children's hearts from this man when he promised them a Christmas tree in the middle of a Montana blizzard?

The pancakes fried up nice and brown and Jenny was even able to warm the maple syrup. Everyone ate their fill, and they had barely pushed their chairs back from the table before Lisa asked if it was time to go to get the tree.

"I don't see why not," Zach said. He didn't like the looks of the heavy gray clouds outside.

"There's the dishes," Jenny reminded everyone.

Lisa and Andy groaned.

"It's going to snow later," Zach said. "Maybe we should go right away."

Lisa and Andy looked at Zach and beamed.

"Well, maybe just this once we can do the dishes after we get back," Jenny conceded.

"You can put them to soak," Andy offered. Soaking the dishes was Andy's favorite way to cope with them. Lisa, on the other hand, carefully scrubbed each dish with a sponge.

"I'll at least clear the table while everyone gets dressed," Jenny said to her children. "And remember double socks today."

Jenny had put on panty hose under her jeans and two flannel shirts over a T-shirt. She figured that should keep her warm enough outside. She figured wrong.

"Don't you have anything warmer than those shirts?" Zach asked when the children had left the kitchen.

It wasn't until this morning that Zach had figured out that the men's flannel shirts Jenny was wearing had to be left from her husband's wardrobe. No wonder the woman wouldn't let them go. If they'd been real flannel, they'd probably keep her comfortable in the cold. But they were the thin, city flannel that was meant for style instead of weather.

"What's wrong with these shirts?"

"Nothing. They're just not warm enough."

Jenny lifted her chin. "They'll have to do."

"You could borrow a sweatshirt from me," Zach offered and then held his breath. "I've got a new one—not even worn—picked it up at a rodeo in Fargo a couple of weeks ago."

"What makes you think it's warmer than my shirts?"

"Those are California shirts. Made for the beach. The sweatshirt was made for North Dakota wear."

"I wouldn't want to impose."

"And I wouldn't want you to catch your death of cold." Zach thought he had the upper hand, but he decided to cinch it. "Who will take care of your kids if you come down with pneumonia?"

"I won't get sick," Jenny assured him. She couldn't afford to get sick.

"Then you'll wear the sweatshirt," Zach ordered. "And the sheepskin coat."

"Oh, I can't possibly—I can't wear your coat," Jenny sputtered. She needed to draw the line somewhere. She was used to taking care of herself. It wouldn't be good to let down her guard and become used to someone doing things for her. She'd have to cope on her own again when he was gone. Besides, she'd always been a fair person. "You will get just as cold as me. It's your coat. You'll need it."

"I can't wear it, anyway, while I chop down the tree." Zach only hoped they found a tree to chop down. He'd look foolish chopping down a thistle bush. "You might as well wear it. If not, it'll just stay sitting on the seat behind me."

Jenny looked at the coat. Maybe she could let her guard down a little. It was Christmas, after all. And the coat was lined with a heavy knotted wool. "That's not real sheepskin, is it?"

Zach grinned. "Imitation."

Jenny walked over and touched the coat. The rough, knobby lining was warm.

"Try it on."

Zach held the sleeves to the coat as Jenny slipped her arms into it.

"Feels like fur," Jenny said. The coat made her

feel warm for the first time in days. She almost felt like purring.

"Now you're ready to go." Zach looked at Jenny with satisfaction. She finally looked like a Montana woman.

Lisa was the first one to spot the trees. After Zach had scraped the ice off the front and side windows, the four of them had squeezed into the postal truck and driven down the road that ran along the fence of the Collins property. Just like Zach remembered from the previous day, the only trees around were at the bottom of the coulee about a half mile past the fence, just as the road turned up the hill to go to the house.

Zach had to give Lisa credit. She had leaned over her mother's shoulder so she could look out the side window. Since Lisa had already insisted Jenny roll down the window on their side, that meant Lisa's nose was cold enough to be red.

"I see one. I see one. I see one. Stop right here." Lisa bounced on her feet as she stood on the floor of the postal truck and half leaned out the passenger-side window.

"We need to pick one that doesn't have any pine cones," Jenny announced as she pulled out a narrow, green book from a bag she carried. She started to flip through the pages. "And it's also good to find one that's at least—" she turned a page "—eight, maybe even nine feet tall."

Lisa seemed familiar with her mother's green book. The girl didn't even look at the book, she just nodded dutifully. "We will, Mama."

"What's that?" Zach eyed the book that Jenny read. He had assumed the bag held cookies or crackers in case the kids got hungry.

"It's my *Montana Guidebook*. It's got a chapter on caring for local trees." Jenny lifted her chin. Mrs. Hargrove had given her the book when Jenny said she wanted to learn more about the area. "I don't know very much about Montana. But the people who wrote this book do. They say there's no excuse for just stripping the land of its trees. A good farmer doesn't do that."

"We're only talking one tree," Zach reminded her as he turned off the ignition. He'd already pulled the truck to the side of the road in an area between two snowdrifts. "That's hardly stripping your land."

Jenny tightened her grip on the green book. "The trees with pine cones are needed to make seeds for new tall trees."

"Well, there is that." Zach nodded.

He didn't have the heart to tell her that it would take more than a few pine cones to make nine-foot pine trees grow on her land. The trees at the bottom of the coulee were hunched over from the wind. He doubted any of them would ever grow more than five feet tall. And those were the lucky ones. Any tree seed unfortunate enough to fall on the top sides of the coulee would never live to grow even to four feet. The wind would see to that.

"I want a tree with an angel hook," Lisa announced as she sat back down on the floor in the back of the postal truck and pulled on her mittens.

"That's just something they put on trees at the lot where we got them in L.A., dear," Jenny said as she sat her book down on the tray that ran along the front of the cab. "These trees won't have them."

"Will they have one of those kissie-toe things?" Andy asked as he crawled up front and held out a mittenless hand to his mother.

"You mean mistletoe?" Jenny asked hesitantly. She had hoped Andy had forgotten about the kiss he'd seen last night. She put her hand in the pocket of Andy's coat and pulled out his missing mitten. "No, the tree won't have that."

"Then how is Mr. Lightning going to learn how to kiss?" Andy forgot about his mitten and just stood in the space between Jenny and Zach.

Zach felt a little hand clamp on to his arm and he looked over to the boy. Andy's eyes were earnest with worry as they looked back at him. Zach would have joked with the boy, but he looked over the little one's head and saw Jenny. Joking might not be the best idea, Zach decided.

"Mr. Lightning doesn't need to learn how to kiss," Jenny finally said firmly as she reached around the truck's gearshift to capture Andy's bare hand. Jenny pulled the mitten on Andy's hand. "Now, be sure you have your coats buttoned up tight before you go outside."

Zach held back his grin until his muscles ached. He could watch Jenny's face blush a hundred times and never grow tired of the wonder of it.

"I'm zipped," Andy said happily as he wiggled back into the back of the truck.

"Me, too," Lisa said as she unhooked the back door.

"Wait at the edge of the coulee. We'll all walk down together," Jenny called as the two children scrambled out. "I need to talk to Mr. Lucas for a minute first."

Jenny wished she didn't blush. "I'm sorry. Sometimes kids say the craziest things."

"I suppose it's because of Christmas." Zach agreed solemnly. It occurred to him that he hadn't been able to get a clear picture of Jenny's eyes last night when they had kissed. The candlelight hadn't given off enough light. "I hear everyone's crazy at Christmas."

"Yes, yes, that must be it." Jenny was relieved he seemed to understand. "They just get excited, and… well, they don't mean anything by it."

"I must say, though, it is a little troubling." Zach turned so that he was looking squarely at Jenny.

"What is?" Jenny turned to face Zach.

Zach reached up to touch Jenny's cheek. It was

cool and smooth as silk. "How can I let your son think I don't know how to kiss his mother?"

"He's talking about air kisses," Jenny whispered. She felt the man's thumb as he rubbed it down her cheek. Her cheek was cold, and his thumb felt like a hot brand, marking her cheek as his own. "The kind you blow across the room."

"Seems an awfully risky way to send a kiss," Zach said softly as he moved closer. "And not nearly as satisfying."

Jenny swallowed. Or at least she tried to—she was having a hard time even breathing. "We need to go get the tree."

Zach must have kissed more than a thousand women. Never once in all those times had he wanted a signal as desperately as he wanted one from Jenny. He didn't want to kiss her unless he knew she wanted him to kiss her.

"Is that what you want?" There, he thought to himself, he'd just put the question out there. He didn't want to have any doubts. "The kids are warm. They can wait a minute."

"No, I don't want to… Yes, I mean…the kids—" Jenny stumbled. She needed to remember the kids. She was going to find a steady, churchgoing man to be a father to her kids. She couldn't afford to be sweet-talked by a cowboy who was just passing through. Besides. "The kids want a tree."

Zach swallowed. Never let it be said he took rejection badly. He was a grown man. He knew the odds. He put his hand on the door handle of the truck and pushed. "Well then, let's go get us a tree."

Before they got to the trees, they all came to a slight indentation in the ground.

"Mrs. Hargrove told me that's where the first house in this area sat," Jenny said. "One of her husband's ancestors settled here by the creek."

Zach walked over to the place. There was a raised edge to the indentation that showed the outline of what must have been the house. Zach guessed the house had been half sod and half stone. It certainly hadn't been very large.

"His name was Jake Hargrove. He'd taken in some children and wanted to live away from the fort," Jenny continued from where she stood. "The kids were part Dakota. Both girls."

"Girls like me?" Lisa asked as she followed Zach over to the ruin and stood where the house would have been. "My age, I mean?"

"We'll have to ask Mrs. Hargrove how old they were," Jenny said.

"I wonder if they went out to get a Christmas tree," Lisa said. "Like we're doing."

"I don't know," Jenny said.

"If they did, they were probably quick about it," Zach added as he looked up to the sky. The clouds were turning dark.

"We'll be fast," Lisa said as she left the old house

and ran toward where the trees were. "I see one already."

The tree was deformed. But Lisa had happily pointed out the one she wanted, and Zach had dutifully cut it, and they had all dragged it up out of the coulee.

"It's got a place for stars," Lisa said as she patted one of the branches.

When they got back to the house, they set the tree up in the middle of the living room. Jenny produced a plastic bucket, and they poured rocks around the tree trunk to make it stay upright. Even with the extra height of the bucket, however, the tree didn't top four feet. It also had a tendency to tilt to the left.

"It's beautiful," Jenny declared loyally when they were finished.

"It's crooked," Lisa confessed, a worried frown on her face.

"Some of the most beautiful things in the world are crooked." Zach anchored the tree deeper into the bucket of rocks. "Remember that leaning tower in Italy."

"Yeah." Lisa smiled. "We'll just have an Italian tree."

Jenny had taken Mrs. Hargrove's camera with them and she'd taken a picture of Lisa, Andy and Zach as they all measured that tree down at the bottom of the coulee. And then she'd taken a couple more of them dragging the tree up out of the coulee. "And I'm sure we'll think of something for decorations."

"We don't have decorations?" Lisa stopped studying the tree and turned to her mother. It was clear that any worry about the tilting of the tree was forgotten. "We have to have decorations."

"We can make decorations," Jenny said firmly. She should have shown her children how to make decorations in the years past. It's just that Stephen never liked the mess that projects like that made and so it was easier to just buy things at the thrift stores.

"But how can we make stars?" Lisa said worriedly. "Stars need to sparkle."

Zach sat down on the sofa to get a better look at the tree. He didn't know whether he was coming or going. He'd looked ahead down the road on the way back from getting the tree just to see if he could make it into Dry Creek. He could tell it would be foolish to leave this house, especially because the clouds had started to grow even more gray.

Of course, no matter how foolish it would be to leave, staying might be worse.

Life had really pulled a fast one on him. Here he was, snowed in with a family that was everything like the family on that Christmas card he'd seen when he was ten. Everyone cared about each other. They even cared about the stray cat out in the barn. And they didn't need a tree to be happy together, but they had a tree, anyway. They made a perfect

Christmas card picture. Sure, the father might be missing from the picture, but the man used to be in the picture. For years and years, this Stephen guy had been the husband and father in this family.

The man was dead and buried. And Zach still envied him like he'd never envied anyone in his life. That man had had it all.

"I bet he never rode a horse, though," Zach said aloud to himself.

"Huh?" Jenny looked over at Zach. For the first time today, he looked a little frayed around the edges. Zach was sitting on the sofa with his shoulders hunched forward and his hands clutching an empty cup that had held coffee.

"Horse." Andy caught the one word that interested him. He had been sitting on the floor at Zach's feet. Now he jumped up and stood at Zach's knee. "Are we going to ride a horse? Huh? Are we?"

"We don't have a horse," Jenny answered her son.

"And lights," Lisa moaned. She was still looking at the tree. "We don't have any lights."

"I can take the lights off those reindeer horns on the postal truck," Zach offered as he stood up. He might not be part of this family, but he still wanted this Christmas to be perfect, Christmas tree and all. "They are on some kind of batteries."

Lisa brightened. "That's right."

"And we can make stars out of aluminum foil."

Jenny started toward the kitchen. "And I have some red yarn for bows."

"Mr. Lightning has a horse," Andy said softly as he watched Zach walk toward the kitchen door.

"That horse is sick," Lisa said in disgust. "You can't ride a sick horse."

Zach stopped himself from promising the boy a ride. It would be a promise he might not be able to keep. Once Thunder was well, they needed to keep driving down to Vegas. He and Thunder were both roving souls. And it wasn't as if Jenny would ever invite him back for a visit. "I'll bring in the reindeer horns. Maybe we can rig you up a horse to ride from them."

"See," Andy said to his sister. "I am going to get to ride."

"That's just a pretend horse."

"I still get to ride it."

Lisa just shook her head. "First you have to help make stars."

Zach stepped into the kitchen. Jenny had opened a drawer on the counter and was pulling out slender tubes. "I know I had tinfoil here somewhere."

"I have some foil in the truck."

Jenny looked up, relieved. "You do?"

"Wrapped around half a dozen plates of cookies."

"I could replace the foil with waxed paper," Jenny offered. "That way your cookies won't dry out."

"I thought I'd bring them in, anyway. The kids will like them."

"Oh, we couldn't take your cookies."

"They're not my cookies. They were meant for Mrs. Brown or Charley. They'd want the kids to have them."

Why was it, Zach asked himself, that it was so difficult to give that woman anything? Even a porcupine had fewer prickles.

"Well, thank you." Jenny pushed the empty tube of foil back into the drawer. Why was it that the man insisted on being so nice? Couldn't he see that she was determined not to let him get under her skin? "I'll pay you for them, of course."

Zach just looked at her as he grabbed his coat off the hook. What was it with this woman? "I can't sell you a plate of Christmas cookies. Besides, I don't need your money."

Jenny was going to point out that everyone needed money, but the man was out of the door before she could. Still, she had made her point. She wanted to keep things on a businesslike level between them. Money helped do that. She didn't like accepting things from him. It made her feel as if they were friends.

No, she admitted to herself, it didn't make her feel as if they were friends. Friends stayed around. They didn't leave and take your heart with them. No, the last thing Zach offered was friendship. At the moment he was a stranger, just passing through, and she would do well to remember it.

She'd do better to bond with that poor cat out in the barn. At least the cat would be around long enough to get her kittens born and settled. Jenny supposed she'd need to find a way to coax the cat into the laundry room before Zach left. They couldn't leave kittens out in the barn without heat, and there would be no one to tend the fire at night once the cowboy left.

Chapter Eight

Zach had a towel wrapped around his fingers and a hot sheet of metal in his hand. It wasn't the best time to be watching Jenny as she watched the sky. He wondered if she knew her blond curls shone with golden highlights as she stood in the thin light that came through the window above the kitchen sink. And the long curve of her neck as she looked up—well, as Zach already knew, it wasn't the best of times for him to be holding a hot sheet of metal.

He'd already burned himself once today when Jenny bent over to pick up a spoon that fell on the floor. Of course, it had almost been worth it when Jenny insisted on rubbing some kind of an ointment on his thumb. She'd been shy about touching him, and Zach had found it more exciting than any flirtation he'd ever encountered.

"Expecting geese?" Zach carefully set the cookie

sheet on the pot holders Jenny had laid out on the counter. The kitchen was warm and the sounds of the children in the living room made him feel a contentment he'd never known. For one brief day he was inside the Christmas picture.

Andy had gone into the living room to fold tinfoil stars with Lisa. Jenny had been doing dishes, until she stopped to look up at the sky.

Jenny turned toward him. "It's below zero out there. There're no geese."

Zach nodded. "I know, but the way you've been watching that sky I figured you must be watching for something."

"I was looking at the clouds." Jenny had resisted the temptation to bring her green *Montana Guide-book* out from her bedroom. Before starting the dishes, she'd carefully read the different cloud descriptions. If she could just match the clouds outside with the right picture in her guidebook, she should be able to tell if it would snow more today. Unless there was more snow, Zach might leave. She didn't want that to happen—for Andy's sake, she told herself. Gray and heavy clouds meant snow. The clouds outside were gray, but she wasn't sure if they were heavy enough.

"Ah." Zach started lifting the cookies off the pan and onto a platter.

"What makes air heavy?"

Jenny hardly recognized the cowboy. He had

flour on his face and a sprinkling of cinnamon on his shirt. He'd tied an old dish towel around his waist. If the cereal people could only see him now, they'd take a whole new set of pictures for the backs of their boxes.

"Moisture, I guess." Zach carefully nudged the angel cookies to the left of the platter so there would be room for a few sugar-cookie trees. He'd never thought he would ever be baking Christmas cookies. "Don't tell me you're worried, too. I thought Andy was the only one."

"Andy's worried?" Jenny didn't like that her son was worried about whether or not it would snow. Of course, Zach had probably mentioned the roads to Andy. "Have you said something to make him worry you'd leave?"

"Me? No. He's not worried about me. He's worried about Santa Claus. Andy's afraid that if it rains instead of snows Santa won't be able to land his sled on the roof because it'll be too slippery." Zach kept his tone light. "It seems he remembers when you tried to fix the roof."

"Oh."

"Something about the roof being slippery because it was raining." Zach took a deep breath so his panic wouldn't show. He knew it was none of his business what this woman had decided to do a few weeks ago. But what if she had fallen off the roof instead of just sliding down the roof a bit? He wouldn't have even been there to get her to the doctor. "I guess that guidebook of yours didn't tell you that you shouldn't be climbing around on a roof in the rain. Especially not a pitched roof like this one. It's dangerous."

"Well, I didn't know the roof leaked until it started to rain for the second time."

"That's what buckets are for." Zach put the empty cookie sheet back on top of the stove. He had one more tray in the oven. "You wait until the roof is dry to work on it. Besides, you shouldn't be fixing your own roof, anyway." Zach bent his head down to open the oven and mumbled the rest. "I'll see it gets done for you."

Jenny didn't think she had heard him right. "But you can't do it, either. Snow's no better than rain. Well, it has to be worse—snow is wet and ice both at the same time. Besides…" Jenny didn't finish. They both knew he would be gone before the snow melted.

Zach swallowed. The hot air from inside the oven felt good on his face. He reached in for the tray of snowman cookies. He might as well say this while he was facing the oven. He didn't expect Jenny would like it. But he had given it some thought. "I've decided—when I go back to Dry Creek—I'm going to give Charley money to hire someone to put a new roof on this house."

Jenny gasped. She forgot all about the dishrag

in her hand. "But, you can't. Why, that's way too much…you can't possibly."

Zach pulled the tray of cookies out of the oven and straightened up. "Consider it a Christmas present."

Jenny dropped the dishrag back into the dish water. "That's not a Christmas present—a Christmas present is socks or a pin—something small. A roof is way bigger than a Christmas present." The warm air from the oven floated across the kitchen toward her. "Besides, you don't even like Christmas."

"Maybe not, but I like solid roofs."

"But you can't pay to have a new roof put on my house. Why, what would Charley and Mrs. Hargrove think?"

"They'd think you were getting a new roof."

No, Jenny thought to herself, they'd think she was getting a new husband. Which was ridiculous, of course. Anyone could see the cowboy wasn't the kind of guy to marry anyone. He would never settle down. He'd just—no, Jenny realized with a start, Charley and Mrs. Hargrove wouldn't think of marriage at all.

She'd been out of the dating game for so long, she didn't recognize the obvious. Maybe Charley and Mrs. Hargrove wouldn't think it, but other people would think the cowboy was doing her favors because she'd been generous to him in the way of women throughout time. A lot of people would think that. "I could never accept a gift that expensive. It'd be hundreds of dollars."

Try thousands, Zach thought. But he wouldn't sleep well nights thinking Jenny might be crawling around up on that roof. And paying someone to do it was the only way. Unless… "If you won't let me pay someone, I'll come back and put a new roof up myself."

Jenny looked at him as if he'd offered to burn her house down instead of seeing that it stayed dry. "I have the children to think of, you know. Not to mention the fact that I have to live in this community." Jenny paused. "I'm afraid you wouldn't get anything in exchange for the roof."

"I wouldn't—" Zach had been scooping the cookies off the sheet and turned too fast. The back of his hand hit the hot sheet. He barely felt the burn. He'd figured out what Jenny was saying, and he didn't like it. Not that he wouldn't have tried to find an angle with any other woman he found attractive. "I can think of the children, too, you know. And I wasn't expecting anything in return for the roof."

Jenny had noticed his wince when his hand hit the sheet. She reached in her pocket for the tube of ointment. "Then why were you offering it?" She held out her hand. "Here, let me see your hand."

Zach held out his closed fist. The ointment felt cool until Jenny rubbed it around on the back of his hand. Then his whole body heated up. "Can't someone do something nice for you just because—" Zach scrambled for a reason "—just because it's Christmas?"

"You're doing it because of Christmas? You?" Jenny obviously wasn't convinced.

Sometimes, Zach decided, a man needed to stay with the cards he'd been dealt, even if they were losing cards. "I have a lot of Christmas presents to make up for. From the past."

"I didn't know you in the past." Jenny held Zach's burned hand while she reached over to the counter and picked up the roll of gauze she'd used on Zach's thumb earlier. She started to unroll the gauze. "You don't owe me any presents."

Zach closed his eyes. Why did she have to make it so hard? "Maybe I've decided it would be too difficult to track down everyone I've known over the years and give them a belated present."

Jenny wrapped gauze around Zach's hand. "So this roof—it's like penance for all your past missed gifts."

"Something like that." Zach closed his eyes wearily. He hoped she never discovered that just because he didn't believe in Christmas didn't mean he'd been stingy in the past. Ever since Zach had started making good money on the rodeo circuit, he'd given some very nice presents to people. Of course, they were usually checks. Some of them had even been for dollar amounts that would be more than Jenny's roof would take. Never, however, had Zach had as much trouble with anyone accepting a present as he was having with Jenny.

"And you're not expecting to sleep with me in return?" Jenny asked the question crisply. She was just making sure they understood each other.

Zach opened his eyes at that. "Lady, you'll barely kiss me. I'm not fool enough to think a roof would get us to where you're thinking."

Zach hoped she'd protest. Hoped she'd say it might at least get him a date. She didn't.

Instead Jenny slowly knotted the gauze on his hand. She didn't even raise her eyes to his but kept them on his burn. "But I don't have anything nearly that expensive to give you in return."

Zach smiled. So it was her pride that was bothering her. He turned his bandaged hand so that he held hers. "At the rate I'm going, maybe you should just give me that ointment in your pocket and a roll of that gauze. We'll figure you've saved me from a life of disfiguring burns."

Jenny looked up and smiled back, but she didn't remove her hand. "Cookie baking can be dangerous."

"I never knew kitchen duty could be so hazardous." Zach couldn't control his thumb as it rubbed the back of Jenny's hand. Jenny had been washing dishes and her hands were still slightly damp from the water. Even damp, Zach wagered they were smoother than other women's hands. Of course, maybe he was just partial to them.

Jenny's cheeks were pink as she smiled. "If you think this is exciting, wait until tomorrow. You can help me with the ham. And—if you really want a thrill—you can help open the can of yams I'm going to bake."

"It can't be any harder than baking these cookies." Zach settled back into holding Jenny's hand.

Zach couldn't remember ever holding a woman's hand before. He couldn't remember *wanting* to hold a woman's hand. He was always too intent on winning a bigger prize. What a fool he'd been, he thought as he squeezed Jenny's hand. He hadn't known what he was missing. He would remember this moment forever.

The warm smell of sugar cookies made the kitchen cozy. Jenny had rolled the dough thin, and Lisa and Andy had used cookie cutters to shape snowmen, angels, bells and trees. Zach had measured the ingredients and helped Andy stir. Everyone had sprinkled colored sugar on the different shapes before Zach slipped the cookie sheets into the oven.

The sky outside was gray, and only a thin light shone through the windows. The electricity was still off but Jenny had lit a candle and set it on the folding table. The glow of the candle cast yellow light all around the kitchen.

Jenny held her breath. She couldn't remember ever having someone sit with her at the end of a day and hold her hand. It should feel innocent, even with the hypnotic feel of Zach's thumb as it traced circles on the back of her hand. But it didn't feel the least bit innocent. It was one of the most intense moments she'd ever experienced. Too bad intense was a mistake.

"Thanks for helping with everything," Jenny finally said to Zach as she gently removed her hand. "You got the tree. You took the kids out to see the cat."

"Of course, we didn't find her," Zach added. They had heard the cat hiss when they entered the barn, but they couldn't find her back amid the hay bales.

"Still, you're making it a wonderful Christmas."

Jenny looked around her kitchen with satisfaction. For the first time, she didn't notice all the things she didn't have. Instead she saw that the folding table still had scraps of tinfoil from the star shapes that Lisa had cut earlier and the kitchen counter was covered with every platter she owned. Each platter was covered with Christmas sugar cookies. Such a wonderful Christmas merited a wonderful present for the man who had helped make it all possible.

"I can think of a better gift for you than a first-aid kit," Jenny said firmly. She was full of good-will. Everyone inside her home would have a good Christmas if it was in her power to give them one.

The light coming in from the kitchen window cast shadows around Zach's eyes. "I'm not expecting anything. You don't need to—I mean, the roof doesn't require a present. It's just because—"

"No, I need a present for you." Jenny closed her eyes. How could a cowboy in worn jeans and a towel apron covered with cookie dough look so handsome? Well, it wasn't his fault she couldn't keep her eyes off him. He'd been good to her children, and she owed him a Christmas present. She did a mental review of the boxes in her bedroom. "Maybe something of Stephen's—"

"No." The word sounded abrupt even to Zach's ears. Jenny's eyes flew open. To hide his confusion, Zach turned and stole a warm cookie from a platter. "I mean, you should save his things for Andy and Lisa. When they're older, they'll want some things to remember him by."

Jenny wondered if her children would remember their father in twenty years. If they did, it wouldn't be because of some sweater or tie.

"He must have been a wonderful father and husband." Zach tried to sound casual as he took a bite out of the cookie.

Zach hated himself for trying to find out more about the man, but the man's very existence bothered him like a scab that wasn't healing right. Maybe someone would let something slip, and Zach could learn the secret that this Stephen had known about being part of a family like this one.

Maybe—Zach didn't dare even hope—but maybe the secret was something Zach could learn if he only had a few pointers. Zach almost choked on the rest of what he had to say, but he said it, anyway. "I wish I could have known him. What was he like?"

"Like?" Jenny's voice squeaked. She never talked about Stephen. He was not only a closed chapter in her life, she'd buried the book, as well.

"Yeah. Did he have any hobbies?" Zach supposed the man liked opera. Women always seemed to like opera. Zach preferred a guitar player in a bar any-time. Still, he supposed he could learn to endure opera. "Anything you and he did for special eve-nings?"

Jenny tried hard to think. She and Stephen hadn't done anything social even in the years before he was sick. Stephen preferred to go out with his male friends rather than stay home with her, and he never wanted to spend the money for a babysit-ter so they could go out together. "We didn't have a lot of money."

"I see." Zach figured that meant they spent a lot of cozy evenings at home putting together jig-saw puzzles and watching videos. The very thought of it depressed him. Zach would have had a better chance of competing if Jenny had mentioned dinners in fancy restaurants and dancing. He could afford to fly her to Paris for a weekend. It was the home things he wasn't sure he'd ever get right.

The outside light was fading in the kitchen, and the shine of the candle on the table was growing more golden. Zach's face picked up the glow of the candle. He was concentrating on the cookie in his hand with an intensity that reminded Jenny of his picture on the back of that cereal box.

It was the cereal-box picture that gave Jenny the courage to decide to tell Zach the truth about Stephen. She wanted to tell someone. She really did. The words always just seemed to stick in her throat. But if she pretended she was still only talking to the back of that box, maybe she could get the words out.

"Stephen—" Jenny began and swallowed. She felt almost relieved now that she had decided to tell someone. Even if that someone was just a cowboy who was on the back of a cereal box. "Stephen was, well, it wasn't so much what he was, it's what he— Well, you know I've told you that he wasn't—" Jenny stopped. Zach had turned and was looking at her. All of a sudden, he didn't look anything like his picture on the cereal box.

"Yeah," Zach prompted her.

"I, ah…" Jenny knew it was her chance. She also knew she was a coward. She didn't know what Zach would think of her if she told him about Stephen.

Lots of men thought any marital unhappiness was the wife's fault. Maybe Zach would think that, too. "I…we got married awfully young."

Zach almost groaned. No wonder Jenny didn't want to kiss another man. Stephen was probably the only man she'd ever even dated. "You must have been very much in love."

"Uh…" Jenny swallowed. She would try again.

Jenny never got a chance. The quiet giggles from the living room had grown louder and finally they were at the kitchen door.

"Mama, come look," Lisa called as she stood in the doorway.

The house was in shadows.

"Oh, I better get the lantern lit," Jenny said. She'd talk to Zach later. It wasn't that she wouldn't have talked to him, she assured herself. It just wasn't the time yet. She'd tell him all about Stephen. And soon. Just not right this minute. She couldn't risk the children hearing about Stephen.

"Mr. Lightning," Andy called from the living room. "Come see the stars."

Zach followed Jenny into the living room, and the light from the lantern she was carrying made the tinfoil stars reflect a thousand lights. The tree glowed with the reflections. Zach had unwrapped the Christmas lights from around the reindeer horns that had hung on the postal-truck hood. He'd then clipped the lights to the branches of the Christmas tree. The battery for the lights was nestled on top of the rocks at the bottom of the tree. So far, no one had turned on the lights.

"They're lovely," Jenny said as she put one hand on Lisa's shoulder and smiled at Andy. "I've never seen so many stars."

"Can we turn the lights on now?" Lisa asked. "It's almost dark."

Jenny had told the children earlier that they would turn on the tree lights when it grew dark. Jenny wasn't sure how much power the batteries had left, and she didn't want to run the batteries dry before it even grew dark.

"Let's have some soup first." Jenny looked at her watch. How had the day gone so fast? "It's almost five o'clock. Then we can read the Christmas story before you go off to bed."

"But that will still be too early," Lisa protested. "I wanted to wrap your present."

Zach had hidden the jewelry box the kids had made for their mother earlier this morning. The jewelry box had really been a small wooden toolbox that Zach had kept his leather-working tools inside. Andy had glued some beach shells he'd found in California on top of the box and Lisa had glued a piece of velvet on the inside of the box.

Wrapping presents, Jenny thought in dismay. "But I don't have any paper. Oh, I knew I wasn't ready for Christmas."

"Wrapping paper isn't necessary," Zach said, hoping he was right. He was wrong.

"Yes, it is," Lisa said, and she looked up at Zach as if he was a magician with a hat that still had a few rabbits left inside of it.

"I don't have any—oh, wait." Zach remembered. "I do have paper. In the postal truck. Mrs. Brown carries around a tube of brown postal paper. And tape."

"Brown paper?" Lisa looked skeptical.

"I think there might be some red stamps and some markers." Zach wasn't sure what all Mrs. Brown kept in the postal bin that ran along the right-top side of the truck.

"We can make Christmas paper," Jenny said in relief. The kids would remember Christmas paper they had made themselves a lot longer than anything she could buy.

"Just remember, you need to go to bed early tonight," Jenny said firmly. "Remember what we said? If you go to bed early, you can get up early tomorrow morning."

And, if they go to bed early, Jenny added to herself, she and Zach would have time to make the presents for the children they'd talked about earlier. Zach had told her his ideas, and she knew the children would love the gifts he had suggested.

"All right," Lisa agreed reluctantly.

"Can I have cereal instead of soup for supper?" Andy asked.

Andy had also asked to have Ranger Flakes for lunch when the rest of them had eaten tuna sandwiches. Jenny had given in then. "You've got to eat more than cereal."

"I can have a cookie, too," Andy offered.

Jenny appealed to Zach. "You talk to him."

Zach smiled. He was glad the cereal executives couldn't hear him now. "Real cowboys don't eat cereal for every meal. They need other things, too, to stay healthy. Maybe you should try some soup tonight."

"Are you eating soup?" Andy asked as he walked over and wrapped his arms around Zach's leg.

"I sure am."

"Okay," Andy agreed. "I'll have soup. And crackers?"

"Yeah, we have crackers. And peaches for dessert." Jenny tried to remember everything she had in the cupboards. She was grateful Stephen's uncle had had the good sense to see that the kitchen stove operated off the propane tank like the furnace did. With the electricity still out, they wouldn't be eating anything warm if he hadn't.

Zach left his hand resting on Andy's head. Zach liked the solid weight of the boy as Andy leaned against his leg. "Let's go set the table for your mom."

"I know where the bowls are," Lisa announced as she led the way.

Supper was by candlelight, and Zach was content. He'd eaten candlelight dinners in five-star restaurants at the top of skyscrapers and on cruise ships. At none of those dinners had the conversation lagged or the soup been cold. But he didn't even have to debate the issue. He wouldn't trade this candlelight meal for any one of the others.

"At least the peaches should be all right," Jenny said quietly.

"It was a wonderful meal," Zach assured her. "Wholesome."

"I could heat up some more tomato soup, now that the stove has cooled down." Jenny hadn't realized that using the oven of the stove all afternoon would affect the burners. It meant they wouldn't stay lit for very long.

"I'm content."

Jenny wondered if she should admit to Zach that she was content, too. She wondered at the ease she felt around him. Earlier in the day Jenny had realized she was relaxing around Zach because he didn't criticize her the way she had expected any man would. Zach seemed to be pleased with whatever she had to offer in the way of meals and household comforts.

Zach was a big change from her late husband. Stephen had been visibly unhappy if the laundry wasn't ironed right or the meals weren't to his liking. No wonder she'd been tired all those years when she'd been married, Jenny thought to herself in amazement. She'd been trying to make things perfect for Stephen. And perfection had been hard to maintain when she had two small children to care for as well.

Of course, Jenny told herself, it was easy for Zach to accept things the way they were. He wouldn't be around long and he probably just didn't care.

"I do know how to cook a good meal," she added in self-defense. "It's just the stove and all. I'm learning."

"We're all learning." Zach pushed his chair away from the table. "Let me get the peaches for you."

"After peaches, I want to make wrapping paper," Lisa said.

Jenny rinsed the dishes from supper and left them in the sink. Amazing how liberating that felt. For the second time today she hadn't needed to rush to do the dishes as if she had something to prove to someone. Instead the four of them sat at the folding table and made wrapping paper.

Andy liked to stamp. He'd stamped a red *FRAGILE* over a length of brown postal paper. The stamp was upside down in some places and sideways in others. Jenny noticed that the confused jumble of it all did manage to look festive.

Lisa was drawing bells with a red pen on another length of brown postal paper.

"I'll need to remember to pay Mrs. Brown for all this," Jenny said.

"I bet she'd like a picture, too," Zach said as he stood up and walked to the kitchen counter. The woman deserved to see them as they concentrated on decorating the postal paper. "You should take one for Mrs. Hargrove and Charley, too."

"Great idea," Jenny said as she accepted the camera Zach handed to her.

Jenny snapped four pictures and pulled them out to dry. She'd taken a dozen or so pictures of the children over the day. There was one of Andy and Zach cutting out cookies. There was one of Lisa and Zach stringing the lights on the Christmas tree.

Each picture Jenny took, she took an extra. One of the shots was for herself. The other one was for a Christmas present for Zach. She'd thought about going through the box of Stephen's ties and sweaters, but even though Zach wouldn't be wearing either one around Jenny, she didn't like to picture him in anything but the clothes he already had. She didn't want to look at the cowboy and see any reminders of Stephen.

Actually, she thought she might take the whole box of Stephen's things and tie it up tight with some postal string before setting it at the back of the large closet in her bedroom. Zach was right. Andy and

Lisa might want to see the things someday, but for now, Jenny wanted it tucked away where she didn't have to see it every day.

Jenny couldn't help but wonder, as she listened to her children giggle while they talked with Zach, what her life would have been like if she had married a man like Zach instead of one like Stephen.

Well—she shook herself—that was a pointless thing to wonder about, and on a Christmas Eve.

Chapter Nine

Zach had never heard the Christmas story read to children. Oh, he knew the story—sort of, anyway. The star. The wise men. The shepherds. The angels. The baby in the manger. But he'd never seen it through the eyes of children.

Zach sat backward on a folding chair with his arms resting on the back. He loved watching Jenny as she sat on the sofa with one child on either side of her and read them the Christmas story. The three of them believed that story had really happened. Zach could tell just by watching them, and he envied them. He wished he knew God well enough to trust him like that.

"And that's why we have hope today," Jenny said as she closed the children's book. "Because a long time ago on Christmas Eve, the baby Jesus was born in a manger in Bethlehem."

"I wish He could have been born in our barn," Andy said.

"Like our kittens are going to be born tonight," Lisa added hopefully.

"Well, maybe somewhat like the kittens," Jenny said with a smile.

"We need to take the mama cat some warm milk," Lisa said as she looked up at Zach. "She'll be hungry."

"All we have left is dry milk," Jenny said.

"That will do," Zach said. "Maybe with some crackers in it."

Jenny had moved the lantern into the living room, and it was hanging from a hook she'd rigged up from the ceiling fan. The lantern gave off a yellowish light that bathed the room in a warm glow. The smell of recently baked cookies still filled the air, mingling with the smell of fresh pine from the tree that sat in the bucket of rocks in the middle of the room. A small present was already wrapped and sitting beneath the decorated tree.

"Will the new kittens have their own star in the sky? When they are born?" Andy asked after a minute.

Andy looked up at Zach when he asked the question and Zach froze. He didn't know anything about that night in Bethlehem. He wasn't able to answer any questions.

Fortunately, Jenny was there on the sofa. She

shook her head. "The star was only for the Baby Jesus."

Lisa sighed. "That's why we have stars today."

"Well, we had stars before Christmas," Jenny said softly. "But none of them were as special as the Christmas star."

"It was the biggest, bestest star ever," Lisa said in satisfaction.

"My star is big, too," Andy said as he pointed to the tree that stood in the center of the living room. "It's that one."

Andy and Lisa had colored their stars. The folded foil stars had been marked with red highlighters and yellow highlighters. Some had flowers drawn on them. One had a horse. They each had a hole poked in their top for a piece of twine so they could be tied to the tree branches. The stars made the lopsided pine tree sparkle with reflected light from the red and green lights that were twined around the tree branches.

The star Andy pointed to had to be at least four inches across. It was so big it hung crooked on the tree branch. A yellow stick figure had been drawn on it with a big circle around its head.

Zach thought the stick figure must be an angel and the circle a halo.

"It's a beautiful star," Jenny agreed as she shifted the arm she had around the boy and gave him a quick hug.

Andy wiggled down from the sofa and walked over to Zach's chair. "Did you see my star?"

"I sure did," Zach assured the boy. "I think it's the best ever. And that's some angel you drew."

Zach could see Lisa roll her eyes from where she still sat on the sofa. "It's not an angel. It's you."

The girl might as well have thrown a thunderbolt at him. "Me? An angel?"

"It's a cowboy," Lisa said as she stood up and walked over to the tree. She touched the star and then looked at Zach. "See. There's the hat."

"You put me on your star?" Zach repeated stupidly as he looked down at Andy.

The boy was smiling. "I put Thunder, too—on the other one."

Andy went over and touched the star with the horse on it before turning to Zach. "Do you like them?"

"They're the best ever," Zach said as he cleared his throat and then blinked. A bit of smoke from the lantern must have got in his eye. "What a wonderful Christmas surprise."

Andy looked at Lisa and they both giggled.

"That's not your Christmas surprise," Lisa finally said. "We've got that planned for tomorrow morning."

Zach hadn't had the breath knocked out of him this completely since he had been bucked off Black

Demon in Fargo last year. He knew his mouth was hanging open, but he couldn't close it.

"We can't tell you what it is," Andy warned. The boy danced in excitement. "It's a surprise."

"Well, I'll be," Zach finally managed to say. "A Christmas surprise for me."

Zach turned to Jenny. He admitted he was a little giddy. Usually the only Christmas gifts he ever got were bottles of booze. "They have a surprise for me."

Jenny had never been prouder of her children. They'd planned a Christmas surprise for a guest in their household without any prompting or guidance from her. Jenny thought about that for a minute, and her pride quickly turned to worry. Her children had planned a Christmas surprise for Zach without her input. That could spell disaster.

Not all men appreciated the same things that children did, and Jenny knew that. Granted, Zach had seemed genuinely touched by the stars. But who knew if he'd react as well to some wrinkled tie made out of paper or a cardboard belt buckle?

"I think maybe it's time for bed now," Jenny announced.

Even though both of her children sat with pleased looks on their faces, Jenny was sure one of them would tell her about their planned surprise when she tucked them into bed. If she knew what the big gift was, maybe she could straighten a few of the corners or iron it or something. She'd noticed that several of the boxes in the corner of the living room looked as if someone had gone through them this afternoon.

Well, Jenny thought, whatever it was, she would do whatever she could to make it better. If she only knew what it was. Unfortunately, neither one of her children would budge, insisting it was a Christmas-morning surprise and surprises were secrets.

"Well, at least show me before you show it to him. Okay?" Jenny pulled the covers up to Lisa's chin and reminded herself to have her scissors and glue handy in the morning. Maybe she should also get out a needle and thread. "Is the surprise made out of cloth or paper?"

"Mom." Lisa rolled her eyes. "It's a surprise."

"I know, sweetie." Jenny bent down and kissed her daughter on the forehead. "I know."

Zach was in the kitchen, sitting at the table and stamping *PRIORITY* on a full yard of brown postal paper. He added a few green snowflakes drawn with one marker that still had ink in it. He decided right then that he needed to start carrying a bigger duffel. Either that or he'd have to tell Mrs. Brown she needed to carry more supplies in her postal bin. He wished he had glitter or velvet or even a red stamp that gave a holiday greeting instead of a postal message. And that was just the stuff at the bottom of his wish list.

Right now, he wished for a whole lot of things.

Ever since he'd seen that star, he'd wished he had time to go to Denver or Salt Lake or at least Billings to buy Christmas presents for this little family. He'd like to buy a princess doll and a tiara with real diamonds for Lisa. She could sell it when she wanted to go to college someday—and with a mind like hers she'd definitely want to go.

Then he'd buy a horse for Andy. And if a real horse would be too much trouble, he'd buy one of those electronic ones that they used in bars. He'd find one with a gentle setting. And, if he couldn't find one with a gentle setting, he'd buy the boy a carousel with a dozen horses to choose from.

And for Jenny—Zach stopped stamping and smiled—for Jenny he'd buy a full-length mink coat. Fake, of course, if she was bothered by the real thing. But something warm enough to weather the worst Montana storm her guidebook ever dreamed could hit.

He'd also buy her a tractor.

But Zach knew there was no time to travel and no clear roads even if there had been time. There was no way to get to the gifts he wanted to buy. So he'd just have to make do with what he had.

"They're in bed," Jenny announced as she stood in the doorway to the kitchen. She had brought the lantern into the kitchen before putting the children to bed, and its yellow light formed a circle around the table and Zach. The Christmas-tree lights had given off enough light for her to see Lisa and Andy to bed. Both children had promised to go to sleep quickly.

"They've had a busy day." Zach didn't know when he'd had a better day himself. He'd certainly never had a better day related to Christmas. He stopped stamping the brown paper and raised it up. "Do you think I should stamp this some more?"

"It looks good." Jenny had never seen a man so taken with Christmas. "I brought the wire hanger you wanted. And the strip of old towel."

Zach admired Jenny standing in the doorway. The red and green lights from the living room backed her silhouette, while the yellow light from the lantern played up the blond highlights in her hair. Her face looked dewy smooth and sculpted. Her eyelashes were thick, and he didn't think she was even wearing any mascara. The shadows hid her blue eyes, and they looked like an ocean at midnight.

Zach swallowed and forced himself to think of the presents he still had to make. The night promised to be even longer than the watch on his wrist indicated. "Thanks for bringing everything. I'd better get started."

Zach had taken his duffel into the kitchen. He'd found a few minutes during the day to slip into the laundry room and pound belt holes in the strip of leather he was planning to use in Andy's gift. The rest of the work would be quiet, and he could do it while everyone slept.

"You're sure you want to cut this up?" Jenny walked over to the counter where Zach had laid out the leg garter and picked it up. The lantern light made the rhinestones sparkle quietly. "This had to be expensive."

The black lace and velvet circle studded with rhinestones looked like something out of a classy department store rather than a vending machine. Jenny counted the stones. Fifteen. "These look real."

"The rubies are." Zach rolled the stamped postal paper up. He'd need the whole table for working. "There's only a couple of them. Of course, they're not high quality."

"And you're cutting this up?" Jenny looked at the garter more closely. Those rubies sure did look genuine. "You can't cut this up—not if they're real."

Jenny frowned. She didn't like the fact that Zach had bought something with actual jewels in it for his girlfriend. A garter was one thing, but jewels! Jewels meant commitment. Maybe Zach's relationship with the showgirl was more serious than he had let on. Of course, he did not owe Jenny any explanations about his relationships with women. Zach and her family were stranded together in a snowstorm. He didn't even want to be here. "I'm sure Patti would want the rubies even if you give them to her after Christmas."

"Ah, well, I don't know when I'll see her now. I mean, she expected me today so—" Zach didn't want to admit to Jenny that he'd lost all appetite for his Vegas vacation.

"Oh, and she won't know what's happened. She'll be worried."

"Not likely."

Jenny felt a little better. "She'll probably see the weather reports about a blizzard here. She'll know your trip might have been interrupted."

"Yeah." Zach didn't want to keep talking about Patti. He knew the showgirl wouldn't worry about him at all. "Do you have that hanger? I think that's the first thing to do—see if I can bend that into a likely shape." Zach looked up at Jenny. "Mind if I use your head to size it?"

"Huh?"

"The tiara." Zach took the metal hanger Jenny handed to him and ran his hands along it. "Good quality."

Jenny sat down at the table.

Zach stood up. This tiara-making business wasn't so bad. He realized he had every excuse in the world to touch Jenny's head. "Lisa's hair is the same color as yours. Very pretty."

"Thank you." Jenny felt warm—too warm for a night like this. It was thirty degrees below zero outside tonight, and she knew for a fact that she kept the furnace thermometer set at sixty-five. She should be shivering from the cold instead of the heat—she barely felt Zach's hands as they circled the top of her head. Of course, it wasn't his hands that were bothering her. It was him. He was six feet of muscle standing behind her chair. She could feel the heat from his body. She wondered if he could feel her heart racing. "It's been quite a day."

"Mmm-hmm." Zach tried to keep his mind on the tiara instead of the fact that Jenny's hair was soft enough to kiss. And thick—her curls would scatter over a pillow like the petals of a sunflower. And to think he used to prefer long hair on his girlfriends.

What was he thinking? Zach pulled his hand back. Jenny wasn't his girlfriend. She wouldn't even kiss him. Well, he didn't think she'd kiss him. He hadn't asked again since this morning. And she was sitting awfully still in this dimly lit kitchen. He put his hand back, this time on her shoulder, and she didn't pull away. That had to be a good sign.

"Women—they say they can always change their minds, don't they?" Zach asked without thinking.

"Huh?" Jenny turned around to look at him. In the shadows her eyes were deep blue and unreadable.

"Ah…Lisa. You're sure she wants a tiara?" Zach could have kicked himself. He rode bucking horses, after all. He was always able to ride out of the chute when the bar was pulled back. He never wavered. He never hesitated. Until now.

Jenny turned back around, and Zach began to gently rub her shoulders. "Yeah, I'm sure. She's talked about it ever since we moved here. I wish I'd known sooner. I could have found one in a store in Los Angeles and brought it with us."

"Yeah."

Zach told himself a responsible, decent Santa would get on with making Christmas gifts and forget about the woman sitting in front of him. "And what do you want for Christmas?"

"Me?" Jenny laughed. "I've been working too hard to think about what I want."

"You need someone to help you."

Jenny leaned back into the man's hands. He was giving her a back rub. It felt wonderful. "I've been thinking of getting a dog."

"A dog?" Zach almost lost his rhythm in the back rub. That certainly put him in his place. He was losing his touch.

"Yeah, someone to chase the rabbits out of the garden come spring."

"You're planting a garden!" Zach had driven through this part of Montana last summer, when there hadn't been a foot of snow on the ground. "You'll need to put down a layer of topsoil first. The wind blew it all off a couple of years ago. Besides, you already have a cat."

"The guidebook didn't mention anything about topsoil." Jenny frowned as she turned around to look at Zach. "It said I could grow anything. And cats and dogs can get along."

When pigs can fly, Zach thought. But he didn't say it. "Potatoes might grow," he said instead. He pressed harder against Jenny's left shoulder. "They don't take much topsoil."

"But I want snap peas and roses. Sort of an English garden. And some tomatoes."

"Oh." Zach moved over to the right shoulder.

Jenny felt as if her shoulders were putty. Warm, melting putty. Zach was massaging them with the palms of his hands. Then Zach moved his hands to the base of the back of Jenny's neck.

Jenny held back the moan that purred deep in her throat. "How'd you ever get so good at this?" Jenny regretted the question as soon as she asked it. A single man like Zach learned to give massages for only one reason.

"My horse," Zach answered. Now, why had Jenny stiffened up like that? There, that was better. "He had a leg injury."

"Ah, good," Jenny sighed.

"He didn't think so."

"No, I don't suppose he would."

The massage left Jenny relaxed and energized both at the same time. "I should help you with the presents."

"We've got time." Zach had never felt this content in all his life. Not when he'd bought his first horse. Not when he'd first won the Pro-Championship title. Not when he'd signed the contract with the Ranger cereal company. Not ever. "I like being here with you."

Jenny heard the words Zach whispered. Suddenly she didn't care that he was a man who was just traveling through. "I like you, too."

"Like as in like, or…?" Zach didn't want to shatter the quiet of the evening by making a false move.

Jenny stood up and turned to face Zach. There were only three inches between them. Then there were two. Then…

Jenny figured some women live their whole lives and never have a kiss like this one. It curled her toes and made her breath stop in her throat. She would have swooned, but mothers with two young children did not swoon.

"Hmm." Zach still had the taste of her lips on his tongue. He was reluctant to let go.

"I think—"

"Don't think."

"I think I need to wrap the Christmas presents."

Ah, Christmas. Christmas had given Zach trouble for years. Strangely enough, for the first time he didn't mind so much. "You can stamp while I finish up on the other presents."

Jenny not only stamped enough brown postal paper to wrap the gifts, she drew red bells on them. So what if the bells grew to look a little like hearts?

It was Christmas, after all, and Christmas was a time for wishes and dreams.

It was even, she told herself firmly, a time for dreams that had no hope of ever coming true. She knew Zach "Lightning" Lucas was just passing through. She knew he wished he were in Las Vegas. She knew he hated Christmas and was just being kind to her and her children. She knew he hadn't been to church in ages. But, even knowing all that, she couldn't help smiling when he walked into the unheated laundry room and came back with the mistletoe in his hand. "We could use this for decorations on the packages."

"It's a pity to waste it," Jenny said. She watched the slow smile spread across Zach's face as she added, "After all, it is Christmas Eve."

Jenny floated to bed that night. She'd had one special night. She'd been kissed. She'd been hugged. She'd been listened to by someone who paid attention.

If she had to keep reminding herself that it wouldn't last forever, that is what she would do. After all, once Christmas was gone, winter would be long and cold. Her heart would have time to forget all about the cowboy.

Jenny listened until she heard the door to the house close. Zach was on his way to the barn.

The night was full dark when Zach made his way out to the barn. He carried an old aluminum pan filled with milk made from powder. He had a small bag of crackers stuffed in his coat pocket. He figured he'd have to start the fire small tonight so that the milk didn't burn on top of the wood stove. That cat was a lot of trouble.

He'd probably have to stir the milk while it heated. Which was okay. He'd already decided to light the kerosene lamp for a while so he could read about the Christmas story in the Bible he'd seen earlier in that room. He wanted to be able to answer Andy's questions when he asked them. And even if the boy was finished with his questions, Zach wasn't. There had to be more to the story than that one night in Bethlehem.

Chapter Ten

Could kisses give anyone a hangover?

Jenny sat in her bed and wondered how she could feel so bad on Christmas morning. Well, technically it wasn't morning yet, she comforted herself as she looked out the window in her bedroom. It was deep gray outside. The wind had stopped blowing. She had a good half hour before she had to get up and pretend everything was well with the world.

It was Merry Christmas time. Hugs and Santa time.

Jenny wanted to crawl into a dark pit and stay there until spring. But—she squinted at the illuminated clock by her bed—in nineteen minutes, she would smile. And she would pretend that everything was wonderful, even if she had to crawl to the Christmas tree on her hands and knees. Christmas was a special time of the year for children, and

Jenny was determined to add to her children's cheer and not take away from it.

It wasn't her children's fault that Jenny had gone crazy last night and thrown caution to the wind. And crazy it was. She'd fallen in love with a man who was only passing through—a man who had not even meant to end up in her house and would have left if the snow had not left them snowbound. He had only been there to deliver a package, after all. He was the mailman. And not even the regular mailman. He wanted to spend Christmas with a showgirl instead of a widow and her two young children. What had she been thinking? The man didn't even believe in God. They clearly had no future.

Jenny felt around in the semidarkness for the bottle of water she kept by her bed. Now, if she only had an aspirin. Or two. She winced. Make that four.

Jenny heard the door to the kitchen open. Zach was back.

Zach was miserable. He would never be able to look at another Christmas card again. Or even a postal stamp—Fragile, Return to Sender, Priority— they would all be signals to him to count his shortcomings in the future.

He was a grown man. He should have known he would have to pay the price for those kisses last night. Never before had he so deeply regretted the kind of man he was.

He'd read enough of the Bible last night to have a glimmer of the kind of man Jenny deserved. Zach wasn't that man. If he had any clue as to how to be a godly, family man, he would take a nail and permanently tack that piece of mistletoe to the doorway of this house. And then he'd beg Jenny to marry him.

But he wasn't good at relationships. He didn't even know how much he didn't know. Maybe when he finished reading the Bible, he'd have a list. But, right now, all he knew was that his list of shortcomings was long. And it wasn't fair to Jenny to pretend otherwise. It certainly wasn't fair to the kids.

Sure, Zach admitted, he'd done all right for a day or two. He'd filled in for Stephen, who should have been here with them. Anyone could follow a good act for a few minutes. It was like riding on a bronc that had been winded by the previous rider. It wasn't a fair test. And it wouldn't take long for Jenny to realize he was a fake.

Zach didn't relish seeing the disappointment in her eyes. He would have to leave. But before he left, he owed them a merry Christmas. He was, for better or for worse, Santa Claus.

Zach was in the laundry room, snapping his white beard into place, when he heard the first whisper. It sounded like Andy. The answer that came sounded like Lisa. Zach hurriedly put the Santa hat on his head. He'd already put the rest of the outfit on—even that belt with the lights.

Then he walked into the living room.

Speaking of lights—Zach walked over until he could reach the battery switch to turn on the Christmas-tree lights. The tree glowed in the early morning light, casting red and green shadows all around the living room.

The tree sat in the middle of the living room, and the lights danced on all four walls. Zach's eyes were drawn to the bulletin board that he'd seen earlier. He'd avoided the pictures on the board yesterday, but now—knowing his hours with this family were limited—he went over to look at the pictures.

He had to smile. There was a photo of Andy dressed as a pumpkin for some reason. There was Lisa in a frilly white dress and almost no teeth. And the zoo—there must have been four or five pictures of the children at the zoo. Andy by the elephants. Lisa by a giraffe. And the beach—there were so many pictures at the beach. In one of them, Jenny was building a sand castle with Andy. That picture was crooked. Lisa must have snapped it.

Zach wondered how many men's hearts were broken on Christmas morning. He wanted to give so much, and he had so little to give.

"What?" Jenny's voice carried from her bedroom. The children were clearly in with her, and a quiet rumble of whispers followed Jenny's first outburst. Zach couldn't make out any of the words, but he could tell a heated discussion was taking place behind the closed door.

Zach wondered if he was about to get his surprise. It sounded like some surprise. He only hoped the wrapped packages under the tree would be sufficient to repay the children for the amount of convincing they were doing. It sounded like an uphill battle was being fought in there.

He wondered what they were giving him that their mother so clearly disapproved of. It must be something like a knife. Mothers always disapproved of knives—as they should. But that couldn't be it. Jenny wouldn't care if he had a knife.

Maybe—and the thought didn't sit well with him—the children had decided to give him something that had belonged to their father and Jenny couldn't part with it. That made sense. Some favorite shirt or tie. Well, she didn't need to worry about him. He would quietly return anything they gave him that had sentimental value.

The voices went silent and then Zach saw Lisa's head poke out of the partially opened door. She looked around and saw him.

"You need to go sit on the sofa," the girl directed him, before giving a worried look back into the bedroom. "We're almost ready."

Andy came out first and ran across the room to settle on the sofa next to Zach. Zach put his arm around the boy before he looked down at Andy's hair. A tiny white feather was sitting on top of the boy's head.

"Dum-da-dum," Lisa trumpeted as she stood in the open doorway.

What on earth...? Zach watched Lisa sneeze. She had a dozen tiny white feathers flying around her. They floated around her before settling to the floor.

Zach decided the children must be giving him a chicken for Christmas. A live chicken. That's all it could be with those feathers. But where had they kept a chicken? There certainly weren't any birds in the barn.

"Dum-da-dum," Lisa repeated as she stepped to the side of the door and waved her arm for someone to come onstage.

What on earth...? Zach's first thought was that there must be a truckload of chickens inside Jenny's bedroom. Tiny white feathers floated everywhere as Jenny stood in the doorway in her—Zach took a second look and started to grin—Jenny was in a red-and white cheerleader's outfit.

"It's a showgirl," Andy whispered.

Zach grinned like a fool. "That it is."

"You told them a showgirl was a cheerleader with feathers in her hair," Jenny accused him as she stood in the doorway to the bedroom. She held a pom-pom in each hand and had an exasperated smile on her face. "Lisa even sacrificed her goose-down pillow so they'd have feathers."

"It works for me," Zach said. He couldn't take his eyes off Jenny. She stood there daring him to laugh. Her blue eyes glinted with steel. Her hair was sprayed stiff and covered with feathers. She was absolutely amazing.

"We have a cheer," Lisa announced as she motioned Andy to join her. "A Christmas cheer."

Zach saw Jenny close her eyes in resignation.

"One…two…three," Lisa counted off before she added, "Now."

The three voices blended. They spelled out the words. "M-E-R-R-Y C-H-R-I-S-T-M-A-S—Merry Christmas to you!"

Jenny kicked her leg up and shook her pompoms. Lisa and Andy just screamed.

"Did you like it?" Andy asked eagerly before anyone else had regained their breath.

"I liked it a lot," Zach answered. Even if he lived to be a hundred, he would never receive a better Christmas surprise than this. "It's the best present ever."

"That's not all," Lisa screeched as she ran to the kitchen and came back with the camera. She handed the camera to Zach before rushing back to the doorway. "You get to take a picture of us, too."

Zach's eyes were blurry and his hands shook. But he snapped two pictures all the same. Now it really was the best Christmas gift possible. He had pictures of Jenny and the kids.

Jenny watched as Zach carefully set the pictures aside to develop. Well, he'd been a good sport about it. Lisa and Andy were still trembling with excitement, although she noticed their attention had moved from Zach to the wrapped packages lying under the tree.

"Did Santa come?" Andy finally asked softly.

Zach swallowed. "Well now, let's see."

"Do we have kittens yet?" Lisa asked.

"I don't think so. Not yet," Zach said. He'd put the warm milk in a dish by his door and it had been gone in the morning, but he hadn't seen the cat.

Since there were no kittens, both children went back to the presents.

It was an hour later before Jenny was able to convince everyone they needed to eat some breakfast. Lisa was pirouetting around the living room, dipping and twirling with her tiara. Andy was proudly strutting with the Stetson hat Zach had given him and the cowboy belt.

Jenny herself had been dumbfounded—Zach had given her his sheepskin coat. She shouldn't accept it. Jenny knew he didn't have another coat with him and even though he claimed the Santa suit would keep him warm until he could buy another one, she still shouldn't take his coat. But she couldn't resist.

It wasn't because the coat was warm and she'd realized winter would be much colder than her guidebook had indicated. No, the reason she couldn't refuse was because when she had the coat around her, she felt as though Zach was with her. The coat carried the woodsy smell of him. It just plain comforted her. And she had a feeling she would need some comforting even before the day was gone.

"I need to have cereal for breakfast," Andy said after Jenny mentioned the meal. Andy swung his twine rope around. "I want some of the cereal that real cowboys eat."

"We might have to eat the cereal without milk," Jenny said. She didn't feel like leaving the living room just yet. "Unless you want milk made from powder."

"Would a cowboy eat that?" Andy asked as he looked up at Zach.

"Cowboys eat whatever's set before them," Zach said. "They get hungry out on the trail."

Andy nodded.

"But I don't know what princesses eat." Lisa stopped pirouetting. Her tiara tilted on her head, but she managed to look regal. "Andy can have cereal, but what will I have?"

"Peas," Zach answered. He was sitting on the sofa telling himself he'd never known a single moment in his life when he had been happier. Watching the kids play. Seeing Jenny wrapped in his coat. It was a perfect moment in time. "Canned peas."

"What?" Lisa looked as him suspiciously. She

even walked over to him and leaned on his knee. "You're teasing me."

Zach brushed a feather out of her hair. "You've heard of *The Princess and the Pea*."

"But that wasn't breakfast, silly." Lisa giggled and rolled her eyes. "That was for her mattress."

"Is that right?" Zach watched Lisa laugh and shake her head. Another white feather floated to the floor. "You mean she sleeps on her vegetables?"

The sun had come up and was shining in the windows. The lights were still steadily lit on the Christmas tree, but the sunshine from outside dulled their glow.

"No, she doesn't," Lisa protested. "Nobody sleeps on vegetables."

Zach gave an exaggerated shrug. "I don't know. Kings and queens do strange things sometimes. I figure princesses might, as well."

"You could have toast and jam," Jenny offered. "And I could fix you some tea the way the English make it."

"I could be an English princess," Lisa agreed, and then leaned even more on Zach's knee as she looked at him. "And you can be my servant."

"Me?" Zach lifted his eyebrows and smiled at the girl. "Well, I guess you're right. A princess does need a servant or two. I would be delighted to serve you breakfast, madame."

"Not madame, it's Princess Lisa."

"Indeed it is, Princess Lisa."

Zach decided to serve everyone breakfast when they were all seated at the table. He put a kitchen towel over his arm and a falsetto tone in his voice. He poured from the right and removed from the left. He made the children laugh and Jenny roll her eyes in merriment.

And then, when Zach almost had his back turned, he saw Jenny twist the cereal box around so she wouldn't have to see his picture on the back of the box.

"A problem with the box? I could remove it from the table if you like." Zach could hear the hurt in his own voice. No wonder men didn't like to be vulnerable—especially over breakfast.

"It's not—" Jenny started to explain. "It's not you. It's me."

"How can it be you and not me? It's my picture on the box." He might be hurt, but he wasn't braindead. No one here owed him anything. Jenny didn't need to spare his feelings. Still, Zach didn't want his heart to bleed in front of the children. Especially not on Christmas Day. He forced himself to smile. "Not that it matters. More toast anyone?"

Jenny took a deep breath and closed her eyes. "I used to talk to your picture."

"What?" Zach had picked up the empty toast plate, and now he held it suspended.

Jenny opened her eyes. "I used to talk to your picture on the back of the cereal box."

"Really?"

"I was lonely," Jenny said defensively. "People pick up strange habits when they're lonely. I mean, it's not as if I knew you then."

"Really?" Zach had never thought of anyone talking to his picture before. "Really?"

"It's not that big of a deal. It's only a cereal box."

Zach started to smile. He almost started to whistle. "No problem. Anyone want more toast?"

Learning that someone made a habit of talking to your picture could boost a man's ego, Zach thought to himself all through the rest of the morning. It made twenty games of rope-the-foot possible with a little cowboy, as the boy learned to twirl his rope. It made ten dances with a princess possible, complete with nine bows and one beheading for displeasing the royal one. It even carried Zach through peeling potatoes and basting the Christmas ham.

It wasn't until Christmas dinner was finished that it occurred to Zach that Jenny might have talked to a box of detergent if it had been sitting on her table when she was so desperate. A woman whose beloved husband was sick would talk to anything rather than confess her worries to her husband.

"I'm sure he was a very special man—your Stephen," Zach said. Christmas, after all, was a time to think of others rather than yourself. Zach wanted her to know she could still talk to him. "It must be hard to have your first Christmas without him."

Zach and Jenny were sitting alone at the table. The children had eaten and fled into the living room to play. The blizzard had ended sometime last night and the sunlight coming inside now was so strong and warm that no candles were needed. The frost had melted on the windows. It was the middle of the afternoon.

Jenny took a deep breath. She owed it to Zach to tell him the truth—the whole miserable lot of it. But where did she start? "Stephen and I would have been married for ten years this coming February."

"What date?"

"Huh?"

"The date. What date did you get married?"

"February fourteenth, Valentine's Day, although I don't see—"

Zach's shoulders slumped. He was right. This Stephen had been a charmer. What woman wouldn't want to get married on Valentine's Day? How was another man ever supposed to compete with that? "You must have had some memorable anniversaries."

"Memorable is right." Jenny hadn't realized for two years that the reason Stephen had been so intent that they marry on Valentine's Day was so he wouldn't have to remember a separate anniversary date. Even with the added help, he hadn't remembered their anniversary for the past five years. "But that's not what I want to say."

"I know you loved him." The kitchen was warm and smelled good. Sunshine streamed into the room, and Zach could hear the children playing in the living room. He wanted to wrap the memory of this moment around him tight so that he could pull it out on some lonely night in the future and remember the time he'd been part of a family.

There was a soft ticking, and it took a minute before Zach realized what it was—he was hearing the clock. The electricity was back on.

Jenny swallowed. "Love is a complicated thing sometimes."

"I'd expect so," Zach lied. He didn't find love complicated at all. Painful, yes. Complicated, no.

"It's not always—", Jenny began, and then paused.

The telephone rang.

"Service is back," Zach muttered. He supposed it wasn't fair, but he wouldn't have minded if the electricity stayed off for another week. Especially not if another storm moved in and kept them all snowbound together. But he'd known since morning that the snow outside was melting. Sure, the road still had a buildup of snow on it, but he might be able to push his way through in the postal truck this afternoon.

"Hello," Jenny answered the phone. "Oh, hi,

Mrs. Hargrove. I can't thank you enough for—oh, yes, he's here." Jenny paused, listening. "No, no he hasn't shown up yet. Yes, I'll call you then." Another pause. "No, no, it was no problem. It was good to have him here. Yes, I'll see you tomorrow, then."

It didn't take a snowdrift to freeze Zach's heart. He already heard a distant roar coming toward the house.

Jenny hung up and looked at Zach. "Mrs. Hargrove sent the county snowplow out to plow our road."

"I didn't think they'd work on Christmas. Isn't that overtime?"

"Double time, but they had to do it. We have the postal truck, and tomorrow is a mail day."

Couldn't the mail just wait for a day? Zach thought. Or maybe a week. Even a month would be okay. "So this is it."

Jenny nodded. "You'll have to drive the postal truck back."

But you can come back then, Jenny thought. There's nothing that says you can't come back. We haven't had nearly enough time to…to what? she asked herself. More time would only add to the heartbreak if he was going to leave, anyway.

"I'm going to leave the reindeer horns and the lights," Zach said. He could hardly speak. How did a man leave when every atom of his being wanted to stay? "Mrs. Hargrove or Charley can pick them up later."

Jenny nodded. "Mrs. Hargrove told me how grateful she was you drove for Charley that last day. Otherwise, he would be here and they would have been apart for Christmas."

"No problem."

Zach willed his legs to move. He could hear the snowplow clearly outside now. There were no more excuses to stay. But he still sat.

"You'll be in Vegas late tomorrow." Jenny twisted a knot in the napkin she held in her hand. Zach had never pretended to be anything other than a cowboy out looking for a good time. Even she knew a widow with two little kids wasn't a good time.

"Yeah," Zach lied. He didn't know where he was going. He didn't care. But he had no appetite anymore for Vegas. A grieving man didn't go to Vegas. He'd rather find a deserted hotel somewhere in the open spaces of Utah and lick his wounds for a few weeks. He might even take the Bible out of the drawer in the hotel room and read up on what a wretched man he was.

A man's boots stomped on the porch before a loud knock came and a call was made through the kitchen door. "I'm the snowplow man. Out from Miles City."

There was a moment of silence.

"He'll want a cup of coffee," Jenny finally said as she stood to open the door.

"I'd best say goodbye to the kids." Zach stood, as well. The dream was over.

Chapter Eleven

"You must be Zach," Mrs. Hargrove said as she opened the door to her house. The warm smell of roasting turkey came floating out into the cold air behind her. "I hear you were one popular Santa Claus. Why, Charley got calls—"

"Calls?" Zach's heart started to pound. He stopped scraping the snow off his boots and just stood there. The snow plow man had told Zach that Charley would be at his fiancée's house for dinner, and it hadn't taken much to find the place.

Mrs. Hargrove nodded. "Mrs. Goussley left three messages telling him how much the cats missed you already and what a great Santa you were."

"Oh." Zach grunted as he started scraping his boots again. The cats. It was always the cats. The one out in the Collinses' barn hadn't even shown itself when he went out to pack up his duffel. Christmas had got the best of him again. Next Christmas he wasn't taking any chances. He'd head to a deserted island, maybe someplace off the Alaskan coastline. Or maybe Iceland. No one went to Iceland in the winter. And if they did, they didn't bring their cats.

"And, of course, the candy canes were a hit," the older woman continued as she accepted the bag from Zach that held the Santa costume. "They always are."

Mrs. Hargrove was just as Zach had pictured her. She had bouncy gray hair and a mouth that didn't stop chatting. Her bright eyes welcomed him like he belonged.

How was she to know he didn't belong anywhere?

"I suppose Thunder is well enough to travel," Zach said.

"Well, yes, but you don't want to head out this afternoon. You won't make it to a town with a hotel before dark. Besides, Charley has a spare room at his place, and we'd love to have you join us for dinner. There's nothing like a fresh turkey dinner with all the trimmings."

Mrs. Hargrove was the picture of hospitality with a red-checked apron hanging over a cotton dress. She had pearl earrings on her ears and orthopedic shoes on her feet. She was looking at him as if he were a long-lost friend.

Zach forced himself to smile. "Thanks, but I'll be moving on. I might make it into Wyoming before nightfall."

"Well, if you're sure." A tiny frown settled on Mrs. Hargrove's forehead. "But I know Charley would like to thank you, and he's not here yet."

"No need to thank me."

"We've got pie, too. Apple and cherry. I've never known a cowboy to turn down a piece of home-made pie."

"That's kind of you, but I'd best be moving on."

"Well, all right then." Mrs. Hargrove reached behind herself to get a sweater and stepped out onto the porch. "Let me just go park the postal truck in its spot."

"I can move it if you tell me where it goes."

"It's easier just to show you," Mrs. Hargrove said with a wave of her hand as she marched off the porch.

"A sweater's not warm enough," Zach called after her. Oh, well, Zach thought, if she didn't care, who was he to make a big deal out of it? He was through taking care of people—and cats—who didn't listen to him, anyway.

Zach followed Mrs. Hargrove out to the postal truck. He'd parked the truck at the curb in front of her house.

"Oh, what's this?" Mrs. Hargrove had already opened the door and leaned into the truck. She reached out for the photographs that Zach had laid out on the dash.

Zach winced. He'd taken the pictures out so he could look at them as he bounced along the country roads back into Dry Creek. "I'll just pack them up. Got my duffel in back, too."

Mrs. Hargrove stepped back, holding all four pictures. She squinted in the sunlight as she tilted the photographs up so she could see them better. "Why, aren't those nice?"

"Yeah." Zach swallowed. He didn't know what to say. Not that there was anything to say. A picture was just a picture.

Mrs. Hargrove looked closely at each picture. Zach didn't have to see the pictures to know what she saw. A picture of Jenny as his showgirl. A picture of Andy roping his foot. A picture of him dancing with Princess Lisa. A picture of him and the children dragging the Christmas tree up from the coulee.

"Well," Mrs. Hargrove said softly as she lowered the pictures and turned curious eyes toward Zach. "Looks as though you had some Christmas."

Zach grunted. "I was just doing what I could to make sure they had a good Christmas."

"I can see that."

"Anyone would have done the same." Zach held out his hand. He wasn't going anywhere without his pictures. "They're good kids."

"Uh-huh," Mrs. Hargrove agreed. She didn't hand over the pictures, though. "I don't think I've ever seen the kids like this—laughing and being silly."

"Well, it's Christmas. You know how kids are at Christmas."

"I suppose." Mrs. Hargrove took another hard look at him as she finally handed him the pictures.

The sun had warmed the air considerably, but it was still too cold to stand outside and talk. Zach hoped that fact would encourage the woman to go back inside. "They're just missing their father."

"The kids?" Mrs. Hargrove seemed surprised. "Did they talk about him?"

Zach shuffled. He hadn't meant to get into a conversation about the man. "Well, no, but you gotta figure he was a good father. Good husband, too. They got married on Valentine's Day, you know."

"No, I didn't know."

Zach knew it was time to go. There were only a couple of hours of daylight left, and he wanted to get closer to the Wyoming border before pulling off the interstate for the night. But his mouth just kept talking.

"Must have been tough when he died," Zach added. What was wrong with him? Then he knew what he wanted to say. He knew the question he wanted to ask someone. "Wonder what made him so special, anyway?"

Mrs. Hargrove looked Zach over once again. He felt her gaze on him. She wasn't unkind about it. She was obviously just thinking.

"What makes you think he was special?" Mrs. Hargrove finally asked.

"I figure he was a pillar of the church or something," Zach stumbled.

"I don't think so. Not from what little Jenny has said."

"Well…I…" Zach stammered. Of course the man was special. "The kids are such good kids, and Jenny—well, Jenny is wonderful."

Mrs. Hargrove nodded. "Funny thing, though. Jenny never talks about her late husband."

"Well, no, but…"

"Kids don't, either."

Zach was silent. Come to think of it, the kids didn't say much about their father.

"And did you ever see those pictures she's got hanging on the wall in the living room?"

Zach smiled and nodded. "They liked the zoo."

Mrs. Hargrove nodded, too. "Ever wonder why there's no pictures of the father there?"

The silence cracked over Zach's head. Mrs. Hargrove was right. There were no pictures of Stephen. "What do you suppose that means?"

Mrs. Hargrove shrugged. "I don't know for sure."

"You think it might not have been so perfect—" Zach cleared his throat. "I mean, do you think a man like me could have a chance? I know I'm not the kind of man Jenny deserves. I've been reading about it all in the Bible and—"

"You've been reading the Bible?"

"Well, I had to stay up and heat milk for the cat, anyway, so I thought I'd take a look."

"And?"

"Some of it's too good to be true. At least, for someone like me, but—"

"The Bible is for everyone."

Zach frowned. Could that be? That didn't seem right.

"If you want to spend some time learning about the Bible, Charley and I would be glad to help you with it. Like I said, he's got a spare room over at his place and there's no lack of odd jobs around for a man willing to work. You could stay a while in Dry Creek. See how things go."

"You'd do that for me?"

Mrs. Hargrove nodded. "I'd do that for the man who can make those kids laugh like that."

"I'm not Jerry Seinfeld or anything. I'm not naturally funny."

"That's what makes it so special." Mrs. Hargrove smiled. "They were happy, not entertained."

"You think there might be hope for me and Jenny then?"

"I'm not the one you need to ask."

Zach figured there was a silly smile on his face,

but he couldn't stop the grin from spreading. "Mind if I borrow the postal truck again? I'll be back in a few hours."

Mrs. Hargrove grinned back at him as she handed him the keys.

"Tell Charley I'll pick Thunder up later."

"Don't worry. That old horse of yours will be fine in the barn out at the Nelson place."

The road back to Jenny's house had just as many bumps as it had the first time Zach had ridden over it. The difference was that this time he grinned a little more at each bump he drove over.

Jenny thought she heard someone drive up to her house, but she wasn't sure. She and the children had been sitting on the sofa with blankets snuggled around them. They'd been out in the barn earlier, but they couldn't find the cat so they came back into the house. Jenny had offered to read to them, but both kids seemed to just want to sit and be quiet.

"I think someone is here," Jenny said softly as she untangled her arms from the blankets.

"Tell them to go away," Andy muttered. "We don't want nobody."

"This is Montana," Jenny chided her son gently as she stood up. "Neighbors are important and will always be welcome in our house."

"If it's a stranger, you should be careful," Lisa

advised glumly. "It's not just snakes you have to watch for around here."

"I'll be careful," Jenny said as she started to walk toward the kitchen. "It's probably just the snow-plow guy again."

Jenny had to step around the Christmas tree to get to the kitchen. The batteries had died on the tree lights, and the stars didn't sparkle anymore. Andy's hat sat forgotten beside the tree. Lisa's tiara was next to it.

Christmas this year had been both the best ever and the worst ever for her little family.

The sun had melted most of the frost in the small window of the outside kitchen door. But the afternoon had faded and the light had never been good on that side of the house. She saw a shape, but she could not tell who it was. She squinted, anyway—those shoulders reminded her of—not that it would be him.

Jenny opened the door. What in the world—?

Jenny tried to form a word, but couldn't for a full minute. Then it occurred to her that many things could explain why this particular man was standing on her porch. "Forget something?"

Zach smiled. "I guess I did."

"Let me know where it is and I'll go get it." Jenny knew it was rude to leave someone standing on the porch, but she didn't want her children to know he was here. He'd only break their hearts two minutes later when he left again.

"Well, I don't quite know where it is." Zach tried smiling harder. His smile was often called charming by women.

There was no smile in return. "We only have the five rooms. And the barn, of course."

Zach looked at Jenny. She didn't exactly look welcoming. In fact, she looked as if she was barely tolerating his presence. Her eyes were guarded. She wasn't smiling. She hadn't invited him into the house and it was cold outside.

All in all, Zach conceded, it didn't look good. But a man didn't ride wild horses because he believed in taking the safe route. Zach reached up and ran his hands around the side brim of the Stetson hat sitting on his head. It was the same gesture he used when he was ready to start a rodeo ride.

"It's more of a question than anything."

"Oh?"

"When you talked to my face on that cereal box, what did you talk about?"

Jenny could hear Lisa and Andy running toward the kitchen. She didn't have much time. "Is this some market-research question? You think your sponsor would like to know? Maybe they'll find some small demographic niche of women who are crazy enough to talk to cereal boxes?"

The footsteps entered the kitchen.

"Mr. Lightning!"

"Santa!"

Two pairs of feet ran to the door and planted themselves beside Jenny.

"You're back!"

"You came!"

Now, this was a better welcome, Zach thought as he looked down at the kids. "Hi, there. Mind if I talk to your mom for a minute?"

"Sure," the two voices answered.

But no feet moved. Three pairs of eyes kept looking at him.

"Alone." Zach swallowed.

"Maybe you could go pick out the books you want me to read to you tonight," Jenny suggested.

"Okay," Lisa said, and started back to the living room. The girl nudged Andy to follow her.

Zach waited until the children were in the living room. "I'm not asking about the cereal box because I care about marketing. I want to know what you were thinking and feeling. I want to know why you don't have any pictures of Stephen on your bulletin board."

"Stephen?" Jenny paused. This was about Stephen?

"Was it because it was too painful for you to have any pictures of him around?"

"No," Jenny answered. "It's just that we didn't have any pictures. Not ones like that. I mean, we

have a couple of formal shots—he needed one for a
business thing once. But that was taken at a studio."

"Was the man camera shy?"

"Stephen? No."

"Then why don't you have any pictures?"

Jenny suddenly felt very tired. She'd never complained about Stephen. Never complained about him
to anyone. She'd told herself she was protecting him.
But now she wondered if she was only protecting
herself.

There was such a long pause Zach wondered if
Jenny was ever going to answer him.

"Because he was never with us," Jenny finally
admitted. She needed to tell someone the truth about
her life. "When we went to the zoo, he went fish-
ing with some buddies of his. When we went to
the beach, he went to a ball game with some other
friends."

"So he wasn't some kind of superfather?"

"Stephen? No. He was barely a father at all."

Zach was beginning to have hope. Maybe he'd do
all right as a father. But there was something even
more important he needed to know.

"And as a husband? How was he as a husband?"

Jenny looked up at Zach. She saw longing for
the children and for her in his eyes. She had never
realized until now that Stephen's lack of interest in
being a husband only added to his lack of interest in
being a father. The two weren't separate. A man

who would make a good husband to her would also make a good father to the children.

Especially, she thought to herself, if it was this man standing before her. She looked at him carefully. She could see the fear in his eyes. The drawn tension around his lips. All pretense was gone from his face. He was letting her see his insecurities and his longings.

Jenny reached up and caressed Zach's cheek briefly. She needed to let him see her as well. All her fears. Her defeats. Her tiredness. "He never loved me."

Jenny closed her eyes. There, she'd said it aloud. Stephen had never loved her.

A moment passed before Jenny realized her fears had not come true. Telling someone the truth about her and Stephen did not cause a crushing blackness in her heart. Instead, her heart felt lighter than it had in years.

Zach reached up and covered Jenny's hand with his. "He was a fool."

"I really tried to make him care." Jenny let Zach draw her into his arms.

"He didn't deserve you," Zach whispered. "You deserve someone better—"

Jenny opened her mouth to speak.

"No, don't answer yet. Hear me out." Zach held her quietly and talked in her ear. He'd never had such an important moment in his life. Every word counted. "I grew up in a family of loners. I'm not the man for you yet. But I'm going to stay in Dry Creek for a while. I have some studying and thinking to do. I'm not sure how it will all end up. I'm not asking you to wait for me to figure it all out. I just want you to know."

Jenny opened her mouth again to speak. She couldn't think of what to say. "I can't—"

"Shhh," Zach said as he released her. "You don't need to answer yet. Just pretend I came back out to ask about the cat."

"We can't find the cat. The kids looked and looked." Jenny stood back and looked up at his face.

Zach smiled down at her. He needed to find out some answers before he was ready. But if there was any mercy left in God's heart at all, he wanted it. "If she's had the kittens, she probably doesn't want anyone to know just yet. Sometimes newborn things need time. Have you fed her this afternoon?"

Jenny shook her head. "I told the kids we'd take some more warm milk out to her later."

"I'll go with you," Zach offered. "She's used to me by now."

Fifteen minutes later, they were all walking to the barn. Andy was holding one of Zach's hands and Lisa was holding on to a loop in the man's sheepskin coat, which Jenny had loaned back to him, so Zach had his other hand free to carry the pan of milk. Both children were asking questions about the kittens they hoped to find.

Jenny smiled to herself as she walked with them. They were all used to Zach. But she knew it wasn't time for her to make a decision about him yet. She would need to know it was right in her mind and in her soul before she could commit to another man. She was glad he hadn't pushed for a decision.

He said he was the one who needed time to be ready for her, but she needed time to ready her heart for someone new as well. It might or might not be Zach. She didn't know if Zach would even want to be with her and the kids when he was done thinking about everything. All she could do was trust that God knew the man's heart.

Zach opened the barn door and they heard a tiny meow.

"It's a kitty," Lisa whispered.

The mother cat hissed at Zach when he put the pan of warm milk down.

"She's not ready for company yet," Zach said as he guided the children back to the barn door. "Sometimes we have to be patient."

Zach looked at Jenny when he said the last, and she nodded. Her heart filled with hope. He was asking her to wait.

Chapter Twelve

Jenny was helping Mrs. Hargrove plan her wedding. They were measuring the space at the front of the church so they would know how much room there would be for flowers. Lately, every Thursday at this time, the older woman had asked for Jenny's help for a few hours while Lisa was in school. Since the pastor's wife had asked if she could sketch Andy for a painting at the same time, Jenny was glad to help. She was beginning to wonder if the stress of planning a formal wedding wasn't too much for the older woman.

Jenny was trying to be quiet because the pastor was having a session in his office. No doubt it was Zach's session. She supposed Mrs. Hargrove liked to work while those sessions were going on because Charley was meeting with Zach and the pastor, too.

"I wonder if they're getting anyplace," Jenny

said softly as she nodded her head toward the pastor's door.

"Charley says Zach is just making sure of things," Mrs. Hargrove said firmly.

Jenny held up one end of the tape measure and pressed it to the wall. "Are you sure we shouldn't measure for the candles, too?"

Mrs. Hargrove was halfway across the room from Jenny, holding the tape taut and taking a measurement. "Charley's the one who mentioned candles."

"If we knew where he might want them, we could take any measurements you need today," Jenny suggested. She didn't know how many different ways they could measure the church. Over the past couple of weeks, she'd helped the older woman measure the church space for flowers, for attendants, for banners and for aisle walking. And it never seemed as though any of the measurements they took were the right ones for any other addition to the wedding plans.

Not that Jenny minded spending time with Mrs. Hargrove. In fact, she had started looking forward to their measuring sessions.

A roar of disbelief sounded from the pastor's office, and both women looked up from their tape.

"Your Zach is a man of firm opinions," Mrs. Hargrove said with a smile for Jenny. "Charley says he has a fine bent for reasoning."

"He's not *my* Zach," Jenny said. She'd thought

he would be. When he'd left her place on Christmas Day, she'd been filled with hope for their future. She thought he'd asked her to wait for him. But even if they were both waiting, shouldn't there be some communication?

Zach hadn't mentioned anything about *them* since Christmas Day, and it had been three weeks. Oh, he'd come by and fixed the roof during a thaw a week ago. And he'd towed her car into Dry Creek so Jasmine Hunter, the woman staying with Mrs. Hargrove, could repair everything that was wrong with it. Zach had even come by so the children could show him their new kittens. Andy particularly wanted to show him the two black kittens. He'd named one Lightning and the other Thunder.

But Jenny may as well have not even been there. The cowboy hadn't said one personal thing to her in all that time. Just because she was waiting for him didn't mean she didn't want to talk to him. She would rather he'd let the roof cave in and the car sit and rust instead of ignoring her. A man with intentions would at least be talking to the woman he was thinking about, wouldn't he?

"He's just trying to be sure," Mrs. Hargrove said softly.

Jenny grunted and looked down the length of the sanctuary to the closed door of the pastor's study. She wondered if Zach was trying to be sure about God or about her. Maybe he wasn't talking to her because he couldn't think of any kind way to tell her that he had changed his mind about her and was moving on.

Maybe he'd written to his showgirl friend and told her that he'd be coming to Vegas, after all. A showgirl had to be an easier romance than a widow with two small children. Zach could easily explain being late for Christmas since Thunder had been running a fever. Of course, the horse was fine now, but the showgirl probably didn't know anything about how long it would take a horse to recover from something like that.

Zach was going to break her family's heart, Jenny thought. The children had finally started to talk a little bit about their father. The night when they had told Zach that their father was gone had been a breakthrough for them. They were finally starting to heal, the way she'd hoped they would when she'd decided to move to Dry Creek.

Jenny felt a surge of anger toward Zach. Her children were going to start grieving all over again when Zach left. They'd miss him when he was gone as much as they missed their father, maybe more.

It wasn't fair. Zach had made their life worse, not better. She should have known he would, she told herself. He'd gotten their hopes up and now he was going to say goodbye.

On the other side of the closed door, Zach was straddling a wooden chair. Pastor Matthew was sitting at his desk, and Charley was sitting in the padded side chair.

Zach didn't agree with the pastor. He thought that the pastor and Charley both must have some of it wrong. Zach hadn't found out where they were wrong; his reading of the Bible hadn't got him to that part yet. But there had to be an exceptions clause. All contracts had them. He could show them the place in the Ranger cereal contracts where the exceptions were; he'd find the place in the Bible if he kept looking.

"But I used to cheat at cards," Zach was saying. "And I was playing for money, not just matchsticks. Sometimes it was big money, too. No dimes or anything."

The curtains on the window were open and sunlight was spilling into the room. It was the middle of the morning, and Charley was shaking his head.

"I keep trying to tell you, but you won't listen," Charley finally said. "There are no exceptions. It doesn't matter if you'd gone out and murdered someone. If you confess the thing before God with repentance, you can still become a Christian."

"Who would I have murdered? Somebody who deserved it?"

"It doesn't matter," Charley said. "It could be anyone."

"Could it be you?"

"Well, technically, I suppose…" Charley sounded a little less sure.

"See, you wouldn't like it if someone murdered you and then you had to sit down next to them in heaven and be all buddy-buddy," Zach said firmly.

"Well, I might not like it, but I'd do it," Charley half shouted as he stood up. "That's what forgiveness is all about."

Zach stood up so he could meet his friend eye-to-eye.

The pastor cleared his throat. "Why don't we take a break and go get a cup of coffee? I have a whole pot in the kitchen."

Charley nodded. "Edith's out there measuring things. I should go check and see if she needs any help."

"I suppose Jenny Collins is helping her again," the pastor said.

Zach just swallowed. He had pledged to avoid Jenny, but it wasn't easy.

"That deal still on?" Zach asked Charley.

Charley nodded. He didn't even need to ask what deal Zach meant; the cowboy asked about it every day. "I've told all the single men that she needs more time. No one is to ask her out until the wedding. You'll all have the same chance with her."

"Is that after the ceremony, after the cake, or when the music first starts?" There was a pause as Zach studied the eyes turned his way. "What?

Don't look at me like that. You both know that Max is ready to go. I wouldn't be surprised if some of the hands from the Elkton Ranch are coming to the wedding just to ask Jenny out, too. We need to have some clarification here, or someone's going to be talking to Jenny while Mrs. Hargrove walks down the aisle. I don't intend to let my chance get away just because I was waiting for the cake to be cut."

Charley chuckled. "I guess you're right. The second Edith is my wife, you men are welcome to take your best shot."

Zach nodded. "Be sure the rest of the guys know."

Charley shook his head. "Just don't ask her out until then. I won't have the guys saying I'm playing favorites."

"You've got my word."

The men were silent for a minute.

"Of course, it doesn't mean you can't sit and drink a cup of coffee together," Pastor Matthew said as he stood. "Just being friendly, you know. Since we all seem to be here together."

Zach suspected the pastor made a pot of coffee every time they met just so they'd have an excuse to ask Mrs. Hargrove and Jenny to join them. He wasn't sure how Mrs. Hargrove convinced Jenny to be there helping her measure something for the wedding every time he had his session, but the older woman had managed it.

It hadn't escaped Zach's notice that he had some friends in Dry Creek. And the feeling went both ways. The fact was, he'd have a hard time sitting down in heaven with anyone who had murdered someone in Dry Creek no matter what the Bible said on the matter. Not that Charley would want to hear that. It was coffee time.

"What are they measuring today?" Zach asked as he and Charley filed out of the pastor's office.

"Floral arrangements," Charley said. "I figure we need lots of floral arrangements. Edith loves the smell of roses."

"It'll cost you a fortune to fill the front of the church with roses," Zach said as the men walked to the kitchen.

"What price can you put on love?" Charley said with a grin.

Zach grunted as he accepted the cup of coffee the pastor held out to him. The funny thing was that Charley meant it, too. Zach figured the least he could do was to buy those roses for his friend. If anyone was going to go bankrupt because of love in Dry Creek, it ought to be him.

Chapter Thirteen

Three months later Jenny stood in a Sunday-school room that had been converted into a woman's changing room for the wedding. Mrs. Hargrove had asked her to be a bridesmaid and Jenny had gladly said yes.

Jenny had thought she'd never willingly attend another wedding, not after her heartache with Stephen. And, yet, here she was dressed in a pink satin dress with puffy sleeves. Mrs. Hargrove's daughter, Doris June, was the maid of honor, and Jenny was the bridesmaid.

"You're sure Mrs. Brown can handle the kids?" Jenny turned and asked for the second time. The post mistress had looked delighted when the children showed up in their wedding clothes to sit with her, but a lot could happen while everyone was waiting for the bride to walk down the aisle.

"The pastor's wife will help her," Mrs. Hargrove said from behind the screen that had been put up. "She's had experience with twin boys."

"I just hope Andy keeps that cat in the box I gave him."

She hadn't discovered that Andy had brought one of his kittens with him until they were already at the church. Fortunately, the pastor had an old box they cut holes in so the cat could stay in there at Andy's feet. The kitten had started to meow pitifully when it couldn't smell Andy anymore, but it seemed content to be in the box next to him.

"I just hope I remember my vows," Mrs. Hargrove said as she stepped out from behind the screen. "The first time I got married, no one expected anyone to write their own vows."

Mrs. Hargrove was a radiant bride, Jenny thought as she watched the older woman smooth down the ivory satin of her dress. There were some beads around the neckline of the dress and fine netting over the sleeves. The woman's short gray hair was curled and held back a little with a pearl comb. She was wearing some lipstick in honor of the day.

"I wish I'd insisted on a veil," Mrs. Hargrove said as she reached up to pat her hair. "In my day, the bride always had a veil, and the thing covers a multitude of problems. What does a groom know about a veil, anyway?"

Jenny smiled. She knew Charley was the one

who had not wanted any veils. He'd told Mrs. Hargrove that he wanted to see her face every second as she walked down the aisle. Jenny sighed. Charley was a man who understood romance.

"You won't worry about anything," Jenny told her friend. "Not when you see Charley waiting for you at the front of the church."

Mrs. Hargrove gave a little smile. "I guess you're right. He promised to prompt me, anyway, if I lose my place in those vows. Would you believe, the man has the whole wedding service memorized? He even knows what the pastor is going to say to us. Charley made him write it out."

"He just wants to remember everything," Jenny said. "Forever."

Jenny had to stop her thoughts right there. She refused to have sad thoughts on this wedding day. She also refused to be even the least bit envious of the happiness of her good friends. She had to admit though that she would remember this day forever, too, and it had nothing to do with Charley Nelson and Edith Hargrove's wedding.

She was afraid this might be the last day she'd see Zach. He was still having sessions with the pastor, but Zach had stood up in church three weeks ago and given a testimony that was so heartfelt it made half of the people listening pull out their handkerchiefs. The cowboy had made his peace with God.

Jenny had given thanks for Zach's decision. First,

for the sake of his soul, of course. But also—and here she had tried to keep her excitement under control—because she'd really thought that once Zach was a Christian he would come to her and *at least* ask her out on a date. She half expected him to drive out to her place that afternoon after church and sweep her up in a knee-bending kiss. But he hadn't. He hadn't even stopped by to inquire about her health or the state of her roof.

After a week passed and Zach hadn't come near her, she decided she had been mistaken. Zach wasn't planning a future with her. He must only be staying in Dry Creek for the wedding. Charley had asked him to be a groomsman, and Zach clearly wanted to honor the older man who had become his friend. Once he did that, though, he had no reason to stay in town.

Jenny knew that Mrs. Hargrove and Charley were doing their best to encourage a romance between her and Zach. She half suspected that the reason a bridesmaid and extra groomsman had been added to the wedding party was so that the two of them would be standing up there in front, getting a close up look at the wedding while standing across the aisle from each other.

It was probably supposed to be an inspiration to them.

There was a knock at the door to the room and someone called out, "It's time."

Mrs. Hargrove took a deep breath and picked up her rose bridal bouquet. "Here we go."

Jenny told herself just to concentrate on the roses. Their smell was the first thing she'd noticed when she'd come into the church earlier. That morning, a couple of floral trucks from Billings had delivered dozens of vases of red and pink roses. The whole front of the church looked like a garden. She'd asked Mrs. Hargrove about the roses, but the older woman only said that a friend of Charley's had sent them as a wedding gift.

At least one man knew how special wedding days were, Jenny thought as she stood beside the door leading into the back of the church. The pianist hadn't started yet, and Doris June was having some last words with her mother before they opened the door and all started down the aisle.

Zach stood at the front of the church next to Charley and Charley's son. They were waiting for the bride to appear, and Charley was nervous. Zach could tell because the older man kept reaching up to loosen his tie.

It was those tuxedoes, Zach thought in sympathy.

He hadn't worn a tuxedo in years. Usually, his dress clothes were a pressed western shirt and one of his championship belt buckles. Zach felt as uncomfortable in a tuxedo as he had in that old Santa suit. Not that he had anything against the red suit, he told himself with a smile. He'd managed to buy it from Mrs. Brown, and he'd only had to pay her twice what it would cost to buy a new one.

Fortunately, his bank account was healthy. He'd just signed another contract with the Ranger Flakes people and he had enough to set himself up raising horses. He hadn't picked out the land yet; he wanted to talk to Jenny first.

He had a lot he wanted to talk to Jenny about after Charley and Mrs. Hargrove were married.

The music started, and Zach felt his own mouth go dry. He hadn't been this nervous since the first time he'd stood at the corral chute getting ready to ride Black Demon. Back then, the worst that could happen would be breaking a bone or two. He had a feeling that before this day was over he could break his heart.

The doors at the back of the church opened, and there stood the women. Zach knew Mrs. Hargrove and her daughter, Doris June, were there, all shining in their satin dresses, but the only one he wanted to look at was Jenny.

Jenny was beautiful. She started walking down the aisle as the music played. She was carrying one of the smaller bouquets that Zach had bought to go along with the vases of roses. Her dress was pink and he swore she looked like a princess. Her face was flushed with excitement and her eyes fixed on— Zach stopped. Had Jenny just looked at Max Daniels?

Leave it to the rancher to sit so close to the front and to be so close to the edge of the pew. Anyone walking down the aisle would have to see Max, Zach told himself.

Of course, Zach told himself *he* was right in front of the church, and Jenny didn't seem to have any problem keeping her eyes off *him*.

Everyone in the church stood. Mrs. Hargrove was beginning her walk down the aisle. Zach was worried Charley was going to stop breathing; the older man had drawn his breath in and had not let it out yet. He was staring at his bride. Zach was almost ready to go give the older man a quiet thump on the back when he heard the old man breath again.

Finally, the three women were standing at the front of the church with them and the guests were sitting down.

Then the pastor started to talk. Zach tried to listen, but he found he had a breathing problem of his own. Jenny was standing in front of the church with him and the pastor was talking about making a life-altering commitment. Granted, Jenny and he weren't the ones making the commitment, but Zach couldn't help but wonder if she was wondering what it would be like to have the pastor say those same words over them some day.

Jenny was focusing on the shoulder of Charley's tuxedo. She wasn't used to being up in front of people, and she had the strangest sensation that people were staring at her. They were supposed to be staring at the bride.

The pastor mentioned how important friendship was in a marriage and how the bride and groom had been friends for so long.

Jenny heard a ripple of movement among the guests and turned to look. Andy was standing at the back of the aisle with an empty box in his hands. Oh, dear. That kitten.

Someone in the third row gasped, and someone in the second row whispered, "Catch it."

Jenny looked back at the bride and groom. They didn't seem to have heard any of the sounds from the rest of the church. Hopefully, someone would catch the kitten and everything would be quiet again. Jenny motioned for Andy to go back to his seat, and she saw Mrs. Brown go to get him.

Then Jenny glanced down. The black kitten was curled up next to Zach's boots. The cat looked thoroughly content.

Mrs. Hargrove was repeating her vows, and Jenny watched her friend's face. The older woman didn't need any prompts as she promised to love her friend Charley for as long as she had left to live.

Jenny had to blink after Mrs. Hargrove finished her vows.

And then, all too soon, the pastor was pronouncing the older couple man and wife.

"Now you may kiss the bride," the pastor said.

When Charley did just that, a cheer rose from among the guests. Everyone was smiling.

Charley and his bride were starting back down the aisle. Then Doris June and her husband were walking down the aisle behind them. That left only Jenny and Zach standing.

Then Zach scooped up the black kitten and held out his arm to Jenny. She started walking with him. At least everyone had turned to watch the newly married couple so no one was watching her and Zach.

"Don't look," Zach hissed after they'd taken a step or two.

"Huh?" Jenny looked up at him. She wondered if the kitten had got away again, but it was curled up in the hand Zach had to his chest.

Even with the kitten in one hand, Zach pulled Jenny closer to him as they walked.

"I want to take you out to dinner," he whispered. By that time, they were almost at the back of the church.

"But there's the reception."

"Not now," Zach said. They'd finished their walk and were standing at the back of the church. "I mean later. I just want to ask you out on a date at your earliest convenience. I'm thinking tomorrow."

By now, everyone had left the aisle, and Jenny felt a tug on her dress.

"You found Thunder," Andy whispered as he looked over at Zach.

Zach handed down the kitten. "I think he missed you."

"He got lost," Andy agreed. "But you found him."

Zach gave a quick smile to the boy, but his eyes were on Jenny when he spoke. "He mostly found me."

Zach could see Max coming closer. And Jenny hadn't answered him.

"I know I'm not a perfect man," Zach said. "And I'm not exactly used to dating a woman like you."

"You have Patti," Jenny said.

Zach never was one to stay down when a horse threw him. "What I'm trying to say is that I'd like the chance to get to know you better."

"How much better?" Jenny asked.

Max was standing right beside them now. Zach closed his eyes. "I want to marry you."

"What?" Jenny asked.

"What?" Max bellowed. "I thought we were all supposed to have a fair turn at dating Jenny."

"What?" Jenny asked again.

It took several minutes for Jenny to begin to understand what the men were talking about. It only took one more second for her to face Zach. "You proposed to me to beat out Max, here?"

Zach shook his head. "I'm not very good with words."

Jenny looked at him in disbelief. "You've dated showgirls."

"But that's not like you and me. I didn't feel—" Zach's jaw was clenched, and he had that fierce look on his face again. "I just thought you should know where I'm headed, that's all. I know you can do better. But I've been meeting with the pastor to learn how to be a better family man."

Jenny touched his arm. "When?"

Zach looked at her blankly. "Thursdays. Same as usual."

"No, I mean when—"

For the first time, Zach noticed that Jenny's face was flushed. Max was still scowling and hovering, but Andy had given the man the kitten to hold so Zach decided the rancher would have to be content with that.

"When will we marry?" Zach asked softly.

Jenny nodded.

Zach felt a slow smile spread across his face. Almost everyone had left this part of the church and had gone down to the basement for the reception. He bent down and kissed Jenny.

Jenny felt the church tilt a little. She heard a growl and couldn't tell if it was the kitten or Max. Then she didn't hear anything but her own heartbeat. Zach was kissing her. Then he kissed her again.

Zach broke away from the kiss and whispered in

her ear. "I forgot to tell you that I love you. I meant to say that before."

Zach looked in her eyes and kissed her again.

Jenny heard purring. Someone really should do something about that kitten. Then she realized that Max, the kitten and Andy had all left. The sound must be coming from her heart.

* * * * *

Dear Reader,

When Zach came into Dry Creek for the first time, he was a bitter man who was disillusioned with Christmas, God and himself. His best friend was a horse and the woman he was hoping to spend the holidays with didn't care if he showed up or not. Misery and loneliness are always more difficult on December 25.

One of the reasons I love to read and write Christmas stories is that everything seems more emotional on that day than at any other times of the year. We all have expectations of the day, whether they are good ones or bad. My expectations go more toward the cookies my mother used to bake when I was a child and the sounds of carols at church. There is a midnight Christmas Eve service that I love to go to each year. As I sit with friends and sing the timeless carols, I celebrate the birth of Jesus and feel connected to Christmas from generations past.

I do, however, have friends who have difficult childhood memories of Christmas and always just want to get through the day. I'm sure you have friends or family members who feel the same. Or perhaps you feel that way, too. One of the amazing things about God is that He loves us all the same— those who bound forward with joy and those who hang back in fear. We are all His on that day.

I wish you all kinds of joy this coming Christmas. I also love to hear from my readers at the holidays. If you get a chance, go to my website at www.JanetTronstad.com and send me an email. If you don't have access to the Web, you can always drop me a note in care of the editors at Steeple Hill Books, 233 Broadway, Suite 1001, New York, NY 10279.

Wishing you a Merry Christmas.

Janet Tronstad

QUESTIONS FOR DISCUSSION

1. Why does Zach Lucas hate Christmas? Have you ever felt the way he does about the holiday? Why or why not?

2. Zach talks about trying to make Christmas special for his family once when he was a boy and they didn't appreciate it. Do you feel that the effort it takes to make Christmas a special day is worth it? Why or why not?

3. At one point, Jenny feels she hasn't made Christmas special enough for her children. Have you ever felt that way? Do you think children have too many expectations of the holiday?

4. How do you make sure that Christ is the center of your holiday? Jenny always reads the Nativity story with her children; is there something else you do in your home?

5. Zach isn't the only one who is uncomfortable with family holidays. How can the church be made more sensitive to this fact?

6. When the family and Zach are snowbound,

they have to make their own Christmas presents. Have you ever done that as a family? Do you think the holiday was more meaningful when people did make their own presents? Why or why not?

7. Jenny moves to Dry Creek, Montana, to start a new life for her children. Have you ever moved somewhere to start over? What was your experience? Did you find the new community welcoming?

8. Jenny wants to be able to take care of herself and her children in this new place. She needs the help of her neighbors, though. Have you ever felt the frustration of needing help when you wanted to be independent?

9. Jenny doesn't want anyone to know how empty her marriage was before her husband died. Why do you think this was? Have you ever been ashamed of something that was not your fault? Do you think Jenny blamed herself for the fact her husband did not want to spend time with his own family?

10. Jenny's son, Andy, wants Santa to bring him a cowboy for Christmas, but really wants a fa-

ther. There are a lot of single parents these days. How can your church help them?

11. Zach is reluctant to tell Jenny how he feels because he thinks she had a wonderful marriage and believes he can't compete with her deceased husband. Have you ever been afraid to do something because you didn't think you would measure up?

12. Even after Zach comes back for Jenny, he knows he needs to spend some time figuring out his life before he will make a good husband. Do you agree that he needed to do that? Why or why not?

For unto you is born this day in the city of David a saviour, which is Christ the Lord.
—*Luke* 2:11

SILENT NIGHT IN DRY CREEK

I have been blessed in my life to have some warm, wonderful aunts (my mother's sisters). This book is dedicated to them:
Wilma A (deceased now but I think of her often), Grace L, Alice N, Mary M and Gladys B.

Chapter One

"You want me to keep an eye on *her?*" Wade Sutton pushed the café curtain aside and looked through the window to the only street in Dry Creek, Montana. Clumps of melting snow lined the rough asphalt road and the one vehicle in sight was an old motorcycle leaning against the corner of the hardware store. A tall, red-haired woman was walking toward that store right now, swinging her arms as if she was on some mission from God.

Wade grinned slightly as the edge of his hand pressed against the cold window. It was a cloudy December day and seeing the woman in her bulky, gray sweater and faded dress made his heart beat faster. He liked a strong woman and he could tell by the way she walked that she was a fine one.

Suddenly, a gust of wind blew the woman's skirt up to her knees. She caught the material before it could go any higher. Now, that was the problem with all the piety in this small town, he thought. What was the point of a woman wearing a dress if she didn't show more leg than that?

Wade leaned forward to see if the wind would blow again.

"Nice looking, isn't she?" Sheriff Carl Wall said, moving the toothpick in his mouth. The two men were sitting in the café with their empty breakfast plates on the table in front of them. It was ten o'clock in the morning and the waitress was back in the kitchen. No one else was around.

"She's a regular movie star." Wade let the curtain fall into place and turned his attention to the other man. He knew the woman couldn't be as pious as she looked. Not if the sheriff had asked him to come up from Idaho Falls to watch her. "What's her thing? Stolen property? Blackmail? Arson?"

Wade was ready to sink his teeth into a surveillance job. Until six months ago, when he'd injured his leg while taking down some drug dealers, he'd been the busiest independent private investigator in the Rocky Mountain area. Now, no one except his old friend here was willing to defy the doctors and consider hiring him while he was still in physical therapy.

"Jasmine Hunter hasn't done anything," the sheriff said as he leaned back. "In fact, she even agreed to be the angel in the Christmas pageant this year, so she's real popular around here."

Wade remembered those pageants. "Then she's just plain nuts."

The annual pageant was held in an old barn on the edge of Dry Creek. The angel traditionally flew over the crowd with the help of a pulley in the hayloft. Wade had been the last kid allowed to swing as the angel. Now, it was always an adult.

"They've retired that leather pulley system you used. The pageant committee put in a whole new rope and wheel job. It's as safe as riding in an airplane."

Wade grunted. He'd take his chances with the old system; he didn't trust anything designed by a committee. Either way, it took nerve, though. Maybe that was why the sheriff had asked him here. "You want me to keep an eye on your angel so she doesn't skip town before the pageant? Is that it?"

"Very funny," the sheriff said without a smile as he leaned forward slightly and lowered his voice. "The truth is, I'm not worried about what she'll do, but what someone might do to her—if you get my meaning."

Wade didn't have a clue as to his meaning. The sheriff's square, homely face didn't give much away. Wade hadn't been able to read Carl's face forty years ago when they were boys, so he didn't know why the man thought he could do it now.

"Has she requested protection?" Wade finally asked. The woman out there walking in the wind didn't look like she'd welcome someone stepping into her business. "I don't think anyone would attack an angel, especially not before Christmas."

"It's got nothing to do with the pageant. And no, she hasn't asked for help. She's too proud. That's why you need to be discreet, so she doesn't know you're keeping an eye on her."

Wade wondered what the angel was up to in her spare time. "This better be good. What is it? Abusive husband? Witness protection? What?"

Wade hoped it wasn't a domestic problem. The holidays brought out the worst in some families. He should know. As a boy, he never had a list for Santa Claus. All he wanted for Christmas was a safe hiding place so he wouldn't meet up with his grandfather's fists.

"There's no husband," the sheriff said as he leaned back again. "Not even a boyfriend hanging around. It's just a hunch I have."

The room was silent.

"That's it?" Wade finally asked to be sure he wasn't missing something. It wasn't only a desire to get back to work that brought him here. His savings were almost gone so he really needed this job, but still—this was Carl. "I remember your hunches. They didn't always pan out."

"This one's different." The sheriff crossed his beefy arms. "You'll see."

Wade lifted an eyebrow. "Well, I hope you and your hunch are going to be around to post bail when this woman hauls me to court for following her around for no good reason. That's what will happen, you know. She'll call me a stalker. Just being worried is no excuse to put a tail on someone."

Wade didn't have much, but he prided himself on being a fierce defender of the law. He didn't take bribes, he didn't look the other way and he sure didn't violate anyone's rights by surveilling an innocent woman for no reason—especially not one who was as good-looking as that redhead. She wouldn't be the only one who would think he was a stalker; he'd half believe it himself. Even Scrooge would hesitate to put a tail on the Christmas angel.

"Now, don't go getting ahead of yourself. I'm not asking you to *follow* her exactly. She's staying out at her father's place—Elmer Maynard. You remember him? I just thought you could keep an eye on her. There's no law against seeing what's in front of your face."

"Elmer doesn't have a daughter." He remembered more than he cared to about his days growing up in this small town. The Maynards owned on the place next to his grandfather's farm so he knew them well. The man didn't have any sons, either.

"It turns out Elmer had an affair back when we

were kids. Not that he knew anything about Jasmine until she showed up in Dry Creek last fall, fully grown and cruising past forty."

So she was around his age, Wade thought in satisfaction. Of course, that didn't mean anything. He made it a point never to socialize with church women and he'd guess she was a staunch one if she'd agreed to swing on that rope in the pageant. Besides, he was here on business.

He went back to the sheriff's comment. "I bet the tongues are still wagging over Elmer having a daughter."

Even as a boy, Wade knew how much Elmer and his wife wanted children. Of course, Elmer's wife was dead now so she would never know that her husband had a kid all along.

The sheriff shrugged. "People can only talk about things like that for so long. By the time Jasmine found the three men who might have been her father and figured out Elmer was the one, well, people had sort of gotten used to her. And Edith Hargrove stood up for her, which helped a lot. She's Edith Nelson now that she married Charley, but I'm sure you remember her."

"Of course, I remember her."

Who could forget Edith? She was a warrior. When he was six, she had knocked on his grandfather's door and announced that Wade belonged in Sunday school. His grandfather had been too drunk to respond and Edith boldly took his silence for agreement. Every week after that, she stopped by to pick Wade up on her way to church. His grandfather never looked happy about it, but he didn't stop her.

Once Wade got over the miracle of someone going against his grandfather, he paid attention in church. For some strange reason, Edith saw potential in him when no one else did. Of course, he knew right from the start that he'd eventually disappoint her. No one could make themselves believe something they naturally didn't. Oh, he might have believed in God back then, but—like now—he just couldn't believe that God was of much use to anyone in this world. Frankly, Wade didn't trust Him.

The sheriff grinned. "Edith is some woman."

Wade nodded. "She's a force of nature, all right."

However, with the state of his bank account, he didn't have time to walk down memory lane.

"The problem is that you can't just pay me to follow someone around," Wade said, bringing the conversation back to what he needed to say. "Unless I'm in danger of getting shot, the county won't want to sign the check. They keep the safe stuff for their own people even if it means overtime."

Carl's face flushed. "About the money—the county doesn't exactly have a budget that—"

"Aww, man." Wade looked across the table at the closest thing he had to a friend. "You're joking, right? I drove all the way up here and you're telling me there's no money to pay for the job."

By now Carl's face was red, but he was sticking to his request. "Hold on. There's money. It's just coming from the city of Dry Creek instead of the county."

"When did Dry Creek become a city?" Wade glanced around in bewilderment. This café hadn't been here when he was a boy. Well, the building had been here, but it had been empty. There might be a couple of more houses behind the hardware store. And he heard they'd painted a mural on that old barn outside of town, hoping to get some tourists. He supposed it was progress, but— "It hasn't grown that much, has it?"

"We don't need to be big to have money."

"Enough to hire me?"

"Of course, you. We don't want a stranger poking around. And, if you're here, you can spend a few days at your grandfather's place. He's the only family you've got. Besides, he's having a hard time and it's Christmas. It'd be nice if you visited him."

Everything froze. Then Wade reached for his wallet. He'd pay for his breakfast and be out of here. "Christmas is just another date on the calendar as far as I'm concerned. If going to see my grandfather is part of the deal, then Dry Creek will have to find someone else."

"Now, don't be a fool," Carl said when he saw

Wade's wallet. "I'm paying for breakfast. I know
how it is when you can't work. And you're at least
entitled to gas money for driving up here."

The sheriff pulled a wad of bills out of his jacket
pocket.

Wade hadn't seen that kind of cash in months.
"Don't tell me you carry that much money around.
Is that the Dry Creek money?"

Carl flushed as he laid the well-worn bills on
the table. "We don't have a checking account yet."

A suspicion started growing in Wade's mind.
Those bills hadn't come fresh from a savings account, either. "Have you ever done this before? Col-
lected money to hire someone?"

Carl was quiet.

"Well, that really settles it. I don't take charity,"
Wade said as he pushed back his chair. Pride was
about all he had left and those bills told the story.
Someone had passed the hat for him and he didn't
like it. "You can tell everyone that I'm doing just
fine."

The two men glared at each other for a minute.

"You can tell them yourself," the sheriff finally
said. "If you're too stubborn to take honest work—"

"What's honest about it? I'm not going to follow
some woman around just so you can give me money
and make me think I earned it."

The sheriff's face softened. "It was either that or
I'd have to deliver a carload of casseroles to your

front step. You know the people around here help their own."

Just then the door to the café opened. Wade looked up and saw the red-haired woman walk into the room. A leather bag swung from her shoulder and the faint smell of some floral perfume swirled around her. As she took a few steps, he could see he'd underrated her looks. Her delicate porcelain skin was rosy from the cold and her auburn hair curled around her face, reminding him of a Botticelli angel with a halo. No wonder the people here wanted her in the Christmas pageant. She was like a picture in some museum.

And then she walked closer and he knew he was mistaken. She was too alive for a museum. Or any celestial gathering if it came to that. He'd never seen a woman like her. Her copper hair was spiked instead of curled like he'd thought at first. And her nose was slightly crooked. She wasn't the angel at the top of a Christmas tree; she was the angel who'd fallen just far enough off the top to be interesting to a flesh-and-blood man like him.

It was a good thing he was sitting down, because he felt a weakness in his knees. Suddenly, he wasn't so sure that he hadn't hit his head in the fight six months ago. He felt a little faint and his heart was acting up. But all he could do was gawk at her like the boy he used to be when he'd lived on the edge of this small town. That same feeling of watching his dreams from afar would pass, of course, but it annoyed him all the same. He didn't deal with dreams anymore in his life.

Chapter Two

Jasmine felt her breath catch. Who was that man? He stared back at her for a few seconds before looking down at his coffee cup. In the moment she met his eyes she could tell he had something to hide. At least that's what it must be because he went pale at the sight of her.

For a second, she wondered if he recognized her from prison. She'd told the people around here that she'd spent time in jail, but she didn't want someone from her past to come and remind them of it. Not when she was trying to be a normal woman instead of an ex-con.

She stood still as she looked at the man more closely. He had a fine-looking face, one she was sure she would remember if she'd seen it before. A dark growth of whiskers covered his chin and his moss-green eyes studied the pattern in the check-ered tablecloth. His blue flannel shirt and jeans were both well-worn, too, as though he spent a lot of time outdoors. And he had a black Stetson hat sitting on the chair next to him.

If it wasn't for the way he held his coffee cup, she would think he was a new cowboy heading out to the Elkton Ranch. But he held his cup loosely. Her old boyfriend, Lonnie Denton, had held his cup that way when he wasn't sure what he'd need to do in the next minute or so. He said it gave him options. He could grab the cup and use it as a weapon or reach for the knife he kept in a sheath against his arm. He'd been proud when he explained that to her and she'd been sufficiently young and foolish to be impressed.

Jasmine mentally shook herself. She couldn't fall apart every time a suspicious-looking man came to town. She needed to leave her past behind if she expected others to forget it. And—most importantly— she needed to stop thinking about Lonnie. He was locked up tight in prison. He couldn't get out and, even though he'd always been unstable, she couldn't believe he would send someone to spy on her just because she'd sent him a pamphlet about heaven in the mail. Granted, it had been a colossal mistake; she'd known that when he had sent her that postcard in response. But that should be the end of it. She had a new life to live.

She looked at the man's sleeve in front of her. She couldn't see the outline of a knife sheath.

"I—ah—" Jasmine started to say and then stopped. She'd forgotten that her voice was raw. It sounded sultry rather than raspy, but her throat was sore all the same.

"Here. Let me get you some coffee," Carl said as he reached over to a nearby table and grabbed a clean cup. "It'll make your throat feel better."

Jasmine had been practicing her songs for the Christmas pageant a little too much lately. She'd taken a leap of faith a few weeks ago and pledged her life to God. She'd been half surprised lightning hadn't struck through the church roof on that day. In a burst of gratitude, she'd signed up to be the angel in the pageant.

She owed God big-time for taking her in. Doing the angel role wouldn't be enough to repay Him, but maybe it would be a start if she did it in some spectacular way. She was considering fireworks. Nothing too loud, of course, but maybe a sparkler trailing behind her as she swung over the audience would add pizzazz to the role.

She accepted the cup the sheriff filled from the carafe and sat down in the chair he pulled out from the table he shared. Then she took two long sips of coffee.

When she'd been at the hardware store just now, she had picked up her mail. She was half afraid she'd get another postcard from Lonnie, but all she'd received was an invitation from the sheriff and his wife.

"Tell Barbara I'd love to come to dinner tonight," she said after she swallowed a gulp of coffee.

The people of Dry Creek had really taken Jasmine to their hearts when she volunteered to be in the pageant. Of course, she didn't have the courage to tell anyone that she'd never seen a Christmas pageant, let alone been in one before. Growing up, her mother had avoided churches and the only thing marking the season in their apartment had been a silver aluminum tree that was perpetually bent at the top.

The sheriff nodded at her proudly. "Dinner's going to be great. Barbara's got some fancy holiday menu going. She's been baking all day."

Jasmine swallowed. Things like that made her realize what she'd missed. Too much of her life had been lived behind bars when other women made Christmas dinners for their families. Not that she could afford to forget all that she'd learned. She opened her mouth to tell the sheriff about knives in sleeves.

"I'd like you to meet Wade Sutton," the sheriff said before she could speak. "He's a friend of mine—grew up around here. He'll be coming to dinner tonight, too—I hope."

The sheriff looked at the other man as he spoke and Wade gave him a slight nod.

Just then Jasmine placed the name. What a relief. "Why, you're the angel! I've heard about you."

The man slouched in his chair.

Jasmine hesitated. Maybe there were two Wade Suttons. This man didn't look like someone who would play an angel. He didn't even look like someone who would smile at the baby Jesus, let alone proclaim His holy birth from the rafters of the old barn. Of course, she'd heard the man was a private investigator, but that didn't mean he had to scowl all the time.

When she had heard the angel everyone talked about was coming to Dry Creek, she hadn't expected someone so solidly...well, male. Now that she was sitting, she could see the snug way his jeans fit along his thigh. Maybe he still had his leg in a cast that she couldn't see because of his jeans. No one had that much muscle, especially not someone willing to fly around on a rope. He shifted his leg slightly and she realized she was staring.

"Sorry," she muttered. "It's just I thought you'd look more like a ballet dancer. Because of the angel thing."

He shot her an incredulous look. "I was eleven."

She felt the heat of his indignant glare all the way down her spine.

"It's nothing. I was just wondering what kind

of legs you had when you used those pulleys. Of course, your legs weren't so—so—" Jasmine felt herself blush. She hadn't blushed in years so she cleared her throat. "Well, the point is people are still talking about when you made your swing overhead. You had to be graceful. And your legs—well, I thought maybe you did something special with them as you made the swing. You know—the way you pointed your toes. That kind of thing. Really, I was just hoping you could give me some tips."

She didn't want to mention the sparkler idea. But even a clue as to the real part the angel played would be welcomed. Jasmine couldn't believe that all she was supposed to do was wave her wings over the shepherds and say a few words. Everything was too plain. She was coming to know a God who parted the seas and thundered from the rocks. He wouldn't have announced the birth of His Son without *some* drama.

"I didn't have much sense back then," Wade finally said reluctantly. "You should ask someone else for help."

"Oh." Jasmine said. He must have done something very special if he was so closemouthed about it. But, if he wouldn't tell her anything, how was she supposed to give a performance that surpassed, or at least equaled, his?

There was a moment's silence.

"How's everything at the hardware store?" the

sheriff finally said a little too cheerfully. "I bet they're doing good business even in these hard times."

"I don't know." Jasmine didn't want to show her disappointment in Wade's response so she was glad the sheriff had started a new conversation. She turned to look at him. "There was a sale on nails. No one was buying, though."

"Things will pick up," the sheriff added. He seemed to be struggling with his words, although she couldn't imagine why. "People just need to be patient in these hard economic times."

Jasmine nodded. The pastor had asked for prayer for the store last Sunday. "I buy as much as I can there."

She tried to do everything that was mentioned in church, including the things that cost her money.

The sheriff turned a little more so she could see his face even though the other man couldn't. Then he winked at her. "There's no need to say anything to the people at the store about the hard times—they might be embarrassed."

"Oh, for goodness' sake, Carl," the other man spoke out. His eyes were smoldering and his jaw was clenched. "You don't need to warn people not to say anything to me. Everybody knows I'm the one who is supposed to get the handout. The people of Dry Creek just can't leave well enough alone."

Jasmine wondered how anyone had ever thought

that man could be an angel. He might not even be suited to being the innkeeper, and that role was written for a surly actor.

"You should be grateful someone cares enough to help you." Jasmine refused to listen to any complaint about her friends in the church here. They were perfect—every one of them.

Although, she had to admit, they might have misjudged on this one. The man before her didn't look like someone who needed a handout. She had pictured him with the watery, timid eyes of someone who was ashamed of needing help. Instead, he almost bristled with pride. And, here she'd contributed six perfectly good dollars to the collection for him.

"I haven't taken a handout since I was a kid," the man said, and then pressed his lips together. "No reason to start again now."

"Well, I'm sure you can work enough to earn it if you want," Jasmine said. "There are still some parts left in the pageant. King Herod, for one. And you could coach me if you would just unbend a little and relax about it."

The man grunted. "Unbend? You should be worrying about things breaking instead of them bending. The church should get one of those mannequins to swing around up there for an angel."

Jasmine blinked. "A mannequin can't proclaim anything."

He shrugged. "Well, it's your funeral."

He wasn't suggesting it was dangerous, was he? She'd seen the pulley system; it was sturdy enough to swing an elephant across the barn.

The man's face didn't change, but he did lift his coffee cup for a drink.

Jasmine bit back her words. He was nothing like she'd expected. She wondered if God had sent him to her as some kind of a test. She secretly thought God should be a little choosier about who He let into His family, so she couldn't fault Him if He wanted to see what she would do when provoked.

"Wade here is Clarence Sutton's grandson," the sheriff finally said in the silence.

Jasmine summoned up a polite smile and looked at the man. "You must be staying out with your grandfather then."

"Not likely." The man's eyes flared for a second and then turned cold.

Apparently that scowl ran in the family along with his rather anti-social attitude. No one could accuse the elder Mr. Sutton of being neighborly, either. He lived next door to her father and the men had feuded for years. Still, Jasmine kept the smile on her face.

"He'll be spending the night at my place," the sheriff injected smoothly. "I expect he'd like to see some of the countryside while he's here, though. I figure he might as well drive out and pick you up for dinner. If that's all right?"

The sheriff smiled again.

"Oh, he doesn't need to do that." She wanted to talk to the man about the role of the angel, but she could do that in a few minutes. She didn't need any more time with him than was necessary, especially since he was so disagreeable. And arrogant. A man like him would probably think he was on a date with her if he drove her anywhere.

"You can't be riding that motorcycle at night," the sheriff continued. "I'd have to ticket you for not having your backlights working and Barbara would be upset with me. It could ruin the whole dinner. Besides, it might rain. Riding with Wade will at least keep you dry."

Everyone was quiet again.

"I might be able to borrow Edith's car," Jasmine finally said. Ever since Edith had gotten married for the second time, she didn't drive her old car very much. Sometimes the car wouldn't start right away, but Jasmine could get out and push it until it did if she had to.

"I can drive you," Wade said, and then added, "It'd be my pleasure."

He didn't sound like it would be his pleasure and that made Jasmine feel better. It definitely wouldn't be a date if neither one of them wanted it to be. And it was a cold night to be pushing a car. Maybe the test God was sending her was to see if she had the sense to stay out of the rain.

"I guess it'd be okay," she agreed.

At least the man didn't have bad breath or anything. And he nodded like he was a sensible person when he wasn't scowling. He might not want to tell her how he'd managed to give such a spectacular performance in the pageant, but if he sat next to her long enough, he might say something about it out of sheer boredom since she didn't plan to put any effort into making conversation with him.

The sheriff beamed at her. "I'm glad you stopped by. It reminds me that I need to invite Edith and Charley, too. Barbara wanted to have the two of you and another couple to balance out her table. Some notion she got watching Martha Stewart on television."

"Oh." Jasmine set her coffee cup down on the table. If the sheriff's wife was watching good old Martha, Jasmine needed to find a hostess gift before she went. She was sadly lacking in homemaking skills, but gift-giving was something important in prison, too, so she'd learned the value of that. "Well, I'll see you later, then."

Wade watched the woman flee from the café before he turned back to his friend. "Are you happy now? You've pretty much scared her away, making her think she's agreed to be a couple with me."

"Oh, she'd never think that. The women have her paired up with Conrad."

"Conrad?" Wade frowned.

"Nelson," the sheriff added. "Edith's his aunt now that she married Charley."

Wade remembered a kid by that name. He came to town during the summers to visit the Nelsons. Wade didn't think much of a man who relied on his aunt for matchmaking. "He doesn't seem like much of a go-getter in the romance department."

The sheriff snorted. "You should talk. I don't see a wedding ring on your finger."

Wade glared at his friend.

"Besides, I'm helping you set up your cover," the sheriff continued like he hadn't noticed Wade's look. "Lonely grandson comes home to be with his grandfather for the holidays. I can hear the Christmas bells ringing already."

"I don't need a cover." Wade gritted his teeth. "There's no reason to follow that woman around. I'm going home tomorrow."

Wade felt hollow the second he said the last. Who was he kidding? He never really thought of his apartment in Idaho Falls as home. His furniture was rented and all that the refrigerator ever held were takeout cartons and a few bottles of soft drinks and water. Half of the time he didn't even get his mail before someone made off with it, not that he had much to steal except pizza flyers and catalogs. All of which had been fine with him until he spent a few hours in Dry Creek again. Now he felt an old stirring, telling him there should be more to a man's life than what he had.

"I don't know," the sheriff said thoughtfully, and for the first time Wade saw real concern on his friend's face. "If she hadn't gotten that postcard last week, I wouldn't be worried."

Wade waited for more, but nothing came.

"Nobody dies from a postcard," he finally said.

The sheriff looked at Wade for a minute. "You remember Lonnie Denton? Shot a gas station attendant in Missoula twelve years ago?"

Wade nodded. "Almost killed the kid behind the counter. All for sixty-two dollars and change. I know a couple of the officers that finally picked him up."

"Well, Denton was Jasmine's boyfriend."

Wade whistled. He hadn't seen that coming.

"It was the only job she pulled with him and she called the ambulance that saved the kid's life," the sheriff continued. "She still got ten years prison time, though. Just got out a year or so ago."

That explained the walk, Wade thought. A woman had to be tough in prison.

"The postcard she got was from Denton."

Suddenly, the sheriff had all of Wade's attention. "I'm surprised they'd let him write to her—since they were in it together."

"He used a fake name for her. But he sent it to Dry Creek and she knew it was hers. She picked it up out of the general delivery mail on the hardware store counter. She showed it to me right away. Told me she didn't want me to think she was hiding anything. Said she'd sent him a pamphlet about the glories of heaven and this is what she got in return. I could see she was shaken, too. He said he'd see her soon."

Wade was quiet for a minute. He didn't like the thought of Jasmine worrying about the soul of a man like that. Not that he was overjoyed about the boyfriend angle, either. "I don't suppose Lonnie is up for parole or anything?"

The sheriff shook his head. "I found out where he was doing his time and called a guy I know who works at the prison, the one west of Phoenix. He said Lonnie had a seven-year stretch to go."

"I guess some people might say soon and mean seven years," Wade said.

"Maybe."

Wade had been an investigator for a long time. Partners in crime often stayed together. Something told him the woman was too perfect. She was trying too hard. And she was clearly nervous around him. All of that chatter about his part in that old pageant was probably just an attempt to distract him from her past. "How well do you know this Jasmine? Did you ever think maybe she and Lonnie are getting ready to pull another job and that's why he wrote to her? Maybe she's here to make plans."

"Jasmine served her time." The sheriff's tone was final.

"She wouldn't be the first one to be sent back to prison. Some folks find it hard to make it on the outside. Even getting a job can be a challenge." Wade stopped. "She does have a job, doesn't she?"

"She sure does. She works for Conrad in that mechanic shop of his. It's only part-time for now, but she's also keeping house for Elmer so she keeps busy."

"Isn't that convenient? Her working for her father and the man she's planning to marry—"

"Oh, she hasn't even gone out on a date with Conrad," the sheriff said. "And, whatever you do, don't tell the women I said they're thinking in that direction. My wife probably shouldn't have even told me. They don't want to scare her off."

Wade wondered what the women in this town thought it would take to scare a thief away from the full cashbox of a local business that was doing well enough to actually have employees. This Conrad fellow might not know it, but he was a target. Dry Creek wasn't Wade's town anymore, but he hated to see innocent folks being set up for robbery. He looked around. "I don't see a cash register here. I suppose the waitresses keep the money in the back?"

The sheriff narrowed his eyes. "I hope you're not accusing Jasmine of something."

Wade shrugged. "I'm being careful, that's all. Just because she's out of prison doesn't mean she didn't do what put her there in the first place."

The sheriff grunted and looked over his shoulder. "Just keep your suspicions to yourself. The women in this town will have my badge if they hear I let you get away with that kind of talk. Besides, Jasmine told me about the postcard. She wouldn't do that if she was planning something."

Wade picked his hat up from the seat beside him. "The real message Lonnie sent was probably in code so it wouldn't matter if you did read it. And she probably figured you would find out about the postcard and she told you so you wouldn't think anything of it. She was just playing it safe. That's all."

"But the people in Dry Creek *like* Jasmine."

Some people had probably liked Al Capone, too. "Of course, they like her. Nobody plans a robbery by going around making themselves unpopular with folks. It attracts too much attention. People watch unfriendly people. They write down the license plate number for their car. They remember where they've seen them. No, nice is a much better cover if you're up to something."

"I think you've been in this business too long. Nobody is planning anything."

"Does Elmer still have that fancy white Cadillac car of his?"

The sheriff narrowed his eyes. "That car is old as the hills by now. No self-respecting criminal would want to steal it."

"Well, let's hope not," Wade said as he pushed his chair back.

"She joined the church, too, you know," the sheriff added.

Wade nodded. That's just what someone would do if they wanted to gain people's trust, but he couldn't say that to Carl. His old friend had never been as cynical as he was. "I'll bet she's joined the choir, too."

The sheriff's jaw dropped. "How'd you know that?"

Wade just smiled as he stood up. He'd seen some sheet music in the bag the woman had on her shoulder, but he didn't mind looking mysterious to Carl. "Just doing my job."

The sheriff and Wade walked out of the restaurant together.

The cold wind hit Wade in the face and he pulled his hat down a little farther over his ears. The sheriff nodded and walked to the side of the café where he'd parked his car. Wade had to walk in the opposite direction.

It had been a long time since Wade had been in the town of Dry Creek. Back then the homes all looked like mansions compared to the weathered old house on his grandfather's farm. He'd spent his childhood feeling second-rate around the other kids here, especially at Christmas. His mother died when he was four and his father went to jail shortly after that, so the only one left to give Wade a present had been his grandfather.

Wade knew a gift was never coming, but it took him years to stop hoping. In the meantime, he was embarrassed to have anyone else know he spent his barren Christmases out in the barn while his grandfather drank himself into a stupor in the house. Maybe that's why he made up stories about imaginary Christmas dinners he claimed his grandfather used to make for them.

Wade smiled just remembering. Every Christmas, he had gone out to the barn and planned the stories he'd tell the other boys about those dinners. He didn't want anyone to feel sorry for him so he climbed up to the hayloft where he kept his mother's jewelry box and her old magazines. That's where he found the picture of the coconut cake with raspberry filling that he said was his grandfather's specialty.

Wade had made it sound so mouth-watering the other kids practically drooled; he'd even agreed to copy the recipe for Carl one year.

But now, looking around at the houses, Wade wondered if some of those kids wouldn't have understood a hard Christmas. The town was very ordinary, maybe even poor. None of the houses were new and, even though each was set back from the main street with a fenced lawn, it was winter and no grass was growing. It felt strange to remember how he used to envy the kids who lived in these houses.

Fortunately, by now he knew a man could have a good life without a family. And Christmas passed just fine with a drive-thru hamburger and fries.

He shook his head slightly so the memory of the red-haired woman wouldn't sit so clearly in his mind. He didn't need to mess up his life by dreaming about her. She was like that coconut cake. Something nice to dream about, but nothing that was likely to ever come his way. He was glad the sheriff had tipped him to the fact that the women around here were planning for her to marry Conrad—that is, if the sheriff wasn't wrong and she didn't end up back in jail instead.

He stopped a minute; he didn't like thinking of her in a place like that. Then he sighed. His radar was good. That probably meant she was guilty as sin. Fortunately, it must also mean the church going was only a facade. If it was, he would have more in common with her than he thought. Suddenly, he was glad he was picking her up for dinner. It wouldn't hurt to get to know her a little bit better. Maybe she wasn't as much of an angel as she wanted people to think she was.

Chapter Three

Jasmine pulled the white curtain back from the kitchen window and looked out at her father's farm. She wished she could just forget about Wade Sutton. The view out this window usually soothed her. Late-day shadows made the deep red barn look almost black. Even though it was winter, there was very little snow. Behind the barn, a mixture of dried wheat stalks and tall weeds spread over the slight hill. Night would be here soon, but she could still see well enough.

Just looking out that far made her eyes feel restful after being in prison for so long. There were no concrete buildings or searchlights in sight. Unfortunately, what her eyes kept coming back to was the new post on the hill. She could barely see it in the gathering dusk, but she knew it rose up in the area to the left of the barn where the barbed-wire fence trailed up the hill.

Most of the wire fence on Elmer's ranch sagged comfortably, but that particular section was stretched tight and kept in good repair. He said he wanted the divide clear between his land and the Sutton place.

Her father was a stubborn man. Clarence Sutton was another.

Several weeks ago, Clarence's old donkey had wandered out of its barn, down the road and into her father's lane. The animal had probably been looking for something to eat, but her father believed his neighbor had deliberately sent the donkey over to do mischief. Clarence, he said, always knew where his animals were and the donkey had a reputation for biting people. It had taken a bucket of oats to lure the donkey back to her barn and Clarence hadn't even come out of his house to say a proper thank-you.

Last week, in retaliation, her father had dug a hole and put a twelve-foot metal cross on the top of the hill that divided the two ranches. Then, as if that wasn't enough, today he'd taken several heavy-duty electrical cords and ran them from the barn up to the cross so he could wrap strands of Christmas tree lights around it. Now, in the evening, he could walk out to the barn and flip a switch and the cross would flash with white and yellow and clear lights. It would all look like a big golden cross that some televangelist would use.

Jasmine shook her head as she heard footsteps behind her. She turned to see her father walk into the kitchen from the living room. He was wearing jeans and a dark denim shirt with snap buttons. His white hair was plastered back and he had a look of glee on his weathered face. "Time to turn on those lights."

"Maybe you should wait and talk to Mr. Sutton before you do that," Jasmine said. "He might not like them and—"

She'd told her father she was going to dinner at the Walls', but she hadn't told him she was being picked up by Wade. The way her father fumed about that donkey of Clarence's, she doubted he'd be any more welcoming to the man's grandson. If everything stayed calm, though, there was a chance her father wouldn't see who was driving the car. He might just assume it was the sheriff behind the wheel.

"I'm celebrating Christmas. If old man Sutton doesn't like the lights, he can just look the other way." Her father picked a jacket off the coatrack by the door. "I got those special outdoor bulbs and I intend to use them—outside where they belong."

It suddenly struck Jasmine that the reason the people of Dry Creek might be so excited she was in the pageant was because they hoped she'd work a miracle between these two men. Maybe she should give it a try.

"It's not right," Jasmine declared when her father had his hand on the doorknob. "Christmas should bring people together. Decorations aren't something you use to annoy your neighbors."

Elmer turned to her. "Of course, Christmas brings people together. That's why I put the thing up there. Besides, an old sinner like Sutton should get down on his knees instead of complaining about Christmas anyway."

"You'll be using a lot of electricity with those lights." Jasmine tried a different argument. She didn't want to hear another list of Mr. Sutton's short-comings. "And they're not energy-efficient bulbs."

"I've got nothing better to do with my money than pay the electric company," Elmer said as he opened the door. "I've already bought you that Christmas present and you won't take the rest."

Cold air came into the room.

"I'm practicing poverty," she said. She was work-ing on all of the attributes of the Christian life. She'd found a pamphlet and she was targeting the hardest ones first. "I don't need more money."

Elmer had started to walk through the door, but he turned around to look at her. "That's why I'm buying you—"

"I don't need jewels, either," Jasmine added quickly. Her father had shown her the picture of a ten-thousand-dollar diamond-and-ruby necklace that he said he was buying for her. *Ten thousand dollars!* She hoped it was an empty promise.

"Every woman needs jewels," Elmer snapped back. "It gives her security. I should have given some to your mother. And my wife, too."

With that, he stomped out into the darkness.

Jasmine looked up at the clock on the wall. She didn't want to argue with her newly found father again tonight. She knew it was guilt that was driving him and she'd have a hard time making him understand.

She didn't care what holiday it was, real people didn't wear necklaces like that. Not unless they wanted thieves to buzz around every time they walked out of their houses. Besides, she wanted to walk by faith. Her father was wrong; a woman wasn't pushed to have as much faith when she had that many diamonds hanging around her neck.

She'd have to talk to her father later just to make sure he understood. In the meantime, Wade would be here in five minutes. She had planned to do a quick check on her lipstick so she stepped to the oval mirror hanging in the hallway.

She didn't know why she was making such a big deal of her appearance since this wasn't a date, but she wanted to look her best. Not that Wade would care if she wore a brown paper bag over her head. Her hand stopped. She wondered if she was guilty of the sin of vanity.

She sighed. She'd never thought there were so many pitfalls in the Christian life. Trying to make oneself worthy of God's acceptance was not easy. People kept saying God didn't care if she was an ex-con, but she just didn't see it that way.

Jasmine took her perfume bottle out of her purse before she realized. Of course, that was it. It was amazing that she hadn't seen it. No wonder Wade didn't offer any friendliness. She was an ex-con. He was a lawman. He probably saw them as oil and water; sin and righteousness—good and evil.

Well, that was probably best for both of them.

She went ahead and sprayed perfume on her wrists. She was determined to be like the other women in Dry Creek and she looked to Edith for inspiration. The older woman wore rose-scented perfume, so Jasmine kept with a light scent. Since Edith wore dresses, Jasmine had bought a couple of plain shifts at a thrift store in Billings. She no longer wore clothes with much color and she kept her shoes sensible.

Jasmine had started to go back to the kitchen when she saw headlights flash through the window. At least her father was still out in the barn. Hopefully, he'd stay out there until she was gone.

She pulled her coat off the back of a chair where she'd placed it earlier. Her coat was the one thing she hadn't been able to replace yet. Oh, well, she thought as she turned to the kitchen door, it would have to do. She shouldn't care what Wade thought about the way she dressed anyway.

Wade wondered what was wrong as he drove up to Elmer's house. On the drive out here, he'd thought nothing had changed in the decades that he'd been gone. The land was just as dry as it had always been and the gravel road had as many ruts. But he'd barely gotten out of Dry Creek before he saw a glowing light in the distance. When he turned off the main road to go down Elmer's lane, he saw that someone had put what looked like Christmas lights on a cross standing on the hill that divided Elmer's land from his grandfather's place.

Wade wondered why anyone would bother with lights way out here in the middle of nowhere since not that many people drove down this county road. The one person who would see the cross most often would be Wade's grandfather. Those lights must shine right in front of the porch where his grandfather sat every evening about now.

Wade started to chuckle as he stopped his car in front of the house. So that was it. The cross would make his grandfather crazy. No doubt about it. The two old men had never gotten along. They must still be going at it.

The back door to the house opened and Wade saw Jasmine standing there. The day had grown darker and light streamed out the door behind her.

Her red hair was spikier than it had been earlier and her black leather coat had what looked like metal rivets along the sleeves. She stood there a minute and Wade almost wished he could keep an eye on her like Carl wanted. Guilty or innocent, she was definitely his kind of woman. It would be a pleasure to watch her awhile.

He sat there, just enjoying the sight of her when— without any warning—a gunshot ripped through the silence. Wade looked over at Jasmine. She seemed frozen in place. With all of the light behind her, she made a perfect target.

"Get inside!" he yelled.

The sound of the shot had come from the north, so Wade bent down and drove his car as close as possible to the doorway where Jasmine had been standing.

"Lose the lights," he ordered when he saw they were still on in the kitchen. He didn't want someone shooting at the windows. He wondered if Lonnie had a problem with Jasmine and had sent someone to—

He shut off his car and opened his passenger door. Then he folded himself down and slid across the seat, stopping to pull his gun from the glove compartment as he passed.

Another shot rang out. That one sounded like it came from the direction of his grandfather's back porch and Wade relaxed a little. His grandfather was probably just shooting at a coyote or something. But a wise lawman didn't assume anything.

The night was dark and now that Wade's car lights and the ones in the house were off, he had to rely on his memory as he tried to sprint to the kitchen door. He hadn't run anywhere since he'd started therapy and his whole leg was throbbing in protest.

Wade twisted the knob and opened the door.

He stepped into the dark kitchen and something soft wrapped around his neck.

"A-a-rgh," he gurgled in protest. The only light in the room was an illuminated clock that hung on the wall and it didn't make anything but itself visible. The band around his neck loosened and he could tell it was an arm encased in leather.

He leaned back a little, preparing to make one of his defensive moves, when he realized he was settled into a womanly softness that was kind of nice. He was breathing better and, now that the lights were off, there was no reason to move. Besides, he could smell the perfume.

Maybe he got a little too comfortable in the dark leaning against her, because she whispered suspiciously. "Is that you?"

Now how did a man answer that? "Depends on who you're expecting."

He felt Jasmine shift her body as she took a step backward. Unfortunately, she didn't warn him and his body twisted to go with her. A muscle cramp in his leg seized him and he could hardly breathe. He clenched his teeth to keep from hissing in pain.

A small glow of light entered the room. Jasmine had reached back and opened the refrigerator door.

"Are you all right?" she asked now as she moved away from him slightly. "I didn't mean to hurt you. I was just—"

"Don't worry about it," he said hoarsely as he reached out to put his gun on the counter so he could massage his thigh. Now he could see why no one wanted to hire him until he'd conquered his leg spasms. He wasn't healing as fast as a younger man would. If a killer had been in the room, Wade would have been helpless to stop him.

"I'm sorry," Jasmine said as she moved closer.

The pain was leaving and in the light coming from the refrigerator he saw her misery. In the darkness, her eyes were pools of worry. He reached out and brushed her cheek, thinking to comfort her. "Who taught you about that defense hold anyway? You're pretty good at it."

"My old boyfriend, Lonnie," she whispered.

He could feel her breath on the back of his hand and it sent shivers down his spine. Then she looked up at him. She was beautiful. Without thinking, he bent his head down. She raised herself up on her tiptoes. He dipped farther down. He knew they were strangers and it was only the relief she was feeling that drew her close. But he was going to kiss her anyway. He just wanted to look at her a second or two longer before he did.

Then, without warning, the kitchen door opened with a crash.

Wade lunged toward his gun. He barely felt the pain in his leg, because of the panic inside. He'd grown soft. He'd assumed his grandfather had been behind the gunshots, but this wasn't the old man. He and Jasmine were going to die and it was all his fault.

"It's okay," Jasmine said quickly.

Wade thought she was talking to him until he saw the man in the doorway more clearly. Even with all of the shadows, Wade recognized Elmer as he stood there, looking ready to do battle, with a barnyard shovel in his hands.

"You all right?" Elmer asked as he flipped on the overhead light switch.

"We're fine," Jasmine answered as she stepped a little closer to Wade.

Elmer arched back like an attack cat.

"Who's he?" he demanded.

The older man didn't sound the least bit friendly, and Wade couldn't blame him. He carefully moved his hand away from the gun on the counter.

"He came to take me to dinner," Jasmine explained.

"He needs a gun to do that?"

"No, of course not." Jasmine took a step away from the counter as though she'd just realized a gun sat there.

"I'm sorry to disturb—" Wade began.

Then Elmer's fierce scowl disappeared. "Why you're little Wade Sutton! I haven't seen you since—"

Elmer stopped and had the grace to look flustered.

Wade nodded. "Since the day my grandfather drove my dad and me away with enough shotgun blasts to rattle the entire county. As I recall, you were mending fence and had a first-row seat."

When he was fifteen, his father had come back from prison. He had lasted two weeks on the farm before he had a knock-down fight with Wade's grandfather. When his father left, Wade had gone with him. He'd never returned to the farm, not even to see if the new wheat he'd planted that spring had yielded the harvest he'd expected.

"Well," Elmer murmured. "You were a good kid even if you and your friends were messing with my Cadillac."

"You knew?"

Elmer grinned. "I could hardly blame you for wanting to sit inside. That Cadillac was something back then."

Wade relaxed. He was glad the man didn't ask about his father. But then everyone in Dry Creek must have heard his father ended his crime spree in a shoot-out with the police a few months after they'd left the farm. It was the day Wade had turned sixteen and he'd begged his father to take him along. He was so glad to have his father back, he would have gone anywhere with him. His father had refused, saying he wanted Wade to stay on the right side of the law and have a decent life.

"Your grandfather always did try to solve his problems with a shotgun," Elmer continued. "I figure that's him shooting at the cross. I saw one of the lights go out so he must have gotten off a good one."

If the shooter was aiming at the cross, it had to be his grandfather. At least that meant it wasn't someone like Lonnie Denton. "You'll have to report it to the sheriff."

"Can't be anyone but your grandfather," Elmer said as he studied Wade again. "The only set of lights coming down the road was yours. It's too dark out for someone to drive in unannounced."

Wade nodded. He supposed that was true, too.

"I'll give the sheriff a call after you're gone. No point in putting it off. I already unplugged the lights and your grandfather never leaves his porch until the seven-o'clock news comes on the television."

Wade remembered. Nothing gave the old man a better excuse to drink than the problems of the world.

"Yeah, well, I guess we should be going." Wade

noticed that Elmer was still taking his measure. Not everyone in Dry Creek would trust a Sutton these days, even if they were willing to take up a collection on his behalf.

"You take good care of my daughter," Elmer said.

Wade looked at Jasmine. Her face was flushed. He wished he'd kissed her even if her father had been crashing in the door. It probably would be his only chance and he'd always regret not tasting her lips.

"I can take care of myself," she said.

Elmer grunted.

"He's just giving me a ride," Jasmine continued. "I have some special lights on order for my motorcycle. I can't drive it at night until I get them."

Wade wondered why she didn't just say she was suffering his company because the sheriff had forced them to ride together. Carl was probably laughing his head off about it right now.

"You shouldn't be driving that bike at all," Elmer sputtered. "A lady should ride in a car. If you don't like driving my old Cadillac, I have a Bentley in the garage, too. And a few others."

"I do fine with my motorcycle," Jasmine said as she spread her hands. "I don't need *things*. Not in my new life."

Wade grunted. He wasn't about to ask any questions just now, but he did wonder what story she'd spun for Elmer. Everyone wanted things. He didn't trust someone who said otherwise.

"I've got my car outside," Wade said as he reached over to pick up his gun from the counter. He moved his leg again and grimaced in pain.

"Here," Elmer said as he held out a hand.

Wade took the help to steady himself. So this is what he'd come to, he thought. Depending on others like he was an old man.

"I forgot you'd damaged your leg," Elmer said. "That's why you can't work."

Wade tried to push the pain away. It was like he figured. Everyone knew about his problem. "I can get a job. Soon."

"Well, until you do—I put in twenty bucks."

Wade forced himself to give a short nod of thanks. He didn't want to have to explain to every person in Dry Creek why he couldn't take their charity. Maybe he'd ask the pastor to put a notice in the church bulletin offering to return the contributions. Maybe then they'd leave him alone.

"You need to take care of your leg," Jasmine said as she led the way to the outside door. She picked up a small jar of jam that was sitting on the counter.

"Hostess gift," she announced proudly.

Wade nodded. For someone who wasn't into things, she sure knew how to spread gifts around. It was probably what made people think she was so sweet.

He picked up his gun and followed her to the door only to look back at Elmer. Apparently, Wade wasn't the only one feeling a little down. "Don't worry. She'll be fine."

The old man didn't say anything.

Wade opened the car door for Jasmine and she slid inside. They were at the gate leading to the main gravel road before he decided he had to know. "So was everyone there when they passed the hat for me?"

"Uh…"

"I'm a grown man. I can take care of myself." Wade looked straight ahead. The heater was going in his car and the dials on the dash were lit up. There was nothing but darkness outside the car.

"You should take the money anyway."

Wade looked over at her. He couldn't see her eyes in the darkness.

"You could consider it a Christmas present if you want," she added.

"If the people here wanted to give me a Christmas present, it would be socks." Wade suddenly remembered the many pairs of socks he'd gotten as a boy from the people in the church here. Sometimes, he'd also get a shirt or a jacket, too. Maybe that's why the money stung so much. He'd already received so much from these people. The kids might have believed his stories about the Christmas presents his grandfather gave him, but the adults knew better. They probably even knew there hadn't been any cake or turkey or apple stuffing.

"If they wanted to give me the money, they could have at least asked me to dig a ditch or something. That's honest work," Wade muttered half to himself. "I can't see where they think following the Christmas angel around could be anything at all."

"What?"

Wade heard the surprise in her voice and could have kicked himself. He was not himself tonight.

"They wanted you to follow *me?*" she asked.

"I could be mistaken," Wade said. "I—ah—it might have been one of the wise men."

Jasmine wasn't paying any attention to him. "I can't believe they'd ask you to follow me. What do they think—that I'm going to steal from somebody?"

"Oh, no," Wade said. Now he'd really done it. "The sheriff made it very clear that no one suspects you of anything. I was to protect you."

"From who? I can take care of myself."

Wade didn't know how to answer that. "The sheriff had a hunch. That's all. He's worried about Lonnie."

"Lonnie's in jail."

"I know."

They were both silent for a moment.

"I don't need anyone to follow me around," Jasmine repeated. "I'm trying to start a new life and be a regular person—"

Wade had the alarming feeling she might cry.

"Well, don't worry," he said. It was the only comfort he could offer. "I'm not doing it."

"I should hope not," Jasmine said, and that was the last conversation they had until she pointed out the turnoff to the sheriff's house.

Wade knew he was leaving tomorrow, but he didn't want anyone to be upset when he did. Especially not Jasmine. He'd been stealing glances at her all the way down those lonely roads. He had the shadow of her profile clearly in his mind. He told himself it was in case he ever needed to pick her out of a lineup, but that wasn't it. He stole another glance at her. He just wanted to remember her.

"If you ever get down around Idaho Falls, be sure and give me a call," he found himself saying. "We could maybe have dinner or—"

She turned to look at him indignantly. "You don't have to ask me out. Or follow me. Or anything."

"Okay, well—" Wade knew when to step away from the firing line.

"Thanks anyway," Jasmine said, none too politely. "It was kind of you to offer."

It was crazy of him to offer, Wade figured. But he'd done it anyway. He supposed it was just because, back in the kitchen, he'd felt some emotion stirring. It was probably all that talk reminding him he'd once been the angel. He'd put that experience completely out of his mind. Who wanted to remember the time they'd mortified themselves in front of everyone they knew? But maybe some vestige of it had clung to his soul anyway.

He pulled the car to a halt in front of the Walls' house. The windows were decorated with Christmas lights and tall wooden candy canes lined the path up to the front door. Light and laughter spilled out the windows.

Even when he'd been in the pageant, he'd dreaded Christmas. Wade wondered if he was ever going to be on the right side of the holiday. He glanced over at Jasmine. He wondered if she knew she had a frown on her face as she marched up the sidewalk to the house. Then he realized he had one, too.

At times like this he wished he had someone to arrest.

Chapter Four

Jasmine had lost what little Christmas cheer she had. She was sitting on the sofa in the Walls' living room with a glass of cold spiced cider in one hand and a piece of stuffed celery in the other. Carols were playing on the stereo system and she'd just let her misery overflow to Edith, the only other person in the room. The older woman was sitting next to her on a straight-backed oak chair.

"Oh, dear, no, we'd never pay someone to take you out," Edith protested.

"Not take me out," Jasmine corrected in the whisper she'd been using to tell the story. "Follow me around."

"Oh, Wade wouldn't do that. Goodness, no. You must have heard him wrong." Edith's short gray hair was tightly permed and her waves shook along with her head. She had a worried look on her kindly face and her white magnetic necklace hung above a red checked housedress in an attempt at seasonal fashion. "Besides, Wade isn't the man we have in mind for you anyway."

"You have someone in mind for me?" Jasmine looked around to be sure no one else had walked back into the living room. It sounded like they were all still in the kitchen putting the finishing touches on that coconut cake.

"Well, just Conrad. You know he's a sweet man. A little shy maybe, but… Of course, it's just a suggestion. For when you're ready to date."

"I don't need to date anyone," Jasmine said firmly. She supposed a husband like Conrad made sense given the fact that she wanted a regular life. But somehow the prospect seemed a little suffocating right now. Of course, he was a good mechanic. She liked that, but— "No one needs to worry about me. Maybe Wade can do whatever he's supposed to do with someone else."

"Yes, well, maybe. I thought he was going to help the sheriff, though," Edith conceded as she rubbed her hand around her wrist. "Maybe he could be a security guard at the barn now that we're setting up the stage. With the pageant being this Monday—"

"Do you want an aspirin?" Jasmine asked. Everyone knew the older woman suffered from arthritis on cold evenings. Her wrist must be hurting.

Edith shook her head. "I'll be fine. And don't

worry about Wade. I'm sure it's just a misunderstanding."

"He said he'd rather dig ditches than have anything to do with me." Jasmine didn't realize how peevish she sounded until she saw a spark of interest light up her friend's eyes.

"Not that I want him to," Jasmine added firmly. "He's just a test from God anyway."

Edith looked a little startled. "In what way?"

Jasmine wished she'd left that last part out. "Oh, you know, old feelings."

She'd already decided that, when she'd almost kissed him in her father's kitchen, it had just been because of the rush of adrenaline that had raced through her after the gunshots. It was a natural response. Guns always made her nervous these days. It had nothing to do with the way Wade's eyes made her feel. Or the way the line of his chin looked so strong. Or—

"I don't know that God sends us people as tests," Edith said gently, interrupting her thoughts.

They were silent for a moment, Jasmine taking a sip of her cider and Edith taking a drink from the glass of water by her side.

"I must admit Wade's a handsome man," Edith finally said. "I can see why you'd be interested."

"I'm not—"

Edith just kept going. "The problem is that he has it in his head he can't really trust anyone. He refuses to even have a partner on the job. Until he does, I can't see him being married. Not happily. And he doesn't have much use for God, either. I blame myself for that."

"You?" Jasmine set her glass of cider down. "How can it possibly be your fault?"

"I should have taken him to live with me and my husband. It wasn't good for him to rattle around in that house with his grandfather. The man wasn't even sober most of the time. He would have given the boy up for a case of cheap wine. I thought a couple of times of making him an offer, but I kept hoping things would get better. How could a boy, living with someone like that, trust anyone?"

"He looks like he turned out fine." Jasmine offered what comfort she could.

"Yes, in some ways," Edith said slowly. "Carl says he's got a spotless reputation. Determined and smart. He never bends the rules. Always by the book. Other lawmen look up to him."

Jasmine swallowed. She wondered why a man like that had been tempted to kiss her.

"He's a good boy," Edith finished. "Even if he hasn't answered the letter I wrote him about his grandfather."

"It sounds like Mr. Sutton cooked some grand meals in his time." Jasmine grabbed at a new topic like a lifeline. She'd been in the kitchen earlier when Barbara had been asking Wade about the cake his grandfather used to bake. The raspberry filling apparently had orange flavoring in it, too.

"That cake is the very reason I should have taken Wade in. I knew back then it was too good to be true."

Just then a burst of laughter came from the kitchen.

"Sounds like they're having fun," Jasmine said.

Edith nodded and started to stand up. "No point in us sitting out here when the excitement's in there."

Wade was holding the frosting spoon in his hand, feeling like a fraud. Carl's two kids had taken Charley outside to see their kittens and he and Carl were standing at the center counter in the kitchen. Two round circles of white cake sat on wire racks. A bowl of raspberries sat beside them.

Carl's petite, dark-haired wife, Barbara, said she'd followed Carl's crumpled up old recipe as best she could but that she had waited for Wade to get there to assemble the Christmas Fantasy Cake. He'd been dumbstruck that she'd baked it.

"You say your grandfather found the cake in a magazine?" Barbara was asking as she turned the bowl of icing slightly. She was standing at the side counter so she'd have room to move around the cake. "I hope that you don't mind that I named it. Did your grandfather call it anything special?"

"All I know is there was a picture of it in *Good Housekeeping.*" Wade remembered his mother's magazine like he'd been holding it yesterday. It was the one thing in the whole story that was true. He wondered how he was going to carefully unravel his lies without destroying Barbara's enthusiasm. "My grandfather really wasn't much of a cook."

"Well, maybe not every day, but on Christmas. Uhmmm," Carl said with a smile as he looked down at his Barbara with love in his eyes. "I used to spend half of Christmas thinking about Wade over there eating that cake. I wished my mother's fruitcake was half as good. And then I found you and you made the cake for us."

Carl gave his wife a quick kiss. "You're a great cook."

Wade felt hollow. "I may have exaggerated the cake back then."

"I wondered how you got the fresh raspberries for the filling," Barbara said with a smile. Her face was pink with pleasure from the kiss she'd received. "Carl insisted they had to be fresh, but all I could find was frozen."

Just then Edith and Jasmine walked into the kitchen.

Barbara turned to Edith. "Do raspberries grow wild around here at all? I know the chokecherries do and I've heard of some wild strawberries over by the Redfern place."

Wade knew he was in trouble. Edith had been inside his grandfather's house. The top of the stove had always been piled high with empty liquor bottles. She must know the stories of cake and turkey dinners had been false. His grandfather could barely make toast. Wade had lived on peanut butter sandwiches and the bruised apples his grandfather bought by the case from a wholesale place in Washington.

"I think raspberries always have to be tended," Edith said.

Wade didn't like standing there knowing she knew he was a fake. But, on the other hand, Barbara was looking proud and content in her ruffled white apron. The smell of the freshly baked cake was still in the air and the frosting was on the spoon she'd given him to taste.

Carl shook the jar of coconut. "Yeah, I always wondered about the fresh raspberries, too. How did your grandfather manage to get them?"

"This whole thing, well—it's—" Wade looked around. He couldn't find words to say what he needed to say so he compromised. "I hope you know how touched I am by this even though it's not really necessary. The truth is—"

Carl stopped him with a hand on his shoulder. "No need to thank us. Just thinking about your grandfather making this cake tells me he has a soft side. That's the first thing I thought of when Elmer called to say your grandfather was shooting at that cross. I said to myself that Clarence Sutton is a good man, deep down inside. I don't think we need to put him in jail—especially not with Christmas only a few days away."

"You don't?" Wade asked in surprise. "Because he'll do it again."

Carl shook his head. "Not if we arrange for him to be under house arrest. And we'll take away his gun. He should have someone checking in on him anyway."

"I don't—" Wade felt the weight of everything. Did he have an obligation? The man had chased him away with his shotgun over twenty-five years ago.

"Oh, not you," Carl said quickly. "We'll have to find someone. That's all."

Everyone was silent. Barbara went back to putting the raspberry filling on top of one of the white cake layers. Wade was trying to think of words to steer the conversation back to the confession he needed to make. It didn't help that Jasmine was there, staring at him like he'd done something wrong.

He was trying not to look at her, but he could see her out of the corner of his eye and he had to stop his head from moving in her direction. He wondered if she thought he had been taking advantage of the situation when he tried to kiss her. Of course, he had been—he'd been doomed to foolishness when he first looked in her eyes.

"Maybe the Covered Dish Ladies could check on Mr. Sutton," Edith finally said. "I mean, we need to go over there anyway—and we understand his problems."

Wade brought himself back to the present. What was she saying? As far as he knew, his grandfather didn't have any problems that required something as sensitive as understanding. Sympathy didn't do much for a drunk. Edith should know that.

"I can hardly deputize you," the sheriff said. "You're all ladies."

"We're not all ladies," Jasmine offered. "I could take a turn delivering something. He's just an old man. Besides, I'd know what to do if—if he started shooting."

"No," Wade said at the same time as the sheriff did.

"If I can't do it," the sheriff said as he handed the jar of coconut to his wife. "I'll ask one of the deputies to come down from Miles City tomorrow."

Wade felt low. He barely remembered the Covered Dish Ladies. They were some kind of woman's group at the church. He couldn't recall what they did, but he supposed they got together and made Christmas cookies or something for the baskets they handed out over the holidays. His grandfather must be on their list for sugar cookies. And, now the old man was on the sheriff's list for people who were more trouble than they were worth.

"It's kind of you to think of my grandfather," Wade finally said as he watched Barbara add the second layer of cake to the first. He wondered how much the Suttons owed their neighbors. He should have asked about his grandfather now and again over the years. It wouldn't have hurt him to send the old man a tin of cookies at Christmas, either. Maybe then he wouldn't need one of the church baskets. Of course, he'd still be shooting out those lights.

"I don't suppose Elmer could just take down his cross?" Wade asked.

"It's almost Christmas," Edith said, aghast. "We can't ask someone to take down their cross on the birthday of our Lord and Savior."

Wade nodded. He could see where this was going. "I know, a man has a right to display religious items on his own property, but—"

"Well, you can take away your grandfather's gun. That will solve it. He's caused enough trouble with that old thing. He shouldn't have it anymore anyway. Not in his condition," Edith added.

Wade couldn't argue with that. A drunkard had no business being armed. "He's probably just worried about coyotes getting to his livestock."

"The only animals he has left are a few chickens and that donkey of his," the sheriff said. "No coyotes will get inside the barn with that donkey there. She's mean enough to take care of a whole pack of them."

Wade felt his heart lift. "Jenny? He's still got Jenny?"

The sheriff nodded. "Don't ask me why. She bites anyone who goes near her."

Wade smiled.

"I forgot about the donkey," Edith said with a light in her eyes. "We still don't have one this year for the pageant. Maybe—"

"That thing bites," the sheriff reminded everyone.

"Not around Christmas," Wade said. She did throughout the rest of the year, but somehow Jenny seemed to know what time of the year it was. She'd even let him rub her ears while he hid out in the barn over the holiday.

"The cake's ready," Barbara said as she finished sprinkling coconut on top of the frosting. "When the kids and Charley get back, we'll be all ready to eat dinner."

Just then, Wade heard footsteps on the back steps leading to the kitchen door. Everyone had returned. Barbara started gesturing for everyone to go into the dining room.

An hour later, Jasmine put her knife across the top of her dinner plate. "Everything was delicious."

They were all gathered in the dining room.

They'd just eaten a roasted pork loin with sweet potatoes and glazed carrots. Barbara had made wheat dinner rolls and opened a small jar of rhubarb jam. It had been a feast.

"I haven't eaten food like that in a long time," Wade said from the other side of the table. "How'd you get everything to taste so good?"

Barbara smiled. "I was able to store the carrots and sweet potatoes from my garden. I think people can tell the difference between those and the ones I get in the store."

"Absolutely," Jasmine agreed as she looked around. If she didn't know better, she would think they were all posing for a Norman Rockwell painting. Everyone sat there with satisfied smiles on their faces and the empty serving platters in front of them showing what bounty they'd had to eat. Barbara had made a centerpiece of candles, pinecones and red berries. She'd even covered the table with an antique lace cloth.

This, Jasmine thought to herself, was what a holiday meal in a home should be like. She was learning to cook, but she realized that was only half of it. A family needed a home, too. She would find it easier to rebuild a tractor engine than to create a home like this. She didn't know what it was about her months in Dry Creek that made her long for a life like she saw in her friends here, but she wanted it badly.

Across the table, she saw Wade move slightly and she looked up at him.

"Oh." If she wasn't mistaken, she glimpsed the same longing in his eyes that she knew was in her own.

Wade gave her a little smile. "Beats frozen dinners, doesn't it?"

Jasmine nodded as her heart sank. A man like Wade would want home-cooked meals if he went to the trouble of getting married. She couldn't bake bread, either, she reminded herself. As for that cake their hostess was carrying to the table, it was pure fantasy to think she could ever do something like that.

The phone in the kitchen rang and the sheriff pushed back his chair.

"Our answer machine is broken," he said as he stood up. "But I'll ask them to call later so I'll be back before the cake's all dished up."

Jasmine watched as Barbara repeatedly slipped the knife into the cake. Then the woman lifted each slice up and slid it onto delicate china plates. The raspberry filling was so red it matched the berries in the centerpiece on the table.

Then the sheriff opened the door from the kitchen.

"Wade," he called. "Come here a minute."

Jasmine couldn't imagine what would require both men's attention when they'd been looking forward to the cake. Then she heard a single word before the sheriff completely closed the door behind them.

"Lonnie," the sheriff had said.

Jasmine looked around her. No one else seemed to react to the name. They must not know.

"Excuse me," she said as she stood. "I'll be right back."

Jasmine felt a tremor in her stomach. Something was wrong and she had a feeling it might be related to her.

Chapter Five

Jasmine put her shoulder to the kitchen door to push it open. She wondered if Lonnie had sent another postcard and the mailman was calling to warn the sheriff. It didn't seem likely the mailman would do that, but what else could it be? Maybe someone else had picked the postcard up from the counter in the hardware store and just now realized it?

"Excuse me, I—" Jasmine repeated as she opened the door.

The sheriff and Wade stopped talking and turned to look at her.

Jasmine stepped through the doorway and let the door close behind her. It was something worse than the postcard. She could tell because both men had changed from dinner companions to lawmen. They had that look in their eyes.

"I thought I heard you mention Lonnie," she said

quietly as she squared her shoulders. She wasn't afraid to face her past. She'd been such a confused young woman. All the men she'd ever known had been losers like her mother's boyfriends. Lonnie hadn't seemed too bad at the time. She'd spent years paying for her foolishness in following Lonnie around, and if she had to pay more she would. It just made her realize how much of a dream it was to think she could erase her past and have a normal life where she got married and grew a garden or made centerpieces out of pinecones. She wondered if women like Edith and Barbara knew how fortunate they were.

"Do you know what he has planned?" Wade spoke first, his voice hard.

"Lonnie?"

Wade nodded. "Is he coming here?"

"What do you mean? He's in prison."

The sheriff cleared his throat. Jasmine looked at him and saw the sympathy in his eyes. "Lonnie escaped a few hours ago. The prison officials saw the pamphlet you sent him in his cell and they remembered the call I'd made checking on him. It seems he marked up that pamphlet a fair amount. Especially the part about the streets of gold and the city on a hill with a cross."

"Lonnie escaped?" Jasmine felt dizzy. "How could that happen?"

"He had to have had outside help," Wade said.

His voice was even, but she could hear the condemnation in it.

It took her a moment to realize what he was thinking. "Well, it wasn't me. I was out there having dinner with all of you."

Wade nodded. "Which seems very convenient."

The counselors in prison had warned her that this might happen. She'd been prepared for people to look at her and only see her past. But that was before she'd found a place in Dry Creek. She'd let down her guard. No one here treated her like an ex-con. She'd become a child of God.

She looked at the sheriff. "Are you planning to arrest me?"

"Of course not," he said with an irritated glance over at Wade. "We just need to know if you can tell us anything about where Lonnie might go. I mean, he's been in jail for a long time. Why did he pick now to escape?"

Jasmine shrugged. "I have no idea. And I don't know where he'd go. Probably the closest place he could find to hide. He's not much of an outdoorsman, so I'd guess a big city. He likes to play pool and he does that to hustle up money when he's broke."

"I'll pass that along," the sheriff said. "In the meantime, we'll have to assign you some protection. Just in case he plans to head this way. The Feds will be here tomorrow to nose around, but in the meantime Wade will keep an eye on you."

A lump was starting to settle in her stomach. She looked up at Wade. "I don't want to put you out."

"No trouble," he said. He'd shaved since this morning, but his face was still grim. His jaw was tense. "I need to keep track of my grandfather now anyway. Since you're both out there, it'll be fine. I'll be around in case anyone stops by."

She wasn't fooled. Lawmen wouldn't be worried about Lonnie just coming by for a social visit. They'd be worried about her helping him. "Am I under house arrest, too?"

"I wouldn't call it that," the sheriff mumbled, but he looked embarrassed enough that she knew that's exactly what a judge would call it.

"Well." She turned to Wade and blinked. She willed herself not to cry. "I guess it's a good thing you're taking me home tonight, then. So you'll know exactly where I am. I suppose you'll want the keys to my motorcycle, too."

"It's for your own protection," the sheriff hurried to say.

Jasmine nodded. She felt real protected, all right.

They were quiet for a minute. Then the sheriff cleared his throat. "Barbara will be expecting us back for the cake."

No one moved.

"Are you going to tell them?" Jasmine asked,

keeping her voice cool. She hadn't realized how bad this situation would feel until the sheriff mentioned the cake. How could she face everyone if they knew what the two men suspected?

The sheriff looked over at Wade.

"I don't see any need to do that," Wade said. He paused and looked right at her. "This might all blow over and no one would ever need to know."

Was that pity she saw in his eyes, Jasmine wondered. She hadn't let one tear escape. He didn't need to feel sorry for her.

"It's just routine," Wade added as he ran his fingers over his hair. Then he looked down. "Policy."

Jasmine nodded. They might as well give her an orange jumpsuit and a number.

"You'll still be able to move around." Wade cleared his throat and looked back at her. "Anywhere local, that is. I can drive you."

"Escort you," the sheriff corrected the other man. "You'll be escorting Miss Hunter."

Wade gave her what would pass for a smile if a person didn't pay too much attention. "That's right. Just let me know if you need to leave your father's place."

Jasmine forced herself to look up at him. His green eyes had darkened. The friendliness he'd shown in her father's kitchen was gone.

"I need to go over to your grandfather's tomorrow morning for the Covered Dish thing," she finally said.

"Well, that's fine, too." Wade's voice was professional. "I'll be around to give you a lift."

Jasmine stopped herself from asking how he'd prevent it if she wanted to run away. With her motorcycle, she could drive across the fields and slip through a fence past the gully east of her father's farm. Wade wouldn't even see her if he was watching the lane or the main road. And, if he did see her, that bike of hers could go where his car couldn't. She would be riding free, just like she'd been when she rode into Dry Creek last fall.

She had a spare key for her bike and, for a moment, the thought of leaving was tempting. But where would she ever find a place like this again? She couldn't run and build a home for herself at the same time. She had a chance for a new life here. She had the church. She had friends. At least, she hoped she had friends. She didn't know what would happen when the suspicions spread. Would people here think she could help a criminal? Still be a criminal?

"Fine," she finally said. She never had been a coward. "I guess we should go have some of that cake."

Wade followed Jasmine and the sheriff back into the dining room. He wished he had never come back to Dry Creek. Or, if he had come back, he wished people hadn't been so kind to him. Barbara making that cake for him was putting him off his game. And then Jasmine—usually, he didn't have any trouble taking a tough line with a suspect. But then he'd never been tempted to kiss a suspect before.

He watched Jasmine's back as she walked to the table. She was ramrod straight and angry with him. He knew he'd come on too strong, but it was either that or forgetting everything he knew about law enforcement and refusing to believe she could be responsible for anything.

As a lawman he had to consider all of the possibilities and it was hard to forget that Lonnie had been her partner. She could have sent him a coded message that helped him escape in some way, or at least given him an incentive to risk everything to get outside. Those streets of gold bothered him. Were they planning another robbery? Even the roll of bills the sheriff was flashing around this morning would be enough to tempt most criminals.

He wished he knew how to look into the heart of a person so he would know what Jasmine was thinking. Was she as innocent as she looked or as guilty as she'd been the first time she was convicted of a crime? He knew better than most how many ex-cons fell back into theft. He was often the one who took them in the second time around and listened to their sorry excuses.

"I gave you the biggest piece of cake," Barbara said as he sat down at the table.

"Thank you," Wade smiled. It was the cake of his childhood fantasies and he was going to have to force himself to eat it. All he wanted to do was take Jasmine home and then park his car at the end of the lane of her father's place. Why did she have to be tied up with Lonnie? Why couldn't she be a nice, ordinary woman like Barbara here? Carl never had to worry about arresting her.

Wade felt the smoothness of the cake on his tongue and tasted the sweet tang of the raspberry filling. He smiled up at Barbara and thanked her again for the cake. The two kids at the table were smacking their lips and demanding more, just like Wade would be doing if he wasn't so troubled.

Then he looked down the table and saw his dear friend, Edith. She wouldn't be happy about him keeping an eye on anyone. It was clear the older woman was very fond of Jasmine. That, of course, was the problem with being a lawman and trying to have friends. He liked things black and white with no shades of gray. He didn't want to have feelings for the suspect.

By doing his job, he was going to upset Jasmine and everyone else in Dry Creek. For the first time since he'd driven into town, he missed the barren feel of his apartment in Idaho Falls. He knew who he was there.

It didn't take long for Wade to leave the Walls' house with Jasmine walking in front of him. The night was cold. Jasmine wrapped her arms around herself to keep warm and hurried to his car. He was still nursing that leg of his so he moved slower than she did. He made it in good time, though, and, as he opened the car door for her, she nodded her thanks and slid into the passenger seat.

The first thing Wade did after he got into the car was to move the dial up on the heater. Snow-flakes were just starting to fall, but they were scattered enough that he could clear them away with his windshield wipers.

He silently turned his car around and started down the sheriff's lane. The car lights shone on the falling snow, making the flakes look like pin-pricks in the darkness. The black shapes of trees lined the rutted lane. It reminded him of stars and that led to thinking about angels, or at least one particular angel.

"I suppose you have to practice for the pageant," Wade finally said when they turned onto the main gravel road. His passenger was squeezed so close to the other door that she would almost disappear in the shadows if it wasn't for her red hair.

"We do it during the Sunday school time," she mumbled without looking over at him. "I can't miss practice. The pageant is on Christmas Eve."

It was Friday night. If the pageant was on Christmas Eve, that meant it was Monday night. Three days away. A lot of escaped prisoners were caught within the first forty-eight hours. Hopefully, everything would be back to normal by the time of the performance since that big barn would be hard to secure at night.

"No one's suggesting that you miss anything." Wade tried to keep his voice friendly, hoping Jasmine would smile a little and ease the knot in his stomach.

Then, just like that, he knew what he could offer to her. "I'll be happy to help you practice for the pageant."

Even in the darkness, he could see her look over at him in surprise.

"You won't want to do the angel swing the way I did," he continued as he steered his car around a low point in the road. "But I can help with your flight angle and things. Some people end up hanging in the air like a sack of potatoes. You'll want to look like you're really flying."

"I changed my mind," Jasmine snapped back. She might be hiding in the shadows, but her voice was strong. "I don't need your help, after all."

The inside of the car was warm by now and Wade lowered the temperature dial. The snow had picked up speed and more flakes were flying.

Wade nodded and looked over at Jasmine. "That's

fair enough. It's been years since I was in the pageant anyway. They probably do it different now."

She was silent for a minute. "It's the same story as always."

"I suppose."

"Timeless," she added.

"No doubt."

She was quiet for a bit longer then she spoke. "Oh, all right, you can help."

Wade wanted to smile, but he didn't. "I don't want to put you out any."

Heavy, wet flakes gathered on his windshield and he started the wipers again.

"If you must know, I could really use the help," Jasmine finally admitted. "Edith has lots of suggestions, but she's never done the flight and I want it all to be spectacular."

"Who has been doing the part until you showed up?"

"They put the angel on hold years ago until they finished the new wheel and rope thing. As I understand it, they've just been using a broadcast system for the 'Fear not' speech. Apparently, it wasn't very effective."

"I wouldn't think it would be," he agreed. "The shepherds need some help in looking awestruck."

"I want them to look happy."

Wade shrugged. "That's one way to go."

He had to admit the young boys who played the

shepherd role were probably happier to see Jasmine as the angel than the shepherds had been when it was him in the role. He'd been only slightly older than most of them and they refused to gaze up at him in rapt adoration.

"What'd you do?" Jasmine asked.

Wade was glad he had her attention. "Trade secrets?"

He could see her nod.

"The only way I could think of to get the right expression on their faces was to throw dimes down on them," Wade admitted. "Everyone loves money and a dime bought a lot back then. I thought they'd look ecstatic."

"You did it when you were overhead?"

Wade shrugged. "I figured the dimes would sparkle on the way down and give a special effect. All their silver shiny surfaces."

Jasmine gave a small smile. "That's a great idea."

"I had the dimes in a bag attached to my leg," Wade explained. He was glad she was thawing. "I went over it a million times in my mind. But, when I was up there swinging, I had trouble getting the bag undone and—"

"Don't tell me you couldn't get it off your leg in time?"

"Worse. I got the bag untied from my leg, but it didn't open right and I was pulling on it in panic and—" He paused. "The bag fell on Alan Perkin's head and it had all those dimes in it. Almost made him pass out."

"Oh."

"It did make the shepherds look up into the sky with fear on their faces, though," Wade said as he heard her chuckle. "And Alan got to keep the dimes so he was okay with it. His mom was mad, but he wanted to get hit again. He was saving up for a new bike."

She was grinning now. "I've been thinking of using a couple of those Fourth of July sparklers. I figure if I tie them to my feet, they'll trail behind me."

Wade knew he had met his match. "They'd look like little stars."

"Exactly," Jasmine said with enthusiasm. "A whole galaxy of them."

Wade nodded. "Just be sure you have the paramedics there. I wish I'd thought that far ahead with Alan."

Jasmine was silent for a bit. "But Dry Creek doesn't have any paramedics. Charley works as a vet some, but—"

"The sheriff can get a paramedic unit to come down from Miles City if we need one. He's entitled to some of the county budget on that." Wade figured the sheriff owned him one. "Maybe he should put the fire department on call, too."

Jasmine looked at him closely. "You're joking, right?"

Wade smiled. "All I can tell you is that I messed the whole angel thing up so bad that folks probably were thinking of calling out the National Guard. Alan was down there, almost passed out on the floor, and the other guys were scrambling around trying to get the dimes. And me, up there knowing I only had one chance at it. I gave a blood-curdling Tarzan yell and swung on that rope like a monkey in the jungle."

"Wow," Jasmine said.

"No one was even looking at the baby Jesus," Wade said. "And people cleared out of the barn before the kids had a chance to sing 'Silent Night.'"

"We're singing that, too."

"I think they sing it every year. It's the last thing as the shepherds and the wise men are looking down at the baby."

Wade turned the car into the lane of Elmer's place. He was glad Jasmine had loosened up around him. It didn't make her more or less guilty, but he felt better knowing she wasn't all knotted up inside. He told himself he would have put as much effort into seeing that any prisoner was at ease, but he knew it wasn't true. Usually, he didn't even talk as he brought someone in. He certainly didn't care if they were in any emotional distress. They were the bad guys; they deserved to suffer.

Wade was parking the car by the house when Jasmine turned to him.

"You're going to want to tell the Feds about my father's cars," she said to him. "He's got about four classics inside the barn that are worth big bucks. There's the Cadillac, a Bentley and a couple of early Fords."

Wade looked toward the big shape to his left. In the night, the barn looked black. "When you say big bucks—"

"I mean, they're worth stealing. I've started helping him restore them, but there's not as much work as I thought there'd be. He's kept them in mint condition. They're almost collection ready. I'd guess he could get a couple of hundred thousand for the lot of them."

Wade shut off the ignition. He'd never had a suspect confess before any crime had been committed. He didn't want Jasmine to put herself in jeopardy, though. "I'll mention it to the Feds, but I won't tell them you know how much the cars are worth."

Jasmine shrugged. "There's no reason for me to steal them anyway."

"It would be theft if you cheated him out of them, too."

"That's not what I meant," she said as she crossed her arms. "My father has offered me the cars repeatedly. He's put me in the will to get everything he owns if he dies. He'd like nothing better than for me to take his beloved cars."

Wade had indigestion. He hadn't even considered how much Elmer had that would pass to his natural daughter, especially if he assigned everything to her in his will. His farmland would be worth a few hundred thousand dollars, too. The streets of gold ended right in the middle of the old man's driveway. Wade hadn't even considered a potential murder in all of this.

"Does Lonnie know about your father?" Wade asked quietly.

Jasmine shook her head and then thought a minute. "Well, he might have known the three names I came to investigate. My mother didn't talk about her affairs. I didn't even know which one of the three men was my father when I knew Lonnie. But my mother had a box of journals and he might have read them. That's where I found the name of Edith's late husband and decided he was my father. But the other two names were there, as well. I didn't even know then who my real father was."

Wade nodded. With the help of the internet, Lonnie could have found out that Elmer was the only one of the three who was alive.

"You don't think Lonnie would do something to my father, do you?" Jasmine asked. She looked up at him with eyes full of worry. "Lonnie's not very stable. I wouldn't want anyone around here to be hurt by him."

Wade shrugged. "With all you'd inherit if Elmer were out of the picture—"

Jasmine gasped. "I don't care about the money."

"Lonnie might."

That turned her quiet. He didn't want her to worry.

"He won't even have the chance to get close to anyone," Wade assured her. "We'll have the Feds all over the place by tomorrow. Lonnie has a better chance of breaking into Fort Knox than he has of sneaking into Dry Creek."

Wade hoped he wasn't lying. He had no idea what the Feds would do. And, they might have some completely different theories as to why Lonnie had broken out of prison. It might have nothing at all to do with Jasmine or anyone in Dry Creek.

"You'll be safe," Wade said as he opened his door.

He walked around to the passenger door and opened it. Jasmine stepped out of the car just as he realized he'd left her alone in the car with a loaded gun in the glove compartment.

Wade stood by the open car door and watched as Jasmine pulled her coat closer to her body. She wasn't making any move to walk toward the house and he wasn't making any move to let her. Finally, Wade reached up and touched her cheek. It was soft and a little damp. She must have been crying when she'd been huddled against the door on the drive out here.

"It'll be okay," he whispered to her as he brought his hand down.

"I'm fine," she said.

He nodded with a slight smile. "I know."

Wade had never kissed a suspect, but he would do it now if he didn't think it would make Jasmine cry even more. She was barely hanging on and he needed to leave her with her dignity.

"I'll be parked at the end of Elmer's lane if you need me," Wade said as he stepped back from the door. Snow was falling in earnest now, but he had a heavy sleeping bag in his trunk that he used on stakeouts like this. "I'll come to the door in the morning, before I go over to my grandfather's."

"You can't sleep outside all night. It's freezing out here. I'll leave the kitchen door unlocked if you need to come inside."

"Don't leave anything unlocked. I'll duck into the barn if I need to."

Jasmine nodded.

Wade watched her walk to the kitchen door and go inside the house. Only then did he head back to the driver's door. He wondered if he'd get any sleep tonight. The next thing he knew he was going to be offering pillows to everyone he arrested and wishing them sweet dreams. When had he turned into a soft touch?

He waited for the light to go out in the kitchen before he started his drive down the lane. He already felt lonely.

Chapter Six

Jasmine stood on the cold wood floor of her bedroom and shivered as she buttoned up her bright yellow blouse. It was six o'clock and the gray morning light was just starting to seep through the blinds.

She'd stood at her closet door for a few minutes before deciding she needed something more powerful than the washed-out colors she'd worn lately. She'd been trying to blend in with the other women in Dry Creek, but the discouraging fact was that she was different. She couldn't be like the other women. Once an ex-con, always an ex-con. From now on she was wearing her boots.

She wasn't going to let Wade get her down, either. He might suspect she was planning the crime of the century. He might even think she was foolish enough to help Lonnie escape from the cell where he belonged. But he couldn't prove anything because it wasn't true. If she had to, she'd fight to clear her name of any suspicion.

After all, she was going to be the angel on Christmas Eve and she wanted people to watch her with a clear mind instead of worrying that she was going to steal their watches the minute their heads were bowed in prayer. Not that they would even think such a thing if Wade weren't around to spread rumors.

In her indignation, she wrestled a little too much with her buttons and tore one of them off her blouse. She went ahead and pinned the gap it left, but it looked kind of puckered so she put on her loose gray sweater so the blouse wouldn't show so much.

She looked odd when she saw herself in the mirror, but she defiantly went downstairs to the kitchen anyway. The day would have to take her as she was; she was tired of trying to change to please other people.

Ten minutes later, Wade was knocking at the back door. She knew it was him because she'd looked out the kitchen window earlier and watched his car slowly coming up the lane. It had snowed during the night and everything was white outside. Her father was in the barn doing his morning chores so she figured it was as good a time as any for Wade to appear. She hadn't figured out how to tell her father that she was being watched so she hoped Wade didn't come to the door with handcuffs or anything like that.

She was cooking and decided to strain the water from her pan of noodles before she made any move to answer the door. Wade could wait. She was getting ready to sprinkle the packet of dry cheese so she didn't want the noodles to sit in the water when they didn't have to. She wasn't much of a cook, but she had heard that most people let their pasta boil too long. She wasn't sure the noodles in the box of macaroni and cheese were that sensitive, but she was determined to do her best.

Besides, Wade was only here to stop her from breaking any laws, she told herself as she walked over to let him in.

"Cooking yourself breakfast?" Wade asked when she opened the door.

"Not yet." For the first time, Jasmine realized how much steam had been caused by boiling water for the noodles. The air coming in from the outside was frigid and immediately everything felt moist, even her face.

Wade's face went from white to pink as the damp air settled over him. His hat had a dusting of snow on it and his coat collar was turned up to protect his neck.

She stepped aside so he could enter. "Cold out there?"

"I'm an icicle," Wade said as he stepped inside

to the mat. He turned and closed the door behind him. Then he pulled his gloves off and started to rub his hands. "I thought my nose would freeze."

"Well, you could have come and knocked on the door," she scolded before realizing that, of course, he wouldn't. "I guess it would have compromised your honor, or whatever it is you lawmen have."

He took his hat off. "I didn't want to trouble you."

If he didn't want to trouble her, he shouldn't look the way he did. The cold made his jaw stand out more than normal. He needed a shave and his eyes were bloodshot. But, even with all that, he looked like a young boy just in from a snowball fight. It was clear he'd enjoyed being out in the cold. He wiped away the few flakes of snow still on his face but, when he'd done all that, he smiled.

"I'm going to fix some coffee soon." She would have offered to fix him a banquet if she had known how his eyes would light up. "You'll be welcome to some."

"Sounds great."

She nodded. Nobody could make better coffee than her, even if everything else was up for grabs.

"It'll be a few minutes," Jasmine said as she turned to walk back to the stove. "I'm in the middle of baking something."

That might have been too optimistic of a statement, but she let it stand.

It wasn't until Jasmine got back to the stove that

she realized she'd be more comfortable if Wade wasn't there to watch her make her version of macaroni and cheese. Especially because the cooked noodles had turned hard and crusty in the few minutes that she'd left them uncovered. And the dry cheese mixture looked like sawdust as she tried to stir it in.

"Smells good," Wade said from where he patiently stood by the door. He had his hat in his hands as snow melted off his boots onto the mat.

She looked over at him. "You can't possibly smell anything. Besides, the noodles are stuck to the bottom."

She took the pan off the stove and tilted it so she could scrape it better. "I don't know what's wrong."

That statement pretty much summed up her life of late, she thought. Everything was supposed to be getting better since she'd become a Christian. Instead, it felt like it was going backward. She couldn't believe someone standing right here in her kitchen thought she might still be a criminal.

She set the pan back down on the stove in defeat.

"Try adding some boiling water," Wade said, and then he hesitated. "Not that I'm any expert on cooking. Usually—"

"I know. Usually, its women that are supposed to be the experts," she snapped back at him. "But not all women know how to cook. It's not something that we're born knowing. Some of us have outside lives, too."

She shouldn't have to spell out that her outside life had been lived behind walls for the past few years.

He looked at her cautiously. "I was going to say I usually eat out."

"Oh. Well."

"I only mentioned the boiling water because I know it sometimes works with things that are glued together. Not that I think your noodles are glued. I'm sure they're good."

Jasmine nodded. "Thanks."

She kept her head down and her hands moving. She really should have made her coffee before she started on the casserole for Wade's grandfather. It seemed she was a little irritable without her cup of brew. Of course, she did have some extra stress. She was the newest member of the Covered Dish group at church and this was the first dish she'd made for anyone. If she hadn't been determined to join every single group the church had, she wouldn't be part of this one anyway.

"If all else fails, you're welcome to the crackers I have in my trunk," Wade said. "They're better with butter, but—"

Somehow, in the time she'd been looking down at the mess of noodles, Wade had moved closer. He'd taken his boots off and left them by the door. He wore thick gray stockings and one of them was unraveling around the big toe.

"Butter. That's what I need," she said as she looked up. "That's what I forgot—that and the milk. It doesn't take much, but it makes the cheese work."

Jasmine set the pan back on the stove. The refrigerator was just five steps away, but she was feeling a little flustered and couldn't seem to move. "Do you always loom over your prisoners like this?"

Wade was standing so close she could count the whiskers on his chin. He stepped back in surprise. "You're not my prisoner. I'm protecting you."

She stepped to the refrigerator and opened the door. "I don't think anyone camps out in freezing temperatures because they're protecting someone."

"I do," he said quietly.

"Yeah, well," she muttered as she grabbed a cube of butter and the carton of milk. "Lonnie isn't coming here. He doesn't even know how to get here." She saw the doubt race across his face. "I know I could have told him how to find me, but I didn't. You're just going to have to trust me on that."

She wasn't looking at him, but she knew if she looked up she would see an expression of incredulity on his face. A lawman could never trust an ex-con, not entirely. She turned to the stove so she wouldn't have any chance of seeing him. "Now, if you'll excuse me, I have some cooking to do."

She was glad he didn't say anything.

Even though he wasn't wearing his boots, she

could hear him slowly walk over to the table and sit down in one of the chairs.

"That leg of yours bothering you?" she asked.

"Not too bad," he said. "I was able to stretch out in the car."

"I'll get to that coffee in a second." She felt a little bad about snapping at him earlier. Even if he didn't need to guard her lane, he'd been uncomfortable doing it.

"Don't worry about me."

"I'm not worried." She looked up and there he was waiting patiently again. "I'm just being hospitable."

He smiled then. A long, lazy smile that made the morning feel warmer even though the sky outside was still gray. "Actually, I thought maybe I could take you to breakfast at the café instead. After we go over and check on my grandfather."

Jasmine felt her spirits rise.

Then he added. "I need to meet up with the Feds anyway and I can't leave you out here alone until we figure out what's going on."

"Oh," she said as she dumped the macaroni and cheese into a small glass dish. So, that was it. "I wouldn't be alone. My father is here."

"I forgot about Elmer," Wade said with a frown. "He'll have to come with us, too. I can't leave him out here alone, either."

Jasmine put the lid on the dish and squared her

shoulders. "He usually goes into Dry Creek when he finishes his chores anyway. He sits in the hardware store with the other guys and drinks his coffee while they all sit around that old woodstove. On a day like today, they'll stay there until noon."

"That sounds safe enough."

"We may as well leave then," Jasmine said.

She had to walk out to the barn, of course, to tell her father that she was going over to the Sutton place with Wade and then into Dry Creek. And Wade had to walk with her because he considered it his duty. At least he didn't say anything.

"You and Wade?" her father had asked when she stepped inside the barn and relayed her message. Fortunately, the man in question was giving her some room and was standing a few yards outside the barn door.

"It's just—" Jasmine started, and then trailed off.

"You don't need to explain," her father said as he grinned. "I know you young people like to spend time getting to know each other."

"It's not like that," Jasmine said in dismay. "We don't want to know each other."

Her father chuckled. "I remember when I was courting. No man comes out this early in the morning—after driving you to dinner the night before—unless he's got courting on his mind. Especially not in the snow."

"Trust me. Wade Sutton is not dating me," she said. "And I think he likes the snow."

Her father just kept smiling. "Wait until Charley hears this. He'll have to put a bug in his nephew's ear if he hopes to step up to the plate."

"Conrad's my boss," Jasmine protested. "You can't say anything like that."

She wondered when the people of Dry Creek decided she was fated to be with Conrad.

"Why? Lots of women marry their bosses."

"I don't," Jasmine said firmly. She hadn't thought any more about it since Edith had mentioned it, but she just didn't think Conrad was meant for her. Oh, he was nice enough—really nice, actually—and… The thought struck her out of nowhere and almost brought her to her knees. She thought Conrad was too nice for her. That couldn't be good, could it? Shouldn't she want to marry the nicest man in the world?

"It wouldn't do any harm for your young man out there to think you might be interested in Conrad, though," her father said as he walked closer to the barn door and peered out. "Men like a little competition."

Wade certainly wasn't the nicest man in the world. He was opinionated and exasperating and distrustful. Besides, she'd promised herself long ago she'd never become involved with a man who

used a gun again, no matter which side of the law
he was on.

"This is not a competition. Besides—" Jasmine
started, but her father stepped out the door and away
from her.

Oh, dear, as if she didn't have enough on her
mind, she was going to have to go out there and
make sure her father didn't embarrass her completely. She waited a minute first on the off chance
that her father would come to his senses and return
before she had to look like a fool racing after him.
She already looked incompetent in front of Wade
and she didn't want to add to the list he was probably keeping of her shortcomings.

Chapter Seven

Wade noticed that the Maynard barn needed a new coat of paint. And there were a few dead weeds gathered against its foundation. It wasn't the first time since he'd been back in this area that he had seen there was a lot of work to be done. The people here were getting old. And not enough men of his age were here to do the hard, physical work of farming.

The fields behind the barn didn't look like they'd been planted last year, either. He never drove anywhere in Idaho or Montana without noticing the fields at the sides of the road. Before his grandfather had run him and his father off the family farm, Wade had expected to live his life right there. He'd always liked to watch crops grow. Even now he missed the itch from the wheat shaft on his skin when harvest was in full swing.

Wade looked up when he saw Elmer walking out of the barn with a big grin on his face.

"Morning," the older man said. "It's good to see you up and around so early."

"Well, I just—" Wade started to explain.

"Don't say anything," Elmer interrupted him. "Jasmine told me all about it."

"She did?" Wade didn't know whether to be relieved or annoyed. It was rightly his job to tell Elmer about Lonnie escaping from jail. But if Jasmine had already done it, so be it. "I don't want you to worry. I've got it all under control."

Jasmine was walking toward them, her arms swinging in that way he'd first noticed out the café window. He wondered what was bothering her now. He couldn't help but wish she was still wearing a dress instead of her jeans and that heavy gray sweater that hung halfway to her knees. There was just something about the sway of a skirt when a woman walked like she did.

Elmer grunted as he looked over his shoulder at his approaching daughter. "A man always thinks that he's got it under control, but sometimes there's more going on than meets the eyes."

"Don't listen to him," Jasmine said when she reached them. Her auburn hair was sticking up here and there and white puffs of air came out of her mouth when she spoke. He was surprised he hadn't noticed the generous curve of her mouth before; he could look at her all day. He forced himself to pay close attention as she continued. "Conrad is only my boss. All he cares about is whether or not I can get that combine engine fixed before it's time to harvest next year. It's in an 8780 and some widow up by Miles City is relying on it—"

"You're working on a *combine engine?*" Wade was stunned. And impressed. When people had said she worked in Conrad's mechanic shop, he thought she was the secretary or the bookkeeper.

"It's only temporary," Elmer jumped in, speaking quickly. "Until she gets married and settles down. And Conrad—"

Wade got it now. "I understand everyone wants her to marry this Conrad fellow. You don't need to worry. I should be finished with her before Christmas."

Elmer's mouth hung open. "Just like that."

"It's okay," Jasmine said as she took Elmer's arm. "It's not what you're thinking—"

"In my day, we did things differently," Elmer said with enough bluster in his voice to wake any chickens that were roosting on the place. "Men treated women with respect and—" All of a sudden he got a strange expression on his face and looked at Jasmine. "I never thought with your mother. I mean, I couldn't marry her because I was—I never thought—and then she had you and I didn't know—"

Elmer finally gave up and hung his head.

Wade felt like he should give the two some privacy, but he was rooted to the ground.

Jasmine gently put her hand on Elmer's shoulder. "My mother didn't have any hard feelings about you. At least, she never mentioned any."

Elmer looked up. "She'd have a thing or two to say to me if I didn't see you were respected, though. That's all I can do now to make up for any of it."

Then Elmer turned to glare at Wade. "You break my daughter's heart and I'll make you wish you hadn't. I don't care what kind of lawman you are."

Wade felt warm inside even though it was freezing outside. Elmer thought he had a chance. "I won't break anyone's heart."

He heard Jasmine draw in her breath as if she was going to say something, but he never dreamed she'd be so upset at what Elmer was thinking that she'd tell the truth.

"Wade has me under arrest," she said. Her voice was clipped and empty of emotion. "There's nothing else going on here."

"What?" Elmer's eyes were starting to bulge.

Wade wondered if the older man was going to have a stroke.

"Now, that's not right," Wade said. "Protective custody would be a better way to say it."

"I don't care how you say it." Elmer found his

voice. "This is still my land and you're not welcome here. I'll thank you to leave."

Wade nodded. He knew how Elmer felt. "It's for her own good. Her old partner escaped from jail and there's reason to believe he might come here."

"That no-account Lonnie?" Elmer asked. "How'd he get out of jail?"

"We don't know," Wade answered.

"They think I might have helped," Jasmine said quietly from where she stood beside Elmer.

"Well, that's nonsense," Elmer said as he turned to her. "Why would you help him? He's the one who got you locked up to begin with."

Jasmine smiled. "No, I'm the one who got me locked up. But, you're right, I have no reason to help Lonnie."

Elmer looked over at Wade before turning back to his daughter. "Well, I suppose he better stay around in case you need help, then. At least he has a gun."

"I'll do my best to protect you both," Wade promised.

Elmer grunted. "I can take care of myself. You worry about Jasmine."

Wade nodded. He understood how the man felt. "We don't even know if Lonnie is headed this way. Jasmine and I going into Dry Creek after we check on my grandfather. We need to meet up with the Feds and we may as well do it there."

Wade had his day planned out. He looked over at Jasmine. "Ready to go?"

She nodded and they walked toward his car.

Wade wished Jasmine would talk to him as they drove over to his grandfather's place. But she just sat there with her glass dish clutched in her hand. He didn't quite understand why she was taking her macaroni and cheese over to his grandfather, but he knew it had something to do with that Covered Dish group at church. Maybe they were trying to get the old man to eat his lunch instead of drink it.

The wooden gate that marked the entrance to his grandfather's farm was hanging crookedly from its hinges. The boards themselves were a weathered gray and splintered so badly they didn't look like they'd last much longer. Deep ruts in the lane spoke of neglect. No one had grated the road in decades. Beside the road, dead grass was rotting under the damp snow.

Wade slowed his car as he drove toward the house. He told himself he was giving his grandfather time to realize he had company coming, but he wasn't so sure he could have driven faster anyway.

The fields beside the lane hadn't been plowed in years. He looked farther out and saw the far field didn't look tended, either. With the proper care, a good crop always grew in that field, even when water was short. He wondered if his grandfather was farming at all. He could have at least leased the land on shares to someone.

"You need to park by the old pickup," Jasmine said as he got closer to the house. "That's as far as we can go."

"What are you talking about?" He turned to look at her.

"The Covered Dish group," she said. "That's as far as we're allowed to go. Edith got your grandfather to agree to that much. We just leave the food in the pickup and he comes and gets it."

"You mean, you do this often?" Wade was stunned. It wasn't just something for Christmas?

"Every other day," Jasmine said with a matter-of-fact nod. "We would do it every day, but Edith said we shouldn't push him."

"You shouldn't have to feed him," Wade said as he stopped his car beside the pickup. He looked around. The house looked almost deserted. There were no curtains on the windows and the paint was chipped off so much that the yellow boards had turned a sickly beige.

What had happened? His grandfather should be prosperous. He'd have his social security payments by now and he'd always talked about his investments. Was he just so drunk that he didn't care?

A figure moved in one of the windows and Wade's stomach clenched. His grandfather had seen them. Wade had to remind himself that he wasn't a boy any longer; he didn't have to worry about taking a beating from the old man inside the house.

Still, Wade thought as he looked over at Jasmine, it wasn't only his grandfather's fists that could be unpleasant. The old man had a tongue on him that was just as bad.

"Why don't you stay in the car here?" Wade said, trying to keep his voice casual. "Let me check on my grandfather and let him know I'll be keeping an eye on him and that shotgun of his."

Jasmine looked up at him and then nodded. "I'm sure you'd like some privacy."

Wade grunted. He wasn't expecting any heart-warming scene inside that house if that's what she meant. "I shouldn't be long."

Wade opened his car door.

"I'll pray for you," Jasmine said just as he started to close it.

That stopped him in midmotion. He bent down and looked inside his car at her. "Don't waste your breath. My grandfather is beyond all that."

Jasmine shrugged. "So was I. But Edith prayed for me anyway."

Wade knew better than to argue with her on this. "Well, do what you want. Just don't expect anything to happen because of it."

Wade stepped back and shut the door before she could say anything else. He knew better than most that God didn't answer people's prayers. He couldn't count the number of times he'd lain in bed at his grandfather's house and prayed for his father to return from prison or his mother to be raised from the dead. By then he knew God had done things like that before. He'd learned about it in Sunday school.

He shook his head. Sunday school just didn't match up with real life.

Wade forced himself to knock on his grandfather's door. He wondered if the old man would even recognize him after all of these years. It might be best for them both if he didn't.

Wade had to wait for the door to open. He could hear the locks being pulled so he stood there and reminded himself he was an officer of the law. Sort of. He and the sheriff didn't have a formal agreement on this, but—

The door opened a crack.

"What d'ya want?" an old man's voice asked.

Wade tried to see inside, but all that was visible was an inch of face with one suspicious bloodshot eye squinting out at him.

"I've come back to—" Wade started to speak when the door opened fully and he stopped.

There was his grandfather. He used to be a giant of a man, but he had shrunk and he seemed to be mostly bone. His hair was almost gone and, what was left of it, was hanging in uneven strands. He was wearing a dingy T-shirt that used to be white and baggy jeans that were held in place by worn black suspenders.

"Sonny? Is that you?"

Wade's heart sank. What was wrong with the old man?

"It *is* you," his grandfather said with joy on his face. "I knew you'd come back someday."

Wade couldn't take it any longer. "Sonny's dead. Remember he died in a shoot-out with the cops. Sonny was my father. I'm Wade."

It was silent on the porch.

Finally, his grandfather looked up at him in puzzlement. "That can't be right. You have to be Sonny. That nice woman you married is out in the car right now. I can see her. Don't know what I'd do without her. I knew you'd come back to see her, even if you didn't want to see me."

Wade stared at his grandfather. He knew the man wasn't joking; he didn't have a sense of humor. "Have you seen a doctor lately?"

"I don't need a doctor." His grandfather reared back and shouted. "I'm as healthy as a horse."

Wade heard a car door shut behind him and he looked around. Jasmine had gotten out of the car. She probably had heard the yell if nothing more.

"Do you need help?" she called.

"I don't know," he answered back as she kept walking forward.

"Have her come in," his grandfather said as

he turned to go inside the house. "I haven't had a chance to visit with your wife for some time now."

"She's not—" Wade said as he followed his grandfather inside. Then he decided that was the least of the old man's worries. He glanced back and saw Jasmine still coming. He'd have to find a moment to clue her in to his grandfather's craziness.

When he turned around, he saw the kitchen counter.

"What in the world?" Wade couldn't believe it. Dozens of casserole dishes were spread all over the counter. Some yellow glass ones. A couple of metal ones. A few black ceramic ones. Red ones. Blue ones. "There must be twenty, maybe thirty, dishes here."

"Edith comes by and picks them up now and again," his grandfather said. "She'll be by soon. I wash them up for her."

Wade was relieved to see, as he stepped closer, that the dishes were at least all clean.

"She must take them to that wife of yours and she fills them up again," his grandfather said with a frown on his face. "I've never figured out that part of it."

"It's the women at the church," Wade said. "They're the ones who bring you the food."

His grandfather looked at him as if he was trying to remember something. "I don't think that could be right. I didn't figure anyone but your wife would do it anyway. She likes me okay, you know?"

Wade nodded. He did remember a time as a young child when his mother had been alive and this house had been happy. Maybe his mother had liked her father-in-law. The old man hadn't been drinking as much back then so he was probably easier to be around.

He looked over at his grandfather and saw him looking up quizzically.

"You should be nice to that wife of yours, son," he said. "She's what keeps this family together."

Wade nodded. He could hear Jasmine on the steps now. Somewhere inside him was a faint hope she would know what he needed to do. He had no idea his grandfather was this bad off. The old man obviously shouldn't be living out here by himself. He wouldn't fare well in one of those nursing homes, though. And, the idea of bringing his grandfather to his apartment in Idaho Falls was ludicrous, of course. What he needed to do was to find someone he could hire to move in and take care of his grandfather.

"Jasmine," Wade greeted her as she walked through the door into the kitchen.

"That's not her name," his grandfather said with a frown. "What is it? Patricia? No, Maria? It was something with an *a* at the end and it was a pretty name."

"Annabelle," Wade finally said. "Her name was Annabelle."

"That's right," his grandfather said in relief. "I knew it was on the tip of my tongue."

Wade nodded as he watched Jasmine look at them in bewilderment. He didn't even know how to explain to her that his confused grandfather was living in a world that had been gone for over thirty years.

Chapter Eight

Jasmine couldn't believe Mr. Sutton was smiling at her. Everything she had ever heard about the man led her to believe he'd greet her at the door with a shotgun instead of an invitation to come in and sit down.

"It's so nice to meet you," Jasmine said as she stepped farther into the kitchen.

The old man began to chuckle. "Why you've known me for years."

The day was gray outside and the house was filled with shadows even though there were no curtains on the windows. She had to let her eyes adjust to the darkness. Then she looked up at Wade to see if he knew what his grandfather was talking about.

"My grandfather thinks you're my mother," Wade quietly said as he stepped closer so only she could hear.

"What?" Jasmine put her hands up to her hair. She might not look her best, but—

"And he thinks I am my father," Wade continued.

"Oh." Jasmine was silent for a moment. "That's why he's so friendly."

"Apparently," Wade said grimly. "He's discovered a love for his family at last."

Jasmine could feel the tension in Wade. She supposed he was disappointed that his grandfather didn't recognize him. She'd never had a grandparent, but she knew some children grew attached to them. And, of course, Wade had been raised by his.

"I'm sorry," she said.

Wade turned to his grandfather and raised his voice. "We need to be going. But I'll come back in a few hours."

"With your wife?" his grandfather asked.

"No, she won't be back."

Jasmine didn't like the disappointment she saw in the old man's eyes. She could visit again, but she didn't get her mouth opened soon enough to say so.

"But she has to come back," Wade's grandfather said, looking a little frantic. "This is her home. It's my fault, I suppose. I should have made you pay more attention to her. I'm your father. I knew it was important."

"It's okay," Wade said as he reached a hand out to put on his grandfather's arm.

"No, it's not okay," his grandfather thundered as he shook the hand off.

Jasmine stepped back. Now, this is the man she'd expected to meet when she walked up to the door of this house. Even in his sagging suspenders, the old man looked fierce.

"She doesn't care—" Wade started to say.

The old man glared at him. "Right here and now. I want you to kiss your wife and tell her that you have feelings for her. If I had made you do that more often, everything would be different."

"It's okay," Jasmine said as she made fluttery motions to the old man. "I'm fine. Really."

"Now, son," the old man said, his voice just as firm as it had been. "Do it now."

"No, I—" Jasmine looked up and saw that Wade had taken another step toward her.

"It's easier," Wade said softly as he bent his head to hers.

No, it wasn't easier, Jasmine thought as she felt his lips on hers. It was just as she had feared. Her heart started to beat faster. Her mind forgot to worry. Everything in her focused on the man kissing her. The man who didn't trust her. The man who—oh, my, she felt as if she was floating.

Everything was in slow motion, but she did her best to pull away from Wade. And then she noticed he looked a little stunned himself. His eyes held hers and wouldn't let go. So she stayed where she was, close enough that she could feel his breath on her face.

"I need to—" She started to say something and then forgot the excuse she'd been going to offer for moving away.

"I know," Wade answered anyway.

"Well, isn't that nice," the old man said in satisfaction as his gaze moved between the two of them. "I can see you're reminded of just how much you love each other."

That made Wade break away. "We're not—"

Jasmine stepped farther away, too. "We certainly are not— I'd never—"

"We need to leave," Wade finally said and he grabbed Jasmine's hand and guided her out of his grandfather's house.

The day hadn't gotten any warmer when they were in the Sutton house, but Jasmine was ready to fan her face even though it was forty degrees outside. What did she think she was doing, kissing a lawman that had more suspicions than he had feelings toward her?

"I'm sorry about that," Wade said as he walked beside her to his car. "I didn't know what else to do and—"

His excuse trailed off.

She turned to him. "Edith will want those dishes back. I'm sure some women in the church are running out of baking pans completely."

There, she thought to herself as she opened the
car door before he could reach for the handle. She
wasn't about to let him know she'd been affected by
that kiss, not when it had just been the easy way out
for him. She watched him as he walked around the
car to the driver's seat. She hoped his leg hurt him.

"I don't know how I'm going to thank everyone,"
Wade said when he slid into the driver's seat.

He sounded so miserable, Jasmine's heart softened. "Just the words would do."

Wade shook his head. "I didn't expect other
people to take care of my grandfather. I honestly
thought he was okay. Oh, I figured he was probably
ornery as always. But I never dreamed he needed
so much help. He probably would have stayed in
that house and starved to death if it weren't for the
church."

"Well, Edith does keep an eye on him. I thought
she wrote you a letter a couple of months ago about
your grandfather. She got the address from Carl."

"I don't always get all my mail," Wade said as
he started the car.

Jasmine wished she had that problem. If she
hadn't gotten that postcard, she wouldn't be sitting here in Wade's car right now. Better yet, if she
hadn't sent Lonnie that pamphlet, he wouldn't have
even written the postcard.

It would have been a pamphlet, though, because
it had been a wonderful tract. She still remembered

the words about how glorious heaven was with its streets of gold and the cross high on the hill. She'd wanted to give it to Lonnie because he liked shiny, gold things. And, if anyone needed God's grace more than she did, it was her old partner in crime.

The sadness of it all made her sigh.

"You have my full apology, of course," Wade said as he passed by the broken-down gate of his grandfather's farm and turned the car onto the main gravel road.

Jasmine looked up and saw the frown on his face.

"You can file a complaint," he continued. "Sheriff Wall should have a form."

It suddenly dawned on Jasmine. "Because of the *kiss?* You're worried because you kissed me when you were on duty?"

He turned and looked at her. "It's only fair that you know you have the option. I was out of line."

"Duly noted," she said.

They were both silent for a moment.

"Not that I regret it," Wade finally muttered, so low she could barely hear him.

Jasmine decided that Conrad was looking better all of the time. At least he didn't make her half-crazy like Wade did. Not that she would consider a man who used a gun to make his living anyway.

"Don't worry. I'm not filling out any form," she said.

"Thanks."

"I have better things to do."

They were silent as they continued into Dry Creek. About halfway there, Jasmine pulled a small mirror out of her purse and tried to make sense of her hair. She had a little tube of mousse in her purse and squirted some into her hands. It was too late to try for curls and she was more in the mood for the spiked look today anyway. That way people wouldn't be so likely to notice the bulky gray sweater that made her look like a refugee from a war zone.

"Nobody's going to take your picture today, if that's what you're worried about," Wade said finally.

Jasmine gasped and jerked up from her mirror. "I never thought about them taking a picture if they arrest me. Can they do that?"

"I meant the press," Wade said. "Sometimes a reporter will get a tip that the Feds are working on something and they'll come along to see what they can find."

"Well, I'm certainly not going to be talking to any reporters. I'm just hoping no one tells everyone that I'm suspected of doing anything."

"Sheriff Wall is very discreet."

Jasmine knew she was doomed. Oh, Carl may not say anything. But someone was going to say something if a carload of agents in suits pulled into Dry Creek. There was no way they'd blend in. And, if

Wade insisted on dragging her all over with him, people were going to ask why.

"I don't suppose you can deputize me," she finally asked. "Just so people think I'm working when I'm with you."

He actually took his eyes off the road to stare at her. "I'm not even a deputy myself. I'm independent."

Fortunately, there was no traffic on the road. They hadn't passed another car the whole time Wade had been driving into town.

"It wouldn't need to be official or anything," she said. "I just don't want to stir up people's curiosity about why I'm with you. Maybe you could ask me to take notes or something."

She looked at him hopefully.

"I guess I couldn't stop you from taking notes," he said. Which was probably as much encouragement as she was going to get, she decided.

"Thanks."

Jasmine knew the Feds were in town the minute they turned the corner and could see the shiny black car parked at the café. None of the local cars were that clean, not in winter with all of the slush on the roads around town. Everyone would know strangers were here.

"I don't suppose you have a notebook?" Jasmine asked as Wade parked his car beside the federal one.

Wade looked at her and then leaned down to open

his glove compartment. "I think I have one in here someplace."

His elbow dug into her knee as he rummaged around in the compartment. Finally, he pulled out a tattered green notebook and held it up triumphantly. It looked as if it'd been chewed up by a dog.

"That's the only one you have?" she asked. "It doesn't look very official."

"I don't take a lot of notes."

"I guess it will have to do, then." She accepted it from his hand.

"Knock yourself out." Wade moved back and took the key out of the ignition. "Don't expect the Feds to say much in your presence, though."

Jasmine nodded.

When they stepped onto the café porch, she looked through the windows and saw three men sitting at a table. Wade saw them, too, and before he opened the door he turned and inspected her. She felt like a bug under a microscope. Then he reached up and flattened down her hair.

"Hey—" she protested.

"It's better without the spikes. Makes you look more innocent."

"I *am* innocent." Of course, now she probably looked like a drowned rat that didn't have the brain-power to help someone escape from prison. Maybe that was what Wade meant by innocent. That she was didn't look capable of committing a complex crime.

"And don't talk too much," he added. "Just smile. Answer all the questions truthfully, but don't volunteer anything extra."

"I don't know anything to volunteer. I didn't do anything."

"Yeah, well," Wade said and, with those encouraging words, he opened the door to the café.

All of the chitchat and silverware noise stopped the minute she stepped through the door. All three agents were dressed in black suits and looked ready for action. Fortunately, their eyes weren't focused on her.

"What took you so long?" they said to Wade in unison.

She turned around in time to see Wade shrug.

"Family business," he said.

She could see the shock on the faces of the agents. Finally, the man who looked the oldest in the group, cleared his throat.

"You've always said you didn't have any family," the man said. "What'd you do, Sutton? Get married?"

Now they all turned to look at her. Jasmine couldn't believe it. Here she was, with her hair plastered to her head and her blouse with a safety pin where a button should be, and they thought she was a bride. No wonder they were looking at her as if she had an extra eyeball in the middle of her forehead.

To make it worse, Wade just chuckled.

"Not yet," he said. "I'll let you know when we sign up."

The agents laughed a little, too, like it was a joke. Which she supposed it was, but it didn't do anything to help her self-esteem. She waited for Wade to mention his grandfather. Or at least say he was the one who had squashed her hair down like it was against the law to have a spike in place.

"Sit down and have some coffee," the older man offered.

"Just as soon as I get her settled," Wade said as he took hold of Jasmine's elbow and steered her to a table in the back of the café.

"But—" she started to say.

"They won't say anything with you at the table," Wade said. "Just order a pot of coffee and I'll be back in time to drink it with you."

"But—"

Wade nodded to the chair in front of her. "If you want to take notes, you can take them from here."

Now that would make her look like an idiot, Jasmine thought as she sat down. She wasn't that keen on hearing what the agents had to say anyway. Not if they were convinced she was involved.

She watched Wade walk back to the agent's table and saw the other men move their chairs so he'd have room to pull another one up beside them. She was surprised he knew these men. How many federal agents were there around anyway? She saw one of the agents slap Wade on the shoulder and she smiled.

Wasn't that nice? He had friends. She hadn't realized that the men he worked with would be his family.

Just then Linda, the young woman who owned the café, came out of the kitchen and walked over. She wore a large bib apron over her jeans and T-shirt.

"Come in to see the sights?" Linda asked as she pulled an order pad out of her apron pocket. She nodded her head toward the agents. "It's not every day we see men coming to town in suits. We women need to enjoy it."

Jasmine tried to smile. "Do you know why they're here?"

Linda shrugged. "I figure they're IRS guys going out to the Elkton ranch. A big place like that gets audited now and again. Whoever they are, they sure look federal."

Jasmine knew she should tell the café owner that the men weren't here about the Elkton ranch. But she couldn't get the words past the lump in her throat. She was afraid she'd begin to cry if she started to explain.

"Want to start with a pot of coffee?" Linda asked.

Jasmine nodded and the café owner went off to get one.

One of the men at the other table laughed and Jasmine looked over. She wondered what they were saying. And what could possibly be funny in the situation. Since she could only hear snatches of their conversation, she did the only thing she could. She bowed her head and prayed God would smite them with the truth.

Thinking of them being brought low like the Philistines had been in the Old Testament, maybe with a few locusts thrown in for extra measure, brought a smile to her lips. She liked to remember that God had protected His children against overwhelming odds. He stood up for the oppressed. Three federal agents, who just needed to see the truth, would be nothing to Him.

Well, make that four, she thought with a broader smile. Wade needed to be convinced, as well. She'd give him an extra dose of locusts.

She'd no sooner gotten deep into prayer before the whole place went silent.

Chapter Nine

Wade almost groaned. He'd been telling the Feds his doubts that Jasmine had helped Lonnie escape when what did she do but close her eyes and start to smile like she was a fool with a secret. She couldn't have looked guiltier if she had pulled a gun out of her purse.

"What's she doing?" one of his buddies asked as he looked across the café.

That made the other two agents turn and stare.

"I think she's praying," Wade said.

There was silence.

"Most folks cry when they're praying," the agent commented suspiciously. "They don't smile like that."

"She doesn't have any food in front of her, either," another one of them observed. "So she can't be saying grace or anything."

"People in this town pray a lot." Wade was tempted to close his eyes, too, just to avoid explaining it all. "Smiling, crying, food or no food—they do it all the time."

"Oh." The agents all turned their heads back to their table.

"You were saying you don't think she meant to send Lonnie the postcard?" one of the agents picked up the discussion they'd been having.

"Oh, she meant to send it," Wade clarified, relieved that everyone had stopped staring at Jasmine. "I just don't think she meant for it to say anything. It was an act of religious devotion."

If they were talking about any other suspect, Wade would be amused. His colleagues all started to frown. They weren't exactly comfortable trying to judge a person's religious sincerity. Neither was he when it came to that.

Fortunately, he'd grown up in this small town and knew a good number of people here believed in God and prayer with everything they had inside themselves. He hadn't envied anyone for a long time, but last night he had started to feel wistful when Edith had blessed the food. It would be nice to believe God cared as much as she thought He did.

"Here's a copy of what Ms. Hunter sent," the agent on his right said as he handed a photocopied sheet to Wade. "The original is at the lab being tested."

Wade accepted the copy of the pamphlet Jasmine had mailed off. He might even read it tonight, he told himself. He hadn't given much thought to heaven lately.

"They're still working on how Lonnie got out," the man continued. "Another inmate went with him."

This was the first time Wade had heard about that. "Well, maybe it was the other guy that had a contact on the outside, then."

"Maybe," the agent agreed with a shrug. "We don't know at this point."

"Do you have someone checking into where the other inmate might go?" Wade asked. The two escapees were probably staying together. Cowards tended to do that. "Maybe it has nothing to do with the pamphlet Jasmine sent at all."

"That's possible. We're just covering all the bases."

Wade felt an elastic band inside him relax. He hadn't realized how tense he'd been. He knew he was pushing it, but he couldn't stop himself from asking. "So you don't really think Jasmine—Ms. Hunter—has much to do with it?"

"She might still be a destination. We plan to get some deputy sheriffs to keep an eye on the roads around here. But it doesn't take much to see that anyone coming into Dry Creek from outside wouldn't know how to find Ms. Hunter anyway.

There aren't even any signs on most of these county roads."

"So you don't think she helped Lonnie escape?" Wade had to be sure.

"Not unless that's in code," the agent said with a laugh as he pointed to the copy of the pamphlet Wade held in his hand. "And so far we haven't seen any streets of gold or crosses on hillsides."

It hit Wade like a brick. There was a cross on a hill. It didn't belong to Jasmine, but—

"Are you okay?" the agent closest to him asked.

Wade brought his attention back. "Just a little hungry is all."

"Well, we're done here. We'll let you get to breakfast. The sheriff will be in touch with you about the deputies that are coming in."

"Good," Wade murmured as he watched the agents each put a ten dollar bill on the table and then stand up to leave.

"We'll see you later, Sutton. Let us know when your leg's better."

Wade nodded. That was about all that he could manage. As the agents left the café, he looked over at Jasmine. Had he lost the ability to see when something was suspicious? He was really slipping and this couldn't even be blamed on his leg.

Wade knew it was past nine o'clock. It was morning, but the sky outside was still gray and the sunlight was muted. Overhead lights had been turned on in the café. Without them, no one could read the menu. He looked around the large room. An old guitar hung on one wall with a plaque of some kind under it. A few snapshots of people were tacked up beside it. The linoleum in the floor was starting to wear in some places and the white curtains did not all match.

This whole town was full of ordinary people and ordinary places. He supposed it was the perfect hiding place for a clever criminal who was willing to put forth a little effort to blend into the scenery around here.

He knew he should stand up and walk back to the other table where Jasmine was sitting, but he was weary to the bone. He had disappointments he couldn't name because he'd never let himself believe his dreams could come true. The truth was he'd started to trust Jasmine. Care about her even. There was no fool like a lawman who should know better.

Someone turned a radio on in the kitchen and the music drifted out to him. He'd have to talk with Elmer later this morning and find out why he'd decided to erect that huge cross on the hill behind his barn. He'd need to know the sequence of events before he went to the agents with his suspicions.

He started to stand up and felt his leg cramp. The table was there so he held on to it for support. Maybe the doctors were right and it was time to think of a new career. And it wouldn't be because of his injury. He'd always said he'd be a lawman until he died, but he'd lost his taste for it. He had no appetite for putting Jasmine back in prison. Or anyone else, for that matter.

He looked up and saw Jasmine walking over to him.

"You okay?" she asked.

"Just my leg."

"Well, we can sit here," she said as she started to stack up the dirty dishes on the table. "I'll just take these back to Linda. She's on a long-distance phone call with her husband. Said she had more pancake batter ready to go if you'd like, though. And eggs with bacon."

"That sounds good," Wade said as he sank back down to the chair he'd been sitting in.

"Do you take your eggs fried or scrambled?" Jasmine asked.

"Fried."

Jasmine nodded and walked away with the dirty dishes. That's what was so confusing, he thought as he watched her go. The bad guys should act bad and the good guys good. It wasn't fair when everything got mixed up and someone who might be guilty tugged at a lawman's heart. Why was she being so nice?

As it turned out, Wade didn't have to wait to finish breakfast before he could talk to Elmer. The older man came over at the same time that Jasmine brought their full breakfast platters to the table. She claimed they had enough to share and went back to ask for another plate for her father.

"I heard the Feds were here," Elmer said when Jasmine walked back to the kitchen.

Just then the waitress came out of the kitchen and the two women started to laugh and talk as they went back through the door to the kitchen together. They were friends, Wade realized with a jolt. There would probably be a lot of people around here who would feel betrayed if his suspicions were true.

Wade nodded to Elmer. "The Feds have to check everything out."

"They're not giving any grief to Jasmine, though, are they?" the old man asked. "I have money, you know, if she needs a lawyer or anything."

"I know you do," Wade said, and he had no doubt the other man would mortgage his farm if he needed to on Jasmine's behalf. That's why it was so important Wade know the truth about some things.

"I've been wondering," he said. "That cross you have on the hill. What made you think of doing that?"

"I'm a grateful man," Elmer said.

"Well, you've been grateful other times in your life. Why did you put the cross up now?"

Elmer thought a minute. "I read an article in the paper about a man who put a statue of Jesus on his farm out by Great Falls. It kind of struck my fancy. A man should leave his mark on this world."

"Do you still have the newspaper article?"

"Well, now, I don't know. I think I gave it back to Jasmine. She was the one that handed it to me."

Wade would have to track down the article, but he felt relieved. It didn't sound like Jasmine had much to do with that cross. "Which newspaper was it?"

"It wasn't one I recognized. Must have been one of those throwaway ones."

Wade's heart sank. Anyone could print up a newspaper and pass it off as a throwaway.

Just then the kitchen door opened and Jasmine came walking out with a dinner plate and some silverware in her hand. "We're all set."

Wade let her sit down and begin dividing the pancakes and eggs before he asked her. "What kind of newspapers can I get around here anyway?"

"Billings is the closest," she said as she slid an egg onto a plate for Elmer. "Unless you want *USA TODAY* or something."

"Your father told me there was some small newspaper—that's where he got the idea to put up his cross."

Jasmine smiled at her father. "That's right."

"You don't happen to know what that paper was, do you? I'd like to read the article."

He watched her carefully to see if there was any trace of panic.

Jasmine just smiled at him. "Conrad gets it at his shop. I'll check the next time I'm at work. I don't know if he still has that issue or not. His place is closed next week because it's Christmas, but after that I should be able to get it for you—if he still has it—" Her voice trailed off. "If you're still here."

Wade nodded. He'd probably have to call Conrad himself and verify that Jasmine wasn't making everything up. He was getting a headache.

"You should stay, you know," Jasmine said suddenly.

"What?" Elmer asked as he looked at her.

Wade was just as surprised, but he was speechless and managed to keep his mouth shut.

She turned to her father. "Since Wade can't work with his leg being the way it is, he should stay. Spend some time with his grandfather. Go bowling with Carl. He'd like that—"

"Carl *bowls?* Where?" Wade asked.

Jasmine turned to him. "He and Barbara are trying to get a league formed in Miles City. Life is short. When was the last time you did something besides work?"

"I do lots of things besides work," Wade defended himself. He couldn't think straight. Was Jasmine saying she wanted him to stay in Dry Creek for a while? Well, of course, that's what she was saying. But why? "I ran in a marathon a couple of years ago. Took second place, too."

"Well, that's good," she said quietly.

He half expected her to ask him to stay again, but she didn't.

"People die in those marathons," Elmer said instead.

"They do not," Jasmine said, but Wade noticed her father didn't look relieved at that reassurance. It was clear the old man didn't trust him.

"I might be able to stay for a while," Wade said just to see Elmer's reaction. "And I'm here past Christmas anyway. With the pageant and all."

Jasmine groaned. "I forgot about the pageant."

"You don't need to do it," Elmer said firmly. "They still have that recording they can use. That works fine for the angel."

"But I want to do it," Jasmine said. "I just need to practice."

The thought of watching Jasmine play the role of the angel made the day seem brighter. "I'll be there to help. You'll want to be sure your halo is securely attached or it'll fall off."

"Don't tell me," Jasmine half asked.

"Yup, it happened to me. Landed right on the donkey's head." Wade nodded. "Kind of surprised the wise men. Made one of them drop their golden beads. They rolled around on the stage. Finally, the innkeeper had to come out with his broom and sweep them up so nobody would fall."

"I remember that," Elmer said with a grin. "The donkey kept shaking its head trying to get rid of the thing. And, of course, he wouldn't budge. Finally, he turned around and dumped the wise men in with the shepherds."

"Which made the shepherds cry," Wade added.

"That's because they used the kindergarten kids that year for shepherds," Elmer said. "My wife told them they were too young for the responsibility."

Wade nodded. "It isn't as easy to put on a pageant as everyone says."

Jasmine just laughed. "No one says that around here. Trust me."

Wade wished it *was* that easy to trust her. He looked at her face, all lit up with laughter, and he couldn't believe she'd ever done anything wrong in her life. But even believing she might be innocent was not the same as trusting. If he trusted her, he wouldn't need to have all of his questions answered. He'd know in the center of himself that she spoke the truth when she said she had nothing to do with Lonnie's escape. He wouldn't need proof.

He shook his head wistfully. How did a man begin to trust when he didn't naturally do it? And, it wasn't just Jasmine; he didn't trust anyone. That's the big reason why he never worked with a partner.

He couldn't get used to having his life in someone else's hands.

Edith used to say that was his problem with God—that he needed to let go and trust God to hold him or he'd never be able to trust anyone else, either. And she'd probably been right.

Usually, that was okay, though. It was just being back in Dry Creek that had him unnerved. It was a place so full of roots that people trusted each other in a way no one did in his apartment building in Idaho Falls. He couldn't even leave his rubber boots outside his door there, fearing some nameless neighbor would steal them. That life might be empty, but, if he had any sense, he'd pack up right now and go back. He didn't need to believe anything new to live there.

But, looking at Jasmine's face, he knew he wouldn't go. He couldn't bear to leave Dry Creek before Christmas. He wanted to see the look on her face as she soared overhead as an angel in that pageant. He had a feeling it was going to be something he'd remember as long as he lived.

Besides, if she was innocent, he didn't trust anyone else to keep her safe. And, if she was guilty, she'd still need him around to convince her to turn herself in. For the second time today, he wished he knew how to pray like he'd done as a boy before he'd lost all trace of faith. If he knew how, he'd close his eyes and pray for Jasmine.

Chapter Ten

Jasmine stood in the small hallway of her father's house. She was checking her lipstick in the mirror and generally avoiding the two men in the kitchen. She had accepted a dinner invitation from Conrad, thus causing herself more grief than if she had announced she was going on a date with an ax murderer from Mars.

"Didn't you say he'd be here by now?" her father called to her. He'd asked the same question three times already.

Wade and her father were sitting in the kitchen and drumming their fingers on the table. They'd been there for the past half hour and she had no desire to join them. They hadn't even turned a light on and it was growing dark outside.

"He said five-thirty," she called back. Conrad had suggested they eat early when he'd seen the scowl Wade had given him in the café this morning. Conrad had come in the door as the lawman went back to the kitchen to pay Linda for their breakfast. By the time Wade came back and saw someone else was seated at their table, Conrad had already asked his question.

Jasmine wouldn't have said yes if she hadn't seen Wade's forbidding look. Just because he thought she was involved in Lonnie's escape, she didn't need to stay locked in her room. She's overheard enough of the conversation he'd had with the agents earlier to know that they didn't think she was in much danger. As they said, no one would even know how to find her unless someone in town told them.

"I think he's coming," her father called out. "Someone's pulling in."

Jasmine took one last look at herself. She'd finally gotten her hair to curl just right. She'd washed it this afternoon and the auburn color was subdued. She was wearing the gray wool skirt Edith liked so well. Her only jewelry was a leather watch so nothing she wore flashed or sparkled. She looked more like a librarian than an ex-con.

Of course, her black leather jacket didn't match the rest of her now, but she made do with what she had. Maybe she could convince her father to give her a sensible coat instead of that necklace for Christmas. Then she would blend right in around here. She might have wavered this morning, but she was determined to look like everyone else in this quiet town. By then she would be at ease with her new life.

Jasmine swung her purse over her shoulder and walked back to the kitchen.

"I don't know what the problem is. I'm not even leaving Dry Creek," she said as she continued over to the refrigerator and opened the freezer. "There are plenty of frozen dinners. Spaghetti. Tuna noodle. Pot roast. You can both help yourself."

"I'll wait until we get to the café," Wade said calmly from where he sat. He was wearing a denim shirt and jeans.

Jasmine gave him a severe look. "You can't follow me. I'm going on a date."

"He has to go with you," her father said with a nod to Wade. "He's only doing his job—keeping you safe."

Jasmine frowned. Sometime while they had been sitting at the table those two must have become allies. "Wade promised to bring you something back from the café, didn't he?"

"Just a hamburger," her father admitted. He looked at Wade. "Grilled onions and pickles on the side. With maybe some fries."

"You got it," Wade said.

"I could bring you a hamburger, if that's what this is all about," Jasmine offered.

"Oh, I couldn't ask you to do that. You're going to be on a date."

"Exactly," she agreed. "And I don't need a chaperone."

"It's for your own good," her father protested. "Even if I don't get a hamburger, I'll feel better knowing there's someone with you to protect you just in case. I know Conrad's a nice young man, but I don't think he'd do too well in a fight."

"We're going out to eat, not to fight," she said as she heard a knock at the door. "That'll be him."

She walked to the door, but before she answered it, she turned back. "You two be nice now."

Neither one of the men answered her as she opened the door.

Conrad had an anxious look on his face. He stood lean and tall, his brown hair slicked back. He stood in the doorway a minute, running his fingers under the black tie he wore with his beige shirt. His black wool coat hung open in the front.

Jasmine was glad she'd dressed as conservatively as she had. She matched him that way.

Conrad didn't seem any more inclined to talk than her father and Wade were. He nodded at both men and then held the door for her as she left. There was some bite to the cold air and they both walked quickly to his car. He opened the passenger door for her and she slid into the warm interior.

"Nice music," she said as Conrad opened the

driver's door and moved into place behind the wheel.

"I knew you'd like it," Conrad said.

Actually, the hymns on his CD were a little slow for her taste, but she figured she would appreciate them more if she listened to the words carefully. The slow rhythm was probably more holy than the stuff she liked anyway. She'd get used to it.

Conrad started his car and backed up before heading into Dry Creek.

"That's some cross you've got up there on the hill," Conrad said as he turned onto the main gravel road. "I could see it on the way out here—even from the edge of Dry Creek."

"It's my father's. Sort of a Christmas thing he's got going."

Conrad nodded. "My uncle put a lit-up snowman on his roof. It's got a mechanical arm that waves all night long. You'll have to take your father and drive by some time. Get the effect."

Jasmine noticed that Conrad kept looking in the rearview mirror, but she refused to turn around.

"Dry Creek should have a contest. Best outdoor decorations," she said, hoping to keep Conrad distracted. It didn't work.

"Is he *following* us?" Conrad finally asked as he turned his head to look behind them.

Jasmine knew it was pointless to pretend she

didn't know who Conrad meant. "I think he's just going to get some hamburgers."

"Because if he's worried about that guy coming to town while you're with me, he doesn't need to. I can take care of an escaped fel—" Conrad stopped. He just realized what he'd said. "Well, I can take care of things. That's the point."

Jasmine nodded. She supposed it had been too much to expect that everyone wouldn't find out what was going on. "Who told you?"

Conrad looked over at her. "Charley heard it this morning from Elmer. But you can't blame them. I heard it from Linda later, too. She knew because the agents went back and asked her to be on the lookout for the guy. If he came to town, they figured he'd go to the café first to ask directions."

Jasmine felt a little ill. She hadn't thought of that. "I hope they didn't tell her to do anything. I don't want anyone to get hurt."

She would need to make it plain to Linda that she wasn't to let on that she knew who Lonnie was if he came by. She should just give him the directions he asked for. Better yet, Linda should close the café for the next week or so. She hadn't taken a vacation since she went to London this past summer with her guitar-playing husband.

But if the café was closed, Lonnie would just go to the hardware store. Maybe they should close for a few days, too. Which would leave the church.

Or the houses themselves. The queasy feeling got worse. No one would be safe in Dry Creek if Lonnie was headed here.

"You okay?" Conrad asked. "I'm sorry if I wasn't supposed to know about that guy—"

"No. It's good that you know. Everyone should know. Everyone needs to leave Dry Creek."

"What?"

"Oh, just for a few days. Until the Feds catch Lonnie."

"We can't all just leave. Where would we go?"

Linda thought of that necklace her father was giving her for Christmas. She could sell it for a few thousand. "Those hot springs. You know, those mineral baths over by Dillion. They have some real deals this time of year."

"People can't afford—"

"I could pay," she said. Her teeth were starting to chatter. It was warm in the car, but she felt a chill inside that wouldn't go away. "We could all go together. It would be fun."

"The whole *town?*"

"Of course. People are always complaining about their aches and pains. It'd be perfect."

Conrad didn't have much else to say for the rest of the drive into town. Neither did Jasmine. She was too focused on trying to remember if she'd passed any pawn shops in Miles City when she'd been there. It would be a pity to pawn a necklace like the one she was getting for Christmas, but it was the quickest way to have money.

If she hadn't been so worried about what might happen, she would have thought more about where she and Conrad were going. She didn't really think about it until they pulled into Dry Creek and she noticed how dark the windows of the café were.

Saturday night was date night at the café and Linda always dimmed the lights and put candles on the tables. She pushed the larger tables to one side of the room, too, so that she could position the smaller tables in strategic places around the rest of the café. She managed to give the illusion of a dozen alcoves each with a private table for two. The Redferns were already sitting at one of the tables, holding hands as they gazed into each other's eyes. The rodeo guy, Zach Lucas, and his new wife were at another.

"Welcome," Linda said in a hushed voice as she walked over to Conrad and Jasmine as they entered the café. She was wearing a black skirt with a white blouse and carrying several large menu sheets. "Where would you care to sit?"

Jasmine wasn't worried about sitting anywhere, but she knew Linda was proud of her "romance corners," as she called them. She even had her radio in the back tuned to a station that played love songs. They had more rhythm than Conrad's hymns.

"Closest to the door is good," Jasmine said when Conrad looked over at her for her opinion.

"By the door, it is then," Linda said as she led them there.

They were barely seated before the door to the café opened and Wade walked inside.

Jasmine knew Linda needed to go seat her next guest, but she wanted to start her thinking about a small vacation. "Have you ever been to one of those hot springs west of here? Where the water bubbles up out of the ground?"

"The mineral baths? I've always thought they look lovely. I think I have some brochures in the back. Don't tell me you're going to one of them?"

"Maybe," Jasmine said. She wondered why she hadn't sent Lonnie a brochure for some vacation place instead of that pamphlet on heaven. At least then no one would think he might come up here.

The truth was, though, that she had wanted Lonnie to get a glimpse of God. Her ex-partner wasn't supposed to break out of jail, but he was supposed to break free of some of the guilt he must feel for all he'd done in his life. She'd do as much for her worst enemy.

"Our special tonight is grilled salmon with lemon sauce," Linda said.

"Sounds good to me," Conrad said as he laid the menu down on the table and looked at Jasmine. "How about you?"

Jasmine nodded. She was barely listening. Thinking of Lonnie made her realize she certainly didn't deserve to be sitting here with a nice man like Conrad. However, as bad as her past was, she'd feel a hundred times worse if something happened to anyone in Dry Creek because of Lonnie.

"You don't know of a place to sell jewelry, do you?" she asked Conrad.

"Me?" He shook his head. "I know a consignment shop that takes old ties, but that's about it."

She reached into her purse and pulled out the crumpled green notebook she'd borrowed from Wade this morning. Then she stood up. "I'll be right back."

Jasmine walked over to Wade. He was sitting at a table across the room. He had a jacket on and she wondered if he wore his gun in a holster under it.

"Don't they ever put the lights on in this place?" Wade grumbled before she even got all the way to his table. She noticed he'd blown his candle out. "It's dark in here."

"It's supposed to be romantic."

He grunted. "It's dangerous as all get-out."

"I forgot to give this back earlier," she said when she got to the table and could offer it to him.

He looked at the notebook in her hand and then up to her. "No problem."

"About my dad—"

He took the notebook and waved her words aside. "Don't worry about it. We've made our peace. I can't blame him for coming on strong. He'd do anything for you."

Jasmine smiled. "I know. That's why I need to find a place that buys old jewelry. I figure you would know one from your work. If you could write down the name and as much of the address as you know, I'd appreciate it."

Wade went very still. "What kind of jewelry are we talking here?"

"A diamond-and-ruby necklace that retails for ten to fifteen thousand, maybe more if there are earrings with it."

"And you want to cash it out?"

Jasmine nodded. "I'd prefer to pawn it so I could buy it back, but I have an idea and it'll require some capital."

She knew she should explain herself more fully. But she just leaned back and watched the war in Wade's eyes. He wasn't sure whether he needed to be suspicious or not. She turned around before she could see what he finally decided. She already knew that he didn't trust her.

"Just list the places," she said over her shoulder as she walked back to the table where Conrad was patiently waiting.

She spent the rest of the evening being annoyed with Wade while searching for things to talk to Conrad about. She knew Conrad was trying to come up with conversation, too. Finally, they both gave up and started to talk about the engines he had in his shop that needed repair. The shop was closed for a long Christmas break, but the two of them would be back after New Year's. They spoke low and kept their heads together so Linda couldn't hear them. The café owner would be appalled to hear anyone talking about engine repairs on date night.

Chapter Eleven

Wade was sitting on the porch at his grandfather's house, watching the sun start to rise. He had his sleeping bag wrapped around him and a thermos of hot coffee at his feet. The deputies wouldn't be in place until tomorrow and he wanted to be sure all was calm until then. No one had gone past his grandfather's house, heading over to the Maynard place, since Conrad had left last night.

Speaking of that man, he was too skinny to be of much use in a fight. And he had a startled, rabid look in his eyes when Wade studied him for too long. It shouldn't, but it made Wade feel good to know the other man was so easily unnerved. He told himself it meant Conrad was too timid for someone like Jasmine.

Of course, she didn't seem to know that. Wade's heart had sunk last night as he saw the two of them lean in and start talking together in hushed voices. Whatever it was they were talking about, it had them both captivated.

Jasmine had even forgotten to come back and get the notebook she'd left. He still had it in his pocket and he'd written an address down for her. Plus, he'd added the name of someone to talk to there just to show he couldn't care less who she ate dinner with.

Oh, who was he kidding?

The whole night had given him heartburn. And he hadn't rushed through his meal so that wasn't the problem. No, it was watching Jasmine and her date that bothered him. He didn't know why she couldn't sit and talk to him with that rapt look on her face.

Not that he should be jealous. He was guarding her, not courting her. Besides, she was halfway to being a suspect and only a fool got involved with one of those.

Wade supposed he'd just been single too long. There was a fine line between being a carefree bachelor and being a hopeless hermit and he might be skidding too close to the latter. Last night had brought that home to him. It seemed like every happily married couple in Dry Creek had come into the café to hold hands and coo over each other. They'd all nodded to him as they passed his table, but he still felt like a freak.

He wondered if it wasn't against the law for a public café to have a night that discriminated against single, dateless people like that. There was nothing worse than sitting alone and eating by candlelight in a room reeking with romance.

At least Linda had been gracious enough to make up a thermos of vegetable soup for his grandfather. And, she'd given him some dinner rolls and a few hard-boiled eggs, as well. The old man had been happy to have them when Wade came to the door last night. His grandfather still called him Sonny, but seemed content to have him around. Wade told himself he'd have to get his grandfather to a doctor after Christmas. And, in the meantime, he might as well clean the place up some.

Not today, though, he thought as he looked at the sky. Today was Sunday and, after he went out to the barn and made sure Jenny was fed, he needed to pick Jasmine up and take her to the pageant practice. One good thing was that Conrad wouldn't be able to best him in giving advice to Jasmine. There was a brotherhood among those who had managed to fly as the angel that others just wouldn't understand. She didn't have to be innocent for him to help in her role as an angel. It was nice that they had something that didn't involve the law.

Jasmine was up and dressed when Wade came to the door. She was wearing a gray sweater over a white T-shirt and blue jeans. Her eyes looked tired and he wondered if she'd spent the night thinking about Conrad.

"Trouble in paradise?" he asked.

She hefted her purse onto her shoulder and turned to scoop up a garment bag from a nearby kitchen chair. "Nothing I can't handle."

"No doubt," he said.

She moved the garment bag and he could see it was slipping.

"Let me," he said as he stepped closer and held out a hand.

"Thanks," she said as she turned to look behind the door and came out with a four-foot tall cardboard cutout.

"Those are your wings?" Wade guessed, not entirely sure.

She nodded. "The kindergartners made them in Sunday school."

"Oh." He looked at them skeptically. "Aren't they a little bent?"

Streaks of silver glitter went the length of the wings and cotton balls were glued here and there on the cardboard. The right wing was the one that curled in at the tip. It looked like it'd fold in a breeze.

Jasmine smiled fondly at the wings. "That's because they're made out of the box that Linda's new refrigerator came in. There were corners and we had to straighten them. Little Bobbie sat on them but we didn't get them completely smooth."

Wade wasn't reassured. "Maybe if you'd added some wire reinforcement."

"I didn't want to risk anyone getting hurt. Besides, wire's too hard for the kindergarten kids to use."

"These wings could fall off," Wade felt duty-bound to point out. "Then what would you do?"

"Well, it's not like I need them to fly. Besides, I'm lucky I didn't end up with a dragon tail. The kids got into this, but some of them didn't know what angels looked like in the back. They'd seen angel pictures from the front, of course, but that didn't satisfy them as to the unseen part of an angel. One boy thought they should be more like dragons in the back."

Wade couldn't imagine an angel with a more delightful back than the one standing right here holding these wings. "At least the shepherds would be awestruck if they saw a dragon, though."

"I don't think I was ever supposed to breathe fire or anything. I think the wings just seemed a little tame to them. They see so many things on television."

"What kind of a world do we live in when seeing a creature with wings doesn't strike fear in a little boy's heart?"

"A world with computer games and movies," she said as she followed him out the door. "Kids haven't been easy to impress since *Star Wars*."

As they walked to his car, Wade looked down at

what he was carrying. "Hey, this is the same bag they used for the angel costume when I was a kid."

Jasmine grinned. "Same bag. Same costume."

"Really?" He remembered what seemed like a zip-up bathrobe made out of white satin. The folds of fabric had gotten in the way of his legs and the whole thing felt slippery. Which was part of the reason he hadn't been able to get that bag of dimes opened like he'd planned.

"They did get a few new costumes donated this year," Jasmine said. "But so far no white angel ones."

"By donated, you don't mean bathrobes?" he said as he opened the trunk.

Jasmine nodded as she put her wings inside. "I understand it's a tradition that all of the costumes are recycled bathrobes coming from local people who don't need them any longer."

Wade grunted. "I would have thought they'd have sprung for some regular costumes during all these years. Bathrobes don't improve with age."

He laid the garment bag with the costume over the wings and shut the trunk.

"Well, they do try to match the bathrobe to the role," Jasmine said as they walked to the passenger door and Wade opened it. "I understand some people even buy their bathrobes thinking they'd make a good costume for this or that part. Of course, it takes years to wear out a bathrobe. And who wants to look like a shepherd?"

Jasmine slid into the passenger seat and reached for her seat belt. Wade closed her door and walked around to open his own.

"If they were going to take up a collection around here, they should have taken it to buy some decent costumes instead of worrying about me," Wade muttered as he took his place behind the wheel.

Jasmine grinned over at him. "Oh, the bathrobes are part of the fun. Besides, it keeps the community active in the pageant."

"I can't believe anyone needs to worry about people getting behind the pageant. Folks used to come over from Miles City," Wade paused as he started his car. "Even some from Billings, I think."

"People don't come to Dry Creek as much as they used to. Not that we've given up trying to get them here. That's part of the reason the pastor's wife and her niece painted that huge mural on the side of the barn. It has some historic significance. Everybody wants to see something special."

"I would think the nativity would be special enough," Wade said before he realized he sounded just like Edith. He sure wasn't one to point fingers at people who didn't go to a Christmas pageant. He hadn't been inside a church for decades and he usually spent Christmas Eve in front of his television.

He turned onto the main road before he realized something. "I didn't see Elmer. Is he coming to practice, too?"

"I think he's avoiding it," Jasmine said. "He went over to visit Charley."

Wade had talked to Charley briefly last night when the other man had brought Edith to the café for a cup of tea. Charley had said then that he wasn't going to this morning's practice, either, so he'd given directions to Wade regarding the angel wheel. The morning was looking better now that it was just him and Jasmine driving down the road. The skies were clear and there didn't seem much chance of snow.

He knew he'd be sorry that he was letting his guard down around Jasmine, but he did want to spend some time talking to her. No matter how this all turned out, he wanted her to know he wished her well.

"Would you mind stopping at the café first?" Jasmine asked after a few minutes.

"It's not open on Sunday, is it?"

"I just want to post a notice next to the door. You know on that bulletin board where they have the menu."

"I hope you're not planning a yard sale or anything." He sounded like a grumpy old man, but he couldn't call the words back so he continued. "Usually you need a permit for something like that."

"Not in Dry Creek." Jasmine's lips pressed tight

together. "This is a town of harmony and peace. We don't bother with the small stuff like permits."

Wade knew he should just nod and agree, but he didn't. "Every town has some problems."

"Not this one," Jasmine snapped back and then blinked a few times. "Well, except for me, of course."

Wade almost pulled off the road and stopped the car, but he was only a few hundred yards from the café so he waited to pull in there before he parked and turned to Jasmine. "What in the world are you talking about? No one here thinks you're a problem. In fact, it's the opposite. Everyone goes around singing your praises."

"That's only because they don't know," Jasmine said, and a tear slid down her cheek.

There was probably some regulation somewhere that told a lawman what he was supposed to do in this case, but Wade had never heard of it. He slid a little farther over on the seat so he could put his arm around Jasmine's shoulder. "It can't be that bad. Whatever it is, we can fix it."

He could feel a silent hiccup shake Jasmine's shoulders.

"I need to post my notice," she said.

"I'll post it for you. You just sit here and hold your breath. That should make the hiccups go away," Wade said.

Jasmine bent down and rummaged in her purse

before she came up with a sheet of paper that she held out to him.

Wade didn't even stop to read it. He just grabbed it and opened his car door.

He was at the bulletin board, searching for another thumbtack, before he actually looked at the paper. "What in the world?"

Jasmine had drawn a map of the Dry Creek area and put a red star where she lived with her father. Then she put in bold block letters: Find Jasmine Here.

He forgot all about the thumbtack and went back to his car. He slid into the driver's seat before turning to her.

"What's this?" he demanded as he shook the paper in his hand. "Are you telling Lonnie how to find you?"

She nodded her head.

Wade's heart sank.

"I have to," she said in a small voice. "If I don't tell him, people could be hurt."

Now she was crying in earnest.

He put his arm out and this time she slid into his embrace.

"Now start from the beginning," Wade said. His voice was gentle and he hadn't even had to think about it. "Tell me what you mean."

It took a couple of minutes, because of a few tears and some lingering hiccups, but Jasmine told him what she'd concluded about Lonnie coming to town and trying to find out where she lived from people.

"He's got a bad temper," she said in conclusion. "I can't have him going around here hurting people if they don't tell him what he wants to know."

Wade smoothed back her hair. "So you figured you'd just tell him what he wanted so he wouldn't need to ask?"

She nodded. "At first I thought about taking everyone to the hot springs over by Dillion. But with Christmas being so close, that wouldn't work. People want to be home. With kids and everything, you know—"

Wade smiled. So that's what she'd been talking about last night. He'd thought she and Conrad had those hot springs planned for the two of them. Which just went to show that a man could be wrong.

"We can post a note if you feel better, but we'll make a fake one. Lead him down a false path. Or maybe just a confusing one."

"I wouldn't want him to go to somebody else's house," Jasmine said.

"We won't send him anywhere but around in circles. If he takes the map off the board, though, Linda might see and be able to call the sheriff's department. That way they'd know where he was headed. There are enough county roads out here to keep him lost for days."

Jasmine nodded slowly. "I guess that would work."

"We'll make a new notice after practice this morning," Wade agreed as he handed the map back to Jasmine. "Save that for something more important."

"I just—" Jasmine looked up at him, her eyes still moist. "The people here don't understand what they have. I know because I've never had it in my life before. This is a special place for me."

Wade nodded. "I know what you mean."

"No one should be hurt here."

Wade knew he was going to kiss her when she said that. He couldn't help himself. He'd made protecting people his life's work, but he never cared about those people, not up close and personal. Not like Jasmine.

He smoothed a tear away and then, with her cuddled close in his arms, he bent his lips to kiss her. He felt the sentiment rush up inside him and he knew he was hooked.

Chapter Twelve

A thin stream of early morning light filtered into the barn and the air was dusty. Weathered boards rose high on each side of the huge structure and the view, as Jasmine made her swing, went from the rafters straight down to the wooden plank floor below. No one was down there, which was a good thing because her fingers were cold as they gripped the ropes that held her aloft. She wouldn't be able to give an angel wave to anyone. And, of course, her hair was a whirlwind of a mess.

But she had her wings strapped to her back and she was soaring.

Better yet, she was happy inside. Not just because she was going to be an angel in the world's best pageant. No, she was all warm and fuzzy inside because Wade had kissed her and he hadn't made any apology afterward or suggested she fill out a complaint

form or anything. Instead, he'd given a big whoop
and grinned at her until she had to grin back.

She looked toward the hayloft just so she could
gaze at him again. He was staring down at the gears,
making sure the wheel worked and her flight was
smooth, but she could still see a slight smile on his
face. Yes, it was a happy day.

She felt the rush of air as she flew back over the
barn. She was glad she didn't have to worry about
her costume because she was still in jeans. She'd
only been up in the angel swing one other time with
Charley at the wheel, but last night the older man
had stopped to tell her Wade would run the contrap-
tion as there was some vet work Charley needed to
do this morning. He'd promised to be at the real
performance tonight.

Wade had read the directions and made a test
flight himself before he let her get in the rope har-
ness. At first, he'd thought she should wait for everyone to come, but she explained how quickly the
kids would get accustomed to her flying and how
she wanted them to look up at her with as much awe
as possible on Christmas Eve.

She swung back to where she'd started and Wade
was there to catch her. Her body landed against
his with a soft thud. He'd braced his feet to catch
her and small bits of loose hay, separated from the
stacked bales, flew up in the air. Wade didn't seem
to mind, though, and he held her for a minute, angel

wings and all, purring in her ear and making her heart race. She looked up at him with a smile. His eyes were warm and he traced her cheek with his thumb.

Jasmine was sure he was going to kiss her again.

But then the door to the barn below opened with a bang and a couple of dozen kids came running inside. Edith followed them and Jasmine knew the older woman would need help so she asked Wade to unhook her so she could go down.

"You could help, too," she suggested as he undid her from the rigging and then helped her take off the wings.

"I don't know much about kids."

"So learn. You were a kid once. It's like that bicycle thing—it'll come back to you." Jasmine leaned the wings against a stack of hay bales. She'd leave them there until tonight.

Wade grunted, but he looked pleased that she was inviting him to help. They both climbed down the ladder to the main part of the barn.

"Oh, there you are," Edith said when she saw them. "I think we need to break up into small groups and practice the various parts individually before we put them all together for the pageant. Wade, can you take the boys over there? Girls, I'll be with you along the other wall. Just give me a second."

Jasmine was not surprised when Edith turned

to her when the kids, along with Wade, started to move into groups.

"You have to tell me all about it," Edith whispered with joy in her voice. "I couldn't wait to hear. It's time you were dating."

"How did you see through everything?" Jasmine whispered back, with a tilt in her voice. She knew Edith had said Wade wasn't ready to trust anyone and she knew he didn't go to church so she'd have to pray for him about that, but eventually, maybe—

"Conrad was so excited," Edith continued, her voice bubbling even though she spoke low. "He said he had such a good time and, of course, you both have so much in common and—"

Jasmine's heart sank. Conrad. Of course.

"He's a good man," Jasmine forced herself to say. She suddenly felt very tired. "The kind of man any woman would be proud to call her friend."

"And he respects you, too," Edith gushed. "That's important."

Jasmine nodded. Conrad was exactly the kind of a man she should pick to gradually get to know and then peacefully marry. He was steady, faithful and safe. He didn't use a gun to make his living and he went to church. He was perfect.

She looked across the barn at Wade. There was nothing gradual or peaceful or perfect about him. Even if he did come back to the church, he'd argue with God. He wasn't the kind of man who could let things go. If he was upset, he would show it.

She lifted her arm to smooth down her hair.

Edith reached into the purse she was carrying and pulled out a CD. "Conrad said to give this to you. He said you'd liked it last night and he meant to give it to you before you left, but—" The older woman raised an eyebrow. "He apparently got distracted."

Jasmine forced herself to smile as she took the CD. "Thanks."

She wondered if she should tell Edith that Conrad had gotten distracted because they were talking about the new combines that were supposed to come to the county fair this summer.

"Charley and I want to have the two of you over for dinner sometime soon," Edith continued, her face pink with excitement. "It won't be quite as romantic as date night at the café, but we'd love to have you."

Jasmine nodded.

"We have a very romantic swing on the porch. I love to sit out there with Charley in the evenings. We look up at the stars."

"Wonderful."

"Well, I better go see to the girls," Edith said as she turned to look toward one wall and then the other. "Wade seems to be doing fine with the boys."

Jasmine followed Edith's gaze. Yes, Wade did seem to be doing well.

* * *

Wade knew he was in trouble. He'd worked a couple of hostage negotiations in his day and he was used to staring down the business end of a gun. Nothing had prepared him for boys in a tangle, though.

"It's not *our* fault they were promised a donkey," a shepherd with the fresh bruise on his cheek said as he pointed his finger at the three wise men. "If we have to walk, they have to walk. The wise men just think they're better than us because they've got that gold and stuff. Everybody knows it's only plastic. You can't even buy anything with it. "

Wade nodded because the boy seemed to expect it.

"But we're coming from *afar*," the tallest of the three wise men whined in protest. His voice was a little nasal. "You shepherds are just up there in the hills like you always are. No one will believe we are from *afar* if we walk up like we were just next door buying something at the store."

"Maybe you came by bus," a different shepherd boy replied. "Then you'd be walking from the bus stop."

The wise man snorted in disbelief. "They didn't have buses back then. Or bus stops, either. I don't think they even had rubber tires for buses. Or gasoline. Or windshields. Or—"

Wade tuned the rest of the list out. The crux of

the problem, as far as he could determine, was that Edith still hadn't located a donkey and the wise men thought some of the shepherds should abandon their flocks and pull a chariot for them as they made their entrance. He wondered if the Romans had chariots at the time Jesus was born. He supposed they did.

Finally, the list ended and Wade leaned over so he could get a better handle on the negotiations. He was bending from the waist and keeping his leg straight, but his muscles were still protesting so he changed position slightly until he found some relief.

"I'm not going to be no donkey," the first shepherd boy declared with his hands curled into fists.

The wise man that had made the list looked at Wade a little smugly. "Tell them they have to be a donkey if that's the part they're assigned. We all need to do the parts we are assigned. Even if it's being a donn-n—key." The boy drew the word out and got a laugh, at least from the other wise men.

The shepherds didn't think it was so funny.

Wade was tempted to call Edith in to mediate, but he figured he wasn't done yet.

Just then the youngest of the shepherds slid in close and whispered in Wade's ear, "They're teasing me because I have to wear a pink bathrobe."

Wade looked at all the boys.

"First off, it's not a bathrobe. It's a costume," he told everyone before looking down at the boy with the complaint. "And pink is just a washed-out red.

Fire trucks are red. That's a man's color. You'll do fine."

The boy didn't look convinced, but he took his thumb out of his mouth.

"Secondly, we *need* the shepherds," he said to the other boys. "Don't think you're not important. If it weren't for you, no one would have been there to gather around the baby Jesus on that night."

"Well, the wise men—"

Wade gave the three of them a stern look. "And, thirdly, if the kindergarten kids could make angel wings out of a cardboard delivery box, you can make a donkey out of something. You've got to be, what, nine or ten years old? You wise men need to figure out how to make what you need and the rest of us will help."

Wade was proud of himself until he noticed that all of the boys were looking at him as though he had disappointed them. "What?"

"I thought you were supposed to be a sheriff," the first shepherd said in disgust. "You should lock those wise men up for bothering us. Disturbing our peace."

"Us? You're the ones who—" the wise man started in.

Wade put two fingers in his mouth and gave a shrill whistle. Everything stopped.

"I need to sit down," he said. "And when I do, I

want you to be in two separate groups. Wise men to my left. Shepherds to my right."

He went to the side of the barn and brought back a folding chair. Then he sat down.

"Left." He pointed since no one except him had moved and then he reversed directions. "Right."

"Are we going to fight?" the bathrobe shepherd asked with enthusiasm.

"No, we're going to do crafts."

Wade remembered, when there were problems with him many years ago, Edith always turned to crafts. She used to say that busy hands were happy hands.

"What do you know about crafts?" the wise man scoffed.

"More than you'd expect, son. More than you'd expect."

The wise men finally went into a huddle a few feet away to talk about how to make a donkey, so Wade only had the shepherds to deal with.

"You could make sheep," Wade suggested as they sat there looking bored.

The boys shook their heads in unison. "We got sheep. Our dogs. We already got the white towels to put on them and everything."

The boys sat there, cross-legged, and in a circle around his chair.

"Being a shepherd is dumb anyway," one boy finally complained.

Wade expected the others to contradict him, but they didn't. They all just sat in the circle looking as if they'd been left out of the fun of the pageant.

"Even the innkeeper gets to talk," the boy continued his grievance. "We don't have nothing to say."

"Well, shepherds are still important," Wade said after a minute. "They have to feed the sheep—"

A couple of the boys grunted, but it wasn't a sign of any enthusiasm.

"—and they have to protect the sheep," he continued.

"Do they have guns?" the bathrobe boy asked. He perked up at that thought. "You can't protect nothing without a gun."

"You should know that, being a sheriff," another shepherd added with some persuasion in his voice.

"A gun is always a last resort," Wade said to the boys.

"I bet a real shepherd would have a gun," the oldest boy challenged him.

"Nobody had a gun in the Bible." Wade was beginning to enjoy himself with these boys. It wouldn't hurt them to ask a question or two. He could handle it.

"That's because they just prayed instead," the bathrobe boy said with a sigh. "That's what my mom always says I should do is pray about it, pray about it, pray about it."

"Well, ah—" Wade cleared his throat. "You should always do what your mother says."

"You mean, we should pray about the wise men?" the boy asked, looking up at Wade with trust in his eyes.

"I don't— I, ah—" Wade stammered. He was no authority on prayer. He hadn't said a prayer since he'd been a boy and pleaded with God to either bring back his mother or his father. He had been so desperate for a family, he'd have settled for Him finding a distant aunt or uncle. God's refusal to answer had shown him one thing. God didn't listen to Wade Sutton so there was no point in talking to Him. How could he explain something like that to these boys, though? They might be bloodthirsty, but they trusted God.

"I haven't prayed for a long time," he finally said softly.

"That's okay," the oldest of the shepherds said as he put his hand out to Wade. "We'll show you how."

Wade didn't know whether to laugh or cry. The boys swept him up into their circle of prayer and tried to share their faith with him. They blessed each of their dogs and told God how they felt the wise men were being unfair and that they needed a donkey. They confessed, they requested, they believed. Wade could see plainly the bottom line was that they believed God was going to come through for them.

He didn't want them to stop praying, but he was nervous by the time they'd finished. Wade hoped they never lost their way like he had, but God wasn't likely to answer their prayers, either. Oh, He might bless their dogs now, but the animals would eventually die. And the wise men were still going to be there tomorrow to lord it over them. Some bathrobes would always be pink and not everyone got to talk. Life didn't always deliver up what people prayed for.

But the donkey! Wade suddenly realized he might be able to do something about the donkey.

"Nobody move," Wade commanded as he stood. "I'll be right back."

He walked over to where Jasmine and Edith were talking to the girls. They were part of some choir that sang in the background during the manger scene. They must be planning a song or two for the time before all the cast sang "Silent Night." He caught Edith's eye and motioned her over to the edge of the circle.

Jasmine had her back to him, but he could hear her voice as she softly sang along with the girls. She had one arm around a little girl and looked as natural as if she was a mother herself. For the first time, he realized what Jasmine had given up during all those years in prison. She should have a home and family of her own. She should be stealing kisses with a husband instead of a stray lawman like him. An unexpected wistfulness stabbed through him.

Then he looked up and saw Edith watching him thoughtfully.

"Do you still need a donkey?" he asked before she could comment. He cleared his throat and frowned.

She nodded. "I was going to stop by and ask your grandfather, but—"

"I'll do it," he said as he turned slightly so he didn't need to meet her eyes. "I saw an old horse trailer beside the barn this morning when I was checking on Jenny. I'll bring her over tomorrow night in plenty of time for the pageant. My grandfather won't mind."

"Why that'd be wonderful," Edith said and he made the mistake of looking back at her. She beamed at him cautiously for a second, but then the wattage gradually increased until her whole face was literally glowing.

"And there's an old bathrobe of mine in the closet at my grandfather's house," he continued as he tried to make his face look blank. No one needed to see his heart hanging out there like it had been. "Maybe we could switch out the pink one."

Edith nodded. "The boys will be thrilled." She paused and turned her head slightly as if she wanted to say something, but all she got out was, "What a great day this is."

"Oh," he added. "If any of the boys ask, Jesus didn't carry a gun."

"What?" Edith blinked.

Wade grinned. That would give his friend something to think about instead of the lovestruck look she'd seen on his face while he'd stared at Jasmine.

The door opened before he got back to the shepherds and Carl walked into the barn. Wade motioned for him to come over and join him and the boys. He knew the sheriff was there to update him, but Carl might have a minute after that to tell the boys that guns never solved anything.

"You want me to say *what?*" Carl asked when they met up in the middle of the barn. The boys were still sitting over where Wade had left them. They couldn't hear, but he lowered his voice anyway.

"Just encourage them to solve their problems *without* guns or their fists. Or arguing—put that one in there, too. Arguing can be bad."

"What am I supposed to tell them to do about these problems then?" Carl looked bewildered.

"Tell them to obey their mothers and pray."

Carl looked at him. "Remember, we're the law around here. Sometimes we need to raise our voices—and do more than pray that things will change."

"I know." Wade sighed. "I just don't want them to turn out like—"

He stopped.

"Like us?" Carl asked.

Wade shook his head. "No, just not like me. You're doing okay."

"Well," Carl started, as if he was going so say something encouraging, but then he looked Wade straight in the eyes. "If you don't like what you've become, then maybe it's time you changed."

Wade was a little startled at his friend's frankness. "I don't—"

Carl waved his words aside. "You've had this chip on your shoulder since we were boys. When you left church all those years ago, you changed. So, God didn't do exactly what you wanted."

"All I wanted was a family."

Carl nodded. "And God gave you a family."

"My grandfather wasn't exactly—"

"I meant the church here. After you ran off with your father, folks spent hours trying to find you, especially after your dad was killed. They put ads in newspapers. They took turns driving to all the little towns in the state where they thought you might have gone. They searched for well over a year. Finally, they figured you didn't want to be found."

Wade was silent. He'd gone over to Seattle and gotten a job as a dishwasher. He'd had no idea anyone in Dry Creek would even miss him.

"It was always easier for you to hide than to let yourself be found," Carl finally said wearily. "I'm not casting any stones. I was the same way for a lot of years."

"But you changed."

The sheriff nodded. "Yes, I changed. That's why I know you can, too."

With that, the two men started walking over to meet with the boys. Wade felt like he was shaken to his core. Had he really missed God's answer to all his boyhood prayers? Was he so busy being angry that he didn't even know what he could have?

He looked over at where Jasmine stood and asked the hardest question of all. Was he going to miss it all again? Was it even possible for a man who'd lived his life alone to trust someone else? If he prayed now, would God even listen?

Wade shook his head; he just didn't know the answer to any of his questions. And he couldn't just listen to his heart anyway, not until he knew about Jasmine and Lonnie.

Chapter Thirteen

Jasmine had seen the sheriff come into the barn and she waited for him to finish talking to Wade before she excused herself from the choir and walked over to the men. If they had something they wanted to say to her, she didn't want them to say it around the children. The little ones didn't need to be reminded that their Christmas angel was an ex-con and still under suspicion of doing something wrong.

Carl met her eyes when she got close.

"Hey, I got those fireworks you wanted," the sheriff said. "I have them out in the car. Got them from a guy in Miles City."

"Did he have sparklers? That's really what I wanted." Jasmine glanced at Wade and saw him smile as he listened.

"You'll have to look in the bag," Carl said with a shrug. "He just gave me what he had."

"I'll help you look," Wade offered as he started to turn.

"Before anyone moves, I have good news," the sheriff said. "I think we're in the clear. The Feds don't think Lonnie is planning to come up this way. They've talked to some of the other prisoners and they believe the other escapee was the brains behind the break. They think the two of them will head down to Mexico. That's the smart thing for them to do."

"Well, that's a relief," Jasmine said. She felt muscles inside her relax that she hadn't even known were tensed.

"It's just—" the sheriff said, and then hesitated. He looked over at Wade. "It's probably nothing."

"A hunch?" Wade asked.

The sheriff nodded and then looked over at Jasmine. "The other thing the inmates said is that Lonnie always used to talk about you. In kind of weird ways. How you were his soul mate and how the two of you were meant to be together and stuff like that."

"He's nuts," Jasmine said. The thought of Lonnie talking about her being with her made her skin crawl.

"Probably," the sheriff said. "Just to be on the safe side, we'll have deputy sheriffs posted around town for a few days. They'll take turns sitting in the café in case Lonnie does come here. And they will also watch the county roads."

"I'm going to post a sign," Jasmine said. "Outside the door of the café. It's supposed to tell how to get to my place so if Lonnie takes it, people will know where he's going."

The sheriff nodded. "We'll keep an eye on that, too,"

Jasmine nodded. Everything was taken care of. "I guess I can concentrate on the pageant, then."

"You better," Carl said with a grin. "Because pulling in those deputies is the best advertising we could have done. By now the whole county knows we've got an angel flying in our pageant again. We could have a real crowd here. I'm thinking we should charge admission."

"Oh, we can't do that," Jasmine said. "I'm sure the church would never agree."

"They could use the money to finally buy some decent costumes, though," Wade said.

"The boys need to realize it's an honor to wear those bathrobes," Jasmine said. "They come from the community—with love."

Wade snorted. "You're welcome to try and convince them of that. I'm taking care of it, but I've got one shepherd who was assigned a pink bathrobe. He may be scarred for life."

"Yes, well, that particular bathrobe was supposed to be for the girl's choir, but we didn't have enough shepherd costumes and—"

"Whatever you do, don't tell the shepherds that

it's a girl's bathrobe," Wade said in mock horror and she laughed.

"I won't," she promised.

With that, the men went over to talk to the boys and Jasmine walked back to sing with the girls. Before she got there, though, Edith asked her to help carry in some new bathrobes that had been donated yesterday.

The sun was brighter this time when Jasmine stepped out of the barn. She looked up and noticed that the gray clouds from earlier in the day were giving way to light white clouds that scattered over a blue sky.

She walked with Edith over to Charley's pickup. Two boxes were sitting in the back of the pickup and Jasmine reached for one.

"Oh, we don't need to carry the boxes in," Edith said. "I thought we'd just pull out the bathrobes we need for today. Not everyone's here."

"Sure, that works," Jasmine said as she started to pull one box closer to the end of the truck bed. There was a strip of bright purple showing in the other box and she put a hand out to that one until she realized it wasn't practical. She could see there were sensible colors in the box she was already pulling toward her.

"These will work good," Jasmine said as she opened the box flaps. "Lots of grays and beiges."

She looked up to see her friend studying her face.

"Why didn't you keep reaching for the purple robe?" Edith asked quietly. "You obviously liked it best."

Jasmine shrugged. "I just thought the other colors would be more suitable for the church's pageant."

It was silent for a minute.

"I notice you don't spike your hair as much anymore," Edith commented.

"Oh, that," Jasmine said as she reached up and ran her fingers through her hair to be sure it was under control. "It is a bit wild and—"

"Dear me," the older woman continued to stare at Jasmine. "I think I've led you astray."

"Huh?"

"I never noticed you stopped looking like you," Edith said, her words tumbling over each other. "You used to wear all those bright colors and, your hair, you even wore those red things in it sometimes."

"Streaks. They were streaks."

"I never meant to make you think that quiet colors were more appropriate in God's eyes," Edith continued in a rush. "Just because I wear them doesn't mean you need to. You don't have to be quiet to be a Christian."

Jasmine didn't know what to say and the older woman was still looking at her.

"And you hate dresses," Edith continued. "I

should have realized something was wrong when you started wearing all those dresses."

"I only have three of them."

"And they're light gray, dark gray and beige," Edith said emphatically. "I bet you hate them all."

"Well, maybe a little."

"From now on, you need to dress like yourself. It's the only way things will work. Remember, God gave us peacocks and sunsets and rainbows."

"I can do peacock," Jasmine said with a grin.

"And let's bring that purple robe inside. Maybe we can find someone to play King Herod after all. I'm thinking he should be in the pageant even if he's just lurking in a corner somewhere acting like he's ready to pounce."

"I thought all of the roles were already assigned," Jasmine said as she pulled the box toward them that had the purple robe.

"Yes, but Wade needs a part," Edith said as they drew the robe from the box.

"I don't think Wade wants to be in the pageant."

"Which might just be the reason he should be. That boy has promise, you know. There's a reason God brought him back to us."

With that, Edith marched back into the barn with the purple robe draped over her arm.

Jasmine walked a little slower behind the other woman. She hadn't minded giving up the color in her wardrobe for God. At least, not much. She felt she should give Him something. Now, if she took the color back, flying as the angel was all she had left to give.

She opened the door and stood just inside the barn while Edith walked over to Wade with the purple robe. She couldn't hear what either one of them was saying, but Wade finally took the bathrobe and put it on so she supposed that was the answer. She wondered why God had brought that man back to Dry Creek.

She knew she should go back and sing with the girls, but instead she walked over to the group of boys that were with Wade. It was amazing how much control he had over the kids. He was so intent on talking to them he didn't even see she was there. She stood and looked at him. She wondered if he knew the boys idolized him.

Wade knew he was in trouble. He'd no sooner announced to the shepherds that he might play the role of Herod than they wanted to be in his army. Which meant they wanted weapons. They knew enough of the story to know that Herod had some kind of army and would have gotten rid of the wise men if he could have found them.

The shepherds were all in favor of anything that would cause trouble for the wise men that were rapidly becoming known simply as *them*.

"There is no us and them," he clarified. "The

wise men are good men, too. And you don't need weapons during the Christmas pageant. Or, after, either. At your age, you don't need them at any time, really."

He heard someone clapping when he finished his brief speech and he knew it wasn't one of the shepherds so he turned to the side and saw Jasmine standing there. She'd fluffed her hair up and she tied the bottom of her T-shirt up in a way that made it look like a blouse.

"So you're the king?" she asked.

Wade felt a little foolish standing there in a purple satin bathrobe that was too short for him and didn't tie right. "I said I'd be willing to stand in until Edith found someone else."

"He's going to die," one of the little shepherds announced solemnly to Jasmine.

"What?"

"He's a king without an army," the boy continued matter-of-factly. "Those wise men could take him—even without their donkey."

"I didn't say I don't have an army," Wade defended himself. "We just use our wits to protect ourselves."

"What's wits?" a shepherd asked.

"Brains." Wade pointed to his head. "My army thinks and plans."

"So you're a pacifist?" Jasmine asked, her voice ringing with delight.

"Uh." Wade felt trapped. "Not exactly. But I've never believed that it solves anything to just shoot things up."

"Like your grandfather does." Jasmine nodded like she understood.

Wade had never talked about his grandfather with anyone, but he wanted Jasmine to know. "He—I—ah—"

He was interrupted by a tug on his robe which was fortunate because he had forgotten he was surrounded by boys. He might want to tell Jasmine about the pain of his childhood, but he didn't want to announce it to the whole kindergarten world.

"Yeah?" he asked the boy.

"We could be a marching army," the boy finally said. "They don't have weapons."

"That's right. They don't," Wade said as he stepped a few feet away from the boys and motioned for Jasmine to follow him. He didn't want to wait until he drove her home to ask her because she might think it was just an add-on invitation. He wanted to ask her like it was important.

"Want to have dinner with me tonight?" he asked.

"The café is closed on Sunday."

"Oh," Wade said, and then pressed ahead bravely. "You could come have dinner with me and my grandfather, then. I'll clean the kitchen up and—"

"That would be great," Jasmine said.

"I'm not much of a cook, really, but I'll do my best."

Jasmine nodded.

"At least my grandfather's been pretty well-behaved," Wade felt compelled to add. "He says he stopped drinking a few months ago and I believe him. There aren't any empties around. And he hasn't been—"

Jasmine's face lit up. "I'll drive my motorcycle over."

"It's not a problem for me to come get you."

Jasmine looked like she was going to protest, but then she nodded even though the glow on her face dimmed.

The shepherds drew him back and, before he knew it, he was teaching them how to march in time with each other. They were hopeless at it, of course, but they were having fun and at least getting the concept of cooperation. If he was going to stay in Dry Creek, he wouldn't mind helping with the Sunday-school kids once in a while.

Whoa, he thought. Where had that thought come from?

Then he glanced across the barn at Jasmine singing with the girls and looked down at the boys gathered around his purple robe and he wondered how long he could manage to stay in this small town. He'd only thought to stay a few days, just long enough to do the job Carl had for him. But, according to the doctors, he wasn't ready to go back to his regular work yet, so if he wanted he could stay for another week or so. Even a month.

He skated around the thought of staying, giving it time to grow or die in his mind. He figured he'd come up with a dozen objections to the suggestion, but not one floated to his mind. He didn't even have a plant that would miss him back in Idaho Falls.

"Well, let's get to marching," Wade finally said, and his troops lined up and faced forward. He couldn't have been prouder of them if they had been officers of the law.

When the pageant practice was over, everyone drove down the road until they got to Dry Creek. Then they parked in front of the church and walked inside. Wade hadn't really intended to go that far with them, but he did. The morning had turned warmer and a nice fresh breeze was blowing. He surprised himself by walking up the steps with the others. If anyone asked him, he would say he was guarding Jasmine. But he knew he could do that by sitting on the steps of the church. He didn't need to go into the building for that.

He took an extra breath when he stepped through the door. So many of his childhood hopes had been born and then expired in this place. He'd learned to pray and then he'd learned his prayers didn't work. Now, he didn't know what to expect. The first thing he noticed was the inside of the church hadn't changed much since he'd been here over twenty years ago. The carpet might be new, but the wooden cross hanging behind the pulpit was still the same.

What did surprise him was that he was greeted like the prodigal son would have been at the party his father had given for him. The past years fell away. It seemed like everyone in the church came up and shook his hand. He knew some of it was because they had been reminded of him recently with the collection of money on his behalf, but they sure sounded sincere when they welcomed him home. He recognized most of the faces from his childhood even if he couldn't remember all of the names.

He didn't quite know what to do with so many well wishes so he was happy enough to have the piano signal that the service was ready to start. He let the words of the sermon wash over him without really listening. He wasn't ready to go quite that far as he tagged along with everyone. Besides, he was sitting next to Jasmine and he was captivated by the way several strands of her hair, down by her neck, were so wispy and, at the same time, reminded him so much of fine-tooled copper.

Before he knew it, church was over and people were heading to the back of the sanctuary for coffee. Wade was swept along with everyone else and, when he got there, Carl came over to give him a new update on the search for Lonnie.

Wade was happy for the contact. It reminded him of who he was.

Carl said a border-patrol officer thought he saw a man matching the description of the other escapee trying to drive through a checkpoint. The officer said there had been another man hunched down in the backseat of the car, but the two persons of interest had taken off before the officer could catch them. The officer knew they hadn't made it across the border into Mexico in that try as they'd turned back before he could give chase. But, he said, it wouldn't take long for two guys to slip through the border if they were determined.

"It has to be Lonnie and that other guy. So there's no need for you to guard Jasmine so closely," Carl said. "I'm sure that'll be a relief."

"Yeah," Wade said absentmindedly.

"Well, at least a relief for her," Carl amended his words with a laugh. "You know women—they need some space."

Everybody needed space. Wade knew that better than most. It should be fine if Jasmine rode her motorcycle over tonight. He went over and told her so and it made him feel like a hero to see the grin return to her face.

When Wade got back to his grandfather's place, he was astonished. The old man had actually cleaned the kitchen when Wade had been gone and set up the checkerboard on the table, hoping to play a game with him. Wade had forgotten the two of them used to play checkers before everything had gone so bad.

Wade agreed to a game, but said he could only play one since he'd invited company for dinner. They sat out on the porch so Wade could keep an eye on the road, but no one drove by and his grandfather actually won. Then he quietly called Wade by his own name.

"I thought you were going to call me Sonny forever," Wade said as he started putting the game pieces back in the box.

"Some days things are more clear than others," his grandfather said with a timid look at Wade. "I don't like to remember the past. It makes me ashamed of how I was. But, when Edith told me she'd asked you to come, I stopped drinking. I wanted to be sober so I could tell you something."

Wade blinked.

Then the old man added, "I'm sorry for the way I treated you. I should never have let things get that far out of control."

Wade had never thought he'd hear his grandfather say that much. He cleared his throat. He didn't quite know what to say. He wasn't ready to accept an apology for all that had happened. His grandfather had not been there for him when he needed him the most.

Then it hit him. "I'm sorry I wasn't here to see

you were taken care of, either. I should have kept track of what was going on."

His grandfather reached his hand across the table and laid it on top of Wade's, but all he said was, "Now let's get ready for that dinner guest of yours. What's her name again?"

"Jasmine."

His grandfather nodded.

Wade knew he'd witnessed a miracle. Of course, tomorrow his grandfather might not remember a word he'd said. But he had stopped drinking. That was a start.

Tonight, Wade wanted to sit out on the porch with Jasmine and tell her what kind of a childhood he'd had. He doubted anyone could really know him unless he opened up about his isolation as a boy. It had been a long time since he'd cared about whether someone got to know him or not. Carl was probably the last real friend he'd made in his life and that was back in grade school. But Jasmine mattered.

He already had one strike against him in her eyes because he was a lawman. In fact, he probably had two strikes because of the church thing. His messed up childhood could be the final third strike and he'd be out of the game as far as she was concerned. But he still had to tell her.

He stood up. He'd bought some canned goods and bread when he drove through Billings on the way here. "This dinner I'm cooking needs to be good. Let's go see what we can find in the cupboard."

"I love sardines," his grandfather said with a grin.

That was the first time Wade could remember his grandfather making a joke. He looked at the older man carefully. Yeah, it had been a joke.

Wade spent the rest of the afternoon looking for a tablecloth and worrying about whether or not he could find glasses that matched. He knew he couldn't turn out a four-star dinner, but he was hoping for homey. He had several tins of a pretty good stew and a packet of English muffins. As long as all he had to do was heat the stew and toast the muffins, he'd do fine.

It felt good to be cooking for Jasmine and his grandfather. He sat down at one point and realized that, for the first time in decades, he was beginning to feel as if he might have a chance at a family.

Chapter Fourteen

Jasmine was living on the edge. She'd told her father that she was going over to the Suttons' for dinner and he'd given her a worried look. She wasn't sure if the look was because of Wade's grandfather's shotgun or Wade himself.

"Men can be dogs," her father finally said. She'd been in the hallway, putting on some lipstick, and then she'd come back into the kitchen to pick up her jacket. She'd taken Edith's words to heart and was wearing a vivid magenta blouse with her jeans. Plus some dangling silver earrings. And, her boots, of course. It felt good to be back in her own skin.

"Not all men, mind you," he added. "But some."

"I'm forty-three years old, Dad. I know about men."

Her father grunted. "I mean, that some men just don't make commitments. They'll break your heart just because they can't help themselves."

"Ah." So her father saw it, too. She sat down next to him at the kitchen table and covered his hand with hers. "It's only dinner. He'll probably be gone right after Christmas."

"That's exactly what I'm talking about," her father said as he reached over with his other hand and patted hers. "You don't know each other very well yet. Wade was a good boy, but it's been a lot of years since he's lived around here. Sometimes when people move away, they find it hard to come back here after living in the big city."

"He lives in Idaho Falls. Not New York."

"Still," he said stubbornly. "I wouldn't want to see you get hurt."

Jasmine knew that, but she still got a lump in her throat when he said the words. Elmer hadn't been her first choice as a father, but he'd opened his heart to her without reservation.

She stood and kissed him on the top of the head. "Be sure and eat something for dinner yourself."

He nodded.

"I won't be late," she said as she walked over to get the jacket that she'd left on the chair by the refrigerator. Then she stopped by the counter and picked up her hostess gift.

She didn't know what to do when people invited her to dinner and things like that so a hostess gift made her feel more confident. That way, if she messed up on some other thing she was supposed to do, it went easier on her. Unfortunately, she'd used her last jar of jam going to the Walls'.

Her backup gift, two candles, didn't seem right. She already knew Wade didn't like to eat by candlelight and, given his grandfather's unsteady nature, a candle could cause a fire.

Finally, her mind had gone to chocolate and she'd grabbed an unopened bag of chocolate chips from the cupboard earlier. She'd gotten the chips one day when she'd convinced herself she would learn to make cookies. Now, with the red ribbon she'd tied on them, they managed to look festive.

"He better be buying you jewels," her father grumbled as he saw her pick up the bag of chips off the counter.

She laughed as she walked out the door.

The sun was starting to set and the air was colder than earlier in the day. Nothing made her feel more alive than slipping her helmet on her head and starting up her motorcycle. She was feeling good as she began the short drive over to the Sutton place.

Her father had already turned the lights on for the cross. As the sun set, the hill turned black against a darkening sky and lit up the cross like a crystal chandelier hanging above everything. She half expected an Italian opera to begin, the cross gave the whole area that kind of dramatic style.

She drove slowly so she could enjoy the cross's beauty. Her father should leave the lights on all year around. She suspected the dramatic nature of the cross would turn lighter in the spring or summer. Maybe it would feel playful. It would be lovely to sit up beside the cross and have a midnight picnic.

She turned into the Sutton lane and was tempted to stop at the old pickup like the Covered Dish Ladies did, but she didn't. Lights were on in the house and it looked friendly.

Before she knew it, she was standing at the door, getting ready to knock when Wade opened it wide.

"Come in," he said.

Jasmine stepped inside and looked around. Someone had scrubbed the kitchen. And something smelled good. And—she looked up in surprise—Wade was looking nervous.

"I brought chocolate," she said as she held out the bag done up with the ribbon. "Well, just chips, really, but I wish it were jam."

Why was it that knowing he was nervous made her feel the same skittering way?

"Thank you. I like chocolate," Wade said solemnly as he accepted the gift.

Mr. Sutton came into the kitchen from the living room and smiled at her. "Jasmine, isn't it?"

She nodded and then looked at Wade.

"He has us figured out," Wade said. "Well, at least, he knows we're not my parents."

"Oh, that's good."

"I don't know." Wade gave a roguish smile. "He's not so likely to give me an order to kiss you."

Wade didn't wait for her to say anything, but he just held his hand out for her jacket. "May I?"

Jasmine handed him her jacket and her heart. She liked this lighthearted, flirtatious side of Wade. His grandfather asked if she'd like to sit down and she did. After a few minutes, the old man insisted he wanted to eat his dinner in the living room by the television so he left her alone in the kitchen with Wade.

She kept waiting for Wade to steal a kiss, but he seemed intent on being the perfect host instead. He brought her herb tea to drink while he finished toasting the English muffins. He brought her honey for the muffin before he brought a casserole dish filled with well-seasoned stew. By the time he had finished serving her, all of her earlier confidence was gone. Her father could have saved his breath warning her about men. Wade clearly wasn't ready to make a move of any kind.

"Did you ever get the fireworks out of Carl's car?" Wade asked when they were finished with their dinner. "I was going to help you and then I got all caught up with the boys and—"

"I thought I'd go over tomorrow and get it," Jasmine said as she folded her napkin beside her plate.

"I'll drive you," Wade said, nodding.

"I thought the Feds decided I was clean."

She regretted the words the minute they were out of her mouth. She was upset with him and she should have kept her mouth shut. They hadn't talked about *it* all evening. They'd just been a man and a woman sitting down to a meal together like it was a natural thing for them to do. But it wasn't natural, not for either of them. And he had not even tried to kiss her.

"They did," Wade agreed. "I just—"

Jasmine felt her heart break a little. "They may trust me, but you don't. Is that it?"

"No, I—" Wade swallowed. "I worry. That's all."

He looked at her with misery in his eyes. He might not trust her, but he clearly wasn't indifferent. She supposed it was hard for a lawman to open up to an ex-con. Maybe they both just needed more time.

"What time is good for you to pick me up?" she asked gently, and saw him relax.

"Maybe around ten. That'll give you time afterward to get ready for the pageant."

She nodded. Her father had been right to worry they were going too fast. She wondered if he was right about anything else. "You've been gone from your place in Idaho Falls for a while now. I suppose you can't wait to get back."

"The post office will only hold my mail for so long," he admitted.

That wasn't exactly a declaration of interest in

staying here, she told herself. "You wouldn't want to miss any mail."

Wade grunted and then stood up. "A man needs more than mail in his life."

He took their plates to the sink and then went into the living room saying he needed to get something. He returned with a thick patchwork quilt made of blue and green squares.

"I thought we could sit outside and look at the cross awhile," he said. "My grandfather has a real good view from his porch."

"I bet you don't have anything like it in Idaho Falls."

"Not even close." He looked at her and his eyes grew warm.

Jasmine thought later that she would always remember sitting on the porch with Wade that night. He wrapped that old quilt around them both and they talked for hours. In the darkness, they were equals. He wasn't suspicious of her and she wasn't defensive around him. He told her about his grandfather. She told him about her mother. They compared old pains and new dreams.

"Carl thinks I have a chip on my shoulder," he finally confided. "Told me so today."

"We all have problems of some sort."

"He said if I wanted to change, all I needed to do was do it."

Jasmine stopped breathing. She knew how important this was. "And do you? Want to change?"

Wade was silent for so long she didn't think he was going to answer. Finally, he said with a raw voice, "I don't think I can change."

Jasmine didn't stay for long after that.

Wade didn't blame her. He watched her walk out and get on her motorcycle and ride down the drive from his grandfather's house. She was right to leave him, of course. A man who could not change, not even when he wanted to, was only trouble and heartache for those around him.

He reminded himself that he needed to check about that light she was expecting for her motorcycle. The front light beamed out strong, but it was dangerous not to have a tail light. Maybe he'd have time to drive into Billings one day before he left. They should have every kind of lightbulb ever made in a town that size.

He wondered how he could trust her when he still had doubts. Of course, the doubts were shrinking, but that was only because the reports from the Feds seemed to clear her of any involvement.

Maybe once the pageant was over he could go get hypnotized or something. A man should be able to change if he wanted to and Wade had never had as much reason to change as he did now. There should be a hypnotist in Billings. If not, he'd go to Denver.

Then he realized he couldn't go anywhere until he made arrangements for his grandfather. And he'd promised some of the shepherds he'd take them someplace where they could see a fire engine. A month ago, he'd had no one to worry about, not even the usual trail of suspects he was doing surveillance on. And now, here he was, a man who was actually needed by someone who wasn't a fellow lawman.

Chapter Fifteen

It was Christmas Eve and Jasmine was looking out the windshield of her father's car. He was driving the Cadillac tonight, its white sides already dusted with snow before they left the house. The leather seats were cold enough to be uncomfortable and she could watch her breath in the light of the dashboard.

"You're sure you don't want me to stop and pick up Wade?" her father asked as he turned from their lane onto the main road. "He'd get a kick out of riding in this old car."

"No."

She'd made her decision. She had to cut Wade loose. She didn't want him to feel obligated to say he trusted her when he clearly didn't. Earlier, when he drove her over to the sheriff's to get that sack of fireworks, she had told him her father would take her to the pageant tonight and that's the way it should be. She was polite about it, of course. Not everyone was able to get over the fact that she was an ex-con. She could accept that. She didn't have to like it, but she could accept it.

Her father cleared his throat. "You're sure? 'Cause it'd be no trouble to stop and get him. He's right next door."

"I thought you didn't approve of Wade anyway."

"Well, but you seemed to like him and he's okay." Out of the corner of her eye, she saw her father turn to look at her. "Actually, I think he might be more than okay."

She shrugged and kept her eyes straight ahead. "He's the law."

She never should have forgotten that.

Her father was quiet the rest of the way. When he pulled up to the barn on the outskirts of Dry Creek, she counted twenty or so cars that were already parked around the place. That was a relief; the children were counting on a good audience for the pageant and it looked as if they were going to get one. More people would be coming later, of course. The snow had stopped and, when she stepped out of the Cadillac, she looked up and saw the stars. Dozens of pinpricks dotted the sky.

It was a lover's sky out tonight.

She forced her gaze back down to earth. A man, he looked like one of the hands from the Elkton Ranch, was standing on a tall ladder adjusting a light that was focused on the mural that had been painted on the barn last summer. She couldn't see his face because his gray Stetson kept it in the shadows.

Whoever he was, he had looped the cord for the light over the top of the high door that led into the loft where ranchers had stored their hay for many generations. The mural, with the figures of the men and women who'd lived in this area a hundred years ago, was a symbol of how connected this community was to its past and she felt good calling this place her home. She was even related to the past now that she knew her father was a Maynard, one of the early cattle families.

"If you need anything before you go up there, you just let me know," her father said as he pointed to the hayloft. The night was still cold, but the snow had stopped falling. "It'll be chilly in that angel costume. You'll be up higher than most people and there's that big door up there in the loft that's probably as drafty as all get-out even when it's closed."

"I'm wearing two pairs of socks," she said to comfort him.

She didn't add that she also had some string in her pocket to help her trail the sparklers from her feet. She'd checked with Edith and the barn would be fairly dark when she made her swing over it so the sparklers should make people catch their breath in wonderment when she passed. It was that initial gasp she was aiming for. That's what the shepherds would have done the first thing when they saw the angel, even before they fell to their knees.

She could almost see the looks on the shepherds' faces. She might not have a lover to view the stars with her, but she had no lack of friends and neighbors in this town. And she wanted to do something special for them to make this Christmas Eve feel holy.

The performers were supposed to arrive an hour early to be sure their costumes were on correctly, so Jasmine opened the door expecting to only see the kids who were in the pageant. But there was a crowd. Of course, the shepherds and the choir girls were all too young to drive themselves so their parents and other siblings had to come at the same time and no one would sit out in their cars in this weather. With nothing to do, the families all stood around, sipping cups of warm spiced cider and talking with each other.

Jasmine scanned the room, making sure Wade wasn't there. She relaxed when she saw he wasn't. She laid her angel robe and the sack of fireworks by the ladder that led up to the hayloft. Then she saw Edith over by a refreshment table so she headed in that direction.

"Where's Wade?" Edith asked when she saw her. The older woman had some white towels in her arms and a frown on her face.

"I can help you," Jasmine offered. Why did everyone need Wade all of a sudden? He hadn't even been in the picture when they started practicing for the pageant.

"These are for the sheep," the older woman laid the towels in Jasmine's arms. "I haven't seen the shepherds and they're going to need them."

"Don't worry. I'll find them."

It didn't take her more than two minutes to do just that. The boys were huddled in a corner talking to their dogs.

"I have your towels," she said as she walked over to them.

They all looked up and then past her. "Where's Mr. Sutton?"

"You mean, Wade?"

They nodded.

"My dog doesn't feel so good," the smallest boy explained. "He needs some medicine."

"I don't know—" she began, and then stopped. The boys were looking at her with such trust on their faces. "Maybe I could get Charley for you. He's a vet."

This didn't seem to reassure the boys so she squatted down to be closer to them. "Charley takes care of all kinds of animals. Wade doesn't even have a pet."

She figured they could see from that which man would be better to call.

Jasmine saw the expression in the boys' eyes change from worry to near adoration as they looked behind her. She guessed what had happened before she saw the shadow on the floor in front of her.

"I have a donkey. That should count for something."

Wade.

Jasmine wanted to disappear. She figured he was looking at her about now so she refused to turn around until he left. She kept still, but the uneasy feeling of someone watching her continued.

Wade stood and watched Jasmine's back stiffen as the boys all scrambled to their feet. He wondered if she was going to face him. He wouldn't blame her if she didn't. She hadn't said they were through before they'd begun, but he could read body language.

He'd never been a quitter, but the thought of trying to change enough to be the man Jasmine wanted seemed as difficult as a blind man trying to jump across a deep ravine with nothing to guide him. It wasn't a lack of bravery; it was just an absence of any clue telling him how to do it. Even the blind man would only fall on his face if he tried to do the impossible.

When Jasmine didn't move, the donkey took a step forward. Wade pulled back on her halter. It said something about him that the only real friends he'd had as a boy had been this donkey and Carl—and he'd lied to Carl so the friend who'd known the truth about him was the donkey. And he only trusted her because she couldn't tell anyone else his secrets.

Wade knew he had lived his life in a small box that didn't require him to trust anyone or, since God always seemed to be pushing back into the picture, any Being, either. Wade believed what he saw and what he heard. He never worried about what his heart told him about people, because he went with his head. That's the way he'd been since he was a boy, but he knew it wasn't enough for someone like Jasmine.

So, he was going to turn around and go. But even though Jasmine didn't want to admire the donkey, the boys did.

"Can I touch it?" one of the boys asked as he stepped close.

"Her," Wade said as he patted the donkey's neck. "Her name's Jenny."

The donkey bowed her gray head until it was level with the boy. Then she looked at him with mournful eyes. She was a shameless beggar even if she couldn't smell oats. "Jenny's a little wet from the ride over here. Let her dry off first."

Jasmine finally turned around. "Just remember that she bites. Don't get close."

Then she looked up at Wade as if he was unfit to be around children—or donkeys, for that matter. "Does Edith know the donkey is here?"

Wade smiled. He would rather have Jasmine scolding him than ignoring him. "Edith told me to tie Jenny behind that curtain in the corner. It seems the wise men are going to ride her first for their chat with Herod and then she's going to be whisked away so Mary can use her for the big entrance."

"The two of you will be busy," Jasmine said as she stood up.

Wade watched as she lifted her arm and tentatively reached out to touch the donkey's coat.

"Actually, your father's going to keep track of her so I can play King Herod."

Just then Edith came walking through with a script in one hand and a little bell in the other. "It's time to get to your places. The pageant starts in ten minutes. Be sure you have your costumes all tied up securely."

"But my dog doesn't feel good," the shepherd boy said.

"Well, put him back with the donkey, then," Edith said. She was counting the shepherd boys as she spoke. Wade could see her lips moving.

The boy with the dog sat back in shock, "But the donkey *bites*."

Wade didn't know if the dog felt the shock from the boy and was reacting to it or if he heard the dismissal in Edith's voice, but he lifted his head from the floor, gave a vigorous yip, and stood up, miraculously healed.

"Attaboy," Wade said.

"Now, get your sheep towels on your dogs and go hide behind those boxes. Those are your hills," Edith said, directing them.

The older woman didn't see it because her eyes were already scanning the crowd looking for something else, but Wade proudly watched his shepherd boys line up and march their way to their hills. They could almost keep step with each other. Then, just before they disappeared behind the boxes, they all turned and saluted him.

Wade smiled and saluted them back.

"What was that about?" Jasmine asked.

"Oh, you know boys," he said. "They'd rather be soldiers than shepherds."

The boys were in mismatched bathrobes, but none of them were wearing pink. The shepherd who had been assigned the offending robe earlier was wearing Wade's old brown robe and looking very pleased with it, probably because the front pocket was partially torn off and no one would ever confuse it with a girl's robe. In addition, each shepherd had an old flour sack tied around his head to keep the desert sun off his face and sandals to keep the corresponding sand off his feet.

Jasmine nodded as she started to turn. "I guess I better get over to the hayloft and get my costume on."

"Before you do—did Carl reach you?" The sheriff had called Wade just before he left his grandfather's place to come here. "It looks like Lonnie is in custody. They caught two men trying to get across the border. They need to do fingerprints to be sure, but they think one of them is Lonnie."

"That's a relief."

"Not that it's for sure." Wade had never been one to have hunches or premonitions of any sort. But he had a buzzing in his head somewhere that made him unwilling to relax. Would Lonnie really go to Mexico?

Yesterday afternoon, the sheriff had dropped off copies of the transcripts from the inmate interviews that the Feds had done. None of the inmates remembered Lonnie ever mentioning Mexico. And just like the Feds had told them earlier, one inmate said that, during the last year, Lonnie had become freakishly obsessed with Jasmine.

"Of course, you can't let it bother you," Wade said. He knew inmate testimonies were notoriously unreliable. "Two deputy sheriffs are on their way here as we speak. And Carl will be on duty, too."

Jasmine nodded. "I better go."

"I'll be up to help with the wheel by the time you're ready to go."

"Charley can help me," Jasmine said.

Wade knew he should let her go. When he finished with his bit as King Herod, he could guard her from the steps leading up to the hayloft and she never even needed to know he was there. He'd just seen the deputy sheriffs step inside the barn so he knew they'd be watching the entrances. There was no reason for him to worry. It's just that he didn't want to miss seeing Jasmine's face when she swung back to the hayloft after she made her pronouncement to the shepherds.

"It won't hurt to have another pair of eyes watching that wheel," Wade said, keeping his voice casual.

Just then they both heard the ring of a bell. That was Edith's signal that everyone should take their places.

Wade was glad Jasmine went rushing off to the hayloft without telling him definitely that she didn't want him there. It wasn't that he was shy about pushing his way in where people didn't want him. He did that all the time with the bad guys. But he wouldn't do it with Jasmine.

The strange thing was, he wanted Jasmine to trust him. She'd never said that her old boyfriend, Lonnie, had been overbearing, but reading those inmate interviews made him think it was a good guess. If Lonnie had been the kind to push her around, Wade wanted to give her plenty of room.

The sounds of footsteps and whispers gradually wound down as the audience took their seats in the folding chairs around the edge of the barn. Wade hadn't been to one of these pageants since the disastrous night when he'd been the angel, but he felt the peace of it all settle into his bones.

Edith had marked off a place for him to stand in a shadowed area near where the wise men passed by. Wade took one last look at the audience and walked over to his post. His last thought before the pageant began was to wonder who in the audience had bought a purple satin bathrobe a decade or so ago. And what they thought now that it was being used in the pageant to help portray a king.

This was what being part of a community was like, Wade thought to himself. It was remembering the kids and the traditions of one's home even when shopping. He wondered if he'd ever belong to a place like that.

Chapter Sixteen

Jasmine paused at the foot of the ladder leading up to the hayloft, her gown and sack in her hand. The lights had just dimmed in the barn and everyone was quiet. A sudden cold breeze blew in from somewhere and she pulled her collar a little more firmly around her neck. Even with that, she was chilled.

She looked over the audience that lined the walls of the barn and wondered how many people here were lonely tonight. Not many, she guessed. She saw a chipped-toothed toddler being held in his mother's lap. Even the men from the Elkton Ranch were sitting together and focused on the pageant. Then the spotlight was gradually turned up and the narration began.

"Jesus was born in the town of Bethlehem in Judea, during the time when Herod was king," a man's voice came out over the microphone. Jasmine knew it was a recorded voice, but it was mellow and it pulled her into the story.

She wondered if Bethlehem was as small as Dry Creek. If it was, she could understand how difficult it would have been to find housing for a crowd of people. It would be like when they held their infrequent rodeos here. Surely they would have found room for a pregnant woman, though. Edith would have seen to it if Mary and Joseph turned up in Dry Creek. They'd be in her own bed if necessary.

The spotlight went over to King Herod as the narrator continued. Wade's purple satin bathrobe was too short and his crown was made out of a painted coat hanger. He'd pushed his jeans up to his knees and he wore plastic sandals. But, as he stood there, his back militarily straight and his eyes scanning the distance as though looking for enemies, he truly seemed like a powerful king of old.

Her eyes could have watched Wade all night, but the wise men shuffled into the scene. They were leading the donkey who had saddlebags tossed over her back. The bags were stuffed to overflowing with plastic gold beads and one particular string was swinging back and forth over the donkey's side and the animal didn't seem to like it.

If that string of beads broke, they could repeat the disaster of the pageant Wade remembered where beads rolled everywhere and people stumbled on stage. Jasmine was tense until she noticed King

Herod casually tuck the string of beads back where it belonged while the wise men whispered together, one of them pointing up at the heavens.

As the wise men continued on their course, King Herod slipped out of sight through one of the side doors of the barn. If it had been anyone else, she would think he was leaving. But, given who he was, she was pretty sure the king was making one final check outside to be sure Lonnie was nowhere around. Even when the Feds told him he could ease up, he wouldn't.

Jasmine blinked a few times. It was too bad that he couldn't trust her.

Oh, well. She decided it was time for her to go and get ready. She'd seen Charley move up the ladder ten minutes ago so he'd be in place. Her cardboard wings were already up in the loft. She looked in her fireworks sack to be sure she'd included a lighter for the sparklers.

Then, she turned to the ladder and began the climb. The ladder was a permanent part of the barn and it had nice wide rungs, which was good because she had her robe and the fireworks in one hand and only had the other hand to hold herself steady as she went up the ladder.

The hayloft was about fifteen feet off of the main floor and, about halfway up, Jasmine turned to look back down at the stage. She was holding one rung and had her feet on another. Mary and Joseph were making their journey, with Mary riding on the donkey and Joseph leading them. By now, the donkey wasn't even bothering to look at all the people sitting around watching her. She seemed more interested in the fake little town she saw in the distance. Jasmine wondered if someone had thought to put oats in the stable.

Jasmine turned back to the ladder and continued. Her father had been right, she decided, about it being colder as she went higher. She wondered if that cowboy checking the outside light earlier had left the hayloft door open when he climbed down.

Her head came up inside the hayloft and she was facing toward the back of the area. Which meant she could see that the door was open. She was surprised Charley hadn't closed it, but he was probably too preoccupied with the wheel. Even in the dark, she could feel the wind blowing around tiny pieces of hay. The bales seemed to shed for some reason she didn't understand. Every time she'd been up here it seemed like there was more hay dust than before.

"Charley," she said as she threw the fireworks sack and her white robe onto the floor next to the opening and braced her arms to lift herself completely up into the hayloft. She was surprised when he didn't answer, but it flashed through her head that he might have gone down to say something to Edith. After all, the angel wasn't on for another ten minutes—longer if the girls' choir didn't increase their speed as they sang "It Came Upon a Midnight Clear."

Jasmine was on her knees by the time she could look around. The stacks of hay bales looked taller than she remembered. And there were fewer of the stacks. The angel wings weren't where she'd left them, but she could see them leaning against a different stack of bales. Someone had been moving the bales around, which was an odd thing to do. She wondered what Charley thought he was doing. At his age, he had no business moving anything that heavy.

And then she saw the Stetson hat, sitting on the floor next to the wheel. It was dark and shadowy in the loft, but she figured the gray hat must belong to the cowboy who'd been fixing the light outside. She stood up and started to take a step toward the hat, but then she stopped. Ranch hands generally had two hats, one for dress and one to wear when they worked. That hat looked new. Something was wrong if a cowboy left his dress Stetson in the middle of the floor like that. This place hadn't been swept up here in years.

Jasmine swallowed her panic. She tried to soundlessly turn to leave the loft when she heard a click. It was just a little sound. But she knew all too well what a gun sounded like when the hammer was pulled back with intent to fire.

"Don't worry. It's me," a man whispered, and her mouth went dry.

She had to turn around and face her past. "Lonnie?"

Her ex-boyfriend stood up behind some hay bales. It was dark and he was both thinner and older than she remembered him, but she would have known his face anywhere. His hairline was pushing back from his forehead and his eyes darted around in a way they had not used to do, but his grin—she would know that grin anywhere.

"It's me, baby," he said. "I came to get you."

"You're supposed to be in prison." Jasmine didn't want Lonnie to know there were deputy sheriffs downstairs waiting in case he came here. Of course, she realized as her heart sank, the deputies would be checking people as they came into the barn. They'd never think of a ladder up to the hayloft.

"You know there's no prison strong enough to stand between the two of us." Lonnie's eyes looked a little wilder than she remembered. He lowered his voice in what probably passed for romantic with him. "We're meant to be together. I missed you, baby."

Lonnie took a step out from behind the short stack of bales. That's when Jasmine saw the guns. He had one in his hand and another one stretching the waistband of his jeans.

"How'd you get here?" she stalled.

Lonnie grunted. "I heard about the pageant in Miles City. Some guys said there was a good-looking red-haired angel who was new to town and she had just found her father. I knew it had to be you. Sounds like you've got a good thing going here."

"What do you want from me?"

"I want you to come with me," Lonnie said as if he was surprised she'd have to ask. "I got the ladder set up and everything. Even got a pickup truck parked outside with clean plates and a full tank of gas."

Jasmine's heart stopped. "I can't go with you."

Lonnie's grin ended. "We don't have time for you to play hard to get. I came all this way to find you. You're coming with me."

"Please, just leave. If you go quick enough, no one will even know you've been here."

"That old man will know," Lonnie said as he jerked his head toward a stack of bales near the one he'd been hiding behind. "He's out now, but he'll come to unless I—"

Lonnie held up the gun.

"No," Jasmine gasped. "You've done enough damage. You can't—"

Lonnie just stood and looked at her. "You've changed."

Jasmine nodded. "Of course, I've changed. What we had all those years ago wasn't a life."

"It was good enough for me," Lonnie said, and

she could feel the chill in his voice. "Are you saying you're too good to go on the road with me now that I busted out of jail to come get you?"

"I'm not saying anything. I'm just asking you to leave here."

Lonnie walked closer to her. "You got yourself another man, don't you? That's it, isn't it?"

Jasmine forced herself not to take a step backward. Lonnie enjoyed making people afraid. So she stood there even when he was close enough that she could smell his sweat. "There's no man."

"Maybe not, but there's something." Lonnie studied her silently.

The girls' choir was almost finished with singing their songs. Jasmine should be putting her wings on. If the angel didn't show, people might come up to see what was wrong and someone else could get hurt. Then Jasmine heard a soft moan from behind the hay bales. She didn't want Lonnie to know Charley was regaining consciousness.

"You should turn yourself in," Jasmine said quickly. The only way she knew to ensure Lonnie's attention stayed on her was to get him angry.

"You'd like that, wouldn't you?" Lonnie growled. "You making a fool out of me?"

Jasmine braced herself for a slap to the face. But then they heard footsteps on the ladder.

"Who's that?" Lonnie hissed as he stepped away from her.

"I don't know."

Then a man called out, "Jasmine."

"It's him, isn't it?" Lonnie said as he took a few steps sideways to hide behind another short stack of bales. When he was almost there, he slid his extra gun across to her. "Pick that up and order your boy-friend to leave."

"I'm not going to do that," Jasmine said. Why did it have to be Wade coming up here? "Not even if you shoot me."

"Oh, I'm not going to shoot you." Lonnie gave a low chuckle. "I'm going to shoot him." He paused. "Dead center. He deserves it for messing with my woman anyway."

"No—" Jasmine whispered.

"And you better be convincing," Lonnie added as he slid into the darkness behind the bales. "Or I'll shoot him just for the fun of it."

Jasmine bent down to pick up the gun. The metal was cold and heavy in her hands. Years ago, Lonnie had taught her how to shoot a gun so she knew how to aim and fire with the best of them. She raised the gun so Lonnie could see she was taking his threat seriously. Then it occurred to her. It wouldn't be hard for her to be convincing in this little drama; it's what Wade had been expecting all along.

She could see the top of the lawman's head as he came to the end of the ladder. She only saw the back of his head now, but he'd need to pull himself up into the loft with his arms and then he'd turn around and see her. Her heart was pounding and she couldn't think of the words to pray. All that went through her mind was, *Please, God. Please, God. Please, God.*

Then it all became clear. *Please God, let Wade think his worst. Make him agree to leave. Let him be safe.*

Jasmine forced back the tears she felt. She needed to play her part well.

Wade pushed himself up the rest of the way into the hayloft. He felt an itch on his neck and thought some hay dust must have filtered down while he was climbing up the ladder. He'd taken his Herod robe off and had to catch one of the wayward sheep and return it to the shepherds so he hadn't gotten here as quickly as he'd expected. Charley would have Jasmine ready to go, though.

A faint sob alerted him. Someone had bit back the sound almost before it was out of their mouth, but he heard it. He was still facing toward the open hayloft door and he saw the short spokes of the ladder that rose just inches above the bottom of the opening.

He let the message of that ladder sink in. His back was already to whoever was in the loft and they hadn't knifed him or shot him thus far. He could start climbing down and they might never aim for him. But Jasmine was here. And Charley.

Wade swung his legs around so he could stand. These days that motion usually made him wince in pain, but he didn't even give it a passing thought. He turned around slowly so he wouldn't startle anyone and finally faced the gun.

He hadn't expected Jasmine to be the one, but she held the pistol steady and aimed at his heart.

They just looked at each other for a few seconds. It gave Wade time to orient himself. The hayloft was full of shadows, more so because of the spotlight shining in the other part of the barn. There were stacks of bales here and there and they'd been moved since he'd been up here yesterday.

"Is something wrong?" Wade finally asked just to give Jasmine space to talk.

Maybe if she said something she would give him a clue about what was happening. Someone must have a gun aimed at her, he finally decided. She stood there completely stiff.

Wade moved his eyes slightly, trying to decide which hay bales hid the person who threatened her. He didn't want that person to know he was looking so he was careful not to move his head.

He looked at Jasmine. It was so dark he couldn't see her eyes. He could see the strain on her face, though.

"I want you to leave," she said, her voice hard and flat.

For a second, it occurred to him that he didn't really *know* there was anyone else in the hayloft. He couldn't see or hear or smell anyone. And then, just as quickly, he realized the reason he knew she was innocent was because he trusted her. *He, Wade Sutton, trusted someone.* In his heart, he was one hundred percent positive Jasmine would never hold a gun on anyone like she was doing now—not unless there was someone else here who was a whole lot more deadly.

It was Lonnie, of course. It had to be.

"I came to help with the wheel," Wade said, sounding as close to a witless idiot as he could. "You need help with the wheel."

"What I need is for you to go back down those stairs and leave me alone," Jasmine repeated.

Wade took a step closer to her.

"No," Jasmine gasped.

Wade noticed the quick flick of her eyes as they went to the hay bales in the middle on his right. So that's where the person was.

"You've got to leave," Jasmine said again, her voice rising a little and sounding desperate.

Wade was measuring the distance from the hay bale to him. It was too far away to risk it. If Lonnie had a gun trained on her, Wade needed to be closer to block it. If he could just get himself a few feet closer.

"I'll leave when I get the wheel set," Wade said, trying to sound normal. "I think one of the spokes needs some grease." He gestured to his pocket. "I've got some in here. Just the thing."

Wade took a small step farther into the hayloft. He didn't want to push too quickly and make anyone nervous. Then, as he started to take another step, he heard something. *Oh, no.* Behind him was the sound of boyish voices and light feet.

He knew Jasmine could see what was happening because he saw the horror reflected on her face.

"No. Go back," she whispered.

Wade turned around in time to see two of the shepherd boys pop their heads up through the opening into the hayloft. Fortunately, they were still facing toward the back wall.

"Go back down those stairs," Wade said. "Don't turn around. Don't come up here. Just—"

Wade heard the rustling of hay off to his side.

"Tell them to come up," the man said, and Wade looked over. So this was Lonnie. The man continued, "They've seen too much."

"They haven't seen anything," Wade said fiercely. "One of them is just worried about his dog. They'll go back down." He softened his voice. "They aren't even going to turn around, are you, fellas?"

Wade saw the little heads shake their heads vigorously.

"I said to tell them to come up here," Lonnie almost screamed.

Wade took a deliberate side step which caused Lonnie to twist and look over at him.

"Leg pain," Wade said with feeling in his voice. He noticed the little heads had known who to obey and were scrambling down the ladder. He wasn't sure what they'd think because they hadn't seen anything and had only heard two men arguing. Hopefully, any adult they talked to would know how to make sense of it all.

"You'll have a dose of real pain if you don't watch it," Lonnie said as he jabbed his gun in Wade's general direction. Then he turned to Jasmine. "We better get out of here, baby. Everything's going to bust loose any minute."

Jasmine stood rooted to where she stood. Wade figured she had to have heard Lonnie. But she wasn't moving.

"No point in looking at Romeo there," Lonnie said as he went over and snapped his fingers by Jasmine's ears. "I'm not going to be too happy if you get us caught again. When I say we need to get moving, I mean it."

Wade couldn't get to Lonnie, not with Jasmine in the range of fire. The only escape he saw was for Lonnie and Jasmine to leave. With Lonnie thinking they were safe. Then he could follow them and take Lonnie when he wasn't around Jasmine. It wasn't a good plan, but Wade didn't know what else to do. Lonnie looked as if he'd be happy to shoot anyone.

"Go with him," Wade whispered to Jasmine.

She started to move toward the ladder Lonnie had used to come inside. The man himself was crowding close behind her.

Finally, Wade saw his chance. He waited for Jasmine to be far enough down the ladder that Lonnie couldn't shoot at her. Then he stepped close, plucked Lonnie up by the collar, and half swirled the man around so he could give him a solid punch to the stomach. The man not only dropped his gun, he bent over trying to get enough air in his lungs.

Bringing down a lowlife was one of the joys of being a lawman, Wade said to himself, as he pulled Lonnie back up. But then, as he thought of what Lonnie could have done, his blood turned cold. The stakes in a fight had never been so high. What if Lonnie had hurt Jasmine?

Wade had rescued countless people from harm and he'd cared about each of them. But to have Jasmine hurt? It couldn't happen.

Chapter Seventeen

Jasmine heard Lonnie's grunt, but she kept scrambling down the ladder anyway. She didn't have a coat and the air was cold. She'd have to get a lawyer, she thought to herself. There was no way to explain what had happened up there, not when Wade had seen her act like she was Lonnie's partner again. She wasn't sure it would be considered a forced situation that she had held a gun on Wade or not. He was a lawman. She could receive an even longer sentence for tonight than she'd served for the robbery all those years ago.

She heard noises at the top of the ladder and glanced up to see Wade standing in the open loft door. Behind him were shadows, but the outside light showed him clearly. His legs were braced for balance. His white shirt was askew on his shoulders like he'd been in a fight. His dark hair was tousled and his eyes so intense they took her breath away.

"Jasmine—" He held on to the door and leaned out a little before saying quietly, "Drop your gun."

Until then, she had forgotten she was still carrying it. Just then she heard a sound to her left and Sheriff Wall raced around the corner of the barn, dressed in his official sheriff uniform and holding his weapon in his hand.

"Drop the gun," Carl commanded. His voice didn't waver. "Now."

Jasmine forced her hand to release the gun and she let it fall to the ground. She wanted to cover her eyes, but she couldn't. She had to keep climbing down. "I'm not armed."

She glanced up and saw that Wade was no longer standing in the hayloft doorway. She felt as if her heart had cracked wide-open. He would always see her as a criminal and she would always remember him looking down on her asking her to drop her weapon. Maybe Lonnie would tell the truth about what happened in the hayloft. Maybe the courts would decide she was innocent. But Wade would always be suspicious of her.

She stumbled on the bottom rung of the ladder and felt the shadows enfold her. The spotlight was focused on the mural higher up on the barn wall and she was grateful to be in the dark. Her feet no sooner touched the ground than she felt the ladder shake. She looked up and Wade was crawling down the ladder faster than she had.

"Easy on the trigger, Carl," he called as he started down.

Jasmine put her hands behind her neck. She knew Carl hadn't asked for the arrest position, but she didn't want any misunderstandings. She turned away slightly so she wouldn't have to face Wade directly when he talked to the deputy sheriff.

"Your suspect's upstairs," Wade announced when he reached the ground and stepped off the ladder. "I tied him up with my belt, but that won't keep him forever."

Carl nodded. "One of the other deputies is on the way up to the loft." He used his head to point at Jasmine. "I had a hunch about checking this ladder and I ended up surprising this one here."

Jasmine winced. *Lord,* she began, but no words followed. When did she become "this one" to her friend, Carl?

"That's not the way it went down," Wade said as he stepped over to Jasmine.

The warm sound of his voice encouraged Jasmine to look up at his face. He was standing closer to the light and his face was visible. She looked carefully to see if he had any bruises after his fight with Lonnie. There were none, but then she noticed his eyes. She'd expected to see pity or condemnation. Instead, all she saw was a steady regard.

Kindness flooded his eyes and there was something deeper that made the tension in her slide away.

"You don't need to keep your hands up," Wade said as he reached up and guided her arms down to her sides. Her skin felt warm everywhere he touched it.

"Hey," Carl protested. "She had a gun. It's right there on the ground where she dropped it."

Wade turned to the sheriff and then back to Jasmine with a smile. "I know she had a gun, but she didn't shoot me. That's got to say something."

"Well, that doesn't mean—" Carl started to sputter and then he glared at Wade. "What's gotten into you anyway? You've been saying all along that she's guilty. Now that we know she is, you turn into her defense counsel."

Wade ran his finger down Jasmine's cheek and she felt safe for the first time since this whole thing started.

"The thing is…" Wade kept looking at Jasmine even though he spoke loud enough for Carl to hear. "I was wrong the whole time. She's not guilty."

Jasmine searched the eyes looking into hers.

"Well, I don't know," Carl said with a frown, but he did lower his gun. Then he stepped over to Wade's side. "I suppose you've got some evidence to support your theory."

"Not a bit of it," Wade said.

"I hope you're not going to say you have a hunch."

"No." Wade looked up at him finally. "It's no hunch. I have no evidence. I just know."

"Now you're just freaking me out," Carl said, and then he looked at Jasmine. "What'd she do? Give you something funny to drink?"

Wade shook his head, but he didn't get much chance to say anything else because a whole crowd of people were crashing around the corner now.

At least, it felt like a crowd of people to Jasmine.

"Are you okay?" Her father was leading the pack and he headed straight for her. Wade stepped aside to let her father through and he wasn't satisfied until he wrapped his arms around her.

"I'm fine," Jasmine tried to speak, but her words were muffled as her father crushed her face into the front of his wool coat. She let him hold her for a second and then she started to squirm. "Can't breathe."

With that, her father loosened his arms and stepped back a little. He was blinking furiously and frowning. "I'm getting you pearls for Christmas, too. To go with your diamonds."

Jasmine gave a half laugh. "No one wears pearls with diamonds."

"Then you'll have to take one of the cars," her father said emphatically. "I have to give you something more."

"You already did," Jasmine said as she hugged him back.

She expected to see Wade standing off to her right because that's where he'd stepped when her father came barreling toward her. But, when she turned, he wasn't there. She looked over the others gathered around and didn't see him. Linda was there. Barbara Wall, looking stricken, was standing next to the donkey. Then Jasmine noticed that Barbara's son was one of the shepherds riding on the donkey. A couple of the Elkton Ranch men were there looking as if they were ready to defend anyone who needed it. But the sheriff and Wade had both gone.

Jasmine figured that meant she was free to go. She stepped away from her father and the chill of the evening made her shiver. She hadn't realized it was this cold. She looked up and noticed the sky was totally black. Clouds had closed off the stars. Where had Wade gone?

"Let's get you inside," her friend Linda said as she stepped forward, put an arm around her shoulders, and started to guide her back to the barn entrance. Everyone else followed them, including the boys on the donkey.

"The pageant," Jasmine remembered with a gasp when she saw the open door of the barn. "We didn't finish the pageant."

"That's okay," Linda said as she kept leading her inside the barn. "Don't worry about anything."

Jasmine's started to shake. She barely made it over the doorway before she started to tremble.

Linda looked up and called someone.

Before Jasmine had time to think, Wade was leading her to a place at the side of the door and putting his coat over her shoulders. She barely had time for the warmth to set in before he had enfolded her in a hug that was almost as strong as her father's.

"Breathe deep," he said as he held her close to him. "Take it in. Breathe it out."

She could smell the scent of him. He must have used some pine-scented soap. She kept taking deep breaths and felt the press of his lips against the top of her head. His arms supported her and after a few minutes she felt her heartbeat match his.

They just stood together.

Finally, Wade stepped far enough away so that he could look down at her. "Are you all right now?"

She nodded.

He drew her back to him for another hug.

By then Jasmine noticed that everyone in the barn was stirring. People were walking here and there, shifting to make room for something. Then she saw that the deputies were bringing Lonnie down the inside ladder.

Lonnie looked scuffed up, but when he reached the floor, his eyes began looking over the people in the barn until he found her. The deputies, one on each side of him, marched him to the door. Lonnie stared at her the whole time and, when he passed by, he suddenly lunged at her.

"I'll get you," he snarled as the deputies pulled him back. "Nobody messes with Lonnie Denton, not even you."

Jasmine didn't say a word; she just sank into Wade's protective shoulder.

"Don't give him another thought," Wade whispered to her as the deputies marched Lonnie out of the barn.

After Lonnie left the building, Carl started down the ladder, too. He was helping Charley make the steps.

"Oh," Jasmine said as she walked toward the two men. "I forgot about Charley."

She could see a bruise on Charley's forehead, but otherwise he looked as if he was okay. "You need to have a doctor look at your head."

She saw Edith making her way over to Charley from the opposite side of the barn.

Wade was right behind her, his eyes on Carl. "Didn't we tell you to bring the paramedics?"

Carl snorted. "Who would think we'd need them? This is a church pageant."

"We're going to drive him to the clinic in Miles City," one of the Elkton ranch hands said.

"Not without me you're not," Edith said as she reached up to touch her husband's face.

"Of course, not without you," the ranch hand agreed. "I'll bring the pickup around."

Charley turned to look around while he waited. His wrinkled face was pale, except for his bruise. His eyes went to Jasmine. "I told the sheriff what happened. I think I heard everything he said to make you hold that gun on Wade here."

The older man gave a nod to Wade. The crowd had grown silent as Charley spoke and his cracked, hoarse voice carried throughout the barn.

Even though Wade had known there was an explanation for Jasmine's actions, he was glad to know Charley had heard Lonnie make the threats.

Trusting Jasmine was getting easier all of the time. He turned to her. "You know you're clear of the law if he said he'd shoot you if you didn't hold that gun on me."

"Oh, but he didn't say that," Charley protested. He was almost out the door, but he turned back to look at Wade. "He threatened to shoot you if she didn't do what he said."

"Me?" Wade felt his whole world shift.

"She wouldn't do it when she thought he'd just shoot her," Charley finished his words, and exited the barn.

Wade could only stare after him. He thought he was doing so well to trust Jasmine without seeing proof that she was innocent. He'd never even imagined that she was doing what she did to keep *him* alive.

Something of Wade's astonishment stirred the other people standing around. He couldn't move. He just looked down at Jasmine in amazement.

Then someone started the sound system again and the music to "Silent Night" began to flow over everyone in the barn. People started humming, but soon everyone gathered their voices together to sing the old carol with quiet reverence. Wade felt resentments he'd held on to for years being washed away as he listened to the simple words being sung by his old neighbors.

When the song was finished, everyone stood quietly. Finally, Pastor Matthew stood and suggested they share a Christmas benediction. Wade bowed his head. He told himself it was just so no one could see him wiping away a stray tear. Even with all of the bowed heads, he reached out and took hold of Jasmine's hand so they could hear the benediction together.

All of Wade's past thoughts about God and love and other people tumbled around in his head and in his heart. He'd been wrong. For all those years, he'd been wrong. He could barely take it in.

Chapter Eighteen

Frost covered the windows on Christmas morning. Jasmine didn't even notice, though, as she sat by the sparsely decorated tree in her father's living room and recited to herself the many ways in which she'd been blessed. She was no longer in prison. She was a child of God. She'd almost been the angel in a church pageant. She had a home and a father who loved her.

She stopped herself. It should not matter so much that Wade was going back to Idaho Falls later today. He'd told her as much last night—his words choppy and confused—but she should have expected it. The bad guy had been caught and there was no one else who needed to be followed in Dry Creek. She'd always known he was a loner.

"We can open the presents later if you want," Elmer said as he brought two cups of hot cocoa into the living room and handed one to Jasmine. He was in his bathrobe. "I'm happy to just sit here for a while."

Jasmine glanced over at her father. "You're not coming down with something, are you? I thought you couldn't wait to give me all your presents."

She pulled her gray sweater more closely around her. She knew Edith expected her to wear bright colors now, but the gray was all she could manage today.

"Yeah, well," her father cleared his throat. "I've been thinking about that ham I got us for Christmas dinner. It's so big that we'll be eating on it for a month of Sundays if we don't do something."

Jasmine shrugged. "We both like soup. Bean and ham is good."

Her father nodded as he set his cup on the coffee table. "We could always invite our neighbors over to share it. I mean, if we didn't want to have to eat as much soup."

"What?"

Her father kept nodding. "Last night made me think it's time to end this feud I have with Clarence Sutton. From all I hear, he's just an old man now. What's the fun in besting an old man?"

"I—ah—" Jasmine sputtered.

"Old Clarence and I, we just need to compromise with each other."

Jasmine finally swallowed. "Well, that would be commendable. Very mature. In a good way."

"It'd be all right with you?" her father asked and she knew what he wanted to know. "If we ask them over for dinner?"

"Wade will probably be gone by then," she said. "He'll want to at least make it to Billings tonight. But I'm sure Clarence would be very pleased to come."

"Oh."

Jasmine smiled at her father. "I know what you're trying to do and it's sweet, really, but—"

Just then they heard the sound of an engine driving up their lane. Jasmine had to stand up on tiptoes to look through the upper window because the panes on the bottom were covered with frost. Her father went in the kitchen.

It was Wade, driving the old pickup of Clarence's, who was coming to visit.

"It's him," her father announced as he came dancing back into the living room and grabbed the largest present under the tree. "Quick, open this."

Jasmine ran her fingers through her hair. She didn't have time to open presents. Not when she looked like a natural disaster.

Finally, her father tore the paper off of the package himself. "Put this on."

Her father pulled a long winter coat out of the box. It was a deep forest green with raglan sleeves and square brass buttons down the front. There was black velvet piping around the collar and the cuff.

"It's beautiful." Jasmine took off the gray sweater.

"Quick," her father said as he opened up the coat, and when she lifted her arms, slid it on for her.

Jasmine was all buttoned up by the time she heard the knock on the door.

"I'll be in the living room," her father said as he nodded his head toward the kitchen. "You go ahead and answer."

Jasmine nodded. She wondered if Wade needed something like a cup of sugar or something. Or maybe he wanted to be sure the Covered Dish Ladies would continue cooking for his grandfather once he had left.

Whatever it was, she'd agree quickly so he'd be gone just as fast. She took a breath and opened the door.

Jasmine felt all her resolve drain out of her when she looked up at his face. All she could do was stare. His eyes were smiling at her in a way that made her want to smile back.

Wade had never seen a more perfect Christmas angel. The green of the coat made Jasmine's hair glow with a brighter copper color. She had some heat in her face and it gave her just the right pink to her complexion. Her hair wasn't spiked or curled, either. Instead it tumbled around her face in joyous confusion. And something swelled in his throat, making it hard for him to speak. He was in love.

"Do you need something?" she asked. "Butter? Sugar? Milk?"

Wade shook his head. "I wanted to give you a Christmas present, that's all."

He watched the disbelief flicker across her face.

"It's not much," he added. "At least not in terms of money."

Jasmine stepped back and let him into the kitchen before closing the door again.

Wade had been nervous all morning. He'd gone to bed realizing he didn't have a Christmas present for Jasmine and there were no stores within a hundred miles that would be open on Christmas day. Just yesterday, it hadn't seemed important. But last night, when his heart broke wide-open, he knew he wanted to give her a present. And not just any present; he wanted something worthy of the emotions that were running riot inside him.

It had taken Wade a while to remember his mother's old jewelry box that was lying with the magazines up in the hayloft of his grandfather's barn. He'd been up there once since he'd been back to check on the magazines and he'd seen the small wooden box.

His mother never had much jewelry, of course. There'd been no money for things like that. But she did have one piece. It was a silver chain necklace with a small amber teardrop on it that she had obviously treasured since she was wearing it in every picture Wade had seen of her.

He didn't have a way to polish the chain, but he did carefully lay it out when he went out to the barn to get it.

Wade didn't have a small gold box like a proper jeweler would have so he finally wrapped the necklace in a piece of tinfoil. At least that was bright and shiny. "I used the ribbon you had on the package of chips. I hope you don't mind."

Jasmine took the present, holding it as if it would disappear any moment.

"I can't believe—" she said as she stared at it and then looked up at him. "We were going to give you ham."

Wade nodded solemnly. "I like ham."

"Yes, but it's nothing like this," Jasmine said as she looked down at the package in her hands. She felt like she had three thumbs and none of them worked. The ribbon was loosely tied around the package so it should slip off easily. It didn't; she had to yank it off. She should have been able to peel back the tin foil. Instead, she ended up tearing it. But, finally, there in the palm of her hand was an exquisite amber necklace.

"Wherever did you get this?" she whispered. The sun was shining through the kitchen window and it hit the tawny amber and made it sparkle in a dozen different golden hues. "It's beautiful."

Wade ducked his head in acknowledgment. "It belonged to my mother."

"Oh," Jasmine said as she looked up. "That's too precious. I can't—"

Wade just reached out and curled his hand over hers, enclosing the necklace inside her fist. "I want you to have it."

Jasmine felt her eyes get damp. She had managed to not cry when Lonnie threatened to shoot her. She had forced back her tears when she'd been arrested. But this—this was too much.

Then suddenly it hit her and all her tears evaporated. "Is this a goodbye gift?"

The kitchen was warm, but she felt cold.

"No," Wade said, and he took a step closer to her.

She took a step closer, too, and before she knew it she was in his arms and she wasn't even trying to stop her tears.

"I have things I need to figure out." Wade spoke low and close to her ear. It was intimate, like his voice was for her only. "But, I promise you this, if there is any way I can do it, with God's help, I'm going to become a changed man for you."

"I don't—" she interrupted.

He rubbed her neck. "I'll probably always be a little independent. And we'll disagree some. And I know you need to get to know me better. But I've already set up meetings with the pastor. I'm not asking you to wait until I'm done with it all. It's something I need to do on my own. Just me and God. I just want you to know one day soon I'm going to come to you a changed man."

Jasmine nodded. That was all she could manage. She'd wait for him forever, but she couldn't get the words out to tell him that.

"And, when that time comes," he continued in his velvet voice. "I'm going to ask you to marry me."

Jasmine's heart skipped a beat—and then another. She swallowed. Had she heard him right? She didn't need to ask because, by then, he was looking down at her with more tenderness in his face than she'd ever seen on anyone's before.

"Don't answer yet," he murmured.

She couldn't reply if she wanted; she was speechless. But he must have seen by her eyes that her heart was saying yes, because he kissed her. And then, when she thought he was going to pull away, he kissed her again.

Epilogue

The feud between Clarence Sutton and Elmer Maynard did not end during that Christmas dinner. Instead of arguing over fences, however, they started arguing over where Jasmine and Wade were going to get married.

Clarence claimed to be turning his west-facing porch into a large sunroom. He said it was perfect for a wedding dance. On the other hand, Elmer pointed out he had an old tent he planned to use for displaying his cars if he ever went to a car show. He figured it could easily provide seating for every man, woman and child in Dry Creek once he set it up in the grass next to his house.

Neither Jasmine nor Wade bothered joining in the initial conversation or the many that followed. They figured the discussions were good for her father and his grandfather. It connected them in a common goal.

And it gave the bride-to-be and groom-to-be time to make plans of their own. As winter dipped into spring, the two of them grew into the habit of spending the evenings sitting together on the porch Wade's grandfather was getting ready to remodel.

Usually, their conversation revolved around the meetings Wade was having with the pastor and the deep contentment he was finding in his new faith. At other times, they talked about the crops he would be planting when spring came. Wade had agreed to stay with his grandfather and care for the old man and the family farm. Jasmine would join them in the house when they were married.

At first, Jasmine had worried about him giving up his career as a lawman, but he assured her he'd lost his taste for sending people to prison. It was time for him to settle down and do what he'd dreamed of doing as a boy. He wanted to plant and harvest crops.

One of those nights, as they sat on the porch and watched the lights shine out from the cross Jasmine's father had decided to run year-round, the idea struck.

"We could be married up by that cross," Jasmine said. She was snuggled close to Wade in that old quilt so she moved slightly so she could see his face. "It would make a great backdrop for an evening wedding. Just as the sun sets we could say our vows."

Wade smiled. "I like it. Besides, that way half of the wedding guests could sit on Sutton land and the other half on Maynard land."

Jasmine laughed as she settled back into Wade's arms. "Our wedding planners might just agree on the spot, too."

"And that will give us other things to think about. Like this—" Wade said as he bent down and kissed her.

Jasmine wondered how one man could make her heart feel this way. He must have kissed her a few hundred times by now and, each time, it gave her that breathless, knee-bending feeling. Granted some of them were thousand-watt kisses and some of them just glowed steady like this one, but they all moved her just the same. She had no idea love could be like this. It was home and family and desire all wrapped up together. She knew his love would keep her warm for the rest of her life.

* * * * *

Dear Reader,

How important is trust to love? That's the key question that faces Jasmine and Wade in this book. Can we give someone another chance? Can we trust them to do better the next time? Sometimes the answer is yes and sometimes it is no.

Whether we're talking about the love between friends, a man and a woman or family members, we all need to know how important trust is to our love. This decision always seems highlighted to me at Christmas. Each time I write a book, I get reader responses. Last year at Christmas I got several letters from people who said Christmas is always hard for them—and it's because they lost their trust in someone they loved and the holiday feelings brought the situation back to their minds and dampened their enjoyment of the season.

If you find yourself in that situation this Christmas, I want you to know that you are not alone. If possible, find yourself a church family to share. Or volunteer to feed Christmas dinner to the homeless, Or buy a gift for a needy child. There are many ways to share ourselves over the holidays.

I love to hear from my readers. If you get a chance, visit my website at www.JanetTronstad.com and send me an email or click in the box on the bottom of the page and go to my Dry Creek Days blog.

If you don't have the use of a computer, you may send me a note in care of the editors at Steeple Hill, 233 Broadway, Suite 1001, New York, NY 10279.

Merry Christmas and God Bless You.

Janet Tronstad

QUESTIONS FOR DISCUSSION

1. The people of Dry Creek took a collection to help Wade Sutton because he was out of work. Have you ever needed help like that and been embarrassed to take it? Is there a way the town could have given the money that would have made it easier for Wade to receive it?

2. Wade always had a lot of pride and he tried to keep his poverty a secret as a child. When he looked back as an adult, though, he realized other people were poor, too. Have you ever had a childhood belief challenged as an adult? Can you give an example?

3. To disguise his poverty as a child, Wade made up stories of presents his grandfather gave him and the good food his grandfather made for them on holidays. Have you ever been tempted to pretend things are better than they are?

4. Edith Hargrove-Nelson arranged to pick up Wade every week for Sunday school. Did you have someone in your life who did something similar for you when you were a child?

5. Edith regretted not doing more for Wade. The

reporting of child abuse has changed dramatically in the past forty years. If you were in her position today, what would you do? Do you have children in your church who you think might come from abusive homes? What do you do?

6. Jasmine Hunter made her first appearance in *A Dry Creek Courtship*. She came to Dry Creek, looking for her father. She hoped her father wasn't Elmer Maynard, but it was. Did you ever wish someone else was your father or your mother? What qualities did you wish for?

7. Jasmine agreed to be the angel in the Christmas pageant because she wanted to please the people of Dry Creek. What have you done lately to please someone? How do you strike a balance with this in your life?

8. Jasmine also had someone in her past who was not good for her (ex-boyfriend who was in prison). Have you had someone in your life who wasn't good for you? What did you do?

9. Wade had a hard time trusting Jasmine because she was an ex-con. Have you done something in your past that still haunts you? Have you ever

had a hard time trusting someone else because of what they've done in the past?

10. Jasmine had difficulty forgiving herself for the past, and even when she became a Christian she still felt she had to do something to deserve it. Has guilt been a problem for you? What would you say to Jasmine at the beginning of the book when she feels this way?

11. Edith Hargrove-Nelson is clearly a strong force in the Dry Creek community. Have you ever been in charge of something like a Christmas pageant? Edith became a little more clipped with people when she was trying to get things done. Do you feel the same when you're doing something like that?

12. Jasmine finally realized Wade just didn't trust her. Can love ever blossom without trust?

When a young Roman woman is wrenched from the safety of her family and sold into slavery, she finds herself at the mercy of the most famous gladiator in Rome. In God's plan, a master and his slave just might fall in love....

"Robin," Ethan said, just before his face appeared in the church belfry's open trapdoor, "come on up. It's perfectly safe."

He reached down a gloved hand as she put a foot on the bottom rung of the wrought-iron ladder.

"How does this thing work?"

"It's very simple. There's a tall pole with a hook on one end. I used it to slide open the trap and then pull down the ladder. When I'm done, I'll use it to push the ladder back up and lift it over the locking mechanism, then slide the trap closed."

"I see."

"Oh, you haven't seen anything yet," he told her, grasping her hand and all but lifting her up the last few rungs to stand next to him on a narrow metal platform. In their bulky coats, they had to stand pressed shoulder to shoulder. "Take a look at this." He swung his arm wide, encompassing the town, the valley beyond and the snow-capped mountains surrounding it all.

"Wow."

"Exactly," he said. "There's a part of Psalms 98 that says, 'Let the rivers clap their hands, let the mountains sing together for joy…' Seeing the view like this, you can almost feel it, can't you? The rivers and mountains praising their Creator."

"I never thought of rivers and mountains praising God," she admitted.

"Scripture speaks many times of nature praising God and testifying to His wonders."

"I can see why," she said reverently.

"So can I," he told her, smiling down at her with those warm brown eyes.

Her breath caught in her throat. But surely she was reading too much into that look. That wasn't appreciation she saw in his gaze. That was just her loneliness seeking connection. Wasn't it? Though she had never felt this sudden, electrical link before, as if something vital and masculine in him reached out and touched something fundamental and feminine in her. She had to be mistaken.

He was a man of God, after all.

Even if she couldn't help thinking of him as just a man.

Will Robin and Ethan find love for Christmas,
or will her secrets stand in their way?
Find out in HER MONTANA CHRISTMAS
by Arlene James, available December 2014 wherever
Love Inspired® books and ebooks are sold.

Love Inspired

An Amish Christmas Journey

by

Patricia Davids

Their Holiday Adventure

Toby Yoder promised to care for his orphaned little sister the rest of her life. After all, the tragedy that took their parents and left her injured was his fault. Now he must make a three-hundred-mile trip from the hospital to the Amish community where they'll settle down. But as they share a hired van with pretty Greta Barkman, an Amish woman with a similar harrowing past, Toby can't bear for the trip to end. Suddenly, there's joy, a rescued cat named Christmas and hope for their journey to continue together forever.

BRIDES OF
Amish Country

Finding true love in the land of the Plain People

Available December 2014
wherever Love Inspired books
and ebooks are sold.

Find us on Facebook at
www.Facebook.com/LoveInspiredBooks

LI87927

Love Inspired
SUSPENSE
RIVETING INSPIRATIONAL ROMANCE

THE YULETIDE RESCUE
by
MARGARET DALEY

MISTLETOE AND MURDER

When Dr. Bree Mathison's plane plummets into the Alaskan wilderness at Christmastime, she is torn between grief and panic. With the pilot—her dear friend—dead and wolves circling, she struggles to survive. Search and Rescue leader David Stone fights his way through the elements to save her. David suspects the plane crash might not have been an accident, spurring Bree's sense that she's being watched. But why is someone after her? Suddenly Bree finds herself caught in the middle of a whirlwind of secrets during the holiday season. With everyone she cares about most in peril, Bree and her promised protector must battle the Alaskan tundra and vengeful criminals to make it to the New Year.

ALASKAN
+SEARCH RESCUE

Risking their lives to save the day

Available December 2014
wherever Love Inspired
books and ebooks are sold.

Find us on Facebook at
www.Facebook.com/LoveInspiredBooks

LIS44637

Love Inspired **HISTORICAL**

Big Sky Daddy
by
LINDA FORD

FOR HIS SON'S SAKE

Caleb Craig will do anything for his son, even ask his boss's enemy for help. Not only does Lilly Bell tend to his son's injured puppy, but she offers to rehabilitate little Teddy's leg. Caleb knows that getting Teddy to walk again is all that really matters, yet he wonders if maybe Lilly can heal his brooding heart, as well.

Precocious little Teddy—and his devoted father—steal Lilly's heart and make her long for a child and husband of her own. But Lilly learned long ago that trusting a man means risking heartbreak. Happiness lies within reach—if she seizes the chance for love and motherhood she never expected…

Montana
Marriages

Three sisters discover a legacy of love beneath the Western sky

*Available December 2014
wherever Love Inspired books
and ebooks are sold.*

JUST CAN'T GET ENOUGH OF INSPIRATIONAL ROMANCE?

Join our social communities
and talk to us online!
You will have access to the latest
news on upcoming titles and special
promotions, but most important,
you can talk to other fans about your
favorite Love Inspired® reads.

 www.Facebook.com/LoveInspiredBooks

 www.Twitter.com/LoveInspiredBks

Harlequin.com/Community

LISOCIAL

Love the Love Inspired book you just read?

Your opinion matters.

Review this book on your favorite book site, review site, blog or your own social media properties and share your opinion with other readers!